SOMEONE TO BLAME

> Dear ~~[scribbled]~~ Nora,
> thanks for reviewing
> J.J. Green. (apologies for the
> writing error; was rushing
> and made a mistake).

SOMEONE TO BLAME

J. J. GREEN

The Book Guild Ltd

First published in Great Britain in 2024 by
The Book Guild Ltd
Unit E2 Airfield Business Park,
Harrison Road, Market Harborough,
Leicestershire. LE16 7UL
Tel: 0116 2792299
www.bookguild.co.uk
Email: info@bookguild.co.uk
Twitter: @bookguild

Copyright © 2024 J. J. Green

The right of J. J. Green to be identified as the author of this
work has been asserted by them in accordance with the
Copyright, Design and Patents Act 1988.

All rights reserved. No part of this publication may be
reproduced, transmitted, or stored in a retrieval system, in any form or by any means,
without permission in writing from the publisher, nor be otherwise circulated in
any form of binding or cover other than that in which it is published and without
a similar condition being imposed on the subsequent purchaser.

This work is entirely fictitious and bears no resemblance to any persons living or dead.

Typeset in 11pt Minion Pro

Printed and bound in the UK by TJ Books LTD, Padstow, Cornwall

ISBN 978 1835740 606

British Library Cataloguing in Publication Data.
A catalogue record for this book is available from the British Library.

To Pat and Chuck.

1

Shay inhaled a greedy breath of the fresh September air, hoping it might rid her of the sharp odour of antiseptic that still lingered in her nostrils.

A cluster of dark clouds gathered on the horizon of the otherwise blue sky as she walked towards the hospital car park where her sister was waiting. Shay was certain Ciara would have a hundred questions to ask. *Best not to say anything*, she thought. *Not yet.* She needed a little more time to let the news sink in first.

She kicked through a heap of gold-red leaves, scattering them across the footpath. Overhead, a row of chattering swallows balanced on a telegraph wire. How ordinary and how just the same the whole world felt. How ordinary and how just the same, yet how completely and forever altered. Like putting sugar in tea; it was still tea, but it was permanently different tea. Quickening her step, she lowered her head, letting the softness of her polo neck touch her chin.

The consultant had given her pamphlets and Shay had them stuffed into the bottom of her bag. She didn't want to know what was in them – not right now. She wondered how she was meant to feel. First Rory and now this. Should she be screaming or crying? Angry? Overwhelmed? She was only numb.

She reached the car and opened the passenger door. As predicted, Ciara threw out the first question before Shay's backside touched the seat.

'So, what's the craic?' Ciara asked. 'What did the EEG test come back with? Were they able to tell you what's wrong?'

'It's hard to explain.'

Ciara started the car and began easing them towards the car park exit. 'What do you mean it's hard to explain? That's not an answer. Spill the beans.'

Ciara drove out of the car park. A splash of rain collided with the windscreen, followed by another, then another.

'Are you going to tell me what they said or not?'

'Starting to rain,' Shay said. 'Those dark clouds finally caught up.'

'Never mind the rain. Spit it out.'

Shay sighed like the whole world was on her shoulders.

'I should've been in there with you,' Ciara went on. 'You should've let me come in.'

Raindrops pattered gently off the windscreen as Ciara began the drive home.

'Some point asking me to drive you and then making me stay in the car. Will you—'

'Ciara, can you just stop?' Shay said. 'I'm not ready to talk about it yet.'

Ciara opened her mouth to speak but closed it again. She drove steadily on, her usually cheerful face creased into a frown.

'I'm just worried,' Ciara said, after a while.

'I know,' Shay said. She leaned her head on the car window, feeling the hum of the engine. 'I am, too.'

*

For the rest of the journey, they stayed quiet and soon they reached home.

The village of Kilcross was located on top of a steep incline overlooking a lough, which wound its way between fingers of flat land and silt and widened on its journey to the sea just a few miles up the coast. Kilcross was pretty much one main street flanked by a haphazard mix of colourful terraced houses, semi-detached houses and a few stand-alone bungalows, with a couple of side streets branching off. Down the decades, the local council had built more housing to pick up the slowly growing population so that two small housing estates were clustered at one end of main street and a third estate was at the other end. On top of that, a few private housing developments had cropped up around the edges of the village during the boom years, creating a bit of a sprawl.

Kilcross's only pub, The Snug, was owned by Ciara and her husband, Joe. It was located halfway down the street, facing Robinson's chip shop where Shay worked.

The village hall was by far the largest building. It sat back from the street in its own grounds, surrounded by a black-and-gold wrought-iron railing. Located three or four doors down from the hall was the grocery shop, owned by Daisy and Rodney McBirney-Smith. It was a small but compact outlet that stocked just enough goods to cater for a basic grocery run and it boasted a freshly baked bread section, a coffee dock and a pretty decent deli.

Ciara drove the car carefully down the street and pulled up in front of The Snug.

'That's us,' she said. 'Home in one piece. Are you coming in for a cuppa?'

'I need to get some bread in McBirney's. I'll call in then.'

Shay turned to Ciara and gave her a hug.

'I'm sorry for snapping,' she said, her voice muffled by their embrace. 'I was glad you were with me today.'

She felt Ciara nod.

Ciara pulled away. 'See you in a few minutes then.'

*

Shay walked up the street to the shop, greeting villagers she met on the way. Orla Ryan with her daughter; Brendan Kelly and Aidan O'Brien gabbing at the doorway of Aidan's house; Ella McMonagle walking her dog. Before going inside the shop, Shay retrieved the mask she'd worn at the hospital, the closest one to hand, and wrapped its loops behind her ears. Not everybody wore masks now, but for her it was a force of habit after a year and a half of pandemic times.

A bell over the door announced her arrival with a jingle. The McBirney-Smiths had a sanitiser near the entrance and Shay helped herself. Rodney was stacking shelves in one of the aisles. He looked up at the sound of the bell and nodded to Shay. She nodded back.

The shop was cosy and warm inside with the aroma of freshly ground coffee. Daisy was at the counter serving Shauna Doherty and chattering away about how fuel prices were going up, while Shauna just nodded.

'It's just terrible, so it is,' Daisy was saying. 'Terrible altogether. I mean, we're still coping with the pandemic and now we've got this to deal with. Is it going to get worse? That's the big question.'

Shay walked to the back of the shop where the fridges were. She passed Mary-Margaret Walsh, known as the village eccentric, who was busy complaining about God knows what to the hapless Andie McBirney-Smith, daughter of the owners.

Shay grabbed a small wholegrain loaf and, as she did, her hand locked into a fist. The bread, enclosed in a paper bag, dropped to the floor with a slap. Shay's body ran cold. Another damned spasm. One of the main reasons she'd been to see a consultant. She winced, pulling her arm towards her stomach to nurse it, and waited a few seconds for it to loosen out. Once it did, she lifted the loaf and made her way to the counter, anxious to leave.

By then, Shauna had managed to make good her escape from Daisy. Shay groaned, knowing she was Daisy's next victim. If only McBirney's had one of those self-service checkouts.

'And how are you, Shay?' Daisy asked.

Daisy's mask was sitting under her nose, a pet hate of Shay's since it defeated the purpose of wearing one at all. Daisy was a loud, burly woman you could never imagine being ignored – or anyone being able to ignore. Her unruly fair hair was kept corralled under a headband and her ruddy face always made it seem as though she'd just come in from digging in the garden.

'I'm doing great,' Shay lied. She took out her wallet and retrieved a fifty Euro note.

Daisy rang through Shay's purchase. 'That's two-forty-eight, so it is.'

Shay handed over the money.

'I suppose,' Daisy said, 'there's no word about Rory… maybe I shouldn't bring it up.'

'Maybe you shouldn't.'

Daisy looked rebuked, but not for long. 'Well, not mentioning it would look like I didn't care and I do. We all do. Just so you know that, Shay.'

Shay faked a smile. *Let me get out of here*, a voice inside her head cried. But until she got her change, Daisy could hold her hostage.

'Did you hear the Gards put out another appeal for information about that hit-and-run?'

'I have to go, Daisy.'

'You know the one that happened at the end of June. At the foot of Campbell's Brae. That poor young fella from Derry, who was going out with the Rafferty girl. They fell out or something and he set off walking home. A dreadful tragedy. Only twenty-three.'

Twenty-three, Shay thought. *The same age as Rory.*

'Awful for the family, so it is,' Daisy said, folding her arms under her ample breast, as she was wont to do when she was getting stuck into a good gossip.

'Awful,' Shay said.

And it was. But at least they knew what happened to their son, which was more than Shay did.

'I hope the Gards find who did it,' Daisy said. 'Driving on like that… a disgrace. I heard the boy didn't die straight away, so if the driver had only stopped and called the ambulance, he might've lived.'

Shay held her breath, holding back the urge to tell Daisy to shut up. As heartbreaking as this story was, she was too hollow to give the poor boy and his family anything.

'Could I get my change, Daisy?' she asked, deciding she was going to leave right then, whether she got the change or not.

Daisy's eyebrows shot upwards and her chatter came to an abrupt end. 'Oh, right,' she said, fumbling around in the till drawer. 'Here you go.'

'Thanks,' Shay said, taking the change from Daisy's outstretched hand.

Daisy looked terribly put out. Shay didn't care in the slightest.

2

'I'm back, love,' Ciara called, as she came through to the bar from a door behind the counter. She quickly slipped on a face mask.

Their house was adjoined to The Snug and there was a door in the kitchen that gave access to the bar.

'Ah, there you are, love,' Joe said.

He was unloading the dishwasher. Ciara walked over to him and gave him a pat on the back.

'How'd Shay get on?' he said.

'Don't ask,' Ciara said. 'She'll be here in a minute; she's just getting something at the shop. Anything I can do while I'm waiting?'

'Aye, I've got a pint of Guinness nearly ready there for George, if you can finish it off.'

'Consider it done. Where is George anyway?'

'Little boys' room,' Joe said. He closed the dishwasher door and set it to go. 'I'm off to change the Carlsberg barrel.'

'Maybe check the Harp one, too, while you're at it.'

'Consider it done,' he said, with a smirk that was detectable even under his face mask.

The trapdoor to the cellar was concealed in the floor behind the counter. Joe lifted it up and, whistling cheerfully, he fixed his hair back into a ponytail before disappearing down the steps.

Ciara put the final touches to a perfectly poured pint of Guinness and set it on a beer mat right in front of George's regular perch.

The Snug was divided into two areas, the bar and the lounge, both separated by a thick stone-clad wall that housed the chimney stack and the wood stove. A single oak-wood counter ran uninterrupted from the bar through to the lounge. The bar side of the establishment was a bit rough-and-ready, with wooden tables and chairs and a granite-tiled floor. The lounge, on the other hand, was slightly more comfortable, with deep-pile green-and-gold carpet, lounge chairs and tables, fixed padded seating along the walls and, at the far end, a shiny wooden dance floor and small stage.

The place was quiet, as it usually was during the day. Later, trade would pick up. Considering the nightmare of the lockdowns, Ciara thought their pub was doing rightly. It was good to be open – good to have a pub at all – and things were finally moving in the right direction, though they weren't out of the woods yet. Masks still had to be worn for working behind the bar and sanitiser had to be made available, not to mention checking if customers were vaccinated, which was near impossible. Mind you, The Snug now had a fab heated outdoor area – built using the Covid grant money – and it was going down a treat. It was an ill wind that didn't blow some good.

A couple of young fellas were carrying on by the dartboard in the corner and Ciara noticed the lone figure of Eoin Devine sitting by the wood stove, staring into the soft glow of the fire, seemingly oblivious to the world around him. Rory's business partner and, according to Shay, a complete shit who'd racked up a load of debt in Rory's name. Was he thinking about Rory right now? Was he worried about him or where he was? Did he feel responsible at all? Or maybe he was just enjoying his drink and Rory hadn't crossed his mind for a second. It didn't seem fair that Eoin was sitting in her pub when her nephew was God-knows-where and his family were half out of their wits trying to locate him. By rights, her and Joe should consider barring the creep.

George emerged from the gents and ambled over to his spot at the counter. 'How's Ciara?'

'Yes, George, how're things?' she said, letting her troubled thoughts recede.

George settled himself on the bar stool. 'I'll tell you when I get some of this down my neck.'

He lifted the glass of black liquid up to this mouth and took a long drink. He finished with a satisfied smack of his lips and wiped the froth from his mouth.

'You should know, Ciara, this is the highlight of my day.'

Ciara smiled. George was the local postman and, every day without fail, when his rounds were done and the post van was dropped back at the Post Office, he called into The Snug for a couple of swallows and a chinwag, after which he'd dander up the street home. Ciara and George whiled away many an afternoon, catching up on the craic and putting the world to rights. Did he know, she wondered, that the villagers nicknamed him "Cliff" after Cliff Clavin from Cheers, because he, too, was a postman who never missed a day in the bar? The funny thing was he kind of looked like Cliff, with his moustache, side parting and slightly protruding beer gut.

'Any craic with you?' she asked, wiping down the silk-smooth wood of the counter with a damp cloth. George always knew what was going on.

'Not much—'

The door opened and a blast of cold air invaded the bar, stealing the heat for a moment and bringing Shay with it. For a split second, she looked at Eoin Devine, throwing daggers, but, still lost in his own world, he didn't notice.

'Oh, there's Shay,' Ciara said. 'I'll talk to you tomorrow, George.'

'Right-oh,' he said.

Ciara lifted the hatch in the counter for Shay to come through and, with Ciara leading the way, they went into the kitchen. Ciara closed the door behind them.

*

Shay plopped her slight frame onto the sofa. Ciara sat next to her. Shay pushed the fringe of her auburn hair away from her forehead. Her face was drained of colour, making the thin scar on her left cheek more prominent. Ciara couldn't help noticing the worry clouding her grey eyes.

'You don't look great,' Ciara said. 'Will I get you a cup of hot chocolate? Chamomile?'

'Nah, I don't feel like anything,' Shay said.

'Are you ready to tell me what they said at the hospital?'

Shay sank into the sofa. She nodded. A faint pulse of dread caught in Ciara's throat. A clock on the wall above the fireplace marked time with a steady tick-tock.

'I've got something called Creutzfeldt-Jakob disease.'

'Crust-filt what?'

'Creutzfeldt-Jakob disease.'

'I… what's that? It's not serious, is it?'

'It's like Alzheimer's—'

'Alzheimer's?'

'On speed.'

'I… this… I don't understand. Jesus, Shay, Alzheimer's? That's not possible. You're only forty, for God's sake.'

'The consultant gave me some stuff to read. I haven't bothered to look at it yet. Not sure I ever want to.'

The pulse in Ciara's throat began to hurt. 'How did you even wind up with a disease like that?'

Shay shrugged. 'I asked the same question. The consultant told me a load of gobbledygook but, honestly, I don't think she had a clue. She even admitted it was a disease they didn't know much about.'

'But they can treat it, right?' Ciara said.

Shay took a pamphlet out of her bag. 'See for yourself.'

Ciara opened the pamphlet. Her heart sank a hundred times over with each word she read. A rare fatal degenerative disease of the central nervous system occurring in one person in a million. Early stages were impaired memory, trouble concentrating, muscle spasms, personality changes; progressing into worsening mental deterioration, blindness; and finally losing the ability to move or speak, and falling into a coma and contracting pneumonia.

'Oh, Jesus, help us.'

Shay lifted her face to the ceiling. 'There is no treatment.'

'Shay, no,' Ciara said, her voice just a croak. 'That can't be.'

'There's no treatment and they've given me about eight or nine months.' Shay swallowed hard. 'When I heard that, I couldn't, couldn't, you know… I remember looking round the room… it was a totally bland, forgettable room with just a few bits of office furniture and an examination couch. And a white medical bin in the corner. I wanted to find something memorable, something that would rise to the occasion. But there was nothing, just this boring room and that fucking bin. So, I made do and I stared at that bin and I thought: I'm going remember it, the bin that was there the day I was told I had months left to live.'

Ciara wanted to be strong for Shay, but she couldn't. She began sobbing. She reached out blindly for Shay's hand and found it. Shay leaned over and clasped her. They stayed like that for fifteen, twenty, maybe even thirty minutes – Ciara didn't know exactly – silently taking comfort from each other.

Eventually, Shay pulled away. Her eyes were glazed and distant. 'I've probably got about six good-ish months left before the disease takes hold properly and I start to lose all sense of myself.'

Fresh tears trickled down Ciara's cheeks. 'I'll help you any way you need; me and Joe, goes without saying, we'll be here for you.'

'I know you will, Ciara. You don't know what it means to have you.' Shay cleared her throat. 'I have another appointment at the hospital next week. They're going to work out a management plan and discuss what they need to put in place.'

Ciara breathed out. 'That sounds good… no, not good… I mean, good that they're going to take care of you.' She cupped her face in her hands. 'I can't believe I'm having this fucking conversation.'

Beyond the window, the sky darkened. The aroma of vanilla wafted from a ceramic candle burner Ciara kept lit to camouflage the smell of stale beer. Voices and laughter could be heard from the bar, the evening crowd starting to gather. The door opened and Joe ducked in.

'I could use a hand out here, love… Christ! What happened you two? You look like…' His brow knitted. 'Don't worry, I can manage for a while yet.'

Ciara mouthed, 'Thanks,' and he left.

'You seem so calm,' Ciara said. 'Why aren't you screaming with rage?'

Shay tightened her lips. 'I'm not calm,' she said. 'At the hospital I was numb, but now, inside, I'm angry, really, really angry, like I want to kill something with my bare hands. Only, I can't give in to it. I have to focus on locating Rory.'

Ciara flinched. Rory was gone – she didn't want to use the word "disappeared". He'd been gone for six weeks. Six weeks and three days, to be exact. They were doing everything they could to find out where he was, so were family members living away, with flyers and press interviews and messages on social media, contacting his friends and even his ex-girlfriend – not that she'd bothered to respond. The Gards were involved, too. They carried out searches near the area where he was last seen, but they formally called that off after three weeks of coming up with nothing. They told Shay to prepare for the worst. She paid no heed and Ciara believed she was right not to listen. Rory was out there somewhere and still alive, and the people who loved him had no intention of giving up believing they'd get him back.

'I have to find him, Ciara,' Shay said. 'Soon. I have to.' Red dots flared up in her cheeks, her eyes flashed. 'This Creutzfeldt thing; what if it takes my memory before he comes back? I might not even recognise him.' She gasped for air. 'What if I'm dead?'

'Don't think like that, Shay. It's not going to happen. We'll get him home.'

Shay squeezed her hands. 'Am I going to forget everything, Ciara? That's what's worrying me most right now. It struck me when I was on my way back from the shop that I might forget the day he was born and how happy I was… or when he started school and looked so cute in his uniform… and his eighteenth birthday party when he got legless and fell asleep in the back garden… and my pride that he started his own business and was working hard to make it a success. Could I forget his gorgeous blue eyes or his handsome face or his sense of humour and the way he lit up the room when he came through the door? Could I forget all that? As bad as it feels waking up every night screaming for him, at least it means I remember.'

'Shay, don't—'

'I can't bear the idea of forgetting a single thing. About Rory, or you, or Joe, your wains, our brothers and their families, our parents, anybody. Whatever I have, I want to hold onto. I want to cling to every single precious little thing that ever happened. I want to forget nothing.'

Shay rasped the last word like it had been cut out of her. Ciara was lost for anything to say, knowing she could give no consolation to this sister of hers who'd scrimped and scraped for years to bring Rory up on her own and who now had this living torment to endure. Yet Ciara didn't want to leave her hanging there with only the horror of those thoughts for company.

'Don't give up, Shay,' she said. 'We'll find him and we'll find him in time. You'll see your boy again.'

Shay nodded. 'I'll see him again,' she said. 'I have to. I just have to.'

3

Shay had the beach all to herself, which was exactly how she liked it. On weekday mornings, it was nearly always guaranteed that Shrove would be deserted. Shrove was on the Inishowen Peninsula facing out to the North Atlantic, right at the mouth of Lough Foyle. The sandy strand of Castlerock and Magilligan Point, at the other side of the lough in County Derry, flickered gold in the distance, while the choppy slate-grey sea dotted with streaks of white surf stretched out to a hazy horizon. A black-and-white-striped lighthouse loomed tall a few hundred yards away.

Shay supposed it was beautiful here, but she couldn't see it that way anymore. She couldn't see it as anything other than the place Rory was last seen.

The wind whipped cold off the waves and Shay could taste its saltiness on her lips. She walked along the edge of the shore, dodging the sea as it rolled up the saturated sand and rolled away again. She clung tightly to her shoulder bag – it was full of flyers and posters about Rory that she intended to circulate later on – and closed her eyes to listen to the steady swish of the waves.

Changing direction, she headed towards the soft sand and coarse grasses of the dunes. She reached a deep hollow in one of the dunes and knelt down, scraping her hand against a rough blade of grass. This was the spot they'd found Rory's clothes, his boots placed on top. Shay clenched fistfuls of sand. Her head went down, tears dripped onto her lap.

Straight away, the authorities assumed Rory had taken his own life. For sure, it looked that way – his clothes and his jeep were left abandoned – but equally, Shay couldn't bring herself to believe it was true. She knew Rory better than anyone and she knew he could never do that. Sure, things had been bad for him before he disappeared, but no matter how bad it got, her Rory would never see suicide as a solution. No, no, he'd never. She was positive he'd gone off to clear his head and figure things out. She had no doubt, no doubt at all, that that was the case. The Gards dismissed her thinking as fantasy. They said when a situation looked like a suicide, nine times out of ten it was a suicide.

Rory was last seen by a couple out for a walk. His jeep was in the car park in front of the beach and the couple said hello as they passed him. But they told Shay and the Gards that he'd seemed lost in his own world and hadn't even noticed them. After his disappearance, the Gards called a search and for three weeks the authorities and volunteers scoured the sea and the shoreline up and down the peninsula. Shay came every day, sometimes on her own, sometimes with Ciara or Joe, or Rory's father, Dan, sometimes with other family members, sometimes with neighbours or villagers. Everybody had been so good.

The search was relentless, but it found nothing and the Gards called it off. They told her they'd done all they could but it was likely his body had drifted out to sea with the ocean current. They commiserated, but she hadn't needed their commiserations. For her, not finding his body was good news. Not finding his body meant there was hope. Real hope. And she wasn't giving up any time soon, especially now, after getting that death sentence from the consultant the day before.

'Where are you, Rory?' she wailed. She hugged herself for comfort, rocking back and forth in time with the ocean waves. 'Just come back, will you?'

Her left hand began trembling and then locked. 'Fuck this.' She squealed with frustration and flexed her fingers to finally get them moving again.

She began sobbing. She sobbed until she was hoarse, until she had no tears left, until she was empty. The far-off call of a gull floated like an echo on the breeze. Her mind began to wander. The thoughts that played out in her head every time she came here crept back like debt collectors returning for another pound of flesh.

Reluctantly, she remembered the last time she saw him, how worried he'd been about the mess he was in. It was a proper mess for sure, but she thought she'd managed to calm him down and reassure him that they'd figure it out somehow. Recalling that time was like forcing herself to walk barefoot over broken glass.

*

It had happened at the start of June and she'd had been relaxing under the shade of the small cherry tree in her back garden, enjoying a rare spate of glorious weather. She'd stopped reading her book and had put her head back to listen to the happy trills and whistles of the birds. The still air felt warm against her skin and she breathed it in. She smiled. This could be heaven.

Her phone suddenly came to life, loud and jarring, shocking her out of the moment. She grabbed it and checked the display. Rory.

'Hi there,' she said, 'what's new?'

'Ma, I thought you were going to be at home today, but I'm at the front door and there's no answer. I need to see you.'

He doesn't sound himself, Shay thought. 'I'm out the back.'

'I'll go round the side gate then.'

Almost as soon as their call ended, Rory appeared in the garden. He was a six-footer, like his father, but that was where the similarity between Rory and Dan Feeney started and ended. Rory was a ringer for his Aunt Ciara – everybody said it, right from when he was a baby. They had the same colour eyes, the same pale skin that burned in the sun, the same chestnut brown hair, same long face and nose, the same thin lips, and almost identical uneven teeth. Even their personalities were similar, both outgoing and bubbly and full of positivity.

Today, though, Rory looked none of those things. Normally a neat and tidy young man, who dressed well and looked healthy, the boy walking towards her was unrecognisable as the Rory she knew. His hair was dishevelled, he was unshaven and his clothes seemed as though he'd been wearing them for a month; in fact, he was wearing lounge pants. His eyes were sunken, surrounded by dark rings, their brilliant blue muted.

He grabbed hold of one of the metal garden chairs and sat down.

'Seriously, Rory, you look like a bag of vomit,' Shay said. 'What the hell's going on?'

'You'd look the same if you had my shit to deal with.'

Shay frowned. 'What you're dealing with? Are you going to tell me?'

'It's all a mess and it's not my fault.' He sucked air through his teeth. 'Not all my fault.' He closed his eyes and a pained expression distorted his face.

'Tell me what's upsetting you. I might be able to help.'

'There's a lot happening. Eoin, he's… well, it doesn't matter.'

His left leg began shaking up and down and he flexed his fists.

'You seem very agitated, son, talk to me.'

'I am talking to you,' he snapped.

'Don't turn on me, I'm only trying to understand.'

Rory rubbed his forehead vigorously. 'I'm sorry, I didn't mean that. I shouldn't take it out on you.'

'So, talk to me.'

'I need money – like, real money. It's the business.'

'Aren't things better now? I know lockdown put the kibosh on it—'

'Ever so slightly.' He snorted. 'There wasn't much use for a street food vendor at festivals and concerts when we didn't have any festivals and concerts.'

'But you got the government start-up grant to do the takeaway food instead, plus you had the money I gave you. And your dad helped out. You could hardly keep up with the orders once you got up and running, or so you told me.'

'That was true… it still is.'

'So, what's the problem?'

'The problem is,' he said, 'there's a load of debt.'

'That doesn't make sense, Rory.'

'I know it doesn't. Eoin was looking after the finances.'

Shay sat up.

'He's good with figures,' Rory went on, 'and I'm not, so I just let him get on with it. We… I mean, I was working all hours, raking in the dough. I was handing it over to him, leaving it to him to pay the bills and build up a profit. I was obsessed with making the business a success and I thought it was going well. Eoin kept telling me it was. Until about three months ago. I accidentally discovered we – there I go with that "we" crap again – I discovered *I* was in debt, Ma. I'm up to my hole in debt.'

Shay could scarcely believe her ears. 'But… I… if the business was doing well, where did the debt come from?'

Rory shook his head slowly, his face ashen. She didn't press him.

'It can't just be your debt, though. It's his, too, right? He's in the business with you. It's business debt, so—'

Rory held up his hand. 'I can't listen to a lecture about Eoin Devine right now. Here are the facts: the debt's in my name, just my name. Eoin hasn't to pay a penny if he doesn't want to. And I can tell you now, he doesn't want to.'

Shay wished she could get Eoin-fucking-Devine by the neck and throttle him. 'How much money are we talking?'

'Thirty grand or, um, closer to forty.'

Shay's mouth fell open. 'Jesus! Forty thousand!'

'I know, it's a fucking shocker.' Rory pressed his fingers into his eyelids and groaned. 'Ever since I found out, I've been wrecking my head trying to think of how I'm going to dig myself out. I've come up blank, though. And I have other shit going on, too – important shit that I need to get my head straight for.'

'More shit than this? Oh God, Rory.'

'I'll tell you about that later. Right now, the debt is what I have to sort out. I wouldn't land all this grief on you if I wasn't at a loss about what to do.'

'I've got about five grand left in my savings,' Shay said. 'I can give you that.'

'Is that all?'

'I work in a chip shop, what do you think? And I gave you money already, remember?'

'What about the money you got when Granda Dunne died?'

'You know I used it ages ago to pay off the rest of the mortgage. And that was only ten grand, even if I still had it.'

'I forgot,' he said, sinking into the back of his chair. 'What about Auntie Ciara, or my uncles?'

Shay looked with eyes that pleaded with him to have sense. 'Come on, Rory. Ciara and Joe are only getting back on their feet after Covid. If they had anything, they'd give it to you, but I know they don't. I'm half afraid to even tell them about this because they'd only want to give you money they don't have. And you know rightly that Covid wrecked the business Mickey and Eddie had together. They might never recover. Your Uncle Paul's just on an ordinary wage and has his own family to worry about.'

Rory swore under his breath.

'What about getting debt advice?' Shay said. 'You can get it free, you know. There could be options… debt management, bankruptcy?'

'Some of the debt, well, um, it isn't exactly on the books. I don't think debt management would be an option.'

A big bell clanged in Shay's head. She was tempted to ask what he meant by some of the debt not being on the books, but she could guess. 'Maybe my four grand could pay the off-books debt, do you think?'

Rory nodded. 'It might, just about.'

'Have you tried the bank?'

'They turned me down. I have them tapped out already.'

Shay bit her lip. 'I'll ask your father,' she said.

'No, don't, I'm ashamed for him to know I've been so stupid.'

'He'll understand. He'll help if he can. And he gave you money before, shure?'

'Aye, but that was to set up a business, not pay off debt.'

'Well, I'm still going to ask him.'

'Okay,' Rory said. 'I'm sickened at myself for putting this on you. I'll make sure to pay back anything you give me. I'm such a dick.'

'No, you're not and don't worry about paying me back. We've all got into scrapes at one time or another and we've all needed help. You're not the first and you won't be the last.'

Rory put his head down. Shay wanted to go over and hug him, comfort him like when he was small, tell him it would be okay, but she resisted.

Another idea came to her. She paused, not sure if she should mention it at all, but then decided to go ahead.

'If your dad isn't able to help, there is one last person.'

'Who?' Rory asked.

'Your grandfather.'

Rory shot an upwards glance. 'What?' His face turned crimson and he looked like he might burst. 'Are you mad? Ask Peter Feeney? You know how much I hate that heartless bastard.' He shook his head vigorously. 'You're talking about somebody who doesn't even acknowledge I'm his grandson.'

'Yet you are his grandson,' Shay said, 'and the man's rolling in money. He can only say no.'

'And no is what he probably will say.'

'If he does, he does, and we'll figure something else out.'

Rory sniffed. He was trying to hold back tears. Shay's heart tightened. She went to him, relenting after all, and put her arms around him. He might be twenty-three but, right now, he might as well have been her little two-year-old crying over a cut knee.

'I don't know what I'd do without you, Ma. I've been so scared.'

'It's okay, Rory,' she said. 'It's going to be okay.'

*

The cold, salty wind pinched at Shay's face. She shivered, lifting herself off the sand and onto her feet. Her stomach felt heavy. She hadn't been hugely successful raising all the money Rory needed – between her contribution and his father's, they raised ten grand, but the visit to Peter Feeney had been a disaster. The money she'd gathered was transferred to his bank account and he told her it was enough to pay off the dodgy debts, with a little left over. That took the worst pressure off. For the rest, he was getting debt advice, so he said. As he put it, he was eating the elephant bite at a time. So, why had he run off?

Her gaze wandered to the other side of the lough. Only a few days before, she had remembered that a ferry sailed across the lough to Magilligan Point. It didn't run in the winter, but it would've been in full swing when Rory went missing. He might've taken it. He might be over there someplace. She tapped her shoulder bag with the flyers and posters inside. That side of the lough was her next destination.

Walking solemnly back to the car, with tears threatening, she took out her phone to make a call.

4

Dull grey light seeped through the French windows of the dining room and rain drummed off the panes of glass. Dan Feeney sat at a long, polished oak dining table. Beside him were documents and files, a plate of sandwiches and some tossed salad. He grabbed an egg cress sandwich without looking up from the report he was reading.

'What do you make of it, then?' Dan's father asked.

'I want to study the figures in more detail,' Dan said, 'but, at a quick glance, the numbers are sending me the right message.'

His father was by the window, his favourite spot to stand at, holding a cup of coffee. He looked his age, Dan thought. Diminished somehow and not the commanding figure that Peter Feeney normally cut. Since making Dan CEO the year before, he seemed a much more subdued man – or was Dan just imagining that? Retirement didn't suit him. Not even at seventy-four.

He was hardly retired, though. Three times a week, he insisted that Dan meet him for an early business lunch in the dining room – not in the study, because his father didn't want the smell of food stinking up his special room – and give him an update on everything going on at the plant. Dan understood it couldn't be easy for this father to let go entirely after starting the business from nothing and growing it into a multimillion Euro powerhouse. Equally, it wasn't easy for Dan to run the show when the old man wouldn't let go and give his son full rein. And though he wanted nothing more than to have the run of the company, he had no choice but to tolerate the update meetings.

'When will you be ready to make a decision?' Peter asked.

'By the end of the week. I'll arrange a video call with them.'

'I'd like to sit in on that call.'

'Nah, it's okay. I can manage it myself.'

'Dan, make sure I'm told about it.'

'Of course, Pop.'

Dan let it slide. He knew it was pointless arguing with a man like his father. And, anyway, he was trying to get back in his good books after their set-to when Dan had taken time off to help with the search for Rory. Dan didn't make a habit of getting on his father's wrong side, but when it came to Rory's disappearance, he made an exception. He didn't care anymore that his father had never acknowledged Rory's existence, but to not give a shit that a young person was missing was beyond low.

Dan's thoughts were abruptly stopped by a knock at the door. The housekeeper came through, pushing a serving trolley.

'Pardon me,' Louisa said, 'I won't take long to clear away the lunch things.'

She began lifting plates and cups, silver platters and cutlery. They clanked and clinked off each other as she loaded the trolley.

'Dear God, the noise of you, woman,' Peter said, in an angry shout. 'You're like a herd of elephants rioting through a shop of Tyrone crystal. Will you stop that fussing and get out?'

'Sorry, sir,' Louisa said.

She gave Dan a panicked sideways glance, even though she'd been on the receiving end of Peter Feeney's sharp tongue a thousand times.

'It's okay, Louisa,' Dan said, smiling. 'We're running later than normal today. These can wait 'til later.'

Looking relieved, she scampered back to the kitchen. Dan's phone buzzed from its place on the table.

'Do those infernal things ever stay quiet?' Peter said, coming away from the window. 'Who is it anyway?'

Dan saw Shay's number on the display and almost groaned. 'I'm going to take this in the hall. It's Shay.'

'What's that woman ringing about now?'

Once outside the room, Dan answered his phone. 'Shay?'

'I'm in Shrove,' she said.

She sounded tearful. He sighed.

'I don't need this, Shay. I'm at work.'

'And you're the boss, so you can take five minutes to talk to the mother of your son – you know, your only son who's missing right now.'

He heard her voice crack. She was about to go into one. He hadn't the strength.

'You're working yourself up again. I hope you're not driving like before. You nearly crashed the car.'

'I'm not driving. I'm on the beach.'

'At least that's something. Make sure you get your head straight before you set off.'

'I was just thinking, Dan, just thinking about that last time I saw him.'

'Why are you torturing yourself? It has to stop and you have to stop ringing me like this.'

'Rory's missing and no one's looking for him anymore,' she said. 'No one comes to the beach anymore, not even you.'

'That's cos we've searched everywhere there is to search.'

'We can do more.'

'And we have done more. Flyers and posters, reaching out to people, media interviews... I even went on the radio. Not to mention the private detective I hired. A solid month of searching and he came up with nothing.'

'It's not enough,' Shay said. 'You don't believe he's alive, that's why you've given up.'

'Fuck's sake, I haven't given up. But I've faced reality. The Gards have him listed as a missing person. It's in their hands now. They're covering all the eventualities and they were very clear with us: there's nothing we can do but wait.'

'Fuck waiting. You just don't care.'

'Come on, Shay, you know I care.'

'Do you? You have Francesca and the twins – you're one big, happy family. What does Rory matter? He's just a bad memory from a silly fling you had when you were nineteen.'

'That's harsh, Shay. I love Rory. I did my best.'

'Your best?' she said. 'Don't make me laugh. You weren't even around for his first ten years. Joe's been a better father to him than you.'

'That's enough. I'm sick of getting the guilt trip. I did what I could...'

The other end went quiet.

'I'm sorry,' she said, her voice calmer. 'I shouldn't have said those things. I'm just so fucking angry.'

'I know,' he said, softy, 'I know. But going to that beach all the time—'

'You didn't try hard enough, Dan.' This time, her voice stayed calm, matter-of-fact.

'What?'

'To get him that money he needed.'

'Aww, Jesus, Shay, not the money thing.'

'No, but it's true. You didn't try hard enough.'

'I gave him ten grand the first time round when he set up the business. And I gave him another five to help with the debt.'

'He needed forty.'

'Francesca and me had just set up that college fund for Sinead and Siobhan. I gave him what I had left.'

'You run a massive company. You have as much money as you want. Why didn't you set up a fund for Rory? Why didn't you borrow the money he needed from the bank? Why didn't you ask that scumbag of a father of yours to pay out for once in his miserable life? There was so much you could've done – far more than I was able to do.'

'You make it sound so easy, but I have a board to answer to and Pop still has a tight leash on the finances. And, honestly, when I talked to Rory, he wasn't freaking out. He really seemed like he was managing—'

The dining room door opened behind Dan and Peter emerged.

'Put an end to that call right now,' he said.

Dan could see his jowls tighten – a sign his father was about to have one of his outbursts.

'Shay,' Dan said, 'I have to go.'

'Right now,' Peter shouted.

'Your master calls,' Shay said. 'Shure, you have to obey. Well, go on then.'

The call went dead. Dan slid the phone into his pocket.

'All this time and you still haven't put your foot down with that woman,' Peter said, going back into the dining room. 'She's nothing to you or this family.'

Dan followed his father, though his thoughts lingered with Shay. He knew she was a good person. Down the years, she'd asked him for little or no help to bring up Rory and, at the same time, she'd never denied him access to the boy. She'd been pretty decent, in fact, and she'd been a seriously brilliant mother. They were so young when Rory was born – clueless about life. But they loved each other, that was for certain, and, who knows, if his father hadn't demanded that Dan cut her out completely, they might've had a chance. He often wondered. His mother had liked Shay, had wanted them to make a go of it. His poor mother. She had passed away soon after Rory was born.

But what did any of it matter anymore? It was all academic now. Academic and heartbreaking.

5

'Shay,' a voice said.

Shay heard it muffled like she was underwater.

'Shay, are you all right?'

The voice became clearer. Shay blinked a few times and lifted her head. She was in a shop, standing at the counter and facing a woman who had the most confused expression. Beside her was a second woman, who looked even more confused and was holding Shay's arm.

'Are you all right?' the second woman said.

'Where, um, I, what happened?'

The first woman began to speak and it was then Shay realised where she was and who the two women were. She was in McBirney's, along with Daisy McBirney-Smith and Louisa Allan, the housekeeper up at Peter Feeney's.

'You came up to the counter with your basket,' Daisy was saying, 'and when you put the basket down, it was like you went into a daze or something. You were staring and saying nothing.'

'I thought for a minute you were going to fall,' Louisa said, 'and I had to steady you.' Louisa pulled her hand away from Shay's arm. 'You seem grand now, though.'

Shay felt her stomach sink. She had to get out of there. She had to get home.

'Sorry,' she said, to the two women, 'I don't feel well. I have to go.'

'Do you want me to call Ciara?' Daisy asked.

'I could drop you at your house,' Louisa said.

'No thanks, I can manage.'

Leaving the basket of groceries on the counter, Shay turned to the door. She could feel the eyes of both women boring holes into her back. She knew she'd be their next topic of conversation. It would make a change from Louisa's usual gossip about the latest news from the Feeney mansion. Shay didn't care who or what they talked about. She just wanted to get home safely.

*

'You look tired,' Ciara said, throwing a log into the wood stove in Shay's sitting room and letting a whiff of burnt wood escape into the air.

'I am,' Shay said. 'I was at Shrove yesterday and after, I went over to Magilligan and Coleraine with posters and flyers. Plus I had a shift at the chippie last night.'

'I don't like you exerting yourself...' Ciara's voice cracked before she reached the end of her sentence.

Shay looked up. Her sister's face was turned away.

'Christ, Ciara, don't cry.'

Ciara sniffed. 'I'm not. I'm grand.' She turned back to Shay, smiling, though her moist eyes gave the game away.

'I'm actually managing fine at work,' Shay said, and she lifted her coffee cup to her mouth. 'Last night was a bit busier than—' The cup dropped out of her grip, falling hard onto her lap. The coffee wasn't warm enough to scald her, but it left a ridiculous damp patch on her jeans.

'Shit,' Ciara said, jumping up. 'Are you all right? I'll get something to dry it up.'

She ran out the door and returned seconds later with a damp cloth. She started patting Shay's lap.

'It just slipped,' Shay said.

She knew fine rightly it was more than that. The look on Ciara's face showed she knew, too.

'How bad is it getting, really?' Ciara asked. 'And don't play it down, be straight.'

Shay breathed out heavily. 'It's getting worse,' she said, reluctantly. 'The spasms in my hands, my left one especially…' She fell quiet.

'Something else happened, didn't it?' Ciara said. 'I can tell by your face.'

Shay shrugged. 'I was in McBirney's today and, for a couple of minutes, I couldn't remember where I was. I mean, I've been going into that shop since Rodney's grandparents were running it, but there I was, looking round me like I'd never seen it before in my life. If nothing else, I gave Daisy and Louisa something to talk about.'

'And you didn't come and get me?' Ciara said.

'You have enough to deal with.'

'No matter what I'm dealing with, you come to me first, don't you get that?' Ciara said.

Shay pushed her hand through her hair and nodded.

'Shay,' Ciara said, 'me and Joe were talking and, well, we think you should move in with us.' She rubbed Shay's back in a soothing up-down motion. 'We could cosy-up the downstairs bedroom. Bring some of your stuff over; fix it up however you like.'

'No way,' Shay said, backing off from Ciara's touch, 'I'm not that bad.' Her heart thumped.

'But the episodes are going to get worse. Everything's going to get worse, you said so yourself.'

'Aww, stop, Ciara.' Her heart beat faster, as though it was pushing up into her throat, and she struggled to breathe. 'I want to stay in my own home for as long as I can, hold onto my life as long as I can, even my horrible job. And what I don't want is to be a burden on you and Joe. It's enough to have you check in with me every day.'

'Never say you're a burden.' Tears dropped from Ciara's cheek. 'I love you, Shay, and I'm here for you.'

All of sudden, Shay wanted to scream – scream her fucking head off. This wasn't fair. Fuck. This just wasn't fair. She was going to die and before she did, her brain was going to be like a bowl of jelly.

'I can't let this happen,' she said. 'Not yet. I'm waiting for Rory. I can't die before he comes back and I can't lose my fucking mind either.'

She wailed. Ciara sat by her side and hugged her so tight she couldn't move. Shay clung to her. Sobs tore from her chest.

After a while, her crying subsided. Shay took a tissue from her pocket and cleaned her swollen face. Ciara stroked her hair and Shay sat in the comfort of her touch, grateful for it.

'I called that Garda O'Connor,' Shay said, sniffing. 'The one who's looking after Rory's case – or supposed to be, anyway.'

'Did she have any news?'

'No, but then she never does. They're doing fuck all to find him.'

'Did his ex-girlfriend ever get back to you? What's her name again?'

'Lorna? She's a dead end, too. She's ignored the DMs I sent on Instagram. I don't think much of her. Where was she when he was getting it tough?'

'I know you said you didn't want to, but should you talk to Eoin Devine?'

'I can't bear the idea of going anywhere near him, knowing about the debt thing. I mean, I just couldn't trust anything he'd say.'

'It occurred to me the other day,' Ciara said, 'that maybe we could get a chat with that Natalie, Eoin's girlfriend. She might be able to tell us something.'

'Umm, it's an idea,' Shay said. 'I've seen her a few times at McBirney's, chatting to that poor, gormless Andie. I could ask Andie if she has her number.' Shay yawned.

'I should let you get to bed,' Ciara said.

'I can barely keep my eyes open.'

Ciara stood up. 'I'll see you tomorrow, shure. I'll call in before your shift.'

'I'll walk you out,' Shay said, pulling herself up off the sofa. 'I need to lock the front door anyway.'

Before they reached the end of the hall, the doorbell rang suddenly, disturbing the quiet of the house.

'Who the hell's that?' Ciara said.

Shay frowned and opened the door without hesitating. She was unprepared for who stood on the step: two uniformed Gards wearing face masks. One of them Shay recognised as Garda O'Connor.

Her temple pulsed. A rush of excitement surged through her veins.

'Garda O'Connor?' Ciara said.

'I knew it,' Shay said. 'You've found him. I knew he was going to be okay. Where is—'

'Can we come in?' Garda O'Connor asked.

'No need, I want to go to him.'

Garda O'Connor put out her hand to touch Shay's shoulder, a fraught look in her eyes.

Shay recoiled. 'Tell me what you're here for.'

'I'm sorry, Shay,' Garda O'Connor said.

'No,' Shay said, not wanting to know what O'Connor was sorry for.

'Rory's body was found at Kinnego Bay...'

Garda O'Connor's voice disappeared into a fog. The only word that mattered was "body".

'That's not true!' Shay screamed. 'That's not true!'

She felt her head go light as the world around her swooned and her legs fell from under her. A pair of arms saved her from hitting the ground.

'I've got you,' Ciara said. 'I've got you…'

6

Not a single cloud marked the flax-blue sky. Shay held her face up to the rays from the sun as they stole through the boughs and yellow-green leaves of a grove of sycamore and beech. A lone crow settled high on an uppermost branch and caw-cawed as its curious head turned from side to side. How peaceful it must be up there. She longed for the freedom to take off from the cold earth. The air nipped at her nostrils as she breathed it in. *This might have been a perfect day*, she thought. *If only.*

Shay dropped her gaze, away from the sky and trees and the crow and back to the ground, back to the graveyard. She was surrounded by her family. On one side were Ciara, Joe and their three children. Mickey and Eddie were on her other side – the funeral had been delayed long enough to let them travel from Australia, permitted now with Covid travel restrictions lifted. Paul and his family were there, too. They'd travelled up from Galway a couple of days before.

At the other side of the grave, near the priest, stood Dan and his perfect family. A little knot of resentment twisted in Shay's gut. Dan looked drawn and tired; Francesca fussed with the twins, who were getting restless. Dan's alcoholic sister, Ursula, was there, too, holding herself together well. Maybe she'd knocked the drinking on the head. Shay saw no sign of their father. Had she really believed Peter Feeney would be there? The knot tightened.

Scattered around, with a half-hearted effort at social distancing, were aunts, uncles, cousins, friends, neighbours, practically the whole village – even the non-Catholics like the McBirney-Smiths and Tracy Johnson, her co-worker at the chippy.

Shay found a little comfort from their presence. She scanned the faces thinking she might spot Lorna, Rory's elusive ex-girlfriend. If she'd come to pay her last respects, Shay might even manage to let go of the displeasure she had for the girl. But no, she wasn't there. Damn her, anyway.

The graveyard was silent apart from random coughs and the drone of the priest's voice as it drifted from the graveside.

'… In sure and certain hope of the resurrection to eternal life through our Lord Jesus Christ, we commend to Almighty God our brother, Rory…'

The priest sprinkled holy water as Rory's coffin was lowered into the blackness of his grave. Yes. His grave. Rory was in a grave. Would be forever. A most terrifying thought sprang into Shay's mind like a jack-in-the-box, giving her a start. This day, she realised, was Rory's last interaction with the world. He was gone, really gone, and from now on, she realised, when anybody talked about him, it would be in the past tense.

'… And we commit his body to the ground, earth to earth, ashes to ashes, dust to dust…'

Shay turned away. She wouldn't look anymore. She breathed in sharply and swayed backwards. The stupid heels of her shoes sank into the newly dug soil. She locked arms with Ciara, noticing her face streaked with stifled tears. Shay's own eyes were dry. They had been since she got the news. She hadn't shed a single tear. All she had was a gaping void in her chest where the pain should swell up from. Better this way, though; better not to feel it.

'...The Lord bless him and keep him, the Lord make his face to shine upon him and be gracious to him, the Lord lift up his countenance upon him and give him peace.'

The mourners said, 'Amen,' in a reverberating rumble that scared the crow from its perch. And with that, Rory was laid to rest. Shay hadn't thought about it before, but it sounded nice that – "laid to rest" – like the person was just taking time out for a bit of R&R, the horror of it completely camouflaged.

The priest said a few words to Dan and Francesca, then crossed to Shay. He made his commiserations and mumbled something inaudible as he left. The mourners began to disperse, with some forming a queue to pay their respects.

One after another, friends and neighbours filed past, keeping a few steps away and stopping to give their condolences, to share Shay's grief for that moment.

As the mourners kept coming, Shay held on tight to Ciara's arm, not daring to let her go in case she'd collapse.

When it came to Mary-Margaret Walsh's turn, the silly woman had the insensitivity to blurt out in a loud voice that Rory must have had mental health issues and maybe if he'd looked for help, he might still be alive. She asserted that she knew this for definite because she was a mental health nurse and had lots of experience with disturbed people. Mary-Margaret was notorious for saying the most outlandish things and people generally let her off. But this was beyond the pale of what Shay could tolerate and she thought she might actually slap her across the face. Joe had to physically move her along.

Third or fourth in line after Mary-Margaret was Eoin Devine. Shay looked him right in the eye.

'I'm sorry for your loss,' he said, as though he was reciting a line from a poem.

He reached out to touch Shay's shoulder and she instinctively recoiled. The insincerity in his eyes pierced her like a knife. And even through her broken despair, she noticed something else, too. The way he was dressed. His clothes were, quite literally, stunning. His suit, his shoes, dark shades propped atop his head, all of it designer gear.

Right behind him was a girl who, despite having her head lowered, Shay knew was his girlfriend, Natalie O'Donnell.

'Sorry for...' Natalie said, in a voice that sounded like she'd been crying. 'Sorry. I'm going to muh-miss him... so much.'

Without as much as a glance upwards, she walked away.

More mourners filed past, with sorrowful word after sorrowful word, until their faces became a blur and Shay stopped noticing who they were. *Let this end*, she begged. *Let this end*.

7

The TV flickered colour and light across the sitting room. Shay was curled up on the sofa, a glass in hand, cushions gathered around and propping her up, a patchwork stole draped over her feet. An empty wine bottle stood tall on the coffee table. A second one, half-empty, was on the floor within arm's reach. Beside it was the local newspaper, open at page six, which featured a short article about Rory. The headline read: *Tragic Death of Young Entrepreneur.*

Shay hopped channels, looking for something and nothing and finally settled on a cookery programme, knowing too well it wouldn't distract her from her thoughts.

The funeral was a week and one day in the past. All her brothers had returned to their respective homes, and life had settled back into its routine for everybody. Not for her, though.

A part of her had died. It had died with her son. Food, it seemed, had lost some of its taste, music sounded more like white noise than stirring chords and harmonies, the colours in the world were duller. All those things that made life bearable, even beautiful, were blunted and bland. She'd lost all interest in life and the living.

Except for the funeral. It played and replayed in her head like it was on an endless loop. A couple of things from that day bothered her in particular. She came back to them over and over, and each time she did, the knot in her stomach that had stuck with her all through the funeral returned. She had it now, right in the centre of her belly, coiling inside her like a snake of seething bitterness.

She took a long drink of wine. She was already past the point of being tipsy and, if truth be told, was closer to being pissed, but that was the goal. She couldn't remember the last time she'd had more than a shandy, so being halfway into her second bottle of white wine was something of a novelty. What did it matter now, anyway? All that keeping focused and willing her disease to stay away until Rory would come back, what good was it anymore? Ciara would be none too pleased to see her in this state – she'd asked her again to come and stay at The Snug. Shay had told her, again, not yet. What was wrong with wanting to stay in her own house for as long as she was able?

The credits rolled up on the cookery show and Shay began aimlessly channel-hopping once more. She stopped at a film she recognised. *The Moving Finger*. Wasn't it a Miss Marple story? Those films were shown all the time, but she didn't hate them. In fact, they were surprisingly soothing, like putting on a pair of comfortable old slippers.

She let her head go back and breathed slowly in and out, hoping to relax the knot in her body.

The funeral. The two things that had bothered her. The first one wasn't so much what was at the funeral, but what wasn't. Peter Feeney. He hadn't come. She knew he wouldn't, knew he didn't care. But somehow, on the day, she resented him for it. How could he do that? Even if he didn't accept Rory as his grandson, he should've been there like the rest of the village. Right to the end, he'd maintained his disdain for Rory. The man was a disgrace – a disgusting, vile disgrace.

The first ad break came on and it was then Shay remembered what *The Moving Finger* was about. She was hardly aware that a tiny light blinked on in her mind. She drained what was left in her glass and filled it up from the nearby bottle. Her head was foggy, and she wasn't sure it if was her stupid disease or the alcohol.

At least what love Rory didn't get from his father's side of the house, he'd had in spades from hers. He could've been in no doubt that he was cherished. Even when all her brothers moved away, they never forgot him on his birthday or Christmas and Rory went to stay with the boys in Australia for three summers in a row when he was at college. Had all that been compensation enough for being snubbed by Peter Feeney? Maybe, maybe not.

Shay gritted her teeth. Who did he think he was to treat her boy like that? She punched one of the cushions and screamed. He could've helped, could've made all the difference to Rory. But, of course, he didn't.

'Fuck you, Peter Feeney. You horrible bastard.'

She supposed she could point a few fingers at Dan, too, if she was minded to. The image of him and his perfect little family standing by Rory's grave came back to taunt her. Rory was only a few months old when Dan pissed off to college. Had a right old time to himself, no doubt. Although, if she was being fair, once he returned home and started working in the family business, he gave Shay money every month with extra at Christmas, Rory's birthday and back to school. Money stopped coming to Shay when Rory turned eighteen and then it went directly to Rory until he finished college and started his business.

Dan spent time with Rory, too, having him to stay for a weekend every month. He kept that up even when he got married, and it was only when Rory himself didn't want to do it anymore that it stopped. Rory told her it was when the twins came along that he got fed up going there. That was probably true, but it was only part of the story. The birth of the twins coincided with Rory turning fifteen and at that age, he only wanted to hang out with his friends. Spending time with his father and baby twins was the last thing any fifteen-year-old would want to do on his weekends.

Over the years, when Shay was worried about Rory, she'd lash out at Dan. But in her heart, she knew it wasn't fair and, bearing in mind they'd been a teenage fling, he'd done good by Rory, all in all. Any anger she felt towards him was never lasting nor deep.

Her ruminations turned away from Dan and focused on the second item, or person, that bothered her from the day of the funeral. This one was even more offensive. Oh, this one made her want to commit murder. Eoin Devine. She clenched the cushion until her knuckles turned white.

'*I'm sorry for your loss,*' Shay mocked. 'Like fuck you were.'

Sorry his cash cow was dead, more like. Shay thought about Eoin's eyes, how they'd contradicted the words of condolences that had come out of his mouth. After what he did; getting the business into all that debt and landing it on Rory.

She remembered the cut of him at the funeral. His shoes alone probably cost more than her entire wardrobe. That man liked nice things, expensive things, and by the look of it, he denied himself nothing. Rory hadn't spent his money on frills like that.

The knot in her stomach shifted painfully. She put her hand across her middle, rubbing it slowly, hoping to ease the soreness.

The debt. Had she done enough to help Rory? Yes, she'd given him what she had. Dan had, too, or so he said – and she'd gone begging to Peter. But should she have sold her house or taken out a second mortgage? That might have been her next move, only she never got the chance. Augh, if she'd known what was going to happen… the thing was, she had been convinced Rory was getting on top of the problem, was seeing his way out, was looking into a debt management thing. It made no sense to her that he'd taken his own life, no sense at all. And yet, the Gards had been right, he had. As much as it broke her heart, she had no choice but to accept the facts.

She gulped down more wine, remembering another thing that bothered her from the day of the funeral. It wasn't as galling as Peter Feeney or Eoin Devine, but it stuck with her all the same… Lorna fucking Duffy. Shay recalled the one time Rory had brought her to the house for a visit. She was a tall, good-looking girl, with a thin frame and straight black hair, which had pillar-box red streaks and a fringe that floated just above her eyebrows. They'd seemed happy together and Shay liked her. She never knew what caused them to split up. Rory never said. But all Shay knew now was that Lorna hadn't been there for Rory when he had needed her most, and she hadn't bothered to be at his funeral. So, fuck her, too – with bells on.

And hang on, it was impossible to forget Mary-Margaret Walsh's performance at the funeral. So what if she was a bit strange in her ways? It didn't excuse the mouthful she came out with at the graveside. That woman! Shay reached for a cushion and flung it across the room, bouncing it off the TV. Where did she get off with saying such things?

Shay put her glass on the floor and got up. She swayed on unsteady feet; nothing to do with her disease, though, and all to do with the skinful of wine she'd thrown down her neck. She leaned on the coffee table to get her balance before staggering up the stairs. The knot inside her was expanding, expanding and moving upwards. She groaned as she got to the landing. She stumbled on in the direction of Rory's room.

She hadn't stepped foot in there since getting the news, but, now, an invisible force seemed to be pushing her towards it. She opened the door as the knot reached her chest. Her legs could barely carry her and she flopped onto the bed. She rolled over, so she was staring at the ceiling and the luminous stars and planets she'd stuck up there when Rory was ten. The room was full of his teenage things: games, books, a PlayStation, a skateboard, his prized collection of Warhammer models – those damned things had cost her a small fortune. Shay had kept the room just as it was when he moved out. She never knew why. And now it was still here and he wasn't.

In an abrupt, unstoppable rush, the knot in her body released and, for the first time since she got the news about Rory, Shay began to cry. Not just cry. She wailed, from the depths of her intestines, from the marrow in her bones, from the blood in her veins. Her body convulsed with the force of her grief as it surged forth. She writhed about on the bed, clutching at the bedcovers, burying her head in them as though doing that might bring her close to him.

She went on like that until she was spent, until she'd cried her eyes dry and her voice hoarse, and every bone and muscle ached. The knot, however, was gone and in its place was something else.

She rolled onto her back again, seeing the stars and planets through blurred vision.

The Moving Finger. A story about a poison pen. At work in a cosy village. An idea took shape.

*

Shay gently closed the door of Rory's room and went to the box room – a space so small you literally couldn't swing a cat. But it was big enough to fit a desk, a chair and a small bookshelf. She made herself comfortable at the desk, noting that she didn't feel as drunk as before. Maybe all the crying had helped or maybe it was because she had a plan.

The plan was simple, possibly even juvenile – yes, very possibly juvenile, and stupid along with it. Her disease could be the cause of this – it impaired judgement, after all – but what did it matter? For the first time since Rory's funeral, she felt as though she was really doing something. Instead of helplessly stewing in bitterness at her lot in life, at losing Rory, at getting ill, she was taking action into her own hands.

Her laptop was open at a blank Word page, the cursor giving her the come-on.

She was going to do this old school. A printed letter in the post. No online stuff. That could get complicated, could be tracked. Drunk as she was, silly as her plan was, she hadn't lost all sense.

A letter was simple and impossible to trace.

She bit her lower lip, her brow furrowed in deep concentration. Then she smiled and, in a flurry, began typing in the middle of the page in Times New Roman italics: *You won't get away with what you did; I'm going to make you pay.*

She stopped and contemplated the words. No, they wouldn't do. She pressed the backspace key until the page was blank again. She gave it another go. *I'm going to tell the world what you did and then it'll be your turn to suffer.* She considered this new version. No, it was terrible.

She erased the second attempt and tried a third time. It was no better than the first two. She tried another half dozen attempts, each one worse than the last. And then, she came up with a form of words she liked. Not too melodramatic, just enough to unsettle the recipient; not too specific, just enough to hint at something their own minds might conjure up from the past; not too verbose, just enough to get the message across: *I know what you did. Be prepared for the consequences.*

Yes, these words seemed right.

Shay had modest expectations for her scheme, though modest expectations would be enough. She would send her poison pen letter to two people – to start with, at least. Maybe she'd decide on deserving others like Lorna or Mary-Margaret Walsh. Or even somebody like Tracy Johnson. Sure, she'd come to the funeral, but Tracy had spoken more than a nasty word or two about Rory down the years – an outworking of her jealousy that Rory had achieved everything her own ne'er-do-well son hadn't.

But those people were for later, if at all. For now, Shay would stick with just the two letters: one for Peter Feeney and one for Eoin Devine.

Her son was dead, gone off the face of the earth like he never existed, and here they were, the pair of them, happily getting on with their lives and never giving Rory a second thought. Christ's sake, that old bastard Feeney was still as sharp as a tack, which was more than could be said for her. Shay didn't intend to sit around waiting for her brain to turn to mush without at least trying to inflict some pain for the harm they'd done to her son.

So, how best to do that when she was sure those men didn't care, not about Rory and certainly not about her. She was sure, too, that when they held their letters in their hands and read those words, it wouldn't for a second cross their minds that it had a thing to do with Rory. Peter rated Rory as nothing and fly-by-night Eoin would by now have written Rory off as a business deal gone wrong and moved to his next venture. There would be no crisis of conscience when it came to Rory. Yes, she was sure of all that – maybe not one hundred per cent sure, but as near as damn it.

However, Shay was sure of something else. Along the timeline of their miserable lives there would be a trail of other misdeeds and victims, lots of guilty secrets, one of which would be of significant enough magnitude as to give them a sleepless night or two. And perhaps that's what they'd think of when they were holding her letter in their hands. She hoped so, and it was why she'd kept the wording vague; to let the letter mean whatever they thought it could mean.

The letters seemed like the best route for her to give them a taste of their own medicine. Were there other routes? She thought about it.

Civil action was a possibility against Eoin. Only, she didn't have any evidence – none that would stand up in a court. And the cost would be astronomical, not to mention how long it would take. She'd be dead and buried before it would even get started. Plus, where was the punishment in that for Peter?

She could go public, of course, and announce to the village what they did. That would give Daisy McBirney-Smith and the village rumour mill enough grist to last a year. Somehow, though, that didn't appeal to her. It had no dignity and probably would cut no ice since neither man gave a shit. And besides, once the village found out she was ill, that she was losing her senses, on top of having lost Rory, people would be inclined to think she was lashing out blindly with no clue what she was doing. They'd end up pitying her, condemning her, laughing at her, but what they wouldn't do was believe her.

Then there was the most direct action: outright confronting Peter and Eoin, venting her spleen and pouring it all out. But what would that achieve? Indifference or more humiliation from the merciless Peter Feeney? A derisory snigger from the cavalier Eoin Devine or, even worse, more of his insincerity?

Fuck all that. She needed a way to make them suffer; a way to rattle them and let them know their past was breathing down their necks; a way to plant seeds of fear that they hadn't got away scot-free and were going to pay the price. And that meant they couldn't know the threat had anything to do with her or Rory. The anonymous letters would do that job. The disquiet, the simmering fear, the brooding tension that they were bound to feel as they waited for the "consequences" would be her revenge. And she was bound to hear about it as the village rumour mill did its thing.

She considered for a second if she might need to send a couple of decoy letters to throw Peter and Eoin off the scent, since their letters would be arriving soon after Rory's funeral. But she decided no; they weren't going to think the letters had anything to do with Rory in the first place.

Shay pressed print twice and the printer on the desk beside her cranked into action. The chemical tang off the toner reached her nostrils as one copy and then a second inched out onto the paper tray.

She took a pair of surgical gloves from a box sitting on a shelf above the desk – she still had a load of them leftover from the first lockdown. She didn't intend to leave any telltale fingerprints. She lifted two white DL envelopes from the top drawer in the desk and placed them in the printer. She'd learned on YouTube how to print addresses on envelopes and did it often for formal correspondence. She followed the steps she had committed to memory and soon had two neatly printed envelopes sitting in the printer tray.

Picking up the one of the pristine pages, she carefully folded it and slipped it inside the envelope addressed to Peter. A perfect fit. She did the same with the second page. The only thing missing now was the postage stamp. Shay kept a supply in the desk drawer. She neatly applied one to the top corner of each envelope. Tomorrow, she'd post these puppies. Not in the village, in Letterkenny – that would widen the net for anybody trying to guess the sender.

Shay took a deep breath. Her job was done.

*

A beam of sunshine woke Shay from her sleep. She slowly opened her eyes, putting her hand up to protect them from the brightness. A pneumatic drill vibrated in her head. She looked around, realising she hadn't pulled the curtains the night before or even undressed. By the stale taste in her mouth, she hadn't brushed her teeth either.

'Fuck me,' she said in a croak.

Shay checked the time. It was only ten. At least the whole day wasn't lost. She gently raised herself, until she was sitting upright, and noticed that she was wearing surgical gloves. She frowned, a movement that sent a bolt of pain across the back of her skull. Then, she saw the envelopes on her bedside locker, and the activities of the night before came rushing back in full technicolour.

'Fuck me,' she said, again.

She threw her legs over the side of the bed. 'I really did it,' she said. 'I concocted a plan for those two pieces of shit.'

She giggled even though it made her head pound.

'What was I at, getting drunk like that?'

She wouldn't do it again for no other reason than it hadn't made her feel any better, not even for a while. All she did was ruminate and get angry and cry. And dream up outrageous schemes.

She needed painkillers.

Grabbing the envelopes, she lumbered downstairs. She threw them on the kitchen table and rolled off the surgical gloves, placing them beside the envelopes. She rummaged around the medicine drawer until she found what she was looking for. As she swallowed down a couple of pills, she eyed the envelopes. She'd throw them in the bin, of course.

She clicked on the kettle for a coffee. The pain in her head began to subside.

The kettle bubbled vigorously to a boil. Shay scooped a spoon of coffee granules into a mug and poured in the water.

She looked back at the envelopes, remembering the thoughts and notions that had swirled around in her mind the night before. She might've been drunk, but that didn't change her reasons for writing the letters. The reasons remained. The reasons were valid.

'Fuck it,' she said. 'What have I got to lose?'

She put the gloves back on and gathered the envelopes. As she left the house, a smile crept across her mouth – a sly, satisfied smile. What was wrong with wanting a taste of revenge? Not a lot and not anything dangerous, just a little bit of the harmless kind? Well, there was nothing wrong with that whatsoever.

8

The phone call with Ursula hadn't gone so well. Peter leaned into his Chesterfield wingback chair and sipped on a snifter of Scotch. A Glenmorangie Vintage Malt, but it might as well have been prison hooch for all the value he was getting out of it this evening. Seemed you had to be in the right mood to appreciate the woody, peaty notes of one of the best whiskies in the world.

He set the snifter on the dark-oak side table and sat forward in the chair. The open fire was getting low. He threw on a couple of logs and golden sparks escaped up the chimney. The flickering glow bathed the room in orange light and shadows. There wasn't a sound apart from the crackle of the wood as it started to ignite. Peter reached for his snifter and sat back in the chair.

Why was Ursula always meddling where she had no business? She was far too much like Aggie, including in her over-fondness for vodka. To give her some credit, she'd cleaned up her act of late, though not before several failed attempts in some very expensive clinics. But the gap the alcohol left had to be filled with something and she was always dreaming up one absurd scheme or other. Her latest was a special mass in the house for Aggie's twentieth anniversary.

When she suggested it to him, he hadn't received the idea well. Truth be told, he'd been overly harsh with her and lost his temper. He'd ring her tomorrow, when the dust settled, and invite her to lunch at her favourite spot, The Links. That would make it up to her. And he might put her off the notion of having the mass, too, while he was at it.

His children had been relatively young when they had lost their mother. Dan, twenty-two; Ursula, just eighteen. That had been tough on them. On him, too, in spite of… everything.

Peter didn't often think about what happened to Aggie, deliberately so. But Goddamn Ursula for resurrecting the whole affair again, like stirring a fetid pool of water with a stick. Those memories, that night, they were in his head right now and as vivid as if they had happened yesterday.

He downed some whisky, recalling the most jarring part of Ursula's call. She was going on about Harry Parkes for some reason. Many, many years ago, Harry Parkes had been his handyman, groundskeeper, driver and anything else Peter needed doing around the estate. Ursula said she bumped into him in town a couple of weeks ago and it was talking to him that gave her the idea of having the anniversary mass. Now, what in the holy fuck could that mean? He pressed the particulars out of her, which wasn't easy because Ursula didn't major on perfect recall or concentration. He managed to get enough, though, and now sifted through the information he'd gleaned as he absently traced his fingers across the arm of the chair.

Harry had mentioned Aggie first, not Ursula. Peter found that notable. "It's hard to believe your mother's nearly twenty years' dead," was what he said. "She was a great woman" and he "took her death hard". He remembered the night Aggie died. "It was unforgettable" were the words he used. Unforgettable. Indeed. *What details exactly*, Peter wondered, *were unforgettable*?

"How's your father getting on these days?" was Harry's next

question. "Shure, your mother's anniversary must hit him hard every year." What had Harry meant? Peter felt his jowls tense. He wanted to lash out at that stupid man.

And then Harry told Ursula that his own wife had died the previous year and he didn't know what kind of state he was going to be in when her first anniversary came round. For a man who hardly knew Ursula and who'd probably never spoken more than a dozen words to her in his life, he had a lot to fucking say all of a sudden. That was strange in itself, but stranger still was the subject matter. Why would he mention Aggie and that night? Now, after all these years?

The clock stuck seven. Peter drained what was left in the snifter and left it back on the side table. He got up off the chair, stretching his left leg, which stiffened up so easily these days.

Maybe what Harry had talked about was innocent enough or maybe it wasn't. Either way, Peter didn't like it.

The door of the sitting room opened and Louisa came through.

'Your dinner's ready in the dining room,' she said.

'Thanks, Louisa,' he said.

'If you don't need anything else,' Louisa said, 'I'll pop off home then.'

'On you go.'

Louisa turned to leave.

'Wait a minute,' Peter said. 'Was there any noteworthy post for me today?'

Louisa hesitated. 'Oh, your post, sir,' she said. 'I'm sorry, but with one thing and another, I clean forgot about it. Most of it was junk mail that I threw in the rubbish, but there's a letter from a charity inviting you to a fundraiser.'

Peter gave her a discerning look. *Did she seem jumpy?*

'I'll bring it to you in the dining room before I go.'

'Do that,' he said, 'and try not to make a habit of forgetting.'

9

Eoin Devine pulled into the drive of the rented semi that he shared with his girlfriend, located half a mile outside Kilcross village, and brought his sporty 4x4 to a stop. He made a pretend smile in the rear-view mirror and ran his tongue across his white teeth, all beautifully smooth and even apart from the canine on the left, which stuck out slightly. People always remarked on how nice his teeth were. They were only one piece in the overall package though. He was a good-looking guy, if he said so himself. He had the height, the square hairline, the naturally muscular physique, the smoky-brown eyes that the women loved – set a bit too close together for his liking, but who was complaining? He had it all.

Only he hadn't. Matter of fact, he had fuck all. Even the landlord had threatened eviction today. He bit his lip. Natalie was going to love that. But bad as all that was, it was nothing compared to… what he'd done. Oh, he had fucked up, royally fucked up, and no amount of con tricks was going to fix this one.

He got out of the car. Icy raindrops splattered down on him from the night sky. The house was in complete darkness. After seven and Natalie wasn't home yet. He unlocked the door and went inside, switching on the light and hanging his jacket on a hook on the wall. His belly growled. He was starving but worry had him too sick to eat.

The post was in the little basket that caught anything pushed through the letter box. He opened the hatch and took out two letters, both addressed to him. One was junk mail, which he tossed back into the basket; the other was a white envelope. He kept it in his hand.

He plodded down the hall to the lounge. All he wanted was to vegetate in front of the TV and escape into some inane show or other. He went through to the lounge and flicked on the light switch. He stopped dead, his heart near jumped out of his chest. Somebody was in the armchair. Natalie.

'What the fuck, babes? You scared the life out of me.'

Natalie was curled up on the chair, wrapped in a snuggle blanket, her eyes red, her cheeks bloated like she'd been crying. A lot. That should have been the cue for a concerned boyfriend to ask her what was wrong, but Eoin didn't think he could handle her shit on top of his.

'You're sitting in the dark, Nat.'

'Was it dark?' she said, lifting her face to his, with a brooding, dead expression that disguised the fact she was beautiful.

The first time he'd clapped eyes on her, he'd wanted to devour her as she was so stunning. Wavy chocolate-brown hair, elegant body, high cheekbones, full lips and blue-grey eyes that stole his heart. He thought she was his perfect match. Physically, at least. Personality-wise, maybe not so much. She could be moody, lazy, entitled – like the earth owed her and it was her boyfriend's job to hand it to her on a plate. She loved the attention of other men, too, so he had to endure endless flirtations and – at least one that he knew of – more than flirtations. Yeah, it wasn't easy being Natalie O'Donnell's boyfriend. Though, in the last few weeks, it had become much worse. She was so withdrawn, indifferent; life seemed to be slowly draining out of her. He guessed he knew why, but he didn't dare ask in case he drove her away. But, he had more to worry about than her self-pity.

'It's freezing in here,' Eoin said.

'What d'you expect? We've no oil left.'

'Oh, shit, that's right.'

'You said you were going to order some today.'

'I forgot.'

Natalie shrugged. She sunk further into the blanket.

'Don't suppose you want to share that blanket with me.'

She gave him a disgusted sideways glance.

'Love you, too,' he said.

He dropped onto the sofa and switched on the TV.

'Are you going to order heating oil tomorrow?' Natalie asked.

'Yes, I'm going to order oil tomorrow.' He flicked down through the channels.

'I can do it,' she said, 'if you give me back that 200 Euros I gave you.'

He didn't look at her.

'You've spent it, haven't you?' she said.

Eoin kept flicking the channels.

'I bet you gave half to your mother. You always put her first, no matter what. She has to get the best, doesn't she, because she was a single parent and she was poor and she was so good to you – boo-hoo.'

'Leave my mother out of it. She's done nothing to you.'

Natalie wasn't quite right. Eoin hadn't given half the money to his mother. He'd only given her forty, enough to get a top-up for her electric meter. The rest he put in the bank to pay a couple of direct debits. But he was good for it. He'd get the damned oil.

'To hell with your mother,' Natalie spat. 'You're nothing but a fucking class-A turd. I'm working my hole off in that horrible shop and you're pissing about spending my money. Why don't you get a job or at least start selling off some of that shite you bought when you were throwing money round like there was no tomorrow?'

'I don't need to sell off my stuff. And I'm not interested in some two-a-penny joke job. I've got the long view in mind, Nat. I'm thinking big. I'm trying to close some deals that're going to set us up, give us the life we want.'

'What a crock of shit.'

She was right; it was a crock of shit. His deals were going nowhere. Maybe one of them had potential, with a push, but it was still a long shot.

'I didn't sign up for this. You made promises and you've kept none of them.'

His head was going to bust. She didn't know what was going on for him, the pressure he was under. He couldn't tell her. He just wanted her to shut up.

'I've done okay by you,' he said. 'Not so long ago, you were living your best life because I was funding it.'

She snorted. 'And we all know where, or who, that was coming from. Not by the sweat of your brow, that was for sure.'

'If you mention that one more time, I swear to fuck, Natalie—'

'What? You'll hit me? Why don't you just hit me? Why don't you beat me to fucking death?'

'Jesus, what a mouthful to come out with? I've never hit you. I never would.'

'I don't care anymore. Nothing matters. And you and all your wheeling-and-dealing, I've had enough. I'm sick of it. I'm sick of you.'

'Don't say that, babes. You don't mean it.'

'I do.' Her voice quivered; she was on the verge of crying.

He started towards her.

'Don't,' she said, putting her hand out in a halt gesture. 'Don't come near me. I can't take comfort from you. You're such a liar, but you think you're so smart and people don't notice. Well, they do. Rory did. In the end, he saw through you.'

Eoin nodded very deliberately, pursing his lips. 'You had to do it, didn't you?'

'What?'

'You had to mention his name. It always comes back to Rory. You talk about him like he was a fucking saint.'

His brain was too overloaded to think about Rory. All that shit was behind him – or it would be if Natalie would knock it on the head. Not that he'd done anything wrong, not really. It was business. It wasn't personal.

'He was honest,' Natalie was droning on. 'Hard-working, decent. More than I can say about you. You just took him for a ride.'

'Give me a break. He was far from perfect and you know it – but let's stop bullshitting each other. We both took him for a ride and you were up for that. Don't forget it. That's who you are, who we both are.'

'Don't tar me with the same brush,' Natalie said, raising her voice. 'I didn't know what was going on until it was too late.'

'Me thinks the lady does protest too much.'

'Fuck you. And it's "doth", you dickhead. If I'd known what was going on, things might've worked out different.'

'I can imagine how you wanted them to work out.'

'What do you mean by that?'

'Nothing. I mean nothing.'

He wasn't going to get dragged into talking about what he thought – no, what he knew – when it came to her feelings for Rory before he disappeared. She didn't press him, he noticed. Maybe she didn't want to go there either.

'I'm doing my best for you,' he said, instead. 'I love you.'

She shook her head. Tears brimmed in her eyelids but didn't spill out. 'If you really mean that then stop the wide-boy nonsense and get a proper job that brings in a steady wage.'

'I'm working on it. Trust me. I won't let you down.'

'Whatever,' she said, pulling the blanket tighter.

He smiled, though a half-hearted smile was all he could manage. It didn't matter. She wasn't looking anyway.

He turned to the white envelope he still had in his hand. He tore it open and pulled out a folded A4 page. His eyes widened. He stared down at the single sentence typed in italics across the middle of the page: *I know what you did. Be prepared for the consequences.*

He gasped, loud enough for Natalie to look over. He felt his body go cold. His heart was racing. Somebody knew. Fuck, somebody knew. How could they? How could anybody know?

'What's wrong?' Natalie asked.

Eoin straightened up. He didn't want Natalie to see him rattled. Ideally, it would be better if she didn't see the letter, but she was curious about it now and if he tried hiding it from her, it would only make her more determined to know what it contained. She'd be like a terrier on the scent of a rat.

'Nothing,' he said, and forced a mocking laugh. 'Some joker taking the piss. Want to see?'

He reached her the letter. She read it. Now it was her turn to gasp.

'What the hell is that? Who'd send such a horrible thing?'

Eoin shrugged. 'It's a practical joke,' he said, faking indifference.

'It's no joke,' Natalie said. 'It's a threat is what it is. I think you should take it to the Gards.'

'Ach, don't be ridiculous.'

'I'm serious, you should report this.'

The very notion of shining a spotlight on himself by contacting the Gards made Eoin's skin crawl. He had to get Natalie off this notion. 'Well, I'm not going to.'

'Do you think it's about Rory?'

'What? How would it be about Rory?'

'Maybe whoever wrote the letter knows how you shafted Rory. It could be his mother.'

Eoin thought he was going to break into laughter – loud, boisterous laughter. Oh, if only he could be certain it was Rory's mother. Wouldn't that be a relief?

'You actually think the woman that works in the chippy wrote this?' he said, keeping his face straight.

'Why not? She probably knows what you did and she's not happy.'

'I think with her son dead, she has bigger worries on her mind. Wise up, Nat.'

He felt his whole body stiffen, as though it was alert and waiting for danger to pass. 'And by the way, I never shafted Rory, so you can stop with that craic.'

'We'll agree to differ on that score,' she said, 'but you shouldn't dismiss that letter so easy.'

'Come on, Nat, it's nothing. People are stir-crazy after all that pandemic shit. This letter's from somebody with Covid brain.'

'Aye, maybe so,' Natalie said, backing down. 'It's only you seemed so worried when you opened it. I thought you were taking it seriously.'

'I wasn't,' he said. 'I was shocked, that's all. I mean, it's random as fuck, right?'

Natalie looked him in the eye, intently at first, then smiling. 'I suppose you're right. It's bullshit.'

Eoin felt his body relax and he breathed out. He'd thrown her off the scent. She returned to her sulk and he returned to the TV. He felt the dryness of the sheet of paper in his hand and squeezed tightly. Despite what he told Natalie, the letter was no joke. Somebody knew. Impossibly, somebody knew.

*

Eoin woke with a jump, his heart beating in his chest like a jackhammer. The room was darker than a miner's boot and it took him a second or two to get his bearings. He reached out for his phone on the bedside locker to check the time. The screen came alive, casting a spooky-blue glow on everything around him. It was three forty-five.

A nightmare had woken him. The same one he'd been having since he was a kid: he was trapped under a heap of wooden rafters as heavy as a house and he was suffocating. The moment just before he drew his last breath of air, the nightmare ended.

Not that it was a nightmare exactly. When he was seven, a stack of rafters really had caved in around him and nearly killed him. His granny had found him, by pure chance, and in the nick of time, too, because he'd lost consciousness. The fussing she did when she found him, and the fussing his mother and grand-da did. They couldn't believe he'd suffered so terrible a thing and they looked after him like he was a fragile bird's egg. The hell of that ordeal never left him and, ever since, the sensations and memories came back in his dreams whenever he was worried.

And he *was* worried.

Eoin switched on the bedside light. Natalie mumbled and turned but didn't wake. He listened to her breathing for a while, getting comfort from its steady whisper. He reached for his smokes and lit one.

That stupid fucking letter was playing on his mind.

He sucked a long, deep drag from his cigarette like it was giving him life-saving oxygen. He tasted the dry bitterness of the butt on his lips and watched the smoke streak blue from the tip.

He mumbled what had been written in it. 'I know what you did. Be prepared for the consequences.'

Natalie gave a little snort and snapped her mouth closed. Funny how she looked like a little girl when she was sleeping, like butter wouldn't melt – as if. Ten pounds wouldn't choke her. He covered her bare shoulder with the soft cotton quilt.

He pulled another drag and absently puffed out smoke rings. The meaning of the letter went round and round in his head – and, of course, the numero uno question was what the sender of the letter had meant by "consequences".

Eoin stubbed out the fag and yawned. He longed for sleep, but his mind was moving faster than Roadrunner on Red Bull so he had no chance. He pulled back the quilt. If he couldn't sleep, he might as well make some coffee. The bed creaked as he stepped onto the floor.

'What's wrong?' Natalie asked, her voice slurred and heavy. 'You all right?'

'I'm fucking-A, babes,' he said. 'Go back to sleep.'

Natalie turned over. She was out for the count again. He envied her. He padded downstairs in bare feet, along the hallway and into the kitchen. The kettle had just enough water in it and he flicked the switch.

The letter was lying on the countertop where he'd thrown it before going to bed – an attempt to show Natalie he didn't care about it. He slid it towards him. The words taunted him. He groaned aloud and the groan echoed off the walls in the silent kitchen, like they were jeering back at him in judgement.

The kettle came to the boil, but he couldn't be bothered with coffee, after all.

I know what you did. Eoin wondered if the sender actually did know. What he had done was so terrifying he still couldn't properly believe it had happened. He took a deep breath as though bracing himself against a tidal wave.

Two months ago, he'd killed a man.

He hadn't meant to – not that that let him off the hook. He was guilty and he was one hundred per cent to blame. It haunted him like some loyal lame dog that limped around after him.

Eoin lifted the letter, his eyes stinging with a mixture of fear and exhaustion. He tore the letter in half. He tore it again. And again. Until it was in tiny pieces.

His chest tightened and began to burn with red hot guilt. Maybe the letter was right, maybe he should prepare for the consequences. He tossed the pieces into the bin. Maybe, after all, it was the justice he deserved.

10

'I should get back to the plant,' Dan said, gathering the papers he and his father had been discussing into his brown leather document case.

'Before you go,' Peter said, 'I wanted to ask you something.' He was standing by the French windows and staring out at the gardens with his back to Dan.

'Okay?'

'Has Ursula talked to you about having an anniversary mass for your mother?'

'An anniversary mass? That's news to me.'

'If she does,' Peter said, 'do your best to dissuade her.'

'Right,' Dan said, in a mumble. Ursula hadn't mentioned anything to him yet, but if she did, he decided he wouldn't do as his father asked on this occasion. In fact, he quite liked the idea. Not that he was going to say that out loud.

'What? No protest? I thought you might be with Ursula on this.'

'I just do whatever you say, Pop.'

Peter turned to look at him. 'You don't seem yourself, Dan,' Peter said. 'You seem distracted.'

'Distracted?'

'Is that wife of yours making more demands? Wanting you to take time off to spend with her and the twins, no doubt. You can't let them dominate. Women need a tight rein.'

Dan sighed. His father wasn't just old school. He was medieval. Dan didn't argue with him when it came to Francesca, but, by the same token, he didn't heed any of his advice either.

'Francesca and the twins are fine,' Dan said.

'Well, there's something wrong with you, boy. Spit it out.'

Dan swore inwardly. 'Apart from the fact that I buried my son a couple of weeks ago, you mean? But you're right, I'm not myself. I heard some bad news yesterday,' he said.

His father came closer.

'I called into The Snug for a quick drink and Ciara McCann told me that Shay's really ill.'

His father raised an eyebrow.

'She's got a disease. It's like a severe type of Alzheimer's, called Creutzfeldt-Jakob disease.'

His father tutted. 'That's what used to be called Mad Cow Disease back in the day. Well, if the cap fits…'

Dan's voice faltered. 'Jesus, Pop, how can you say that? She's dying.' Hearing the words out loud gave him a shock. He felt an aching pang in his heart as he suddenly realised that once Shay was gone, that whole part of his life, that little family of his that never was, would be gone, too. Wiped out. And so quickly.

'Is she sure?' Peter said, coming over to the table.

'She's sure.'

'Well, that's life.'

Dan's eyes pooled with tears. 'That's life?' he said. 'That's all you can say?'

'What do you want me to say? It's very sad, but we have nothing to do with her.'

'She's the mother of my son. I've known her my whole life… I care about her.'

'We don't know Rory was your son.'

'My God, Pop, you need to stop making statements like that. Rory was my son. I know he was. And I'm only after burying him.' Dan clenched his jaw. He was in danger of breaking down and that was a major no-no in front of his father.

'You know I'll never believe that. You should've had a DNA test done, like I always told you to. That would've settled the matter.'

'Maybe I should dig him up,' Dan said, gripping the side of the table to stop himself from shouting, 'and get that test done.'

'There's no need for that kind of talk,' his father said, his eyes flashing a harsh look. 'Get a hold of yourself.'

'Get a hold of myself? Right, get a hold of myself.'

Dan thought his head might blow clean off his shoulders with the force of the rage inside him. His father could be a cold bastard – the coldest.

Peter's eyes fell to his feet. 'I know you're hurting. I'm not made of stone, but carrying on like this isn't going to help. You have a job to do, so go on with you, now. Get back to the plant.'

Dan grabbed his document case and, getting up from the table, marched to the door.

'You did ask,' he said, pressing on the door handle, 'what was bothering me and I told you. Expect me to stay distracted for a while as I deal with the loss of my son and the approaching death of his mother. And don't ask again.'

With that said, and not giving his father a chance to have the last word, he left.

Once in the hallway, he fell against the wall and let out a long, shaky breath. He gave himself a moment to calm down and when he felt a little better, he straightened up.

He began walking towards the front entrance when Louisa came running from the direction of the kitchen.

'Mr Feeney,' she said, slightly out of breath, 'I've been hoping to catch you.'

Dan stopped. Please God, she wasn't going to land him with some domestic crisis. He didn't think he could cope with another problem.

'You know how your father has me open his post for him,' she said.

Dan had forgotten about this arrangement, which was surprising because it had caused a fair bit of tension when Peter first put it in place. Dan didn't quite trust Louisa to be discrete about what she might discover in Peter's letters. She was a cousin of Daisy McBirney-Smith, who was known as the worst gossip in the village, and some folks said Louisa was a close second. She'd never been caught out carrying stories though, so Dan had no proof of disloyalty. And Peter was so adamant that it was beneath him to open his own correspondence and that Louisa wouldn't dare betray him. In the end, Dan lost the argument and the arrangement remained in place, never to be mentioned again.

Until now.

He gave Louisa a nod by way of encouragement to continue.

'Well, this came in yesterday,' she said, handing Dan a white DL envelope. 'You were gone before it was delivered. I didn't know what to do about it... it... it's so strange. I gave your father his other post from yesterday, but I decided not to let your father see this. I thought I'd better show you first.'

Dan frowned. He opened out the sheet of paper from the envelope. He had to do a double take to believe what he was reading: *I know what you did. Be prepared for the consequences.*

He checked the envelope. Nothing out of the ordinary; a standard stamp and a Letterkenny postmark. Who could've sent it? What did it even mean? Somebody with an axe to grind against his father? There was no shortage of people he'd crossed in his time.

Louisa hovered beside him, nervously rubbing her hands.

'You did the right thing,' he said.

He saw her face relax.

'Thank you,' she said.

'I can look after it from here.' He slipped the letter back into its envelope and tucked it into a pocket in his document case.

'I was hoping you would.'

She made to move away.

'Ah, Louisa,' Dan said, 'I don't need to tell you to say nothing to my father about this.'

'Wouldn't think of it.'

'And for that matter, say nothing to anybody else either. It's probably some silly prank – just nonsense.'

'I never talk to anybody about what happens inside these walls.'

She spoke the words emphatically. *Too emphatically*, Dan thought.

He eyed her. She eyed him back.

He pondered how best to handle the letter, wondering whether to take it seriously or ignore it. It seemed so… so infantile. Certainly not a threat. But then again… However, if he took it to the Gards, he was convinced they'd laugh him out of the station. Or even if they didn't, what could they realistically do about it? Then, of course, there was always the chance it was real. What if it referred to something his father did that wasn't legal? That might have been what the letter meant by "consequences". In that case, the Gards were the last people to involve.

The best thing might be to do nothing. If it was a wind-up, it would go away on its own. If it was serious, which was improbable, then whoever sent it would be certain to make contact again. Dan would keep a lookout for that.

'If you see anything strange like this again,' he said, 'just do what you did this time.'

'Bring it to you and not your father?'

'Exactly.'

'I'll be sure to,' she said.

Dan left the house, got into his car and started the engine. He sighed heavily as he set off down the half-mile-long driveway. He'd have a chat with Francesca when she came back from her conference. It'd be good to get her take on the letter.

He sighed again. 'I need this like a hole in the fucking head.'

11

The chip shop shifts started at four o'clock and ended at midnight, or at one o'clock on Fridays and Saturdays. Tonight was Friday. Shay looked at the wall clock. Only half eight. Time felt like it was going backwards. The smell of cooking oil from the fryers saturated the air. She knew she'd go home with that smell on her hair and skin. Her Covid mask only seemed to make the greasy stench ten times worse.

Shay was chopping onions, lettuce, tomatoes and gherkins, while Tracy Johnson was busy cooking up a phoned-in order, throwing a handful of onions onto the hot plate beside a sizzling beef pâté.

Tracy was a dull girl with one of those faces that always looked slightly confused by what was going on. However, behind that unsuspecting face was a very unpleasant person.

Shay gave her a sideways glance and thought about how Tracy could never bear to hear Shay mention Rory or his achievements. She had practically willed his business to fail when Covid hit. "He'll sell nothing now" were her words, if Shay remembered correctly. Was Tracy gloating now that her son was still alive while Shay's was in the ground?

A pang gripped her heart. Rory shouldn't be dead. She slapped the chopping knife down harder than she needed to. Maybe Tracy deserved to get a nasty surprise in the post, after all. Shay hadn't entirely ruled out that possibility.

At least Tracy was keeping quiet – for now, at least. A small mercy since she was a person who had opinions on every subject under the sun, and opinions that weren't exactly informed or rational. It had come as no surprise to Shay when Tracy declared she was an anti-vaxxer. She had stopped wearing a mask as soon as the first lockdown was over, even when she was working. Worse, she believed – and had the evidence to prove it, apparently – that the pandemic was a hoax engineered to gain more control over ordinary people. This was from a woman whose mother had died from Covid. She also believed – again with more "evidence" – that the Covid vaccine planted microchips in our bodies. The silly woman had even gotten off her lazy ass to go to anti-vax protests.

Shay dropped three large scoops of chips and two battered cod into a basket in the fryer and they sizzled when they hit the hot oil.

Morbid thoughts – more pressing than her irritation with Tracy – returned to her mind. In the not-too-distant future, she knew she'd have to pack in her job. Even though she hated the job and would leave it in a heartbeat, it did give her some semblance of normality, the pretence that things were the same, and she wanted to hold onto that for as long as she could. She hadn't breathed a word to Tracy about being sick and not only because she didn't want the woman knowing her business. Tracy's brother-in-law owned the chippie and Shay knew she'd go blabbing to him. Shay wanted to be the one to tell him and at a time that was right for her.

The fish and chips in the fryer began to turn brown. As she stared at the bubbling oil, Shay wondered about her letters. Nearly a full week had passed since sending them. She itched to know if they'd arrived with Peter Feeney and Eoin Devine; how her pair of targets had reacted; whether they were worried at all; and, best of all, who they blamed. She grinned. They deserved every bit of discomfort the letters might bring their way and she hoped it would be a lot.

It was then she realised Tracy was talking. She'd finally, inevitably, broken her silence.

'Did you hear that there's a whole pile of refugees just moved into The Seven Swords in Letterkenny?' she said.

Shay put her head down and gave the fryer basket a shake. Was she really going to have to listen to this shit? The refugee situation was Tracy's second favourite subject after Covid. Needless to say, her views on refugees and anybody "not from here" were as dumb as her views on the virus.

'They're taking over the whole town, so they are, and they're making the place look bad.'

Shay breathed out through her teeth and scooped three portions of chips into bags.

'The local businesses are saying they're losing money and there's hardly any tourists because of them. Where's it all going to end, that's what I want to know?' She plopped the meat pate and onions onto the lower half of a burger bun. 'Do you have the salad ready for the burger?'

Without looking at Tracy, Shay practically shoved a plastic bowl containing the chopped salad into her hands.

'They've been stealing out of the shops, you know,' Tracy went on. 'They're all thieves. As if they don't get enough from the government. Fuck's sake, the government treats them better than they treat us. I heard they—'

'Tracy, stop,' Shay said. In spite of all her troubles, or maybe because of them, she found herself unable to listen any longer. 'Tracy, I don't know if you realise it, but I don't agree with a single word that comes out of your mouth. Ever. About anything.'

Tracy swung round, her usually confused expression now mingled with disbelief. Her mouth hung slightly open. She was literally speechless. Shay knew this outburst could get her sacked if Tracy had mind to complain to her brother-in-law, but all that would mean was she'd have to leave the job a bit sooner than she wanted to and that might be worth it if she could give this ignorant, racist bitch a piece of her mind.

'Everything you say,' Shay said, 'is wrong, uninformed and offensive. You're what's called a fascist. And if you don't know what that means, look it up – preferably not on social media. You don't speak for me and don't ever think you do.'

Shay spoke clearly and didn't once raise her voice. She was so calm she could've been talking about what she had for breakfast.

Tracy looked like she might blow a blood vessel, but the bell above the shop door jangled cheerfully, interrupting proceedings. In came Andie McBirney-Smith.

The two women stared at each other until Tracy lowered her eyes. Shay could tell she was unsettled, probably not used to being on the receiving end of such a dressing-down. Shay, on the other hand, felt surprisingly buoyant.

'Get the order finished,' Shay said, to Tracy.

Shay turned towards Andie.

'Hi, Andie,' Shay said, smiling.

'Aww, hi,' Andie said, bowing her head.

Poor Andie, with her tousled, straw-like hair. The girl was nearly six feet tall, but she looked smaller because she stood with a stoop, like she was trying to hide. If that's what she was doing, it worked, because it was easy to forget she was there at all. She was such a shy girl, it seemed to hurt her to speak in front of people. With parents like Daisy and Rodney, it was little wonder she retreated into the background. Daisy talked enough for Rodney, Andie and half the village put together, though Rodney hadn't exactly taken a vow of silence either.

'There you go, Andie,' Tracy said, her voice much more muted than usual. 'Two fish and chips, one cheeseburger and chips.'

'We paid over the phone,' Andie said, her face turning red above her mask.

'I know,' Tracy said. 'You do that every week.'

'Enjoy your food,' Shay said.

Andie nodded and scuttled away.

'That's one weird wee girl,' Tracy said. As soon as she had the words out, she squeezed her lips together as though stopping in her tracks. 'I only mean, she's, you know, she's—'

'Whatever,' Shay said. 'I'm going to the storeroom.'

She left Tracy to her own company, thinking how she very much liked this new assertive her – a person who took no shit. She smiled, but no sooner was the smile on her lips than it dropped away. A shiver rippled down her back as she remembered not so long ago taking a lot of shit.

It was back in June, a couple of weeks after Rory dropped the bombshell about the debt, and she'd paid a visit to Peter Feeney. All of Rory's life, the miserable old bastard hadn't given him as much as a Christmas card. Christ's sake, he'd never even acknowledged him as family. But he was rich and Rory was in need and she figured that maybe he might do this single act of kindness. If only she'd been her new assertive self during that encounter. Things might've turned out very differently – or was that just wishful thinking?

*

Louisa, Peter Feeney's dour housekeeper, had shown Shay in and pointed her to an ornate chair, before leaving to let the master of the house know his guest had arrived.

Shay sat down, feeling very small and unsure in the expansive entrance hall. Crystal chandeliers hung from the high ceiling. A wide staircase curved along the far wall, disappearing around a bend. The beige carpet was deep and soft enough to sleep on. Select items of furniture were placed at well-chosen locations: a console table, a coat stand, a stand-alone full-length mirror – all of them oozing refinement and luxury. A generous porcelain vase filled with white and orange lilies sat proudly on the occasional table, their subtle fresh aroma teasing the air.

Funny how the place didn't look much different from the last – and only – time she'd been there. Then, she was seventeen, and she and Dan had come to tell his parents she was pregnant. That day was seared into her memory. Peter Feeney hadn't just shamed her; he'd broken her. She'd left the house with his voice shouting at her never to darken the door for as long as she lived.

Now, she was back.

Her stomach swirled and gurgled. This was a bad idea. She shouldn't have come. Her face mask felt too hot against her mouth. She probably didn't need it anyway – Louisa hadn't been wearing one – but best to be told that than have Peter Feeney use it as an excuse to put her out.

On the opposite wall, above the curved stairs, was a large portrait of a woman. Now, there was something that had changed since Shay's last visit. The woman in the painting had been alive then, although not much longer. Rory was barely a toddler, she had tragically died. Fell down those very stairs. The village rumour mill said she was drunk and slipped. Poor woman. Everybody knew she had a problem with the drink. *No wonder,* Shay thought, *being married to Peter Feeney.* He had her so brow-beaten, you wouldn't have wished her miserable life on your worst enemy.

Louisa returned. 'Come with me, Shay.'

Shay followed her along a corridor, not a word passing between them, until they reached a large oak door. Louisa opened it and moved aside to let Shay step through. She closed the door behind Shay, leaving her in what seemed to be a study – the kind of place you saw in films in the house of a mogul: floor-to-ceiling bookshelves, heavy oak desk, dark-green leather suite, deep-pile maroon carpet, French windows. The air was heavy with the smell of wax polish and leather.

Peter Feeney was seated, king-like, on a desk chair of the same style as the suite. He didn't get up, didn't indicate that she sit down, didn't smile or say a word of welcome. She remained standing at the door. Her stomach gurgled for another time and she swallowed hard, willing herself not to throw up. She was like that terrified seventeen-year-old again.

'You have five minutes to say whatever it is you have to say,' Peter said. 'And take off that mask, will you? I want to see your face when you're talking to me.'

She did as she was told.

'Thanks for seeing me, Mr Feeney,' she said. She took a deep breath. If he was giving her five minutes, she wanted to make every one of those minutes count. 'Rory... you know Rory... is twenty-three years old and, for his whole life, I've never asked you for anything.'

He leaned his chin on his hand, like a philosopher deep in thought, and raised one eyebrow. He peered at her from goat-like eyes that nestled under a pair of bushy white eyebrows. She could tell he knew where this was going.

'I'm here today because I need your help, Mr Feeney. Rory has grown up to be an industrious, upright young man. He worked hard to earn his college degree and even harder to set up his own business, all on his own, and he was doing well... until Covid.'

She paused, trying to gauge if he was reacting at all. There was nothing, only an awkward moment where she wished she could fade into the wall and disappear. Her left hand tightened.

'Covid, um, pretty much destroyed his business,' she went on, 'but he's a resilient boy and he came up with a new idea that would work, pandemic or not. The new business is succeeding, only all the disruption since the start of the pandemic has left its mark. He needs money to—'

Peter started shaking his head.

A reaction, finally, though not an encouraging one. Shay's

hands were sweating, her mouth was like sandpaper. She pressed on regardless.

'Rory needs money,' she said, hearing a slight tremble in her voice, 'to pay off some business debts. I'm here to ask you for thirty thousand Euros.'

She and Dan had gathered ten Euros between them, and she needed Peter to pay the balance.

'It would be a loan, of course,' she went on, 'that Rory would pay back, with interest if you so wish. Will you give him thirty thousand Euros?'

There. She'd said it all. Wasted no time; kept well within his five-minute deadline. Here was the moment of truth. She waited, seconds drawing out like hours, her heart about to explode, as he kept his philosopher's pose. Finally, he moved. She let out her breath.

'Well, Shay,' he started, clearing his throat, 'I knew this day would arrive. All those years ago when you came to our house with Dan and that boy growing inside you, I knew someday you'd be back with the begging bowl.'

'But I—'

'Hush!' Peter put up his hand like a traffic cop stopping cars. 'You'll be quiet while I speak.'

Shay bit on her lip.

'You Dunnes are no good. Never were. I remember your grandfather and his brothers. My father warned me against them. You're lazy folk; you have no gumption within yourselves to make anything of your lives. Bottom feeders, depending on other people to keep you alive.'

He stopped and pulled a pristine handkerchief from the breast pocket of his jacket. He wiped his forehead and dabbed his flushed cheeks. Shay thought he might be having a heart attack, one of those slow-build ones. If he did, she would walk out of there and tell no one.

'Can you even begin to imagine my utter dismay,' he continued, 'when Dan told me you were having his child? Do you have any sense of what it felt like? My only boy and a Dunne? I said to him the child probably wasn't even his. People like you don't care who they lie down with, but the gold-digger in you would think you'd hit the jackpot with the likes of Dan.'

'I nev—'

'What did I tell you?'

Shay breathed in and out, counting to four each time. She was so incensed she thought fumes had to be coming out of her nostrils.

'He insisted the child was his. I told him that wasn't the point. He wasn't going to marry you and give your offspring a claim to what I built with my own hands.'

'My son's a good man who works hard,' Shay said, unable to stops the words from pouring out. 'He's no bottom feeder.'

'And yet, here you are, asking for money on his behalf. I might've thought better of him had he come here himself.'

She wanted to kill him, take something with weight like an iron bar and actually beat him to death. She felt humiliated all over again. 'He told me he'd never come near you for anything,' she said, just above a whisper so as to disguise her anger. 'He doesn't even know I'm here.'

Peter shrugged. 'He has more sense than you.' He got up and came towards her.

'Please, Mr Feeney,' she said, 'I'm begging you to do this one thing for him.'

'It's time you left,' he said.

Panic descended on her like a cloud of dust, so strong she nearly choked. 'Please, Peter, please help him.' A teardrop spilled out onto her cheek. 'This is so important to him. He'll give you back every penny.'

He looked at her with disgust. 'Pull yourself together.'

'Help him, please?'

'Stop making a spectacle of yourself.'

Shay felt more tears land on her cheeks, leaving them moist. Peter went to the door and opened it, calling for Louisa.

'Get her out of here,' he bellowed.

Louisa reappeared and took Shay's arm. Shay went with her willingly, resigned to failure. She stole a last glance at Peter. She was convinced she could see a smirk on his wretched face.

Louisa walked her to the front entrance, saying nothing and keeping her gaze straight ahead.

When they reached the door, Louisa opened it. Her face softened.

'I'm sorry,' she said. She gave Shay's arm a gentle squeeze. 'He's nothing but an auld bastard.'

Shay stumbled away, cursing every fibre of her being for ever having thought Peter Feeney would show compassion for Rory.

12

'There you go,' Daisy said, setting down a hot mug of coffee on a coaster. 'Help yourself to biscuits.'

'That's lovely, Daisy,' Louisa said, lifting a chocolate digestive from the plate in the middle of the table. 'So, where is everybody tonight?'

'Rodney's at choir practice,' Daisy said, 'and Andie's about there someplace. Up in her room, probably.'

'She needs to get out more with people her own age,' Louisa said.

'Shure, don't I know. But she's as odd as two left shoes and she won't go anywhere. And I'm fed up trying to get through to her.'

'I thought she might come out of her shell a bit when she started palling about with that Natalie girl.' Louisa bit into her biscuit, feeling it crumble in her mouth.

'Me too,' Daisy said, 'but Natalie's never invited her to go on a night out and Andie's too much of a mouse to suggest something herself. She's got no gumption at times. I feel like giving her a good shake, so I do.'

'She wouldn't say boo to a brick,' Louisa said, her mouth too full. 'She's too soft.'

'Exactly, she's not pushy enough. I've told her she needs to push more, but will she listen?' Daisy raised her eyes to heaven and tutted. 'Anyway, tell me, any craic from the big house?'

Louisa took a sip of coffee and smiled. The two of them loved nothing more than a good gab about the goings-on at Peter Feeney's.

'There's something juicy, isn't there, Louisa? I know by the look on your face.'

'You have to keep this one between us.'

Daisy nodded. That was good enough for Louisa. The village pinned Daisy for a slabbermouth, but Louisa knew a different side to the person who stood behind the counter every day. Daisy was well able to keep her lips sealed when it was called for.

'So, it was about five… no, six days ago,' Louisa said, 'and I was going through the post, like I do every day, and guess what?'

Daisy eyes widened in anticipation, like they were about pop out of their sockets.

'He got a letter – an innocent-looking letter in a plain white envelope – and, well, you're not going to believe this.'

'What?' Daisy nearly squealed.

'It was one of them, what do you call them, a threatening letter… no, a poison letter.'

'Holy Lord!' Daisy whistled. 'Now, there's a surprise and a half. A poison pen letter. Imagine that. What did it say?'

Louisa recited the contents as best as she could remember, before finishing off her biscuit.

'Sort of vague, isn't it?' Daisy said. She lifted her coffee mug up to her mouth. 'I thought it might have accused him of something.'

'That's what I thought, too, cos I'm sure there's plenty he could be accused of, but then I thought maybe it was better this way.'

'How do you mean?'

'Well, won't this way make him think the worst?'

Daisy said nothing for a few seconds as though she was letting

Louisa's words sink in. And then she started to laugh – a wicked, delighted laugh. 'Oh, that is clever, so it is.'

'He deserves it, doesn't he?'

'He deserves it all right.'

Louisa sipped some more on her coffee, savouring the moment with her cousin. Daisy was savouring the moment, too, it seemed. After a while, she spoke up.

'Might not be the only one who deserves it,' Daisy said. 'I could think of one or two more candidates who could do with a wee shake-up like that.'

'Me too. There are a few rats in our community I'd like to see squirm.'

Daisy ran her finger down the side of her mug. 'I'd love to know who sent it, wouldn't you?'

'Wouldn't I just.'

'It has to be somebody local.'

'I'd say so,' Louisa said. 'Then again, Peter Feeney knows a lot of people from far and wide, so it's not necessarily a local.'

'Well, my money's on a local,' Daisy said.

'I wonder if anybody else got one.'

Daisy shrugged. 'I'm sure we'll find out soon enough.'

'Aye, I'm sure we will,' Louisa said. 'For now, we'll just keep a lid on it and wait and see what happens.'

13

'Thank God to be home,' Francesca said, exhaling loudly. 'Those conferences are so exhausting. And then having to stay the extra days to fit in that guest lecture – yuck.'

'It's good to have you back,' Dan said, driving out of the airport short-stay car park. 'I've missed you; the twins, too.'

'And I missed you guys,' Francesca said. 'I can't wait to see them.'

'I'd have brought them with me, only your plane was going to be delayed and I didn't fancy keeping two live wires amused in an airport lounge.'

'I hear you.' Francesca yawned and leaned back on the headrest.

'I told Dee to let them stay up 'til we came back, so you could put them to bed yourself.'

'Nice.'

She closed her eyes and put her hand on his knee. Dan turned onto the roundabout on the dual carriageway and set off in the direction of Derry. Raindrops fell haphazardly against the windscreen before the wipers cleaned them away.

'How was the trip anyway?' he asked.

'Same old, same old. I swear, Dan, some of my fellow psychologists have more problems than their clients. It'll be nice to get back to the normal world with you and the girls.'

Dan sneaked a glance in her direction before returning his eyes to the road. Francesca was a strong-minded woman who took shit from no one. Some men, his father came to mind, might find that off-putting but not him. She was statuesque with platinum blonde hair tightly cropped in a pixie style. His father didn't approve, of course – said she had a haircut like a man's. Not that Francesca gave a monkey's what he thought.

'I've something I've been dying to tell you,' Dan said. 'I wanted to save it 'til you got home.'

Francesca sat up. 'What's happened?' she said, her voice worried. 'Is it the girls?'

'No, no, it's nothing bad, just kinda weird.'

'Sounds intriguing.' She relaxed again. 'Do tell.'

'About a week ago… yeah, it was a week ago today… Louisa showed me a letter that came in the post for Pop. You'll never believe what it was.'

'I'm too tired to guess – just tell me.'

'A poison pen letter.'

Francesca was suddenly upright again. 'A what? Oh my God.' She laughed.

'What's so funny?'

Dan indicated right and manoeuvred the car onto the Foyle Bridge.

'The idea of your father getting a letter like that. I can imagine how he reacted. He must've had steam coming out his ears.' She laughed again.

'He doesn't know anything about it.'

'What do you mean?'

'I didn't let him see it. I intercepted it.'

'Dan? Was that wise? If he finds out you did that, he'll come down hard on you.'

'I've no intention of letting him find out.'

Francesca tisked. 'What did the letter say anyway? Can I see it?'

'I don't have it anymore. I was going to keep it 'til you got back, but then I thought it might be best to destroy it for fear of anybody getting sight of it. I ripped it into pieces and burned it.'

'But what did it say?'

Dan recalled it as best he could from memory. 'What do you make of that?'

'Umm, it's very general.'

'That's what I thought. Do you think it's a real threat?'

'Well, I can't be one hundred per cent, but, honestly, I don't think so. A real threat would be more specific.'

Dan took the road straight on at the end of the bridge. Another half an hour would get them home. The rain was falling harder now, drumming off the roof of the car, and the wipers speeded up.

'That's what I hoped you'd say,' he said. 'I thought it might have come from somebody Pop wronged in the past, but I'm more inclined to think it's a hoax. I've told Louisa to let me know if any more suspicious letters arrive.'

Francesca laughed again.

'What's funny now?' Dan said.

'It's fascinating, don't you think? Sending a letter like that. I wonder if whoever sent it has sent one to others or if this is the only one?'

'I never thought about that, though I don't see why that's fascinating.'

'No? It's like a social experiment, don't you think? If you sent that same letter to a group of people, it'd be so interesting to study their reactions. The variety of ways they'd read into that set of words. Would they be angry, confused, worried? Would they laugh it off? Would they feel victimised for no good reason, or would it stir up some guilty secret? There are so many tantalising possibilities.'

'You mightn't be so tantalised if you were on the receiving end of this experiment.'

'Possibly. You still have to admit, it's a genius idea. I only wish I'd come up with it.'

'You can't mean that.'

'Why not? What's the harm, really?'

Dan considered Francesca's take on the poison letter. Maybe she was right. He smiled, warming to her way of thinking. Yeah, the letter was harmless. All the same, he'd keep his Pop in the dark.

14

Natalie pulled her red puffer jacket up around her face. The sky might have been clear, but the day was bitter cold, too cold for early October, and even though it was afternoon, frost still lurked in places the sun hadn't managed to touch. She walked alongside Andie.

Natalie didn't have a lot in common with Andie, but beggars couldn't be choosers. Natalie wasn't from the village originally and she didn't know anybody. She and Eoin only moved there because they wanted to rent a whole house to themselves and Rory had told them they could get a place in the village for the same rent as a pokey apartment in town. Natalie met Andie in the shop not long after she moved there. Andie was the first person her own age she met and she was friendly, uber friendly. She even complemented Natalie on a coat she was wearing. Every time Natalie was in the shop after that, Andie struck up a conversation. Natalie thought she seemed lonely, desperate for a friend. Natalie was a bit lonely, too, and – if she dared to admit it – she liked the attention she got from Andie. They became friends; not best friends or even good friends, just casual friends that hung out now and then.

'I wish we didn't have to meet up outside,' Natalie said. 'It's fucking Baltic. I'd rather be in your cosy bedroom, tucking into a load of munchies from the shop.'

'Me too,' Andie said, her nose red at the tip, 'but you know Mammy says it's too soon after lockdown to let non-family back into the house. And at least we don't have to wear masks out here.'

Natalie groaned.

'It's nice to be meeting up at all, though,' Andie said. 'It's ages since we did.'

To Natalie, Andie was like a child inside a woman's body. She was so naive, gullible even. She still lived with her parents and even her job was in her parents' shop. She'd never had a boyfriend and the only bar she'd ever been in was The Snug. Her bedroom was like a teenager's: posters of pop bands on the walls, cuddly toys everywhere, a Hannah Montana quilt covering her bed. It was ridiculous. Only, the thing was, Natalie liked being in Andie's room. She found it comforting in a weird way, like an escape from real life.

'The shop's been busier than ever,' Andie was saying.

'Same at my shop,' Natalie said. 'Endless customers – moaning fucking customers.'

'Are you still fed up there?' Andie said.

'Sick to death. I mean, you must be pissed off, too, right?'

'I dunno, I don't mind it that much. It'll be mine someday.'

'Don't you want to do other things, go other places?'

'I never thought about it. There are good things about working there as well as bad. And shure, look at you, why're you just working in a shop, same as me, when you could do other things or go other places?'

Natalie pursed her lips. 'Touché, Andie.'

A green *An Post* van rolled by and beeped the horn. Postman George. Natalie rolled her eyes. Andie waved. They rounded a corner and took a road to the right, which veered farther from the village.

'Do you want to hear something totally mad?' Natalie said.

Andie's face brightened. Natalie noted how she never failed to be excited by her stories. Natalie got a buzz from that and she smiled.

'Do you know what a poison pen is?' She knew she shouldn't really spill the beans about Eoin's letter but keeping it to herself was burning a hole in her.

'Did you say a poison panda?'

'A poison panda? Where did you get that from?'

'I thought that's what you said.'

Natalie breathed out a heavy puff of air. Sometimes talking to Andie was like talking to a block of wood. 'Pay attention, will you? I said, "Poison pen". You don't know?'

Andie shook her head.

'You are so thick.' Natalie raised her eyes to heaven. 'It's a person who sends anonymous letters to people and the letters say something nasty or threatening.'

Andie perked up. 'Is that a thing?'

'Eoin got one.'

'Holy shit!' Andie leaned closer, her eyes dancing in her head. 'Eoin got a letter like that? What did it say?'

'It only had one sentence. "I know what you did, be prepared to..."' Natalie stopped. 'No, it's: "I know what you did. Be prepared for the consequences." What do you make of that?'

'"I know what you did. Be prepared for the consequences". Oh my God. And what was it he did?'

Natalie looked across at Andie to check if she was serious. Bless her dumb heart.

'Andie, you're missing the point. It's not really about what Eoin might or might not have done – especially in this case, cos all it says is: "I know what you did". That doesn't mean anything.'

Natalie's mind went to Rory – he was never far from her

thoughts. An ache pressed down on her heart. She recalled her suspicions that the letter was about Rory and that his mother might be the culprit. Eoin had dismissed the idea. So had she, more or less. She had no intention of sharing any theories with Andie, not that the girl had the brain to understand anyway. For Andie's benefit, Natalie was going to downplay the letter.

'But why send a letter?' Andie asked.

'To be vindictive, to scare the shit out of the person who gets it.'

'So, he hasn't done anything, and the sender doesn't really have to know if Eoin did anything or not.'

'Suppose so.' *Good*, Natalie thought. Andie was downplaying it all by herself without any prompting.

'Umm.'

'Eoin's not bothered, though. He thought it was daft.'

'He's not worried at all?'

Natalie shook her head.

'Would you be worried if you got one?' Andie asked.

'What? You don't half talk shite.'

'Umm.'

They came to another road junction and drifted left back in the direction of the village. The sun had dipped a little lower in the sky and a sharp breeze had picked up.

'I saw you at Rory Dunne's funeral,' Andie said. 'You looked really sad.'

Natalie didn't want to think about the funeral.

'You miss him a lot, don't you?'

'Maybe.'

'Do you think Eoin knew about you and Rory?'

'Fuck's sake, Andie, all you do is get your kicks from talking about my life.' Most of the time Natalie liked that – it was maybe even why she put up with Andie at all – but, sometimes, it could be a massive pain in the hole.

'I'm sorry.' Andie looked scolded and put her head down.

Natalie tutted. 'Don't go huffing. You need to toughen up, Andie.' She pushed her hands deeper into her pockets, seeking warmth. 'Eoin hasn't a clue I cheated on him. He'd lose his shit if he did. I was going to tell him before, you know, before Rory…'

'Went missing?' Andie said, coming out of her huff.

'Right. Then there wasn't any point telling him after that. I just let it go.'

'Are you and Eoin getting on okay now?'

'Naw, not really. I'll let you in on a secret.'

'What?'

There it was again, Andie's fascination with Natalie's life.

'I ended up falling for Rory,' Natalie said.

'Oh my God, you got serious about him?'

A pang of guilt and longing – a sickening combination – rose in Natalie's heart, making it hurt to swallow.

'I did, I got serious about him.'

Natalie remembered how it had started out, in November the year before. It was just a physical thing, just sex, but it wasn't long before it changed for her and she fell in love with him. She loved him like she had loved no one else, not even the way she had loved Eoin at the start. When Lorna and him split back in February, knowing he was a free agent got Natalie thinking that their relationship had a chance to become something more. She'd wanted that. She'd longed with her whole heart he had, too.

Andie looked stupefied, her mouth hanging open. 'Really? It's so romantic, like something from a movie. Did he fall for you, too?'

For a stupid girl, Andie had an uncanny knack of hitting the nail on the head at times, which sort of creeped Natalie out. She considered the question. Did he fall for her? For a little while, Natalie had thought so. She had even fantasised that maybe he'd been the one who ended it with Lorna so he could be with her. She had been waiting for him to tell her he loved her and wanted her to be with him, and only him.

But if she'd thought the end of him and Lorna was going to mean the beginning of something deeper for him and her, she couldn't have been more wrong. If anything, the end of him and Lorna spelled the end for him and Natalie, too. She saw less and less of him in the months after the break-up with Lorna, and the few times they were together, he was so distant. He talked a lot about how busy he was with the business, working every hour with no time for much else. Then, about a month before he disappeared, he finished with her. Her body tightened as she tried not to remember the night he had dropped his bombshell – the worst night of her life.

She thought she'd die and she had nobody she could tell. Not even Andie because she didn't want Andie seeing her that way. She had to keep the pain to herself, carrying it around every day like an elephant on her back. And now he was dead.

'Oh, he fell for me, for sure,' Natalie said. 'He told me he wanted us to make a go of it.'

'You never said.'

'Umm, well, I didn't want anybody knowing 'til we were ready to make our move.'

They were nearly back in the village.

'But why did he take his own life when he was so loved up with you?' Andie blurted out.

Andie had hit another nail on the head – with a merciless blow at that.

'I don't know,' Natalie said, snapping. But course she did. He wasn't loved up at all. He never had been.

Andie put her head down, huffing again. Natalie let her stew. They were silent for the rest of their walk and when they reached the main street, Andie said her goodbyes and was gone.

Natalie continued walking, in the direction of her house.

Now alone with her thoughts, she answered Andie's question about why Rory took his own life. Because she was sure she did know the answer. Or she was as sure as she could be without having been told by Rory himself.

Money. It was down to money. Money and that damned business. They nearly went under because of lockdown, but then Eoin came up with an idea for a new direction. He was so pleased with himself and said they were going to rake in the dough once it took off – which it did, she guessed, because he started throwing cash around like it was confetti at a wedding: buying the 4x4, splashing out on jewellery and designer clothes for the both of them, eating out in posh restaurants, clubbing and getting high. He even bought a pair of handmade Italian shoes, which she personally thought were ugly.

Drops of freezing cold rain landed on Natalie's forehead at the same time as a hot tear splashed onto her cheek. It soon turned as cold as the raindrop.

It was only when Rory went missing that she found out the truth. The money hadn't been coming from just business profits. Most of it was debt. A shedload of debt. Eoin had maxed out credit cards, bank loans, doorstep lenders, payday lenders, even loan sharks. He'd left no stone unturned. But the terrible thing was that he borrowed every penny in Rory's name. Eoin himself was clean. When the chickens came home to roost, as they were certain to do, it wasn't going to be in Eoin's hen house.

Up until that point, Natalie had no clue about any of it. No, definitely not. She had no clue. As the reality of what Eoin was telling her sank in, she remembered being horrified, disgusted. At herself. At Eoin. She completely lost it with Eoin. She went on a rant, lashing out, hating him for leaving Rory in the shit. There she was, broken, pining for Rory, sick with worry, and now she was being told that it was probably Eoin's fault that Rory was missing.

Eoin tried explaining he'd never planned for things to go so badly wrong. He'd expected the business to do well enough to cover the borrowing and for things to work themselves out. Only they didn't.

Nothing he said could calm her.

She couldn't believe he'd really been so stupid as to believe the business could stay standing under the weight of so much debt. He came out with some crap about it not being his finest moment and that business was like that – ruthless, cut-throat and sometimes people got hurt. He honestly didn't think he'd done anything wrong. He was such a rat bastard.

More rain splattered across her face and the sky darkened. A voice in her head taunted her. *But Natalie, are you really being honest with yourself?*

She didn't know what it meant.

Oh yes, you do. Come on now, you know.

And so, she did. But no, no, no, she couldn't go there. She couldn't bear it.

The rain was falling steadily. Natalie would be soaked to the skin by the time she got home. She didn't give a monkey's fuck. She didn't give a monkey's fuck about anything anymore.

Despite what she wanted, her mind dragged her back anyway, back to that last night she met Rory – the night he ended it. If only she'd known how wretched he was feeling, how bad things were, she could've done something, said something. But she didn't know. She had no clue.

*

Seven o'clock. The end of Natalie's shift had come and not a minute too soon. She was meeting Rory and couldn't wait. She hadn't bothered to spin Eoin a line about meeting the girls after work. When she didn't come home, he'd put two and two together and he could just like it or lump it.

She made a pit stop at the staff toilet before leaving to change into a pair of three-quarter-length jeans and a cropped satin top with a tie waist. She touched up her make-up; just some lipstick and a dash of mascara and eyeliner to accentuate her eyes. She rubbed her lips together and fluffed her hair. She looked at herself in the mirror, liking the end result.

'Now you stay cool when you see him,' she said, to her reflection. 'Nice and cool so you don't look like you're mad about him.'

She left the toilets and used the escalator to get to the ground floor. She walked towards the entrance and was about to step outside when she felt a tap on her shoulder. Natalie turned round to see Rory. She hadn't even noticed he'd been standing just inside the entrance. He was looking gorgeous in a white T-shirt and a pair of tight black Chinos and she was trembling with excitement. She just melted at the sight of him. Fuck trying to be cool. She flung her arms around him and kissed him.

'Hi there,' she said.

She slipped her arm around his waist and he responded not by slipping his arm around her, but by giving her a peck on the cheek. He was so cold, aloof. It was impossible not to notice, though Natalie tried with all her might.

They began walking, rounding the corner at the end of the street.

'It's so good to see you,' she said. 'I missed you like mad. Did you miss me?'

'Let's get to the car,' he said, without a glance. 'I need to talk to you.'

He speeded up and she did likewise. She touched his hand and he pulled it away, forcing it into his pocket. A sick feeling of dread seeped into her stomach.

'You look tired,' she said. 'Are you okay?'

'I'm grand.'

They got to the top of Linenhall Street and crossed Ferryquay Street to Pump Street.

'Want a cigarette?' she asked, half-jogging to keep up.

'No thanks.'

She put the cigarettes back in her bag. Her heart was breaking, so slowly and quietly it was barely noticeable.

'It's so warm and lovely, and it'll be bright for hours yet,' she said. 'It'd be lovely to take a spin to the beach. Maybe down to Inch like we did before.'

'I don't think so, Nat.'

At the top of Pump Street, they turned right into London Street and then straight on until they got to Bishop Street.

'Jesus, Rory, what's the rush? I'm out of breath. Can't we stop for a drink somewhere? It's supposed to be a date.'

'This isn't a date,' he said. 'Can we just get to the car? It's in the car park here.'

Natalie stopped. There it was again, that sick dread. 'What is this if it's not a date?'

Rory turned round. 'I don't want to do this in the street. Come to the car.'

'Do what?'

Though did she really need to ask? She knew what he meant. She might want to pretend she didn't, but she knew. Last time they had met up was May and now it was the end of June. He hadn't answered any of her calls or texts in that whole time. When he got in touch to suggest they meet up, it was completely out of the blue. She was desperate to believe it was a good sign. It was impossible to believe that now.

He started walking again, in the direction of the car park. She followed. They reached the car and got in.

Natalie thought she might throw up. She sat in the passenger seat, staring straight ahead. The sick dread had now reached her chest.

'This is hard for me to say,' Rory said.

'Then I'll say it,' she said. 'You're breaking up with me.'

'I'm ending it, yes, though it's hardly breaking up. We weren't in a proper relationship, were we?'

'We weren't?'

'We were an affair, cheating on Lorna and Eoin.'

'It's still a relationship.'

Natalie imagined screaming abuse and slapping his face. Then she imagined begging him to change his mind and kissing his face. All the while, she sat motionless, not as much as blinking.

'What we had,' he said, 'what we did, it was, you know, it was just infatuation – a fling. Surely you knew it wasn't serious. If you thought it was anything more, I really am sorry, and if I've hurt you, I never, ever meant that.'

A fling, she thought. To him, what they had together was a fling. To her, it was everything.

'It was always going to fizzle out. It was never going to last.'

Why not? she yearned to ask.

'You're not even with Lorna anymore,' she said, not above a whisper. 'And I always said I'd finish with Eoin.'

'Which I always said not to. And for the record, I'm not with Lorna anymore because she found out about us and ditched me. I love her and I don't know why the fuck I cheated on her, but I did and I destroyed what we had, and all I want is to have her back.'

Natalie couldn't believe what she was hearing. Every word that came out of his mouth was like a piece of glass being pushed into her skin. And, worst of all, he was almost in tears – because he'd lost Lorna.

A sound came out of her mouth, a dry, hoarse grunt that didn't sound human.

'I have to go,' she managed to say. She fumbled for the door handle.

'Stay where you are,' Rory said. 'I'll take you home.'

'No, I don't want you to. I don't want another thing from you.'

'Don't be like that.'

'Don't be upset, you mean? I should make it easy for you and say I'm fine and happy and no hard feelings, right? Wouldn't that be the decent thing to do?'

She could hear her voice crack, but she forbade herself to cry. All she wanted now was to get away from him, away to somewhere she could lick her wounds.

'Nat, I'm so sorry. Let me drive you back to Kilcross.'

'I'm going to ring Eoin. He'll come and pick me up.'

'I don't think you'll get him.'

'What do you mean?'

'He told me he had plans for tonight, something special. He didn't say what.'

Natalie frowned. He hadn't told her about any plans – not that it mattered.

'I'll get a taxi then.'

'That'll cost you a fortune. There's no need.'

'There's every need. Now, let me have some say in how this ends. Let me go.'

With that, she finally got the door open. She left the car and left Rory, not able to bear giving him as much as a backwards glance.

15

Sifting through the junk in the attic was proving to be a bigger job than Shay first thought. She'd pay for the exertion tomorrow and her body would be aching. She didn't care. She wanted to keep going, get it finished. It was a job she'd been putting off for as long as she could remember, but, now, time had caught up with her.

The attic ran the length of the house and was spacious enough for somebody of medium height, as Shay was, to stand upright. Two skylights, one at either end, leaked in some dull natural light from the foggy afternoon outside, and three electric bulbs placed at intervals along the ceiling chased the shadows back into the farthest corners. The air was stuffy and smelled dry and stale, like nothing alive could survive there long. A layer of dust covered just about everything, even the air, and miniscule specks performed an endless dance in the bars of light under the bulbs. Her mobile phone was perched on a wooden box and Shay had it tuned into the afternoon show on Highland Radio to kill the deathly silence of the forlorn old roof space.

She had the attic's lost treasures organised into three different piles: one for recycling, which was by far the biggest pile; one for any pieces she thought family or friends might want to have; and one for the junk that just couldn't be salvaged and would have to be dumped.

She could hardly believe some of the things she'd found so far. Toys, videos and even a VCR; a game console bundled together with a bag of matching games; endless boxes of clothes – Shay couldn't fathom why these had been hoarded away instead of being sent to a charity shop; broken furniture and lamp stands; Rory's first guitar with not a single string left on it; a stack of books and, in the middle of them, Rory's all-time favourite, *Barnaby Buckle and his Amazing Discovery*; a dozen or so soil-encrusted plant pots; a garden hose in perfect condition that Shay had hunted the house for but never found; and box files of accounts, bills and papers.

Under a bag of clothes, Shay found a dress mirror with a crack that ran all the way from the top to the bottom. She remembered how Rory had kicked off his boots and accidentally sent one of them flying into the glass. The crack was instant and the mirror was ruined. Superstition stopped her throwing it out, but the days of storing it were at an end and she walked it over to the recycling pile.

She caught her reflection, eerily murky in the long-discarded glass. The disease inside her hadn't reached the outside yet. She still looked the same as she had for the majority of her adult life: the bump in the middle of her long, thin nose – she touched it, remembering the slap from a camogie stick that had caused it; her oval face and freckled skin, with more wrinkles than ten years ago; and her David Bowie teeth, as Ciara liked to describe them because the two front ones leaned inwards. She was fairly much business as usual, but she knew that was changing.

Shay sighed. She left down the mirror and went back for the bag of clothes, dragging them across the floor to the recycle pile and carving a trail in the dust as she went.

The most surprising find was Rory's first bike – she was sure it was long gone. Its little Postman Pat bell was still attached. She remembered like yesterday fitting it and Rory jumping up and down as he waited for her to finish. She pulled the bell's lever and heard it clanging. The memories returned like a landslide, powerful enough to nearly smother her. She didn't even notice she was laughing as her mind replayed the image of Rory racing around the garden, overdoing it on the bell ringing and nearly colliding with their cat because he hadn't properly mastered the breaks.

Shay ran her fingers over the bike's handlebars, feeling the cold roughness of the neglected metal. It would have to be recycled. Maybe the materials would be used for some other useful object – maybe even another bike for another little boy. She yanked off the bell and placed it gently on the family and friends pile. Her heart couldn't bear to let it all go. She pulled the lever again and, suddenly, without any warning and with more force than a summer rainstorm, she burst into tears.

She raged at the circumstances of her life. Rory – gone. His funeral almost three weeks since. The death sentence she'd been given and so little time to make the most of what was left. Her whole world had turned into a nightmare. Mere months ago, she had been contented – happy with her life of modest achievements. She wasn't complaining about what she had nor was she striving for more. So why was it all being taken away? How could that be happening?

When her tears eventually subsided, she was worn out. She dabbed her eyes with a tissue and grabbed a bottle of water she'd put next to her phone. Finding a place to sit, she drank the water greedily, relishing its taste, so fresh and invigorating – everything the attic, or her life, wasn't.

She put her head in her hands and let her thoughts stray to their pet subject these days. The letters. About two weeks had passed since sending them and there wasn't a whisper. A few times, she had come close to calling Dan and had had to stop herself.

After all, what could she say that wouldn't sound suspicious? The silence, the not knowing gnawed at her like a toothache.

It occurred to her that the letters might not have worked. Peter and Eoin might've taken one look at their letter and laughed it off as a joke, never giving it another thought. If that was the case, where did it leave her?

An idea percolated in her addled brain.

What if she sent a follow-up letter? If she did, what would that look like? She wasn't sure and she'd have to be careful not to say anything that could lead back to her. It might be enough to send the same letter again; getting the letter a second time would show them this problem wasn't going away.

Then there was the possibility of widening the net. She'd considered it before and dismissed it. Maybe it was worth revisiting. It wasn't like there was a scarcity of deserving candidates.

Shay stood up and dusted off her jeans. The little rest had done her good. She'd give the letters more thought later on. For now, there was the attic to clear.

16

'I think that's us for today, Pop,' Dan said, 'unless you have anything else?'

'No, I haven't.' Peter stretched his leg and winced.

'Are you okay?' Dan asked.

'Stop fussing like an old maid,' Peter said. 'It's just old age. It comes to us all.'

Peter saw the reproached look on Dan's face. A face that had his mother's eyes – long and shaped like almonds. He had the height and dark skin of his mother's family, too, and a bush of short fine hair that sat like a halo on his high forehead.

'You haven't forgotten about coming over to ours for dinner on Sunday.'

'Yes, yes, the usual monthly invite. I'll be there – if you don't postpone again.'

'Give it a rest, Pop,' Dan said. 'You know why we postponed last weekend. And we did invite you to our alternative plans.'

'The month's mind mass for Rory Dunne? Not for me. And the mass was actually on the Saturday, so you didn't need to disrupt our usual Sunday arrangement.'

'We set aside Sunday as a special day to visit Rory's grave and go out for a family meal. As I say, you were invited. It was really nice, actually.'

Peter sighed heavily.

'Well,' Dan said, 'Francesca's doing your favourite this Sunday: roast beef with all the trimmings.'

'At least that's something.'

And there it was, another look on Dan's face. This time, hurt. Dan was far too sensitive. His mother's fault. Aggie had spoiled him. And his sister. He couldn't make a decision on his own. Peter was compelled to have these meetings with him two or three times a week, just to keep him right.

Dan stood up, tucking his document case under his arm. Peter had bought it for him the first day he started working for the firm. He liked that Dan used it so much.

'I'll walk you to the door,' Peter said, sliding his hand over his still thick, but white hair. 'It'll help me get this bloody leg moving again.'

He hated that his leg was so prone to seizing up. He was as healthy as a bull apart from that.

They reached the door. Dan hesitated.

'Umm, did Louisa say how long she was going to be off when she phoned in sick?' he asked.

Peter threw him a quizzical look. 'Louisa? Why are you so interested in her all of a sudden?'

'No reason.'

Dan seemed flustered. *The boy would never make a poker player*, Peter thought.

'If she has Covid, like she thinks she might, she'll be out for another week or more.'

'That long?' Dan's brow furrowed. 'Umm, do you want me to look after your personal post? I know she usually does that.'

'My post? I can manage that myself until she comes back.'

'Are you sure? I'd be happy to, ah, you know, handle it.'

'No need.'

'But you don't like having to—'

'Dan, just go. I'll see you on Sunday.'

Dan reluctantly made his goodbyes and left. The front door closed with a loud bang that echoed off the vast walls of the entrance hall.

Peter went into the lounge and lowered himself into his Chesterfield. The post that Dan was so worked up about sat on the side table where he'd left it that morning. He plopped the bundle of envelopes on his lap.

He waded through invitations, advertisements and charity appeals, tossing them aside. Then, he saw a plain white envelope without any corporate or organisation logo. He opened it and extracted the letter inside. He didn't know what he'd been expecting, but what met his eyes made his mouth gape open.

'What in God's name…?'

He read the single sentence on the otherwise blank page: *I know what you did. Prepare for the consequences.*

At first, he couldn't comprehend what he was reading. Sure, he understood the words. But the meaning of them, the meaning of sending them to him, was beyond his grasp.

'This is ridiculous.'

He checked the envelope. It had only his name and address, printed, a stamp and a local postmark. He examined it. Not Kilcross but the next village over. He turned the letter itself around in his hand, scanning it closely for any marks. Like the envelope, it had nothing revealing. He read the sentence again. They knew what he had done.

Did they indeed?

His head pulsed with a far-off hint of rage.

The author of this letter could be nothing other than foolish or exceedingly brave. No one who knew Peter Feeney would dare send him such an abomination and expect to go undiscovered or unpunished. When he found that fool or hero – in the end, they amounted to much the same thing – he would ruin them. And he would take pleasure in doing so.

Peter curled his thin lips over his teeth in a grimace. The throb in his head intensified as his rage crawled closer. Goddamn it. Who did they think they were dealing with here? A country yokel who couldn't spell "cat"?

He was far from the boy he had started out as; from a family of nine and never knowing from one day to the next if there would be food on the table, going to Scotland at fifteen and hard-grafting it on the building sites, eventually finding his way into the engineering business, then putting himself through night school to earn an engineering qualification. And after fifteen years of excruciating toil, coming home with the experience, the knowledge, the contacts and the money to set up on his own. It took guts to do that; it took a man of granite to do that – an exceptional man.

'This is the work of somebody with too much time on their hands,' Peter said, aloud. 'I should treat it with the contempt it deserves. I should throw it away and never give it a second thought.'

Peter squeezed the letter in his fist. He wouldn't tell Dan. The boy would panic and become a nuisance. No, he would keep his own counsel.

His rage subsided, only to be replaced with a deep and nagging disquiet. Sitting there alone in the empty house with his thoughts, he longed for the company of others for once.

17

A frenzy of sounds, whirring machines, hammering, sawing and clanging metal hit the ears of Mary-Margaret Walsh as she opened the door to the workshop. The open-plan room was crammed with workbenches and cupboards and shelves and the air carried a mix of odours: glue, paint, wood and that fresh laundry detergent she loved the scent of so much. This was where the hospital ran a programme for the outpatients. They came here every day, like they would a regular job, to learn skills and to make things, all with the hope that the experience might improve their lives.

Mary-Margaret had no respect for the programme. She knew it was doomed and could achieve nothing. She'd been working at St Bart's with psychiatric patients ever since she had qualified as a nurse and she was far too aware of what they were like. Half were chancers; weak, lazy people, strung out on alcohol or drugs or pretending to be messed up in the head so they could sponge off the state. The other half were genuinely mad and the best that could be done was to drug them into oblivion and keep them locked up. Either way, the workshop programme was a waste of money. The hospital could save itself a few quid if they listened to her – as if they ever would.

There was one good thing about the workshop, though. She could make use of it for her own benefit. One of the workshop activities was to repair donated clothes. The first task the patients had to do was wash them. They had an industrial-sized washing machine and a dryer, no less, specially for the job. Mary-Margaret's own washing machine was broken. It didn't make sense to buy a new one when there was one right here, in the hospital.

Mary-Margaret scuttled to the far side of the workshop, a backpack slung over her shoulder. She kept an eye out for Tony, the workshop supervisor. He always shooed her away if he caught her, so she tried to time her visits to when he was likely to be on a break.

She reached the washing machine safely and threw the backpack to the floor. She smiled. Her little helper was exactly where Mary-Margaret hoped she'd be. Her small, frail frame was hunched over a pile of old clothes and she seemed lost in her own wee world.

'Hello, Sally,' Mary-Margaret said, loudly. 'How are you on this fine Monday morning?'

Sally jumped the height of herself. Mary-Margaret laughed, pushing her horn-rimmed glasses up on her nose and fixing her face mask to keep it under the glasses frame. She hated when her breath escaped and fogged up the glass.

'Oh God,' Sally said. 'Nurse Walsh. I didn't see you there.'

'What're you up to today then?' Mary-Margaret said. 'Keeping out of trouble, I hope.'

'Am I in trouble?' Sally frowned. She started fidgeting with her face mask.

'Only a bit.'

Fear clouded Sally's eyes. 'I haven't done anything.'

'Don't worry, I'll not tell.'

Sally stopped fidgeting but the fear didn't leave her eyes.

'Your face mask is crooked, dear,' Mary-Margaret said. 'Here, let me fix it.'

She reached for the ear loops and gave them a hard tug, pulling the mask up to Sally's eyes. Sally winced.

'Something wrong?' Mary-Margaret asked.

'Nothing, Nurse Walsh.'

'Good girl.'

Mary-Margaret took a tiny bottle of sanitiser from her tunic and doused her hands, before returning the bottle to its pocket. Funny how the world got so obsessed with using the stuff during the pandemic. She'd been using it for years, not just at work, and she carried it with her everywhere. There were germs all over the place, on every surface imaginable, and she had no intention of being contaminated.

'Do you want to do me a favour, Sally?'

Sally's eyes grew wide. 'Umm, I don't—'

'Oh, come on, why are you acting like a scared rabbit? Do you want to help me or not?'

'I'm afraid to get caught.'

'How are you going to get caught? All I want is some clothes washed. If you throw them into the machine, no one's going to be any the wiser. And I only have a small bag, no bed sheets or quilts this time.'

'But Tony—'

Mary-Margaret pursed her lips. Sally was getting tiresome. 'Now, listen here, missy, you don't want Tony finding out you've been taking some of the charity clothes home, do you?'

'I never did. Don't say that.' Sally's hand started shaking. She pulled her tousled hair back from her face.

'No, that's right, you didn't take any clothes, Sally. But they're going to believe me if I tell them you did, aren't they?'

'Please, Nurse Walsh, you wouldn't do that.'

Sally was on the verge of breaking down. Mary-Margaret contained a grin. This was too easy. She had Sally exactly where she wanted her. Now she only needed to reel her in.

'Calm down,' Mary-Margaret said, rubbing Sally's arm. 'You're all right. You know I'd never do anything to get you into bother.'

She gave Sally a minute to settle, continuing to rub her arm.

'That's better,' she said. 'You okay now?'

Sally nodded.

'Good, that's more like it.' Mary-Margaret lifted her backpack from the floor. 'Now, go on and be a pal.'

She pushed the bag into Sally's hands and Sally took it, without a word of resistance. Mary-Margaret pushed her glasses back up on her nose. If there was one thing she knew, it was how to handle these fragile excuses for human beings.

'When do you think you'll have them ready for me, Sally?'

'Tomorrow?'

'Oooh, tomorrow? Really?' Mary-Margaret said. 'I'm not on shift tomorrow.'

'Today?' Sally said, sheepishly.

'Today would be great. You knock off at four, don't you? I'll call for them then.'

'Do you want them ironed, too?'

'That would be so sweet, thank you.'

Mary-Margaret turned on her heels and walked out of the workshop with a bounce in her step. If she'd been able to whistle, she'd have been giving it her all.

As she got to the end of the corridor, she almost collided with Orla Ryan. Mary-Margaret's contented little moment ended abruptly. Orla Ryan lived in Kilcross not far from Mary-Margaret, but she was also a ward manager at the hospital. She was shaped like a beach ball and had beady eyes that nestled into her chubby face like raisins pressed into dough.

'Mary-Margaret,' Orla said, 'you nearly knocked me over.'

'Sorry,' Mary-Margaret said.

If they were in McBirney's shop right now, Orla would just be another customer. But at work, Orla had authority over her and Mary-Margaret hated that.

'What're you doing down here?' Orla asked.

I could ask you the same thing, Mary-Margaret thought.

'It was my break,' she lied. 'I was out in the garden getting some fresh air.'

Orla squinted. 'Umm, is it even your break?' Orla glanced behind Mary-Margaret's shoulder. 'The outpatients' workshop is down here.'

Mary-Margaret felt her face go red. That bitch. It was like she had a sixth sense.

'You better not be up to your old tricks,' Orla said. 'You won't get off so lightly this time. I mean that.'

'I'm offended you'd think that.'

Orla snorted. 'Don't come the innocent with me. Remember, I'm keeping my eye on you.' Orla began walking away. 'And get back to your ward.'

Mary-Margaret watched her take off like a bullet down the corridor. Why was she always rushing about like the building was on fire? And why was she always snooping in places she shouldn't be, popping up when Mary-Margaret didn't want her to? The horrible woman was the bane of Mary-Margaret's life.

She set off to her ward, the bounce in her step gone.

*

Mary-Margaret opened the front door, exhausted but relieved her long shift was over. Those run-ins with Orla-bloody-Ryan really took their toll. The incident earlier that day had been churning around in her head like a wash in one of Sally's machines and had ruined the whole shift. Still, she was off for the next week and that was something to look forward to.

She set her backpack on the ground. At least she had something to show for her troubles. Another successful laundry day: her clothes were washed and ironed – complements of the dim-witted Sally.

She sprayed her hands with sanitiser from a spray bottle resting on the small console table near the door and picked up the post that lay strewn at her feet. She shuffled through it: a couple of junk letters, what looked like an electric bill and a plain white envelope that gave no clue as to what was inside.

That piqued her interest.

She put the other the letters on the table near the door and opened the white envelope.

18

George Grant was in McBirney's. Rosie had made broth for their dinner and she wanted him to pick up some rolls on his way home. And to brighten up this dull Monday evening, maybe a couple of custard slices wouldn't go amiss either. If Rosie didn't want hers, he'd not let it go to waste.

He was at the back of the shop where the bread was. Andie McBirney-Smith was nearby stacking one of the shelves with biscuits and crackers.

'How're you doing, Andie?' George said, putting four crispy rolls into a paper bag.

Andie stopped what she was doing and put her head down. *Odd wee girl*, George thought. Rodney came through from the door that led to the storeroom.

'How's George?' he said.

'How's Rodney?' George answered.

'Have you not finished those shelves yet?' Rodney asked Andie. 'Hurry up, will you? I want you to help me clean the dairy fridge this evening, ready for a new order coming in tomorrow morning.'

George saw Andie's head droop even lower, if that was possible.

Daisy was having a right old gab with Louisa Allan and Francesca Feeney up at the counter, and Matilda Johnson was floating around the aisles with one of the wee wheelie basket contraptions. Even from the back of the shop, George was still able to catch what the women were saying.

'Are you feeling better, Louisa?' Daisy said.

'Grand now,' Louisa said. 'I was back at work again today.'

'You'll have been missed at the house,' Francesca said.

'I think it's my dinners Mr Feeney misses,' Louisa said. 'I thought I had Covid so I didn't want to take a chance going near him.'

'Very wise,' Francesca said.

'People are far too worried about Covid, so they are,' Louisa said. 'There was no need for half the panic the government put on us. I hardly even believe there was a virus.'

'Oh, the virus was real,' Francesca said, 'but the pandemic's put a big strain on us, that's for sure.'

'When we were in the lockdowns,' Daisy said, 'we did our best and we pulled together. We looked out for each other. Since they've been over, it's all changed. We've lost that strong community spirit. It even seems like people are on edge lately, gone a bit haywire.'

'That's interesting,' Francesca said. 'Tell me more about what you've noticed.'

George tutted. Whatever about Daisy and Louisa, he thought a person of Francesca Feeney's position in the community would've known better than to be standing in the local shop taking part in the gossip.

'I'm not sure I can put my finger on it,' Daisy said.

Before anybody could say another word, the conversation was interrupted by Matilda Johnson.

'I wouldn't mind getting my basket checked out,' Matilda said, 'if it's not getting in the way of what you're doing there, Daisy.'

Ouch. Even George felt that one. He shuffled closer to the counter to wait his turn.

'No need to be like that,' Daisy said. 'I'll serve you right away.'

'Have you a problem, Matilda?' Louisa asked. 'Cos you're standing there like you're chewing on a mouthful of sour sweets.'

'Is that right, Louisa?' Matilda said. 'Well, you're standing there not even wearing a mask, but looking at me like I'm the one with the problem.'

'Steady on there,' Daisy said.

'And you're no better,' Matilda said, turning on Daisy. 'You've got that mask sitting on your fucking chin. Are you brain-dead? You're as bad as my sister. Why aren't you being careful?'

'Now, listen here, I won't have you—'

'You realise Covid has killed people,' Matilda said. Her voice cracked.

Daisy's face went purple and she looked embarrassed. 'There,' she said, pulling the mask up over her mouth and nose. 'Now, it's all right, Matilda. I'll get your things checked out for you.'

'You know what,' Matilda said, 'forget it. I'll get my groceries elsewhere.'

With that, she stormed out of the shop, leaving her wheelie basket on the floor. When the rattle of the slamming door subsided, silence descended. The three women looked at each other.

Rodney and Andie appeared behind George.

'Are things all right, dear?' Rodney asked.

Daisy pulled down her mask and looked like she was about to speak when a scream rose up from outside. George, Rodney, Andie and the three women piled over to the window. On the street, in the fading light of the evening, Matilda Johnson and her sister, Tracy, were at war.

'I've been looking for you,' Tracy shouted, stomping towards Matilda, her eyes wild.

Matilda had a confused expression, mingled with a bit of fear, George thought. No wonder. Tracy was like a charging elephant.

'If you have something to say to me,' Tracy screamed, pointing her finger, 'why don't you just say it instead of being a sneaky bitch?'

'What're you talking about?' Matilda took a couple of steps back.

'Don't insult me; you know exactly what I'm talking about. You blame me, I know you do, but I won't take the blame. It wasn't my fault she died.'

'Are you talking about Mammy?' Matilda said.

'You think me being vaccinated would've made a difference?'

'I don't want to talk about this and certainly not in the street, in front of all and sundry.'

'But you won't let me into your house because I'm not vaccinated, so we'll have to do it here.'

'No, we won't. We've nothing to talk about. You're stupid and there's no talking to stupid.'

'You think I went to that march and brought Covid back to our parents. You think it's me that gave them Covid.'

'Go away, Tracy. Go and get some help. You really fucking need it.'

'Don't you dare dismiss me or make out I've got something wrong with me.'

'Why're you bringing this up now? What's made you so angry all of a sudden?'

'Why am I… are you fucking serious? Like you don't know? Don't take me for a fool.'

'Tracy, you are a fool. Now, leave me alone before I call the Gards.'

Matilda started walking to her car, which was parked a few yards from the shop. Tracy followed, still shouting, still demanding answers. Matilda ignored her all the way and got into her car without another word. She sped off, leaving Tracy standing in the street, alone and fuming and with nowhere to spew her rage.

Tracy walked away, unsteady on her feet and like somebody shell-shocked.

'Dear God,' Rodney said, 'what was all that about?'

George was asking himself the same question. He wondered if maybe he knew and it was to do with the same thing poor old Sarah Maguire had brought to his attention on the Friday before. He dearly hoped he was wrong.

'Highly entertaining,' Francesca said.

George glanced at her, unamused.

'That right there is what I was talking about,' Daisy said. 'The whole village has gone haywire.'

19

Mary-Margaret peeked into the envelope. Inside was a folded page. She shook the page out onto the table without touching it and, dropping the envelope, she sanitised her hands again, before lifting the page.

Nothing about the harmless exterior of the envelope could have prepared her for the horror that lurked within. The words, so few of them, struck her like a bolt of vengeful lightning from the heavens.

Mary-Margaret let go of the letter and lowered herself onto the floor. Her hallway, lovingly decorated in pinks and whites, the gateway to her home, the safest place in the world, had been violated. She sank deeper into the cerise carpet, trying to take what comfort she could from its soft, spongy pile.

The letter sat a foot away, innocently resting on the carpet, whiter than snow. Reluctantly, she reached for it, lifting it with her thumb and index finger like it was some disease-ridden object. Maybe she'd read it wrong. She checked. She hadn't. She recoiled with a gasp. It was there in black-and-white print. It was undeniable: *I know what you did. Prepare for the consequences.*

'Oh, dear Jesus,' she wailed. 'What *is* this?'

Somebody was out to get her. Mary-Margaret scrutinised the offending letter in her hand and felt panic edge closer like darkness at dusk. She bit furiously on the inside of her cheek. A thousand questions fought battles in her head – questions she could only guess answers to. She was certain of one thing, though. The letter was referring to her extracurricular activities at St Bart's.

Damn whoever sent it. They didn't know their asses from a black hole in deep space. She was a good nurse, probably the best. She understood the patients better than anyone else in her profession. She could sort the chancers from the genuinely sick and she knew what worked for both. Tough love. No pandering. The Sallys of this world were better off because of her approach. When she had Sally do her washing, that was never to take advantage. What that said was: "I'm giving you responsibility, like I would anybody else." That was a good thing.

A quiet meow jerked her out of her meanderings. The apple of her eye, her well-fed tomcat, all black except for a patch of white on his front left paw and another on his right eye, ambled towards her.

'Oh, Twiffles, there you are,' she said. 'Where have you been? Up having your nap? Did you hear Mum-Mums being upset? Come here, my darling. Give me a hug.'

She gathered him in her arms, her unwelcome letter still held between her fingers, and squeezed him hard. He felt comforting, like the carpet, though not quite so accommodating. He wriggled away from her clutches, giving a little snarl.

'Mercy, Twiffles, don't be so cold. I need your support here. You're my only family.' She pushed up her glasses with her index finger.

Family! She snorted. Not that they would've been much better than Twiffles, if they'd still been alive. There had only ever been Mother and Father, and an aunt who'd lived in England she had met once growing up. Mother and Father had been no-nonsense sort of people who wouldn't have approved of her wallowing and whimpering. They hadn't approved of very much altogether. Lord knows, she might have been a happily married woman with her own family if… there hadn't been a thing wrong with Drew, the only man who had ever taken an interest in her… but Mother and Father wouldn't… She slammed the wall with the side of her fist, rattling a cat-shaped ceramic ornament hanging over her head.

Agh! No point re-treading that tired old ground. More pressing matters were at hand. Mary-Margaret forced herself back onto her feet and leaned against the wall. She felt dizzy – probably stood up too soon.

'Did you see what the bad postman left for poor Mum-Mums, Twiffles?'

But the cat was disappearing with a haughty trot through the kitchen door.

'You're hungry, my darling. Really, how can you think of food after what's happened to Mum-Mums today?'

Mary-Margaret trotted after Twiffles into the kitchen. The heat was stifling, a little too much, but Mary-Margaret tolerated it that way for Twiffles' sake. He liked it warm.

'I suppose I'll have to get you food even though I need to talk about this.'

She waved the letter in Twiffles' direction, before putting it on the countertop. She took a pouch of gourmet cat food from the fridge and emptied it into a stainless-steel bowl. Twiffles clawed at her hand as she returned the bowl to its usual spot.

'Bad boy, don't tear my skin off.'

She filled another stainless-steel bowl, a larger one, with cold water from the tap and left it beside the food.

'There you go now, fed and watered. Mum-Mums spoils you, doesn't she? If only my problems were so easy to solve.'

She went back to the letter and read it again, as though the words might change with further examination. They didn't, of course. They stayed exactly the same.

'Oh, Twiffles, who sent this sick thing?'

The cat paused, purred and continued eating.

'Oh, you're so right, my darling, it's truly awful.'

Twiffles munched at his bowl. Mary-Margaret slipped off her air-cushion sole shoes and wriggled her toes.

'You may not realise, Twiffles, but my particular profession is extra special, even within nursing. General nursing is important, too, of course, but it's basic in its own way. The world is full of sick people. They need primary care... general nurses give them that care, and the patients get better or they die. End of story.'

She straightened herself and took a deep breath.

'Mental health nursing is far more subtle and mental health nurses like me have a much more difficult job to attend to. People outside my profession simply don't get this. What am I saying? The people *inside* my profession don't get it. They don't know the best way to deal with these patients. Not like I do. And I get persecuted because of their ignorance.'

She took off her glasses and set them on the counter beside her. She wouldn't wear them for the rest of the night; they were hurting the bridge of her nose. Mary-Margaret could see perfectly well without them – the lenses were clear glass, after all. She only wore them because they gave her an air of sophistication and helped camouflage the slight turn in her left eye.

'When I leave a patient alone at some far corner of the grounds after a walk, that's never intended to scare or confuse them. I leave them there because I know they have it in them to find their way back. It encourages independence.'

Her voice was low, almost a whisper, as she struggled to contain the loathing that was rising inside her like a high tide in a storm.

'If I hold their medication back from them at times, it's only because I know they can do without it. Or when I give one of them a bit extra, if they've been a bit hyper all day, it's only to calm them down and help them get a good night's sleep. There was that one time the patient didn't wake up again, but that wasn't my fault.

She was ready to die anyway. And besides, nobody thought for a second it had anything to do with the medication.'

To distract her mind for a moment, she pulled out a spray can of pine-scented air freshener from the cupboard under the sink. She walked the perimeter of the kitchen, spraying as she went. Twiffles was dearly loved but, like all cats, he could be a bit stinky.

As she sprayed, the fragrance from the pine soothed her. She could nearly imagine herself in the woods in Swan Park down in Buncrana, feeling patches of warm sun through the leafy branches, hearing the happy chirping of birds, her feet pressing into the cushiony cool moss on the ground.

Her kitchen was calm again, her brain able to think. She left the can back under the sink.

Twiffles had finished eating – his bowl licked clean – and he was lapping at the water.

'Mercy, Twiffles, you've finished all your dinner. I'm glad this whole ugly business hasn't put you off your appetite.'

Twiffles purred, stretched and then swaggered out of the kitchen. Mary-Margaret let him go. Perhaps best to shelter him from some of the trauma of what was happening. She threw the letter another glance and asked the golden question. 'Who sent it?'

Her sense of panic tried to creep back. Who indeed? Her instinct leaned towards Orla Ryan. Although, all of Orla's gossip and lies about her had turned her co-workers against her, so now none of them liked her and that meant any one of them could be the culprit. Then again, Orla had spread malicious rumours about her to people in the village, too. It was possible one of them was guilty.

Mary-Margaret was too exhausted and distraught to think straight. She needed a good night's sleep. And as soon as she could, she'd make it her business to chat to the person who was her only concrete connection with the letter. George Grant. And maybe even he wasn't above suspicion.

20

George Grant had his small green *An Post* van parked up in a lay-by a couple of miles outside Kilcross. The lay-by was a secluded spot – or as secluded as you could get in a country place where everybody knew everybody – and George used it to take his morning tea break. He'd been the postman for the area since he left school at the age of seventeen and he was no young buck now, so he knew his round well enough to sleepwalk through it – which was a good description of how he got through it most days.

A piping hot cup of tea from his Thermos flask was set on top of the dashboard, the rising spirals of steam causing the windscreen to fog up. George pulled a cold cheese toastie from a paper bag on the passenger seat and crunched into it, relishing the salty taste of the congealed cheese inside the soft toasted bread.

'Lovely,' he mumbled, through a full mouth. 'Better hot, but still lovely.'

He slurped some tea and took another bite and another.

Popping the last morsel of the toastie into his mouth, he retrieved a teacake from the bag. He'd really like two of these, but Rosie forbade it. "Bad enough eating one of them", she'd always say. He tore off the foil wrapper and pushed the whole tea cake into his mouth in one go. That was another pleasure his wife forbade, but she wasn't here, was she?

He savoured the last of the tea cake as the chocolate and cream melted in his mouth and helped himself to a refill from the flask.

'Now, let's see what we have today,' he said, getting out of the van, his tea in his hand.

He climbed into the back with all the post, plonked his tea down on the metal floor and closed the doors. He began sifting through the deliveries for the next stage of his route. His search was fast, efficient; his eye, keen.

'Dear God,' he said, 'not again.'

A red letter for the Quinns from Eircom. The Quinns never paid anything until they had to.

'Wonder what this is about.'

He held up an envelope addressed to Matt Roddy and tapped on it to see if he could reveal the letterhead. He only caught the bottom part, but it was enough for him to figure out it was from the hospital in Galway. Matt maybe getting called back for a check-up after his cancer treatment – hopefully nothing more serious.

George moved aside some packages. It was impossible to tell what was in them, so he didn't give them a second glance. Then he spotted what he was really looking for: a plain white DL envelope with no markings apart from the postmark. This one had Brendan Kelly's name and address printed on it and George set it aside.

He took a sip of his tea that by now had cooled down and kept going through more letters, gleaning more intel as he went until he came across a second plain white DL envelope.

'Ciara and Joe McCann,' he said, sniffing.

George shuffled though the rest of that day's deliveries but found no more of the white envelopes. Taking out a soft-backed micro notebook from his trouser pocket, he added the two new names and the date, the twenty-second of October, to the list already on the page and tucked the notebook back into his pocket. He was in no doubt what lay inside the seemingly harmless envelopes. He was in no doubt because he had a role in the community that made him privy to all sorts of hidden goings-on. And it was old Sarah Maguire who'd given him the heads up on this particular mystery. She'd stopped him the Friday before, exactly a week ago, and showed him her letter, still in its plain white DL envelope. He was shocked, but mostly he was baffled. Who would send an eighty-year-old woman a letter like that? A poison pen letter? It was nasty and cruel.

In all his years, he'd never seen the likes of it. How could such a thing be explained?

After seeing Sarah's letter, his first thought was to report it to head office. They were bound to have some policy or other to take care of the situation, even one this messed up. But he put the brakes on that idea. He didn't want to jump the gun and look silly in front of his superiors. So, instead, he decided to wait to see if any more showed up. He hoped there'd be none. But he was wrong.

The count now sat at six, including the two today. He didn't know if he'd delivered letters to anybody before the day Sarah got hers. He hadn't exactly been paying attention to bog-standard white envelopes up to that point. But there was a good chance he had missed at least one. He had a niggling feeling that maybe Peter Feeney got one around the time Sarah did. After Tracy Johnson's outburst at McBirney's on Monday evening, he suspected that could be another one. And if today was anything to go by, the damned thing was only getting worse.

It was high time he bit the bullet and went to head office. To hell with what they'd think. He was sick of carrying the whole thing. The stress was way above his pay grade.

He reached for the letter addressed to the McCanns and stuffed it into his trouser pocket. He'd hand-deliver this one when he paid his usual visit to The Snug later on. There was no way he could just drop that in the postbox for Ciara and Joe to find.

For now, though, it was time to get his shift over and done with.

*

George usually reached Mary-Margaret Walsh's side of the village around noon. Mary-Margaret lived in a cottage set apart from the main street and across from the Post Office where George collected his postbags every morning. He was about to push her post through the letterbox when the door suddenly opened, leaving his hand stretched out in mid-air. Mary-Margaret stood before him.

George recoiled. On a typical day, she was neatly turned out, wore sensible shoes and kept her short blonde curls set so tight they looked like they'd been baked in an oven overnight. The Mary-Margaret standing before him today was still in her nightclothes and her hair was standing on her head as though it had lost a fight with a pack of dogs. Judging by the wilder-than-normal stare in those bright-green eyes behind her glasses, George guessed she'd had no sleep for a while.

'Mr Grant,' she said, 'I've been trying to catch you since Tuesday morning and now it's Friday. Where've you been?'

'There hasn't been any post for you,' he said, 'so it'd be easy to miss me.'

'Ah, right, okay. Well, I need to have a word.'

'Okay, do you want me to come in?'

'No, yes, oh, I suppose it would be better. And a mask... could you put on a mask?'

George stepped into the darkened interior of the house and pulled on a disposable mask he kept handy in his tunic pocket. A whiff of cat pee mingled with a sort of pine smell caught in his throat, despite the mask, and he coughed.

'Put out your hands,' she said.

He did as instructed and she sprayed sanitiser on his palms and about his person, before leading him into the sitting room. The blinds were closed, letting in only a tiny crack of daylight. Even in the dimness, he could see that the whole room was decorated in varying shades of pink. A fat black cat with a couple of white spots jumped off the sofa when they came in and hissed as it scarpered out the door and up the stairs.

'Take a seat, Mr Grant,' Mary-Margaret said, pointing him to the sofa where the cat had been.

Reluctantly, he did as she asked. Mary-Margaret sat on the edge of one of the armchairs and donned a face mask from the nearby coffee table. She couldn't have looked more uncomfortable if she'd been sitting on a cactus. George noticed she was wringing her hands over and over again.

'Mr Grant, I'm sorry to drag you away from your work but I must speak to you.'

George said nothing, but nodded to signal that she should go ahead and talk. He thought he knew what had her so up in ends. Hers was one of the names in his notebook.

'How do I explain?' she said, fixing her glasses over her mask. 'You might… but maybe you might not be able to help at all. See, when I got it, I just couldn't understand why… it's not the kind of thing that should happen to a person, and I've been up to high doh, really, it's been terrible, for me and Twiffles. I don't know… oh, oh, dear, you'll think me mad.'

She was wandering. He was going to be here all day at this rate. He prompted her.

'Not at all, Mary-Margaret,' he said, raising his eyebrows in encouragement. 'It's okay, tell me what it is.' He itched to cut to the chase and say outright, "You want to tell me about the poison pen letter," but he couldn't give the game away.

She sprang up, wringing her hands again and pacing across the floor to the wall and back to the armchair.

'I'm listening,' George said.

'Okay, okay, right, this is what happened. I got a strange letter, a very strange letter, and I wondered, um, if I could trace the sender somehow.'

So, it was about the letter. He feigned surprise. 'Why don't you let me have a look at it?'

'Would you? Thank you, Mr Grant.' She pulled out a creased white sheet from the pocket of her flowery housecoat. 'Here. Read that.'

George took the sheet. It was exactly the same as Sarah Maguire's and no doubt the same as the one he'd stowed away for the McCanns – the same as all the others.

'Have you come across a scenario such as this before in your professional life?' she said, pacing over and back and fidgeting with her mask.

'Never,' he said. "Until a few days ago," he didn't add.

Mary-Margaret whimpered. She fiddled nervously with her glasses. 'Somebody wants to do me harm. I need to know who sent this.'

George was suddenly worried about her. Everybody knew she was a bit of a bin lid, but this was extreme talk even for her. He was in a tricky situation, though. He couldn't stay here all day and, at the same time, he couldn't leave her in this state.

'Mary-Margaret, why don't you sit down a while?' he said, trying his best to sound comforting. He stood up so they were at eye level.

'What?' Mary-Margaret said, staring like she was noticing him for the first time.

'Sit down here and I'll get you a wee cup of tea.'

'Tea? Something herbal. That would be nice.'

She lowered herself onto the sofa and George left the room. In a kitchen that was pink and white everywhere, from the worktop surfaces to the cupboard doors to the floor tiles, George made the fastest cup of tea in the history of tea-making. All the while, he could hear her talking to the cat, even though the cat was upstairs. Once the tea was ready, he legged it back to the sitting room.

'Here you go, Mary-Margaret,' he said, taking her arm with his free hand. 'Have some tea and let yourself settle. Come on now.' He put the mug in her hand. 'And don't forget to take off your mask before you drink that.'

'Mr Grant, you're very kind. I feel a lot better.'

'Okay, that's good to hear. Let me take this letter to my head office and see what they can do.'

He could see relief wash over her like a ray of sunshine coming through a cloud. She hugged her tea mug with her hands and sniffed.

'Do you think they'll be able to help me?'

'Oh aye, Mary-Margaret, they'll be able to help, you know, so don't worry. Everything's going to be all right.'

He lied. He hadn't a notion whether reporting to head office was going to do any good. But, for now, all he wanted was to keep her from jumping off the nearest bridge, and that he appeared to have achieved.

21

'Joe.' Ciara tapped him on the shoulder. 'I need a quick word.'

'Shoot,' Joe said, without looking round.

'I mean, in private.'

He turned round with a bewildered expression. 'Eh?'

'Yes, Joe, in private.'

'But I'm tending to the customers, love.'

'Like now. It's hardly Temple Bar on a Friday night, so you can spare ten minutes.' Ciara nodded in the direction of the clientele. 'They all know to shout if they need a refill.'

Joe shrugged.

The pair nipped into the kitchen, Joe a little slower on his feet than Ciara on account of a limp he had sustained from a car crash a few years previously. Ciara pushed the door almost closed, leaving it slightly ajar so they could listen out for anybody in need.

'George had a surprise for me today,' Ciara said. She handed Joe a folded-up piece of paper. 'Take a gander at that. It was addressed to me and you.'

Joe puffed out his cheeks and slowly released air through his lips as he unfolded the paper. His brow knitted together. '"I know what you..."' He looked at Ciara. 'I don't understand. What is this? Who sent it?'

'George says it's a poison pen letter. He says we're not the only people to get one.'

'But...' Joe paused and scrunched up his face. 'No, I still don't get it.'

'It means somebody's trying to threaten us.'

'Ah, that's fucking stupid, love. And you said there were other letters. Wouldn't that only go to show this isn't really about us? Look, whoever sent it isn't saying *what* we did. They're probably not saying what anybody else did either. They're keeping it loose, hedging their bets. This is a load of auld shite.'

'Is it, though?' Ciara eyed Joe keenly. 'What if this is for real? What if everybody who got a letter has a secret to hide and whoever's sending the letters knows their secrets? It's not that far-fetched in a tight-knit community like ours. I mean, a person like Daisy McBirney-Smith hears everything that goes on.' She pursed her lips. 'Can we afford to take the chance it's not serious?'

'But we don't have any secrets?'

'No? Come on, Joe, what about our creative antics with the spirits?'

Ciara and Joe ran a decent establishment; they worked hard, paid their bills and suppliers on time, paid their taxes. But their one transgression, to keep the costs down, was mixing the good but expensive spirits with a few drams of potent but cheap *poitín*. It did no harm. The customers still got a nice blast and her and Joe were able to make their bottles go further.

'Fuck, now I get you.' Joe tutted. 'But no. We're very tight-lipped about that. Not even Shay or the wains know.'

'Right, but we get the *poitín* off Mackers Donaghy and maybe he's not so tight-lipped.'

'He'd never blab. Shure, it would do him as much harm as us. He's the one making it without a licence and selling it round the country. Just because you don't like him, love, doesn't make him a slabber.'

Ciara rubbed her chin. Joe was right. Like him or not, Mackers had been selling the stuff for years and had never been caught. 'Bollocks. It has to be a customer then.'

'They're all locals; they're all friends.'

'You're too trusting, Joe. It must be one of them.'

'There's no way. And how would any of them even know?'

Ciara's eyes narrowed. 'Remember that night, about a year ago, between the lockdowns,' she said, 'when we had a late one. We closed up the bar and brought a crowd into the kitchen.'

'Was it the night Kevin Moran won twenty grand on the lottery?'

'That was the one. The drink was flowing and so was the *poitín*. Kevin got up to go to the toilet and his legs gave way on him.'

'Aye,' Joe said, with a chuckle, 'he was paralytic. Everybody was in stitches.'

'Except for his wife and his son's girlfriend,' Ciara said. 'His wife was going on about how there was no way he could be so drunk.'

They were interrupted by a shout from the bar that sounded like Mark Connolly. 'Where are ye, Joe?'

'On my way, Mark,' Joe shouted back.

'But the girlfriend,' Ciara said, tugging Joe's arm, 'the girlfriend said that's what *poitín* does to you: the rest of you's sober but your legs are pissed.'

Joe grimaced. 'Do you think the girlfriend's writing these letters then?'

'Not necessarily her, but if she told somebody who told somebody – you get what I mean. Whoever's writing the letters could've heard things about people.'

'Jesus, Joe,' Mark called again. 'Come on, man.'

'Fuck it, Ciara, I have to go before they start a riot.'

'I know, I know, love, but tonight, after we close, the first thing we're going to do is get shot of any *poitín* on the premises and whatever spirits we've already mixed.'

'That's gonna cost us.'

'Better losing some stock than our licence. If there's consequences like the letter says, I don't intend for us to suffer them.'

*

The bar was getting rowdy and one of the customers was up at the counter shouting for the barman, 'Jesus, Joe, come on, man!' Natalie wanted another drink, too, but she was happy to wait a while. Anyway, she had other things on her mind.

She swirled her glass in a circular motion, causing the half-melted ice cubes to clink off the sides. She drained what was left of her vodka and coke and set the glass back on the beer mat. Eoin was meant to meet her, but he was late. She didn't mind. At least The Snug was a warm place to wait. And besides, she wanted some time alone – time to think.

She absently bit at her nails, which were usually perfectly manicured but not these days. Everything was falling to shit. Eoin was fucking useless. The life of luxury he'd promised her was never going to happen, she knew. Now she was the sole breadwinner on a fucking minimum wage. She'd had to ask for more hours, yet more, and it still wasn't enough. A little five-foot-nothing girl like her wasn't built for graft like that.

Eoin kept saying they were just going through a blip, that he had a few deals on the horizon. But she knew he was bullshitting her just the way he bullshitted everybody else. Well, fuck him. He was going to have to get a job, any job, and start bringing in some money. If it was good enough for her, then it was good enough for him.

She scowled. Maybe she didn't care if he couldn't make good on his promises. After Rory, after the real thing, Eoin was like a fake gold necklace tarnished with age. She didn't want him, not really. Part of her still cared about him, but she wasn't in love with him anymore. She was only hanging around because… well… because she was too demoralised to pick herself up and go it alone.

She glanced at the bar. Joe McCann had returned and was serving his thirsty customers. She felt a pang, remembering how fondly Rory used to talk about his Uncle Joe. A large chocolate-brown curl flopped over her face as she nudged her glass.

Of course, Natalie had another problem and one that bothered her more than her personal finances. The letter that had arrived in the post the day before had hit her like a thousand volts of electricity. She hadn't breathed a word to Eoin – she didn't want him knowing. She was sure it was more or less identical to the one he had gotten.

She shivered despite the warmth from the stove. The night before, she'd lain awake – sick at the idea of getting such a letter. She guessed she knew what the letter was driving at. Either she was being called out for cheating on Eoin or she was being targeted because she was Eoin's girlfriend. Eoin had got his letter because of what he did to Rory – Eoin didn't accept that, but she was sure of it – and now she was being tarred with the same brush. Whichever of the two reasons it was, the poison pen didn't know the whole story. They didn't know Rory had broken her heart. And they didn't know that she had nothing to do with Eoin's shady dealings. It was so unfair. The annoying voice in her head popped up again. *Oh, really? It's unfair, is it? Come on, who are you kidding?*

The bar door opened. Eoin was finally here. He smiled over and tipped his hand to his mouth like he was raising an invisible glass. She nodded and lifted the half-pint glass, now with an inch of water where the ice had melted. He'd know the half glass meant she wanted a vodka and coke. As she watched him approach the bar, she knew her life with him was all but over. Nothing was the same since losing Rory and finding out about the debt. Nothing mattered. Maybe she should just accept her fate, fair or not, and prepare for the consequences the letter promised.

22

Tracy leaned against the pebble-dashed wall of the chippie and took a strong drag of her ciggy. It was too bloody cold to enjoy her smoke properly, standing out here on the street, freezing her arse off. Why were smokers the bad guys? The ones who had to get offside and go somewhere uncomfortable? Seriously, the world was just fucked up.

Of course that Shay Dunne would never let her have a ciggy indoors, not even in the storeroom, not even if there was a blizzard. She was too fucking woke to give a person a break. She was more unbearable than ever these days, so ill-tempered and always having a go about the least wee thing. Tracy was sick to death of her. She had a good mind to make a complaint about her to Steven, ask him to get shot of her.

Right enough, it might be a while before she could go running to Steven for a favour after the barney she had with his wife on Monday. Not that that was her fault. Matilda shouldn't have sent that letter. Who the hell did she think she was, anyway, sending weird letters like that? If she had a fucking problem, she should have the guts to say it to her face instead of being so sneaky.

Tracy gave the pebble-dash a kick and a little white stone flew off and landed on the footpath. The streetlights suddenly came on;

not even six and it was getting dark already. She hated the long nights.

She took a final pull from her ciggy and was about to go inside when, coming up the street, she clapped eyes on Harry Parkes. That was him coming to collect his order, no doubt. Harry was a true gentleman; always ready with a pleasant word and a cheery greeting. He was a right age now – had to be in his eighties. Only lost his wife last year and he lived on his own in a cottage a few miles outside the village. His children lived in Derry and Letterkenny and visited him a few times a week, so it wasn't like he didn't have people looking out for him.

Tracy waited for him to reach the chippie as he shuffled up the street.

'How's you, Harry?' she asked.

'How're you doing, dear?' Harry said, and he patted down the few strands of white hair that were left on his bald head. 'It's a nippy one.'

'Tell me about it,' she said.

The bell over the door jangled as she held it open and waited for Harry to go inside. Before she followed him, she saw a silver Bentley Flying Spur go past, slow and quiet, like one of those big cruise ships. In the backseat was Peter Feeney; in the front was Vincent, his handyman.

'Driving Miss-fucking-Daisy,' Tracy muttered, before turning back to Harry. 'Shay should have your order ready,' she said, closing the door and slipping her mask on.

She looked to the back of the shop, expecting to see Shay at the fryers, but she didn't. She went up to the counter… still no sign of Shay. She looked through the hatch. And then she saw her.

Shay was lying in a heap on the floor, making moaning sounds.

'Oh my God,' Tracy said, dropping to her knees. 'Shay, what happened?'

Shay mumbled something. Tracy couldn't make out what, but she was in too much of a panic to care what she was saying. She jumped up again, trying to decide what to do.

'Stay here,' she said to Harry. 'Something's wrong with Shay. I'm going to get Ciara.'

*

Shay opened her eyes. The first thing she saw was Ciara. She put her hand to her head. The back of her skull ached.

'You're awake,' Ciara said. 'Thank God.'

'I feel like I was hit by a train,' Shay said, tasting the dryness in her mouth. 'What happened?'

'You took a dizzy spell at the chippy.'

Shay knitted her brow and tried to remember. She shook her fragile head.

'Tracy came racing into the bar to tell me, then me and Joe brought you back here and you passed out.'

'That's all a blank,' Shay said, slowly realising she was in Ciara's downstairs bedroom.

'As soon as we got you into bed, you went to sleep,' Ciara said. 'I called the emergency number your consultant gave you. They told me if you didn't wake up within an hour, I should call the ambulance.'

'Aww, fuck's sake. How long was I out?'

'About twenty minutes,' Ciara said. 'They want you to go to the hospital tomorrow so they can give you a once-over.'

Shay nodded, unhappily.

'Tracy was flapping about like a fish out of water,' Ciara was saying. 'She was in a terrible state altogether.'

'You didn't tell her what was wrong, did you?'

'Did I bollocks –I played it down.'

Shay turned on her side to face Ciara. Ciara rubbed her

shoulder. They stayed like that for a while, no words passing between them.

'You're going to have to tell Steven Robinson, you know,' Ciara said, eventually.

'And as soon as I do, he'll give me my marching orders. He won't want to risk me having an accident on his property.'

'He's going to know soon enough that something's not right.'

'Well, fuck him. I don't care,' Shay said, snapping.

'No need to jump down my throat, Shay.'

'For pity's sake,' Shay said, raising her voice, 'can't you understand that I want to keep working up until the last possible moment? Being at work helps me feel normal, even though I hate it, and it's better than sitting around waiting to die.'

Ciara winced and pain flashed in her eyes. 'Don't say that.'

Shay stopped herself. 'I'm sorry,' she said. 'I don't mean to be so hateful.' She sighed. 'I'm just so angry. I keep thinking, "Why me?" It's not fair. Then, other times, it's like, fuck it, I don't give a shit. I've nothing to live for anyway with Rory gone. I mean, just the idea of being alive and not being able to remember him, it's unbearable.'

Ciara nodded. She was trying to hold back tears.

'The more time I have to myself,' Shay said, 'the more those thoughts go smashing around in my head, over and over and over and never leaving me alone. At least work's a bit of a distraction.' She pushed herself up on the bed. The headache had subsided. 'I know I'll have to tell Steven – but not yet.'

'I get it,' Ciara said. She squeezed Shay's hand and sucked in a breath. 'Don't get mad again, but do you think it's time to move in with us, like I mentioned before? I know we talk every day and you send me a text before bedtime every night to let me know you're okay, but I don't think that's enough anymore.'

Shay shook her head. 'Can we not talk about this? Not now.'

'Okay. Not now. But soon. And will you stay here tonight at least?'

'Only if you promise to not say another word about doctors or diseases or anything remotely connected to them.'

'Cross my heart,' Ciara said.

They both smiled.

'I feel really hungry all of a sudden,' Shay said.

'You're in luck. There's some yummy chilli and rice left over from lunch.'

'Sounds like exactly what I need.'

*

Half an hour later, Shay found herself sitting in front of a plate of rice and chilli, with a couple of slices of warm garlic bread on the side and a pint glass of water. Ciara was opposite, tucking into an egg salad sandwich and a glass of beer.

'Don't you need to get back to the bar?' Shay said. 'I'll be all right, you know. You don't have to babysit me.'

'The bar can wait for another hour or so yet, and Joe has Fly Gillespie giving him a hand in the meantime.'

'I'm nothing but a nuisance.' Shay put down her fork.

'Shut up, Shay Dunne. Billy Moore, full drunk and refusing to go home at closing time? That's a nuisance. You, my brilliant sister, are not.'

'He's still doing that, is he?'

'Oh, aye, the man doesn't know when to stop.'

Shay smirked.

'There's something I want to show you,' Ciara said. She went to the kitchen dresser and opened a drawer. Shay watched with curiosity as her sister took out a folded-up sheet of paper.

'What do you make of this?' she said. 'George Grant delivered it today.'

Shay took the paper and her eyes stopped dead on the words printed across the middle. She choked. What she saw was impossible. It couldn't be. She flailed about in search of her glass. Ciara put it in her hand.

'Shay?' Ciara said, panic in her voice.

Shay gulped down a mouthful of water. 'A bit of chilli caught in my throat.'

'Who knew my chilli was so potent?' Ciara said.

'You can't put a price on that,' Shay said in a croak.

She took some more water and rubbed her face, before picking up the paper again. Maybe she'd been mistaken. Maybe her eyes were playing tricks. She willed it to be true as she looked again at the page. She willed it.

But no.

There wasn't a doubt.

She stared at the words. Impossible as it was, they were practically the same words she'd written in her letters to Peter Feeney and Eoin Devine, except for a few irrelevant differences. Right about now, she'd be doubting her own sanity if wasn't for the fact that Ciara could see those words, too.

'So, what do you think?' Ciara asked.

'I, I… honestly, I'm lost for words,' Shay said, which was the absolute truth.

'We've been wondering who could've sent it.'

Shay was, too. Her brain went into overdrive, as much as it could these days. Was it possible she sent it? In a blackout caused by her illness? It would have had to be one seriously long blackout to print the letter, address the envelope and then send it off in the post. No, that was ridiculous. And, anyway, no matter how fried her brain got, she'd never do such a thing to Ciara.

She remembered how she'd toyed with the idea of sending more letters – a follow-up one to Peter and Eoin, or casting the net wider to other targets. But she hadn't followed through with that plan in the end. She didn't think the follow-up letters would achieve her goal and it occurred to her that more targets might only detract from the goal.

Whoever was responsible for this letter, it wasn't her.

'George told me other people have been getting them, too,' Ciara said.

Shay's head was spinning in a storm of disbelief. 'Did he tell you who those other people are?' she said. 'Like, did he mention anybody that might be connected to us, or Rory, maybe?'

'What do you mean?'

'I dunno, one of the Feeneys or…?'

'He didn't mention any names. It's probably confidential.'

Shay ransacked her brain to make sense of what she was hearing. There was no way this was the handiwork of another poison pen that had randomly started to write letters at the same time she did. The likelihood of that was a billion to one.

So, that could only mean it was a copycat, somebody who'd managed to find out about one of her letters, and who, for whatever reason – for kicks, revenge – had piggybacked on her scheme.

'It's mad how the letters have stayed quiet,' Ciara was saying. 'How we haven't heard about them, the way tongues wag about here.' Ciara sucked her lower lip. 'I suppose anybody who got one didn't want to let on. I know me and Joe don't want to go round telling all and sundry.'

Shay was only half-hearing her sister. If a copycat was at work, it meant her letters had reached their destinations. That, at least, was more information than she had up to now, though she still had no idea about the impact, if any, the letters had had on Peter and Eoin. Frustration gnawed at her. The copycat's letters weren't supposed to exist. It was all wrong. All she'd wanted was for Peter Feeney and Eoin Devine to fall foul of some suffering. These damned copycat letters could derail that – for the same reason she'd rejected sending letters to more targets herself.

'I reckon everybody's going to know about the letters soon, though,' Ciara said. 'Especially when George reports it to head office.'

For the first time since Ciara revealed the letter, Shay came out of her head and properly listened.

'What? Why? It's… that's just silly. Why would he do that?'

Shay squirmed. The whole ridiculous situation was getting worse. She could get found out. Or worse, her plan for Eoin and Peter might come to nothing.

'He has to report it,' Ciara said. 'Those letters are scary.'

'You think they're scary?'

'Well, they are, aren't they? They're making a threat.'

Shay's stomach sank. Was Ciara right? She supposed she was. That had been her intent for Eoin and Peter, after all. But Ciara. And Joe. Oh, she never meant in a million years for them to be the victims.

'If there are lots of people getting letters,' Shay said, scrambling to somehow diminish any power the copycat letters had, 'isn't it less and less likely the sender knows anything at all?'

'Aye, but would you take that chance, that's the thing?' Ciara said, putting her hand up to her mouth. 'Me and Joe think we might know what our letter's about.'

Shay looked at the agony in Ciara's face as her sister fessed up to mixing the spirits with *poitín*.

'Do you think we're terrible?' Ciara said.

'No, you're not terrible,' Shay said. 'How could you be?'

But she, Shay, was terrible. How could she let Ciara and Joe go through this? Maybe she should bite the bullet and come clean. That was the right thing to do, the fair thing to do, for Ciara and Joe. To put their minds at rest.

She rehearsed what she might say. *Look, Ciara, you have nothing to worry about. I started this whole thing and the letter you got is bogus bullshit from a copycat who's just fucking with people.*

There would be questions from Ciara, but that would be okay, and Ciara would understand and would never breathe a word.

'Ciara, I want to—'

'What kind of person would do this?' Ciara said. 'To deliberately set out to frighten and upset people?'

Shay paused.

'You'd have to be some twisted piece of shit. If I could get my hands on them, I'd wring their fucking neck.'

In all her life, Shay didn't remember seeing Ciara so angry. Perhaps now wasn't the right time to confess. Perhaps there would never be a right time to confess.

23

The Bentley Flying Spur pulled away from the house. Peter was stretched out on the luxurious leather recliner seat in the back, while Vincent, his all-round handyman, navigated them out of the driveway.

'Will I take you straight there, sir?' Vincent asked, eyeing Peter in the rear-view mirror. 'Or do you need to stop off for anything?'

'I don't need to stop for anything, but take the road through the village, will you?'

Peter was in a stinking mood. He hated having to attend the annual Chamber of Commerce dinner and usually had Dan go in his place. But this year, the boy had some other event on and he'd simply refused to welch on it, no matter how hard Peter pressed. So, now Peter was left to do the job.

The truth was that the dinner wasn't his only vexation. There was that letter. The letter he hadn't been able to throw away, even though he should have.

His past wasn't exactly the most savoury. It hid many a ruthless deed done in the name of business that he might expect to pay for. That said, he wasn't in the slightest bit worried about any of those transactions, for he knew his tracks were well covered and there was no proof of anything – just word of mouth and his word against whoever else's word. No, none of that lost him as much as a wink of sleep.

The car eased out onto the road and in the direction of the village. The sky was dark blue and turning into night, with the last of the light fading like a halo behind the horizon. The river slept still and quiet in the valley below Kilcross, winding in glassy streaks through jagged slivers of land. Peter peered down at it as he continued to ponder the letter.

He knew exactly why he hadn't thrown it away.

There was one occurrence from his past, one he couldn't square away so nicely, and he was becoming more and more convinced with each passing day it was that occurrence the letter dared to flaunt in his face.

He took out a comb and smoothed down his hair as his mind took him back in time. Back to thinking about Aggie.

She was a doomed woman. Beautiful once. So much so he'd lost his senses when he first clapped eyes on her. How he'd pursued her, even when she'd been courting somebody else, even when she'd spurned him. He won her in the end – he was a man who rarely lost – though he paid dearly for that particular conquest. He never could have known the life that lay ahead for them – how she was going to be destructive. Her and her damned drinking. She started when the children were very young. She was one of those secret drinkers who hid bottles all round the house. Peter thought there was something so detestable about that, creeping around and sneaking a swallow here and there, slowly getting intoxicated. Right enough, he found it equally detestable when the children got older and she began drinking out in the open. The whole village knew. Everybody in their social circle knew. He'd lost count of the number of times she'd humiliated herself and him at public engagements.

Peter sank into the soft leather of the car seat, relishing its musky aroma.

The woman had even dared to have an affair – dear Lord, the nerve. Peter had had to come down heavy on her and the adulterer. What was his name again? Christopher something, an old flame from when she had lived in Glasgow. Peter had been forced to punish her severely for her dalliance. He did the one thing he knew would hurt her most. He banished her from the house, signed her in for a stay at St Bart's and, for six whole months, didn't let her see the children. He hadn't wanted to, but she needed to know that no one betrayed him like that.

As for Christopher, his boss was a long-time business acquaintance of Peter's and he'd arranged it so Christopher no longer had a job. Soon after, Christopher moved back to Scotland, never to return. Aggie's drinking only got worse after that. The story was bound to end in tragedy. And one night, it did.

Vincent took a left onto the village main street – a street Peter knew every inch of, like it was something he owned. He knew every person living in it, too. Every last one of them. He scowled.

The car approached the chip shop on the right-hand side – the place Shay Dunne worked. She'd never made anything of herself, that girl. He was glad Dan never married her. She was probably in there now, serving up chips.

It was as the car drove past that Peter saw him. Tracy Johnson was holding the chip shop door open to let a man go through.

Peter sat up straight, his eyes narrowed, and it was then he realised why he hadn't thrown away the letter. The man at the door of the chip shop. Harry Parkes. The link with that one occurrence from Peter's past. Harry Parkes, as discomforting as backache: a problem that had no medical cure, that flared up now and again, and that never properly went away.

As Peter remembered Harry's encounter with Ursula, his jowls tightened. All that talk of Aggie and her anniversary. On its own, it was unsettling. But then getting the letter as well. Both were too much of a coincidence not to be connected, surely. Or was he overthinking it, with paranoia getting the best of him?

He needed more time to think it through and decide, once and for all, who had sent that accursed letter. And once he did, oh boy, once he did, he'd make it his life's mission to hunt down the sender.

24

'I'd love to have seen Pop's face when you said you couldn't go to the chamber dinner,' Ursula said, sniggering.

'I said the exact same thing,' Francesca said, 'didn't I, Dan?'

Dan puffed his chest out. 'What's that wife of yours got you doing now?' he said, imitating his father's voice.

The three of them collapsed into stitches.

They were enjoying coffee after a delicious three-course meal that Francesca had ordered in from Bertrand's. Everything came prepared and oven-ready. No effort required. It was a far more appealing option than slaving in the kitchen all evening to cook a dinner that wouldn't taste half as good. All Dan had had to do was put the twins to bed while Francesca set up the dining room.

'He'll be enduring the after-dinner speeches by now,' Ursula said. 'He's probably got a fake smile on his face – you know, the one where he looks like he's having a shit – and inside he'll be cursing every single person in the room.'

'He makes me go every other year,' Dan said, 'so I don't feel one bit guilty.'

'Nor should you,' Francesca said.

The chamber dinner couldn't compare to dinner with his wife and sister. He swayed to the soft Motown sounds coming from the speaker in the corner. The low light in the room was soothing and, if he didn't watch himself, he risked falling asleep. He poured some more coffee, wishing he could have a beer instead. Not tonight. No booze when Ursula was visiting.

'I'm surprised Pop didn't say anything to you about the anniversary mass for Mum,' Ursula said. 'I know he doesn't want it to happen.'

'He did, actually,' Dan said. 'He asked me to put you off your notion.'

'Oh. So, are you going to do that?'

'Behave yourself, Ursula,' Francesca said. 'We'll be the first ones at the church.'

Ursula smiled.

She looks tired, Dan thought, *and thinner than usual*, but she was still sober and that was the important thing. The therapy was helping.

'How about we move into the lounge and watch a film?' he asked.

'Sounds perfect,' Francesca said.

They got up from the table and started towards the lounge.

'Is Pop still in the dark about that weird letter he got?' Ursula said, taking up her favourite spot on the corner sofa.

'One hundred per cent he is,' Dan said, clicking on the TV and sitting down, 'and that's how I intend to keep it.'

'And you have no clue who sent it?'

'I couldn't care less. They haven't followed up with anything so, as far as I'm concerned, it's nothing more than a hoax.'

'But aren't you curious, even a bit, to know who was behind it?'

'Nope. Francesca has a theory, though.'

Dan began searching Netflix.

Ursula turned her head. 'You have to tell me, Fran.'

Francesca sat down next to Dan.

'I've no proof. I shouldn't be saying.'

Ursula rubbed her hands together. 'Tell me. Go on.'

'I thought it might've been Shay Dunne.'

'Shay? Aww, come on, Shay wouldn't do a thing like that,' Ursula said.

'Exactly what I thought,' Dan said. 'Anybody got a film preference?'

'You pick,' Francesca said.

'Why would you think it was Shay?' Ursula asked.

'Something she said at the funeral. She commented on your dad not having the decency to show up.'

'None of us thought he would. I'm sure it was no real surprise to Shay either,' Ursula said.

'I agree, but it was the way she said it. She didn't raise her voice or anything; she was very quiet and, at the same time, intense.'

'How would you expect her to be after losing Rory?' Dan said.

She was devastated, he knew, like he was. He put the remote on the sofa, not interested any longer in finding a film.

'I wouldn't blame her for sending him the letter,' he went on. 'I reckon I'd even commend her, but I'm with Ursula. Something like this isn't Shay's form.'

'I think the fact that he didn't even go to the funeral,' Francesca said, 'when practically the whole village turned out might've been a "last straw" type of thing.'

Dan could see Ursula was coming round to the idea. He wasn't swayed.

'My guess is that this a hoaxer and they've sent letters to other people in the village. I mean, at the start, Fran, you were the one that didn't think it was a threat.'

'I've changed my mind.'

'What about that madness with the Johnson sisters at the start of the week? You witnessed it yourself, Fran. What if that was to do with another letter like Pop's? Why would Shay send a letter to one of the Johnsons?'

150

'Oh my God,' Ursula said, 'you think another letter was sent?'

'We don't know about any other letters,' Francesca said. 'And the row between Tracy and Matilda could've been about anything. It's a bit of a stretch to connect it to a poison letter.'

Dan thought about it for a minute. Maybe she was right. 'Okay,' he said. 'By the same token, it's a stretch to connect Shay, too.'

Francesca reached over and stroked his face. 'Let's call it quits. I'll give up my theory and you give up yours.'

Dan nodded. 'What about that film then?'

25

Saturday night and The Snug was buzzing. Ciara was relieved to see it. Lockdown was well behind them and their customers were making up for lost time. Tonight, a country band was playing – a husband-and-wife duo who knew how to get the crowd going. Between the band, and endless chattering and guffaws of laughter, the noise was deafening. Ciara knew it would be at least two hours after closing time before her ears would stop ringing.

When it was busy like this, Ciara and Joe had a system where she worked the bar side of the counter and Joe, the lounge. Fly Gillespie was always at the ready if they needed an extra pair of hands.

'Will you get two Guinness and a double vodka and coke for Paddy there, love?' Joe shouted into her ear. 'I'm going to top up the wood stove.'

'Will do,' she said.

He pecked her on the cheek and rushed off.

As Ciara poured the Guinness, the band finished a song and the lounge crowd cheered and clapped.

The singer breathed heavily into the mic. 'This next little number,' he said, 'is one y'all know. So, ladies and germs, grab whoever's sitting next to you and get out on the floor.'

'Can I grab this hunk here?' a woman shouted.

'Just you leave him alone, Maggie,' another woman, standing by the bar, shouted back. 'My husband's off limits.'

Laughter rippled across the room as the band struck the opening chords of "Jackson". A rousing applause went up.

'Give me a Powers and ginger and two Harp when you get a chance, Ciara,' a customer called over the music.

'Comin' up, Gerry,' she called back.

She brought the double vodka and coke to Paddy and started pouring a pint of Harp.

'That was wile carry-on with the Johnson sisters,' Gerry said to Ciara.

'Wile altogether,' she replied, giving a short answer. It was too busy to get stuck into a lengthy conversation.

Mark Connolly was standing at the counter next to Gerry. 'I was driving past when it happened,' he said. 'I saw the whole thing. I thought Tracy was going to tear Matilda's head off.'

The two of them sniggered.

'Everybody's on edge these days,' Gerry said. 'I don't know what it is. Maybe there's something in the water.'

'It must be Covid,' Mark said. 'Why not? We're blaming it for everything else.'

Ciara poured the second Harp and went to fix Gerry's whisky and ginger. She thought about her weird letter and how George had said there were others. Was it possible one of the Johnsons had got a letter and that triggered the row? It struck her that more strange incidents could be coming down the pipe before this whole business was over.

Joe returned from topping up the stove and picked up an order from another customer.

Ciara leaned over to Fly. 'Could you lift a few glasses for me?'

'No bother, Ciara.'

She finished serving Gerry and was about to unload the

dishwasher when she spotted Andie McBirney-Smith coming in from the outside door.

'Here for the usual, Andie?' Ciara pre-empted what she was going to say.

Andie nodded. Ciara bagged Andie's parents' Saturday-night carry-out while the girl waited near the end of the counter. Dressed in an old tracksuit, her mop of hair loosely tied back from her face, she stood with her shoulders hunched up and her arms folded, keeping her eyes trained on the floor to avoid the gaze of whoever was around. *God help her*, Ciara thought. She was a sorry sight. She was so under the thumb of her bossy parents – taking orders from them day after day and running all their errands. And here she was on a weekend night, sitting in with her old pair when she should've been out doing her own thing with people her own age.

'Hi, Andie,' called a young lad from a group behind her, 'you're looking sexy tonight.'

The rest of the group laughed. A dying look washed over Andie's face. She didn't say a word in her defence. Ciara didn't come to her defence either.

'There you go, young lady,' Ciara said. 'Six cans of Carlsberg; six small bottles of Babycham. I've put it on the tab.'

Ciara handed over the carry-out.

'You know, you shouldn't let people talk to you like that,' Ciara said.

'It doesn't bother me,' Andie said. 'I don't care what they say.'

Ciara raised an eyebrow, surprised at the defiance in Andie's voice, slight as it was. Andie scampered off.

As she left, somebody passed her in the doorway. He was in such a hurry, he nearly knocked Andie over. Ciara saw it was Brendan Kelly. He and his wife were regulars in The Snug on the nights they ran the "Twenty-Five" card drives. But tonight wasn't a card night and Brendan was alone. He seemed out of sorts, too, Ciara noticed, as he pushed his way towards the counter.

'Is Kevin Moran here?' he said in a loud, gruff voice, slamming his fist on the counter. A thunderous expression contorted his face.

Brendan was known as a 'civil fella', the kind of man who always met you with a smile and if he couldn't do you a good turn, he wouldn't do you a bad one. This aggressive behaviour wasn't like him at all. And he was very drunk, which wasn't like him either.

'Are you all right, Brendan?' Ciara asked.

Joe came over. 'Ciara, love, we need more—'

'Is he here?' Brendan shouted. 'If he is, I'm going to fucking kill him.'

'Jesus, Brendan,' Joe said, 'settle yourself. I'll get you a drink.'

'I never stole a thing in my life,' Brendan ranted, 'not a single thing. If he thinks he can get away with accusing me, he's got another thing coming. Where is he?'

'Who're you talking—' Joe started.

'Kevin Moran's not here,' Ciara said. 'But Joe's right, settle yourself.'

Brendan wasn't listening. His eyes were wild and darting all around. He jostled space for himself at the counter, nearly toppling Tony Cassidy off one of the stools.

'Fuck's sake, Brendan,' Tony said, light-heartedly, 'you nearly spilled me pint.'

'Did you do it?' Brendan immediately rounded on the man.

'Wise up,' Tony said. 'What're ye on about?'

'Did you?' Brendan pointed to Tony's wife.

'Did I, what?' Tony's wife asked.

'You leave her alone,' Tony said, putting his pint on the counter and getting to his feet. He was suddenly sombre and squared off against Brendan. Brendan seemed oblivious.

'Or you two.' Brendan turned to Ciara and Joe. 'Do you think I'm a thief? You better have proof, I swear to fuck. I'm getting my solicitor.'

Customers began to notice the kerfuffle. Ciara could feel an edge in the air, displacing the previous high spirits.

'We don't know what you're talking about, Brendan,' Joe said, 'but—'

'That happened years ago and Moran knows it. He was there when the company cleared me. They saw it wasn't my fault. It was a numerical error. A simple, stupid bastard error and...'

Brendan looked around, his eyes mad and dancing in his head. He suddenly let a roar out of him and reached out. With a sweep of his arm, he cleared the countertop. Everything went flying, crashing into whoever happened to be standing in the way. The customers jumped back off their stools, some of them falling over, others crying out. Dozens of glasses and bottles landed on the granite tiles with a deafening smash, shattering into a thousand shards. Their contents splashed out like an ocean wave, leaving a pool of liquid. The sharp stench of spilt beer and spirits filled the air.

The bar fell into a tense silence, although the revelry in the lounge continued oblivious. The customers formed a circle, wide enough to avoid the mess on the floor, with Brendan in the middle. He wasn't shouting anymore, only standing there with his fists clenched and breathing heavily through his nostrils like a bull about to charge.

Ciara stood open-mouthed. She looked at Joe. He cranked into action and ran out from behind the counter.

'You're going home, Brendan,' Joe said, grabbing him firmly by the arm.

'What?' Brendan said. He looked confused, as though he'd just woken up.

The outside door opened. All eyes turned. It was Brendan's wife, Mairin, wearing a onesie with a coat thrown over it. For a split second, a startled look flitted across her face, then surprise gave way to relief.

'Oh, thank God,' she said. 'There you are.' She raced over to Brendan, crunching through the glass. She looked down. 'Shit, did he do this?'

'Too right, he did,' a customer called out, 'and he owes me a drink.'

'He owes us all a drink,' another customer shouted.

'What the fuck, Brendan?' Mairin said.

'I couldn't find him,' Brendan said, swaying slightly.

'You better get this man home,' Joe said, 'before somebody gives him a hiding.'

'Don't worry, that's what I'm here to do,' Mairin said.

'There's nothing to see here,' somebody shouted out in a mock officious voice. 'Move along, folks.'

Laughter rippled. The tension was banished. Ciara let out a deep breath.

'I'll help you out with him,' she said.

'Could I get a drink down here, Joe?' It was a customer from the lounge.

'Fly, will you help me clean up the floor?' Joe asked. 'Then I'll get refills for everybody who had their drink spilled.'

'Send me the bill for the broken glasses,' Mairin said, 'and the drinks.'

'We'll do that,' Ciara said, 'but, for now, let's get him out of here.'

She and Mairin grabbed Brendan round the waist and walked him out of the bar. He came with them willingly, mumbling as he walked.

'I'm so sorry,' Mairin said. 'What a disaster.'

'It's only a few broken glasses,' Ciara said. 'It'll be grand.'

The night air seemed to revive Brendan and the women didn't have much of a struggle getting him safely secured in the passenger seat of Mairin's car. Mairin closed the door and went round to the driver's side.

'Thanks for helping, Ciara. And let me know about the cost of the damage.'

'You know, I don't think I ever saw Brendan in a state like that. It's not like him.'

'Naw, I know,' Mairin said. 'I don't know what got into him. He was in bad form all week, but he wouldn't say why. Then, tonight, we were having a few drinks in the house and he got up, no warning at all, and said he was coming down here to settle a score with somebody.'

'Fuck's sake.'

'I didn't think he was serious 'til he ran out the door with the keys for his van. I was so worried he was going to crash, I got in my car and followed him.'

'Well, he didn't find who he was looking for and just as well.'

'Who was he looking for anyway?'

'Kevin Moran.'

'Kevin Moran? What the fuck?'

'Well, shure, it's over now,' Ciara said. 'Are you going to be okay to drive? You said you'd been drinking.'

'I only had a bottle of beer and that was over an hour ago.'

Mairin got into her car and drove off, waving to Ciara as she went.

As Ciara watched the car disappear down the main street, she had to wonder what had triggered Brendan's rampage. Her stomach knotted and she felt slightly sick. She guessed she probably knew.

26

'What can I get you?' the barista asked.

'Double espresso,' Eoin said, handing her the exact money, 'and it's for takeaway.'

'Can I get your name?'

He was scrolling on his phone and giving the barista only enough attention to place his order, but being asked for his name caused him to stop and look up. All he wanted was a coffee, a simple transaction – in, out, gone. But they needed his name. It was bullshit.

'Heathcliff-Amadeus,' he said, smirking. 'If there's enough room on that espresso cup for it.'

The barista threw him a go-fuck-yourself look and walked off to prepare his order. Eoin moved to the end of the counter to wait. Leaning on a high stool, he returned his attention to his phone, checking the latest news on the local radio site. He did that daily now. Slowly, he inched down the list for the day, scanning each headline, looking out for that very specific news item he hoped to never find. He was close to the end, nearly home free.

Another customer came and stood nearby to wait for his order. Eoin glanced up for a second before returning to the phone. He was all but done when he saw it. The last headline bar one. The phone nearly slipped out of his hand. The headline he'd dreaded was finally there before his eyes.

He clicked on it, his index finger shaking so hard he could barely land it on the link.

Sweat trickled into his eyes as he read the first paragraph. The words floated on the screen, as though trying to escape, but he managed to read enough to justify his panic. His breath quickened. He had to get out of there, back to the car where he could think.

Hoping his legs would carry him, he made a beeline for the door. The voice of the barista calling out, 'Espresso for Heathcliff-Amadeus,' rang in his ears as he left the shop.

He staggered to his car, glad it wasn't parked too far away. His head was about to bust. Hadn't he known that shit back in June would catch up with him? The weird letter had said as much; it was the hammer waiting to fall on his head, the someone who could rat on him at any time. Though, as the days passed, he saw the letter less as a threat and more like a hoax. Yet the news headline – that was no hoax. That was real and it left the letter meaningless.

What happened in June should never have happened at all. It was so fucking stupid; *he* was so fucking stupid. And, like any other unexpected disaster, the lead up to it had given no clue as to what was on the horizon.

*

He'd had a great plan in place. For the first weekend in forever, Natalie wasn't working the late shift on Friday and was off Saturday and Sunday, too. With the hotels and restaurants open again, he'd thought it would be a brilliant surprise to book them into a lovely place in Rathmullan. He imagined it in his head to be perfect. Dinner on Friday night, walks on the beach on Saturday, an outdoor beach party on Saturday night, a leisurely lunch on Sunday before going home. Natalie had been so down in the dumps lately, this weekend getaway might be just the tonic.

He was standing at the Millennium Forum, across from the store where Natalie worked, his gaze trained on the entrance. The street was busy, full of noise from the traffic and the steady stream of shoppers strolling by. The warmth of the day still lingered in the air and it wouldn't be dark for hours yet. The night, as they said, was still young.

A ripple of excitement ran down his spine, his impatience getting the better of him even though he'd only been there a few minutes. He checked his watch – nearly six. She shouldn't be much longer.

And then he saw her. She was at the store entrance. Another ripple ran down his spine. He lifted his hand to wave and was about to dash across the street. He froze, not wanting to believe his eyes. Someone, a man, came out behind her. Natalie threw her arms around him and they kissed.

A lump welled up in his chest as he watched. He tried telling himself it was a friendly greeting, but that was total bullshit. Their kiss went on forever – or so it seemed. And the worst part was who she was kissing.

Rory.

It was fucked up. His business partner and his girl. How could they betray him like that?

They hadn't seen him; they'd been too wrapped up in themselves. He slid back into the foyer of the forum, his legs like jelly, the ripples in his body from shock now and not excitement. He watched through the glass doors as they bounced up the street, her arm around his waist, until they disappeared around a corner.

He was crushed; it was like he'd been dropped off a skyscraper. He leaned against the wall in the foyer and breathed deeply.

He thought about how he saw Natalie every day, Rory nearly every day, and he had never guessed from either of them what they were up to. Did they laugh when they were together at how stupid he was?

It took a few minutes before Eoin could steady himself. His brain was in a fog and he didn't know what he should do next. Go home? Hang about town? Pay his mum a visit? Or what about taking himself off to Rathmullan as planned? Why the fuck not…

*

The sun had disappeared long ago, leaving behind a hint of pink in the deep-blue sky. Eoin was stretched out on the bonnet of his 4x4, a half-empty bottle of vodka in his hand. His eyes were still wet from a new batch of tears. He sniffed and took another swig from the bottle. His stomach clenched. How could they do it to him? How could they? If he hadn't seen it for himself, he never would've believed it.

He let his eyes close and he listened to the waves in the distance, splashing over and back on the sand. The beach was quiet now, thank fuck. Everybody gone apart from the odd local out walking their dog.

So much for wanting to surprise Natalie; he'd been the one to get the surprise. Right about now, they should've been settling into their hotel room for the night after a tasty meal and a few drinks. Instead, he was drunk and alone and she was… well, he didn't want to think about where she was.

Eoin snorted. 'Well, here's to you, babes,' he said, helping himself to a slug of vodka.

He pushed himself up on his elbows. Clusters of little lights winked across the lough from Inch and Fahan. Rolling off the bonnet, he climbed into the back of the 4x4. The air was colder now and he was dog tired. Lying down on the seat, he pulled his jacket around him and closed his eyes.

He woke with a start, his mouth as dry as dust and his head so sore that he thought it would shatter if he touched it. For a moment, everything was a blank and then it all came rushing back. Natalie and Rory. And he was in his car in Rathmullan.

He checked his watch. Two in the morning. Fuck. He rubbed his face. He didn't fancy staying there all night. He could stay in the hotel, though it would be a horrible experience without Natalie. Besides, it was too late to check in now, anyway. All he wanted was to go home. Natalie would probably be asleep at this stage so he could just slip into bed. He got out of the car and stepped into the driver's seat. He wasn't drunk anymore – he had a hangover instead, but he was still under the influence. What did it matter? He knew he was *compos mentis* enough to drive and the roads would be quiet at this hour.

Eoin set off, carefully navigating the narrow street that took him out of the seaside village. He yawned and widened his eyes. The betrayal scene returned to his thoughts and stubbornly refused to go away. Hurt stirred in his stomach and stabs of pain darted across his chest. He didn't know who to be angry at more, Natalie or Rory.

After a half hour, he reached Letterkenny without having met a single other car. He bypassed the town and continued in the direction of Kilcross. The traffic began to pick up slightly, so he decided to take the old route instead of the main road. It was narrow and full of twists and turns, but he expected it to be traffic-free. Another twenty minutes or so would have him home.

They'd shafted him, Natalie and Rory. No doubt about that. And getting shafted by somebody he cared for – oh, he felt that right to his bones. All the years of his father letting him and his mother down, breaking promises, forgetting birthdays, showing up drunk if he showed up at all. Who the fuck wanted to be made to feel like that again?

Only this was worse because Natalie was his girl. He thought they were the real deal, that they might get married some day. In spite of all their problems, he couldn't imagine being without her – even now, after what he had seen. He loved her, no matter what she did.

But Rory Dunne. Rory was a different story. Man, the shafting he was getting in the business was good enough for him. If Eoin had ever had a moment's guilt about the spending and the debt, he needn't bother anymore because Rory deserved everything he got and then some.

Eoin yawned again and his eyelids flapped closed. The car veered left slightly. He quickly corrected it.

'Shit,' he said. 'Stay awake, fool.'

He put down the window and let the cool night air hit his face. He hadn't far to go, maybe ten more minutes. He pressed down a smidgen on the gas pedal.

Suddenly, the view from the windscreen changed. He'd driven straight into a fog bank. The car lights barely carved out more than a few yards of road as a thick mist billowed past.

'Mother of fuck, this is all I need. I can't see a bastard thing.'

The question was: what was he going to do? Should he confront Natalie? Accuse her outright? No. Bad idea. She could use that as her excuse to leave him altogether. He could just pretend it had never happened and let it run its course. Yes, that might be the ticket. If he said nothing, she'd come back to him once she got this silly fling out of her system and was fed up with Rory. Because that's all this was – a silly fling. He was one hundred per cent definite about that.

He eyes threatened to close and he shook his head quickly to throw off his sleepiness. He was about five minutes from home. The fog was thicker now, if that was possible.

A couple of miles from the village, the road took a sharp left and Eoin had to swing the car aggressively to negotiate the curve without going into the ditch – his approach had been too fast, he knew.

How long had they been carrying on? Was it days or weeks? Months? Longer? Was it why Lorna got offside—

'Jesus!' he screamed.

Something blue flashed in front of the windscreen. Then, there was a thump and a jolt. He stamped his foot on the break. The car skidded and screeched to a stop.

Eoin's heart was beating in his ears and his hands were stuck to the steering wheel like they were part of it. He'd hit something. Oh God, fucking fuck, he'd hit something. *It's a dog or a rabbit*, he thought. It had to be.

He climbed out of the car, his entire body shaking to the point of convulsing, and stumbled to the rear. The tail lights melded into the dense fog, making a creepy crimson glow like he was on another planet. The world around him made no sound, as though waiting for him to make his discovery.

Eoin stepped away from the car, peering into the eerie fog, willing there to be nothing.

And then he saw him. The trainers first, then the legs, then a windbreaker that – even under the red light – Eoin knew was blue. He stopped, not daring to get closer. He stared at the heap that was a human being. The body was motionless, stiller than the sky in a heatwave. He was dead. He was definitely dead.

'Oh Jesus, whu-what have I done…?'

He reached a shaking hand into his jacket pocket, fumbling for his phone. He'd have to call the Gards. The vodka from before sloshed about in his stomach. He swallowed hard, hoping it would stay down.

The road was empty as far as the fog would allow him to see and there wasn't a single house light. He listened. It was quieter than outer space, as though the fog had sucked all sound into it.

And then, the wrong sorts of thoughts began swirling in his head. If he made that call, what would happen to his life? He could say goodbye to everything he'd built so far. He could say goodbye to Natalie, too. This would destroy any chance he had of keeping them together. And what about his mother? How would he look out for her from a prison cell? She wasn't doing so great these days and she depended on him. His only reason for coming back from London was so he could be near her.

Eoin walked around his 4x4, checking for damage. From what he could make out, there was a dent in the passenger-side fender and the plastic cover of the indicator was broken. Nothing that couldn't be fixed and made good-as-new.

He found himself putting the smartphone back inside his pocket. He saw it happen as though watching somebody else. His stomach gurgled and the vodka came dangerously close to exiting his body.

He took a last quick scan of the road. Up. Down. Nothing.

'Fuck this,' he said, his voice cracking.

Before he knew it, he was back in the driver's seat and tearing away with a screech of the breaks. Without as much as a glance in the rear-view mirror, he put distance between himself and his dreadful deed.

*

The memory of that night back in June was sharper than a surgeon's scalpel and it cut as deep. As Eoin sat in his car, all these months later, he knew in the depths of his soul that the game was finally up. The news report on his phone left no room for doubt. He read it again – not that he needed to, as every word was etched in his brain.

Using evidence found at the scene, the Gardaí investigation into the hit-and-run had identified the make and model of the car involved. This, the report said, would help them narrow their search and identify the driver responsible.

Even though he'd had his car repaired – the dent and the indicator cover, as well as a scratch on the paintwork that he hadn't even noticed on the fateful night – it wouldn't matter. Eoin had to face facts: as sure as the days got shorter in the winter, it was only a matter of time before the knock came to the door. The time for dodging and wide-boy antics was over.

27

A whole weekend had passed since Mary-Margaret told George about her letter and she'd seen neither hide nor hair of him since. She couldn't stand another day of trying to cope. The longer she waited, the worse she got. She couldn't function. She'd even had to take sick leave from work and that was unheard of. She could barely eat and at night, she lay awake looking at the ceiling, enduring her fretting, clamouring thoughts until the sun came up.

Today, she was so out-of-kilter, she hadn't even bothered to rise from her bed. Half twelve and she could hear Mother's voice admonishing her, even though Mother had shuffled off her mortal coil long ago. Oh, surely this was an extraordinary situation and she could be excused for lingering in bed for once, couldn't she?

Twiffles caterwauled from the other side of the bedroom door.

'Mercy, Twiffles, leave Mum-Mums alone, will you? She's not well.'

Earlier on, she'd heard him tearing up something downstairs – God knows what. She was positive he wasn't hungry; she remembered putting food in his bowl before bedtime. She knew he just wanted attention and she wasn't going to give him any. She was the one needing attention for a change.

The curtains were drawn, letting in only a dreary, sickly light. She hadn't opened the window in ages and the room smelled like the donated clothes they took in at the hospital workshop. Dirty laundry lay scattered across the floor and the armchair in the corner, and unwashed plates and mugs were stacked up on the dressing table. Her bedside locker was strewn with prescription meds – none of which she'd acquired on prescription: temazepam and triazolam for sleep; diazepam and duloxetine for anxiety; flupirtine and co-codamol for headaches. She was close to overdosing and yet not one of them had done its job. On the bed, within arm's reach, was a can of pine air freshener that had done her more good than all of the meds put together. Its spray helped calm the pandemonium in her head, not to mention mask the staleness of the room for a little while.

Everything was a mess, turned upside-down – her house, her life. She was living a twenty-four-seven nightmare, for pity's sake. And all because of that letter. That awful, hateful letter – it loomed in her mind like some tower stretching forever upwards into the sky.

Mary-Margaret's agonised thoughts turned to the only subject they were able to focus on and that was her number one suspect. She'd figured from the start what the letter was referring to. It could be nothing other than her unorthodox methods of helping patients. And with that being the case, she had come to accept that there really was only one culprit.

Twiffles meowed again and scratched impatiently at the door. Mary-Margaret reached for a book from the drawer in her bedside locker and flung it with full force at the door. The book bounced off the wood with a bang and Twiffles screeched and belted down the stairs.

'Get the fuck out of here, my darling! How many times do I have to tell you? Mum-Mums is sick.'

Mary-Margaret began to cry. Tears came hard as angry thoughts flapped about in her mind like a flock of startled birds.

She lifted the air freshener and pressed the nozzle, breathing in the pungent woody scent and allowing it to take her down a notch.

Her number one suspect had inflicted her with this pain. Oh, that horrible, horrible person. Orla Ryan. It was Orla Ryan. She ticked all the boxes: never off Mary-Margaret's case at work; skulking about, watching and prying. Like that time with Tina, the young patient who'd botched a wrist slashing – how was it they found it so difficult to do it right? Well, Mary-Margaret had only been taking a wee look in Tina's bedside locker, just out of idle curiosity. Nothing more. And what were the chances that Orla Ryan would come in at the very second Mary-Margaret was holding Tina's necklace? That woman had an uncanny knack of showing up at times that could seem compromising for Mary-Margaret. She was not going to steal that necklace, but, damn it, Orla Ryan made it seem that way.

She was a nosey cow. Mary-Margaret hated her. Mind you, Orla made no secret that she didn't like Mary-Margaret either.

Orla was too stupid to understand the nuance of the special relationship Mary-Margaret had with the patients. Why couldn't she mind her own damned business and keep her nose out of Mary-Margaret's affairs? And to stoop to such a juvenile, maddening, nasty trick like the letter.

Mary-Margaret sunk her head into the pillow and thumped the bed with her fists, stifling a scream. She was going to explode if she had to go on like this. She was tired of waiting for George Grant to come back with an update.

And then she stopped. Why was she even waiting for him? What was he going to tell her anyway? She knew what she needed to know. It occurred to her that she didn't have to go on like this. She bolted upright. Her mind was suddenly clear. She knew exactly what she was going to do.

She grabbed her glasses, out of habit, and jumped out of bed, pulling on her housecoat over her pyjamas and pushing her feet into her slippers. Her hair was like a whin bush, but she paid no mind. She stuffed the can of air freshener and a tiny bottle of sanitiser into the pockets of her housecoat and dashed downstairs. Twiffles was curling in and out between her feet as she got a plastic bag from one of the drawers in the kitchen and packed it with a carton of eggs and a handful of tomatoes. Twiffles meowed and rubbed against her leg. She gave him a push away and pulled a burgeoning bag of waste food out of the mini compost bin by the back door.

'Twiffles, it's time I ended this,' she shouted. 'Time that woman got a piece of my mind. You wait here 'til I get back.'

Mary-Margaret ran out of the house, ranting and raging, out past the garden gate and out onto the road in the direction of the main street.

'She's going to be sorry,' Mary-Margaret screamed.

A couple of women were chatting outside the Post Office and Mary-Margaret glared in their direction as she marched past. They stared back, open-mouthed.

'She sent it,' Mary-Margaret shouted at them. 'Oh yes, she sent it.'

On she raced, shouting the whole way. People began coming to their doors to see what all the commotion was about. Mary-Margaret saw them, but didn't give a single damn. She had one thing and one thing only on her mind.

When she reached the main street, Cyril Wilson was climbing into his Massey Ferguson parked near The Snug. He stopped and looked over.

Does he know about the letter? Mary-Margaret wondered. *Does he know Orla sent it?*

'I'm not letting her get away with it,' Mary-Margaret yelled at him, 'and I won't let you get away with it either if I find out you had anything to do with it.'

Ciara McCann was outside The Snug chatting to her sister, Shay.

'Mary-Margaret? Are you all right?' Ciara called.

Mary-Margaret didn't stop to answer. For all she knew, Ciara and Shay were in cahoots with Orla Ryan.

The pavement was rough and cold under her slippers and tiny pebbles jabbed into the soles of her feet, but she ploughed on regardless until she reached the other end of the main street where Orla Ryan lived. By the time she got there, it seemed as if the whole village was out of their houses having a gawk. Had they nothing better to do?

Mary-Margaret set her bags at her feet and banged on the front door of the Ryan house with the force of a battering ram. She had the wherewithal to push her glasses up and give a few blasts on the air freshener, sucking in its life-saving perfume.

'Open up, Orla Ryan. You did it. I'm not going to stand for this. Open up, now.'

The door swung open. Alec, Orla's husband, stood there, six foot tall with arms like shovels and a black beard that needed grooming.

'What the…?' he said, startled and angry all at once.

'Where is she?' Mary-Margaret screamed, trying to force her way into the house.

'Hang on there,' Alec said. He put his arm across the frame of the door and blocked her way. 'You're not coming in here 'til you settle yourself. What's the problem?'

'I want to see Orla. She sent the letter and she's the one going to pay the consequences. Not me!'

Mary-Margaret became aware of a crowd gathering. They were mumbling and chattering among each other.

'Will you all just shut up and go back to your houses?' Mary-Margaret screamed. 'I've got private business to attend to here.'

'My Orla's done nothing on you,' Alec said, 'so why don't *you* go back to *your* house?'

Anger rose from Mary-Margaret's stomach like a tidal wave building up from the deep. She let the air freshener drop to the ground with a clang, knowing she was too far gone for it to do her any good now. She picked up her bags and stepped away from the door.

'You asked for this,' she shouted, close to breaking down in tears.

She lifted up the bag of waste food and swung it overhead a few times before letting it go. It whizzed through the air like a bullet and – splat, bang! – hit a window of the Ryan's house, dead centre. The bag split open and the oozing, decomposing contents burst onto the glass. It slowly slithered downwards onto the windowsill, leaving behind a trail of half-rotted chunks of vegetables. A teabag stuck to one of the panes.

Alec Ryan could only stare in shock at his newly decorated window.

'What the hell is going on?' a voice asked from the middle of the bystanders.

Mary-Margaret knew that voice. She swung round. There was the portly Orla Ryan standing with a loaf and a pound of butter in her arms. The tidal wave inside Mary-Margaret gave way. She reached into her second bag and found an egg.

'You bitch, I'm going to kill you,' she howled.

She flung the egg in Orla's direction. It landed right on top of her head with a crack. Mary-Margaret threw another, this one bouncing off Orla's shoulder and falling to its death on the pavement. Mary-Margaret lunged straight at Orla, who looked dumbfounded. She grabbed Orla by the collar and started to shake her back and forth. The butter and the loaf Orla was carrying dropped and the butter went plop when it hit the concrete. And just as Mary-Margaret was about to push Orla to the ground to join the butter, she suddenly felt her body being lifted up. Alec Ryan had his arms around her waist and was holding her tighter than a straightjacket.

She roared with rage. 'Let me go, you bastard. I want her.'

Her glasses askew and spit flying in every direction, Mary-Margaret kicked and flailed against Alec's grip, catching the loaf with her foot and sending it bouncing along the footpath.

'Phone the Gards, somebody,' Orla cried. 'For God's sake!'

'They're on their way,' a voice in the crowd said.

'She's really lost the run of herself this time,' another voice said.

Mary-Margaret was so immersed in her rage, everything became blurry and distant. She couldn't even form words anymore so she just kept screaming. Her head wanted to explode and maybe it did, because, next thing she knew, the world started to fade and disappear.

'Watch her, Alec,' somebody in a faraway voice said. 'She's passing out.'

28

Ciara giggled. 'Mary-Margaret's meltdown yesterday keeps popping into my head. When the teabag stuck to the window, that just killed me.'

Shay stretched her legs out on the sofa, trying to find a comfortable position. Not that that was easy because every bone in her body ached. And now she had Ciara banging on about Mary-Margaret, which meant it was only a matter of time before she started on about the letters.

'It's leaking out around the village now,' Ciara said. 'That folks have been getting poison letters and that Mary-Margaret's little display yesterday was because she got one.'

Shay cursed inside. 'I suppose Daisy McBirney-fucking-Smith told you that,' she said.

'She did, as it happens. It would explain the carry-on of Tracy Johnson and Brendan Kelly, too, though, wouldn't it?'

The bloody copycat – not that anybody but her knew it was a copycat – had the village in chaos and Shay was disgusted.

She could just about cope with the Mary-Margaret incident. Even when the Gards showed up, it was more comical than serious. And maybe Mary-Margaret deserved a bit of a scare from the Gards after what she said about Rory at the funeral.

After all, hadn't Shay even considered sending her a letter at one point?

She leaned up on her arm to take her meds and swallowed them down in one go with a mouthful of water. *For all the use they were doing*, she thought. Probably nothing more than a placebo or, if she was lucky, a sedative to keep her from going mad while her unwanted new friend attacked her brain. She dropped back onto the sofa and breathed out.

Truth was, Shay wasn't bothered that Tracy had got a letter. There was another person who could do with a kick up the ass.

But the hassle the letters brought to Ciara wasn't so easy to shake off. Ciara's anguish when she first got her letter seemed to have blown over. Even the incident in the bar was sorted. Brendan Kelly had come down to the bar the very next day, shamed-faced and apologetic, and had paid for all of the damage. Despite that, Shay felt sick to her core and wished it had never happened. If there was any chance of her coming clean with Ciara, that right there was another good reason to keep shtum. She was filled with shame and regret. Shay wondered how many other letters were out in the village, causing misery. This thought gave her more cause for shame and regret.

The letter-writing plan had been the one thing that was supposed to give her some succour when everything else in her life was turning to shit – and now it was turning to shit, too. Bile burned in her chest.

'What do you make of it all?' Ciara asked. 'I wish we could find out who's doing it.'

'Could we change the subject?' Shay said. 'I'm not feeling great.' This was true, but it wasn't the reason she wanted to talk about something else.

Ciara immediately got up. 'Do you need me to ring the hospital?'

'I'm not that bad,' Shay said, 'just tired. Don't be getting worked up.'

'Can I get you anything? A wee blanket to throw over you or a painkiller?'

'It's okay. I don't need anything.'

Ciara sat down reluctantly, that familiar cloud of worry over her eyes. Shay's stomach sank. Seemed like all she was doing these days was bringing trouble to Ciara.

'Shay,' Ciara said, taking in a deep breath, as though preparing herself for what she was going to say next. 'Shay, I don't want you putting me off again, but we have to talk about your living arrangements. You can't stay here on your own much longer.'

Fuck. Shay didn't want to talk about that either. 'This is what I get for telling you I'm tired,' she said. 'Save it, Ciara. I mean it.'

'You keep putting me off anytime I bring it up. Don't you see I'm scared something's going to happen to you here? So is Joe. It's time you moved in with us.'

Shay exhaled heavily and let her head fall back against the arm of the sofa. The clock ticked loudly on the mantelpiece, time ebbing away, second by second. Its calm steadiness was maddening.

'You just don't get it,' she said. 'Once I move in with you, it'll be the beginning of the end.'

'You—'

The doorbell rang, saving Shay from any more of Ciara's good intentions.

Ciara went to answer it. Shay listened as her sister opened the door. A few friendly words were exchanged between Ciara and the caller. Shay recognised his voice. The front door closed and Ciara came back to the sitting room.

'That was George,' Ciara said. 'Look what came for you.'

Ciara held up a plain white envelope. Shay's mouth dropped. She was another victim of the copycat – a victim of her own treachery. Was somebody up there having a laugh? The irony wasn't lost on her.

'Will I open it?' Ciara said.

'Is there any point? We know what's in it.'

'Just in case,' Ciara said, tearing the envelope open anyway.

Shay waited and then read Ciara's face. 'The same as the others.'

Ciara sat down on the end of the sofa. 'Fuck's sake,' she said, her face strained, 'as if you haven't bother enough. You don't need this shit.'

Shay agreed, but not for the same reason as Ciara. The copycat and not the letter was her problem. Oh, if she could find that copycat, she'd choke her.

'Don't worry about me,' Shay said. 'I'm not going to take that letter seriously.'

Ciara's face relaxed. 'Really? You're not worried?'

Shay shook her head. 'Not about the letter.'

'Well, I'm grateful for that, at least.' Ciara put the letter on the coffee table. 'You know what George told me there now? Mary-Margaret Walsh was admitted to St Bart's. She's a patient in the very place she worked.'

The shock of this unexpected turn of events sent a shiver down Shay's back. 'I thought the Gards would send her home with a slap on the wrist. She'll be okay, won't she? She'll get out and be able to go back to work?'

'I dunno, George said she was in a very bad way.'

Shay swore to herself. Was this her fault? Did she have to take responsibility for Mary-Margaret's troubles even though she hadn't actually sent her a letter? Because the copycat wouldn't even exist if it wasn't for her. Guilt nagged.

'I don't get why people are reacting so badly to these letters,' Shay said, trying to reason that guilt away. 'I mean, they're not accusing us of anything.'

'They don't need to,' Ciara said. She put her head down.

And then Shay understood. She understood with that deep, cloying dread you get when you know you've done something terrible and forever irrevocable. She recalled Ciara's account of getting the letter and how she and Joe had immediately thought it was about the *poitín*. The letter didn't have to accuse them of that. They arrived at that conclusion on their own. But wasn't that the very reason she'd phrased the letter how she did? She hadn't wanted to outright accuse Peter or Eoin of anything. She'd wanted to leave it open, present it as a suggestion and let them do the rest of the work.

'We're all guilty of something,' Shay said, her mouth dry, 'isn't that it?'

Shay thought her wording of the letter had been so clever. Now she saw how stupid it was. Not only had she made it easy for the copycat, but her words left it wide open for everybody's imagination to run rampant. This was okay if it was just Peter or Eoin, but not okay if it was other people.

'Jesus, Shay, you look like you're having a turn,' Ciara was saying. 'Your face actually looks green.'

'I'm okay,' Shay said. 'I'm not going to pass out.'

Ciara's eyes were swirls of fear. She touched Shay's arm.

'I'm really okay,' Shay said.

Ciara seemed to settle.

'You'd think,' Shay said, 'that when news about the letters spread, it'd take the threat out of them.'

'That everybody would see them as a hoax?' Ciara nodded. 'I don't know what anybody else thinks, but me and Joe, we didn't want to take any chances, you know, about the *poitín* thing. Letter or no letter, we are guilty.'

That wasn't what Shay wanted to hear.

'Maybe it'll just fizzle out, do you think?' she said.

She wanted reassurance, even if it wasn't true.

Ciara shrugged. 'George says they're still arriving.'

Shay wailed inside.

'And another thing he told me,' Ciara said, 'is that the Post Office has reported it to the Gards.'

'The Gards? Why the Gards?' Shay knew he'd told his head office, but bringing the Gards in was a new development. An alarm bell rang in her head, just loud enough to let her know it was there.

'Head office insisted on it, George said.'

'Oh!' Shay's throat tightened and the alarm bell got louder. 'I didn't realise they'd take it seriously.'

'George gave them a list of everybody who got a letter, as far as he's aware, and they're going to start an investigation. He said he'd keep me in the know.'

'Will you keep me in the know, too?' Shay asked.

Ciara nodded. 'This is giving me such a bad feeling,' she said, quietly, 'like something terrible is going to happen any day now.'

29

The house was empty. Natalie was going out with work friends after they clocked off – that's what she'd told him anyway, though he found it hard to trust her anymore – and wouldn't be home 'til at least nine. For the past hour, Eoin had sat propped up on the windowsill in the bedroom, chain-smoking what was left of the fags in his pack and gazing out at the lough below. The water was smooth and even, like polished silver, and the surface caught the last patches of blue-white sky that were slowly disappearing into the night darkness. He envied the stillness down there.

He touched the cool glass of the windowpane. Soon, today would be gone forever. Eoin felt its passing like a death; his heart heavy, melancholic. He wanted to die with it – but that wouldn't happen.

The news report the day before had changed everything. There was no more hiding. He knew it'd be better in the long run for him to come forward and, hard as it was, he'd called the Gards that very evening and confessed. They were on their way right now, no doubt.

He was terrified of what was to come but, terrified or not, this way was the only way. It's what his Grand-da would've have wanted him to do. As much as the old man used to preach about doing whatever it took to look out for number one, he would've stopped short of covering up a hit-and-run.

Yeah, this was the only way, whatever the consequences.

He laughed dryly. The letter he got; it had mentioned consequences, hadn't it? It hadn't been far wrong.

A glass ashtray, overflowing with butts and ash, was within arm's length. He stubbed out his fag. A cloud of blue-grey smoke lingered in the air. The choking stench made him cough. His throat was dry and sore, but that wouldn't stop him smoking.

His arrest was going to hit his mother hard. That bothered him. A lot. He'd tried to tell her it was about to happen, to prepare her, but chickened out. Of course, what bothered him more was who was going to look out for her and help her money-wise when he went to prison. Shame burned in his chest.

His morose thoughts turned to Natalie. He'd written her a letter and left it on her pillow, explaining himself as well as he could, telling her it was best they end their relationship. It killed him writing that, but he knew it had to be done. He imagined her coming back later that night to a deserted house, how she'd call out that she was home and wander into each of the downstairs rooms. When she could see no sign of him, she'd go upstairs. And all she'd find was the letter on the pillow. She'd be horrified when she found out the truth. She might cry or, more likely, she'd scream with rage. And she'd call him every name under the sun. The most he hoped for was that she'd eventually understand – that she wouldn't hate him.

He ran his tongue across his near-perfect front teeth and lit another cigarette. A random memory of Rory visited his thoughts. He wondered what his Grand-da would've made of all that. Would he have said "all's fair in love and war" or would he have said that Eoin pushed the "looking-out-for-number-one" maxim too far? More importantly, what did Eoin himself think?

Rory's death had rattled him, that was for sure, and no one could deny it was a total heartbreak. Yeah, that was a fucking disaster and unexpected, too. Who could've known Rory was going to kill himself?

The question was, did he feel responsible? The truth? Now? Right here? With only his soul and his reflection in the window to answer to?

Well, no, he didn't. That was on Rory and if Rory hadn't been man enough to face his troubles, like Eoin himself, maybe he shouldn't have been trying to piss with the big boys. Rory did what he did because, in the end, he was weak and – in the first sign of hard times – he broke. He'd have done that anyway, with or without Eoin.

Eoin rubbed his eyes.

The knock finally came to the door. He took one last look out of the window, but there was only darkness in the sky now and the tiny wavering lights from the far side of the lough. He grabbed his fags and, standing up straight, he turned to face his future.

30

A gentle rapping came to the door of her private room. Mary-Margaret didn't bother to answer. In these places, the staff just walked in whether you gave them permission or not. She should know. After all, just a few days ago, she'd been one of those staff. The door inched open and in peeked the last person on earth Mary-Margaret wanted to see.

'Can I come in?' Orla Ryan asked.

Mary-Margaret threw daggers with her eyes. 'As if I can keep you out?'

'Of course you can keep me out,' Orla said. 'I'm not one of the nurses assigned to you. I'm a visitor and you don't have to see visitors, if you don't want to.'

Mary-Margaret snorted, pushing her glasses up the bridge of her nose.

'Will I leave?'

'I don't care what you do.' Mary-Margaret folded her arms and turned to face the blank white wall.

'I brought you some chocolates – cherry liqueurs. I know they're your favourite. And a few magazines.'

Mary-Margaret could murder a box of cherry liqueurs.

'I'll put them here for you,' Orla said.

Mary-Margaret turned her head slightly and saw Orla leave the flat red-and-gold chocolate box on the bedside locker, along with some glossy magazines. Those items were the only bit of colour in the whole room. Everything else was white or grey, from floor to ceiling. Not that there was much in the room apart from the bed, the locker and a small built-in wardrobe where her bits and bobs were stored.

Orla plopped herself down at the end of the bed.

'How're you feeling, Mary-Margaret?'

'Exhausted,' Mary-Margaret said, and so she was. The medication they were giving her was sucking the life out of her.

'I hear Dr Lawlor's looking after you.'

'Dr Lawlor couldn't look after a goldfish.'

'Aww, God, Mary-Margaret, don't say that. She's a great doctor.'

Mary-Margaret had less time for the doctors in St Bart's than she had for the nurses. It was an indignity to be under their care, being one of their patients.

'But who's looking after my cat? My Twiffles?' she asked.

'What?'

'Twiffles. I told Dr Lawlor and the nurses there was no one at home to take care of him. They all ignored me. He had food and water in his little bowls when I left, but that was two days ago. They'll be all gone by now. If I wasn't drugged to the eyeballs, I'd be panicking.'

'I can take care of him,' Orla said, and her eyes, hovering over the top of her face mask, seemed genuinely kind. 'Would you like me to? If you give me your house key, I can go in and put food and water out for him every day.'

'Really? I mean, you'd do that? That would be such a weight off my mind. I've been so, so worried about him.'

Mary-Margaret leaned over and opened the locker drawer where she had her key stored, along with other personal items. She handed it over and Orla took it and put it deep into the pocket of her tunic.

'I'll only have to look after him for a few days anyway,' Orla said. 'You'll be allowed home soon.'

'I hate being here. I want to go home now.'

'I don't blame you. At least you have a room to yourself and, as you know well, not many patients get that. They decided it might not be a good idea for a member of staff to be among the patients, even though you're a patient, too, but you know what I mean.'

'I'm not a patient,' Mary-Margaret said, almost spitting out the words, 'not like them. I shouldn't be here. I shouldn't be getting treated like I'm one of them.'

She pulled off her glasses. After all, they had no practical purpose and they were getting on her nerves.

'Now, don't upset yourself. We all know you're not like the other patients.'

'I didn't do anything wrong. They had no right to lock me up here like a dog.'

'It's only for a few days. You'll be out and back to normal then.'

'Are you going to press charges?'

'What?'

'After what I did, are you—'

'God's sake, Mary-Margaret, you know I wouldn't do that. Alec wanted to – he was so angry – but I put my foot down.'

Mary-Margaret breathed a sigh of relief and might even have cried if she hadn't been so dulled by the medication.

'Thanks,' she said, begrudgingly. 'And I'm sorry about… you know.' She looked over at the locker. 'Maybe I will have one of those chocolates.'

Orla smiled and handed her the box. Mary-Margaret tore off the plastic wrapper and left the box on the bed. She grabbed a bottle of sanitiser from the bedside locker and doused her hands before opening the lid. She extracted one of the silky, cherry-shaped sweets and popped it in her mouth. The taste was like nothing on earth as she let it melt on her tongue.

'What made you do it?' Orla asked. 'Why did you go for me like that?'

Mary-Margaret wanted Orla to shut up. She pretended not to hear and went on enjoying her sweet, relishing that first hint of the sour liqueur as it began to ooze through the melting chocolate.

'Alec said something about a letter,' Orla went on. 'Did you get one of those poison pen letters?'

Mary-Margaret had broken through to the Kirsch-soaked cherry. If only Orla would shut up and let her savour the moment.

'Did you, Mary-Margaret? Did you get one?'

"Knock it off, Orla," was all Mary-Margaret wanted to say. But no, Orla was going to keep on and on. She was so easy to hate.

'If you did, you shouldn't let it upset you, you know. You weren't the only person to get one. Other people in the village did, too, and the Gards are looking into it. It's all just a hoax and nothing to worry about.'

Mary-Margaret chewed on the delicious, pungent cherry. So, she hadn't been the only one. And the Gards were involved.

'Do they know who's been sending them?' Mary-Margaret asked, curiosity getting the better of her.

'I don't think so, but they will soon, I'm sure.'

The chocolate and the cherry were gone and Mary-Margaret was left with the bitter-sweet aftertaste. Maybe she could have another.

'You thought it was me, didn't you?' Orla said, and one side of her mouth turned up in a tiny smile. 'You thought I sent it.'

Mary-Margaret looked at the chocolates.

'So, what is it you think I know?'

She squirmed.

'Tell me then.'

She suddenly wanted Orla to get out.

'Are you going to keep it to yourself? Aww, come on, what got you so worried?'

The door opened and a nurse came in.

'Time for your medication, Mary-Margaret... oh, Orla, I didn't realise you were in here.'

'I was visiting Mary-Margaret, Jill. She's not just one of my staff; she's my neighbour, too.'

'I never knew that,' Jill said. 'Isn't that lovely, Mary-Margaret?'

Mary-Margaret grimaced.

'I'll get out of your hair and let you get on with things,' Orla said. 'I was about to leave anyway.'

Mary-Margaret waved as Orla exited. She was glad to see the back of her, even though she'd promised to look after Twiffles. That definitely lifted some of the worry. Though, there was still the letter. She didn't care if others had gotten one.

If Orla hadn't sent it – and Mary-Margaret believed her when she said she hadn't – the question was: who had?

Mary-Margaret dropped down on the bed as Jill took her blood pressure. She eyed her. Could Jill be the one? Or another person on the staff? Or was it somebody else in the village?

Oh no, she screamed in her mind, because she was too drowsy to scream out loud, *the whole damned thing was starting all over again.*

31

The phone vibrated inside the pocket of Shay's apron. She was due to start her shift and was in two minds about answering. She checked anyway. A number she didn't recognise. Probably some cold caller looking to sell her life insurance. Wouldn't that be funny?

'Sorry I'm late,' she said to Tracy, rushing behind the counter and hanging up her bag and coat.

'Well, you're here now,' Tracy said, without looking up. 'I have the fryers heating.'

Tracy wasn't exactly taking her on these days, only as much as she needed to for work purposes. She hadn't even made mention of Shay's fainting spell the Friday before, and it didn't seem she'd said anything to her brother-in-law either, which was a relief. Shay didn't want awkward questions or Steven Robinson giving her the heave-ho, not before she was ready to go on her own terms.

Shay grabbed her apron. 'I'll get some quarter pounders from the storeroom.'

'Get some chicken breasts, too, while you're at it,' Tracy said.

Shay's phone rang again. She pulled it from her pocket and glanced quickly at the display. The same number as before. Maybe it wasn't a cold caller. She decided to answer this time.

'Hi,' a woman said, 'am I speaking with Shay Dunne?'

Shay didn't recognise the voice. Damn, it was a cold caller after all. 'You're not selling something, are you? Cos whatever it is, I'm not buying.'

'I'm Lorna Duffy.'

The phone almost slipped from Shay's hand. 'Lorna? You mean…'

'Rory's ex.'

Rory's ex. The same ex who had left Rory high and dry in his hour of need. The same ex who had ignored her DMs on social media when she'd been searching for Rory and wanted to speak to everybody, anybody, who might have information that could help. The same ex who didn't even go to his funeral. Now, she'd decided to get in touch. Now, when it didn't matter. She had a nerve. Shay wished she could muster up the words to express how much she hated her so she could vent them down the phone. She immediately regretted not having sent her a poison pen letter after all.

'Are you still there? Missus Dunne?'

'What's keeping you, Shay?' Tracy called. 'I need that chicken.'

'I'm still here,' Shay said into the phone, not hiding her disgust.

With her free hand, she gathered a pack of chicken breasts and a bag of quarter pounders and tucked them under her arm.

'Is it convenient to talk?' Lorna asked.

'I'm at work, but I can give you a minute.'

And a minute was all Shay intended to give her.

'Maybe I could ring you when you're not at work. It'd be more private.'

'Now will do,' Shay said, her words sharp as a knife.

Shay walked back to the shop and threw the frozen food on the prep counter. Tracy gave her a disapproving glance.

'Um, okay,' Lorna said. Shay thought she heard a sigh. 'This is hard for me. I've been building up the courage to ring you for a while.'

The bell on the cafe door jangled. First customer of the evening.

'I suppose I'll have to get this along with doing everything else,' Tracy said, rolling her eyes and going to the counter.

'Build up the courage?' Shay scoffed.

'Well, you know, because it didn't end well between me and Rory.'

'That's not the only problem I have with you, but, yeah, I do know that it ended. Not how it ended, only that it did.'

'I can imagine why you have a lot of problems with me.' Lorna breathed heavily. 'And I'd like the chance to explain…'

Shay could hear what sounded like crying. Shay felt no compassion. The bell jangled again and a couple entered the shop. Tracy was busy with the order for the first customer and this time she signalled to Shay, her face like thunder.

'I loved him,' Lorna said, her voice thick. 'We were… well, that's what I want to explain.'

Instead of being moved or swayed by what Lorna was saying, she found she was offended, downright insulted. And how dare she claim to love him after everything?

'Lorna,' Shay said, 'I'm running out of time here so get to the point.'

'Oh.' Lorna said the word like it had been delivered alongside a slap to the face. She sniffed. 'I'm sorry. Right, okay, I was ringing to ask if… if I could meet you.'

'God's sake, Shay,' Tracy whispered. 'Serve that couple, will ye?'

Shay breathed in sharply, hardly believing her ears. 'Meet me? You want to meet me?'

'I really hope you'll say yes,' Lorna said. 'That would mean everything.'

'I have to go.'

'Please will you contact me to let me know?'

'Will do.' Shay ended the call without a sign-off, without allowing Lorna a sign-off. She had zero intention of contacting her.

She returned the phone to her pocket and headed straight for the customers.

'What can I get you, folks?' she asked, sanitising her hands.

She gave the customers a big smile that hid the turmoil inside. She wanted to punch something, punch and punch and fucking punch. Her beautiful boy was gone and this girl had the gall to ring her and ask to meet. If Lorna thought Shay was going to go along with that, she could think again.

32

'Natalie,' Andie called from downstairs, 'there are guests at the door for you.'

Natalie's skull was lifting from a headache she'd been nursing since the day before. Andie knew it, too, which made it all the more hateful that she was shouting. Andie could be such a pain in the arse at times. Although, it would be fair to cut the girl some slack for she'd come to Natalie's rescue and found her a place to stay after the landlord kicked her out. How quickly everything could fall on its ass. Eoin was gone three days and, in that tiny space of time, her whole life, such as it was, was gone, too. Gone as good as dust in the wind. And she was left with the shock of the hit-and-run that she still couldn't process. Jesus! Eoin had run a man over and left him for dead. What the actual fucking fuck? It looked like he might go to jail. Eoin in jail. None of it felt real. No wonder her head was about to explode.

Natalie rolled out of bed and dragged her carcass downstairs. She peeked in the door of the living room. The guests, as Andie called them, were cops. They were standing in the middle of the floor – a man and a woman. The woman cop was sort of squat and she had shoulder-length red hair, and a red face to match. The man cop was tall and lanky and skinnier than a whippet. They were like one of those comedy duos you saw on TV.

'There you are,' Andie said. 'The Gards want to see you.'

Andie left the room, mouthing "What the fuck?" as she brushed past Natalie.

'What's this about?' Natalie asked, dropping onto a beat-out armchair and reaching for a pack of fags that were lying on a glass-topped coffee table. 'Is it about Eoin? I already gave you my statement. It was a short one. I don't know anything about the hit-and-run.'

The living room was small and what little furniture there was had seen much better days. The reek of stale beer and last night's burgers and chips wafted from the threadbare carpet. Natalie hated the room. It reminded her of being shit-kicking poor, of where she came from. She was back at square one and it depressed her in a way she'd never been depressed before. And though she deserved it – she knew she had to atone, after all – it still sucked.

Both cops took a seat on the sofa and perched their peaked caps by their sides.

'We're aware of Mr Devine's case,' the female cop said, from behind her face mask, 'but that's not why we're here. I'm Garda Duggan and this is my colleague, Garda O'Hagan. We want to ask you about the poison pen letter you got.'

'How did you know about that?' Natalie asked. The nosey bastards pried into everything that wasn't their business. She slipped out a fag and lit it with the red plastic lighter she had stowed in the pack.

'We've a list of people who got letters,' Duggan said, 'and your name's on that list.'

'What? There's a whole list?' Natalie said. She knew about Eoin's letter, of course, but hadn't heard there were others.

'We're going to talk to each name on here. You're the first person we've approached.'

'Where did you get the list?' Natalie said, pulling on her fag.

'Ms O'Donnell,' O'Hagan said, in a southern accent, 'we'll ask the questions, if you don't mind.'

Natalie threw him a hard look.

'We'd like to see your letter, if we could,' Duggan said.

Natalie shrugged. She thought for a second, trying to remember where she had put it. With moving into the cottage, her stuff was all over the place.

'I think it's in my tote,' she mumbled. 'That's where I packed most of my letters and documents. I'll check.'

The tote was in the kitchen. She balanced her fag on a chipped ceramic ashtray and went to locate it.

She wasn't one bit happy that the cops were sniffing around because of that stupid letter. Bubbles bounced around in her stomach, making her queasy. What could they want to know? Whatever they were looking for, she had nothing to tell. For her, the letter might've been unnerving at first, but since there had been no follow-up, she had come to see it as a load of bollocks – an idle threat sent by somebody who had no clue – and it didn't worry her anymore. It was her conscience she had to answer to. That was her judge, jury and executioner. If the letter had done anything, it was to force her to face up to what she knew already. So, when it came to the cops and answering their questions, it was fucking-A, as Eoin would say. And yet, those bubbles in her stomach wouldn't settle.

She carried her bag back to the sitting room and rifled through the pockets, taking out envelopes and papers and plastic pouches containing more envelopes and papers. Eventually, she found what she was looking for, still inside its envelope and neatly folded in half.

'Here you go,' she said.

Duggan put on surgical gloves and reached over for the envelope. She took the letter out and O'Hagan leaned closer so he could get a gawk, too.

'Same as the others,' Duggan said.

Natalie grabbed her fag and sat back in the armchair, trying to look hard and like she didn't give a shit. Her head pounded like a hammer on a tin roof and her stomach still bubbled away. How she wished she could crawl into a dark hole, away from all the noise and the light, and just sleep.

O'Hagan put the letter and envelope into a plastic bag.

'Do you have any idea who might have sent this?' Duggan asked.

'Haven't a clue,' Natalie said, flicking ash into the ashtray.

'What about the letter's content? Do you know what that might be referring to?'

Natalie shifted in the armchair. She shook her head vigorously.

'Nope. Not a clue,' she said.

'The day the letter arrived,' Duggan said, 'did it have any significance? Was it an anniversary, a birthday?'

'The date doesn't mean anything to me.'

'I'm going to read out some names,' O'Hagan said, 'and if you recognise any, I'd like you to tell us. Okay?'

Natalie nodded. She took a final pull from her fag and stubbed it out. The squashed butt, all on its own in the ashtray, looked pathetic. Like her fucking life. Her hand was shaking slightly. She threw a sly glance at the cops. Had they noticed that shake? Of course they had. Them fuckers were trained to notice everything.

'The first name here is Eoin Devine, your boyfriend,' O'Hagan said. 'He's on our list because he told us he got a letter when we interviewed him after his arrest. We can safely assume you know him, so we've taken the liberty of ticking his name.'

'Sure, but he's my ex-boyfriend, not my boyfriend.'

Duggan pounced. 'Ex-boyfriend? Why did that happen?'

'As if it's any of your business.'

'Your attitude isn't very helpful,' Duggan said, taking that superior tone Natalie often got from authority figures. 'We'll decide what is and isn't our business.'

Natalie squinted at Duggan, begrudging the fact that the cop would get the better of her and she'd have to answer the question. 'I don't like telling a complete randomer like you about my personal life, but what choice do I have? He finished with me, if you're so dying to know. He wrote me a letter and, in it, he finished with me.'

She didn't add that she had considered contacting him – she wanted to know if he was coping okay. In the end, she had chickened out. Thinking about Eoin stuck in jail made her heart ache, in spite of what he did and in spite of their relationship being over. His life was fucked and hers was in the same general location.

She found it hard to stay looking tough in front of the cops. Why wouldn't they just go? Tears filled up inside and she fought with all she was worth to hold them back.

'Do you still have the letter he wrote?' Duggan asked.

'No,' Natalie said, with a snap.

She lied. His letter was in her tote, too, in the same pouch where the poison letter had been. No way was she going to hand it over. Eoin's letter was too personal, too private; the cops had no right to see it.

'When did he write you the letter?'

'The night he was arrested, I came back home and found it on my pillow.'

'Did he say why he was breaking up with you?'

'Are you stupid? What do you think? The letter said he was going to prison and we didn't have a future together.'

Duggan just nodded, showing not an ounce of compassion. Natalie sneered. She could nearly smell their disrespect. They were rummaging through her feelings like sifting through cast-offs at a car boot sale. They didn't care what state they left her in, so long as they got what they wanted.

'You lived with Mr Devine at Braytop View,' Duggan said. 'The landlord told us you moved out. Any particular reason for that?'

'I'm really enjoying our heart-to-heart.'

Duggan gave a stare that almost said, "You're on your last chance."

'If you really want to know,' Natalie said, 'the bloody landlord kicked me out the day after Eoin was arrested. We owed rent and I hadn't the money to pay it. Though I'd have left anyway cos I couldn't afford the place on my own.'

Natalie's voice was breaking, ever so slightly – the way a tiny crack would show in a piece of glass. It would only take the slightest nudge and the whole thing would shatter. She didn't want to shatter in front of these two.

'And you moved in here, not with family?'

Natalie cleared her throat and composed herself. 'I still haven't mustered up the courage to tell my family what's been happening,' she said.

Truth was she longed to go home to them but didn't dare. She was too ashamed that they'd see her sunk this low, plus she didn't want to bring worry to their door.

'This place belongs to Andie's parents,' she went on, 'and no one lives here. Andie's letting me crash rent-free 'til I sort out what to do next.'

Nothing in this world was free, of course. Staying there meant she had to put up with Andie for hours every time she came over. It just added to her hell.

'Curious,' Duggan said, 'that you wouldn't go to your family for help?'

'No, it's not curious. I don't want to give them any grief. My mother doesn't keep so well.'

'Okay, we'll leave it at that,' Duggan said. 'Let's get back to the list.'

O'Hagan began to read out the names. Natalie couldn't believe how many there were.

'Are any of those familiar?' he asked.

'I recognise a few, but I'm not from here originally and I don't know many people. I recognise Shay Dunne and Peter Feeney. Eoin was in business with Rory Dunne and he talked about his mother and his Grand-da – Rory hated him.'

'What about any of the other names?' Duggan asked.

'Ciara McCann and Joe – the people who own the pub – they're Rory's aunt and uncle.'

Natalie put her hand across her forehead to cool it down.

'Anybody else?'

'I don't know any of the rest,' Natalie said.

Her voice was beginning to sound pleading. She so badly wanted them gone. Duggan and O'Hagan looked at each other.

'I think that's it for now,' Duggan said.

'What do you mean "for now"?'

'We might want to talk with you again as the investigation goes on – that's routine.'

'Oh, right,' Natalie said, trying not to show her relief.

'We'll see ourselves out,' Duggan said.

This time, her face seemed to say, "I don't expect you to walk us to the door." Natalie matched it with one that said, "I wouldn't do it in a million fucking years."

The front door had no sooner closed behind the cops when Andie appeared.

'What was the craic with them?' she asked, dying for news. 'Were they questioning you about Eoin?'

Natalie shook her head. She grabbed another fag and lit it – she was lighting these things like she was in a smoking competition.

'They wanted to know about that poison letter I got.'

'The letter?' Andie said. 'Why would they want to ask you

about that? Are they investigating it? Are they trying to find out who sent it? Did they—'

'In fuck's name, Andie,' Natalie said, resisting the temptation to slap her across the face, 'you really need to get a life if this is how you get your kicks.'

Andie's face fell.

'Aww, come on,' Natalie said, 'can't you see I'm exhausted here? They've been interrogating me and now you're doing the same. I can't take it.' She flicked ash into the ashtray and fell back into the armchair. 'I'm not doing well. My head feels like there's a pneumatic drill pounding a hole in it. I need more painkillers.'

'I'll get you some,' Andie said. 'I brought you a load of them from the shop so you'll not run out.'

Andie went to get the painkillers, leaving Natalie with her thoughts.

I know what you did. Prepare for the consequences. She might not see the letter itself as a threat anymore, but its words were imprinted in her brain like an engraving on a brass plaque – an eternal reminder that she'd actually done something wrong and now she was paying the price. Finally, she was getting her comeuppance, and not before time. Her mouth curled into an ironic smile. It was clever, in a twisted way, that the poison pen left the wording vague enough to drive a person mad with their own dark thoughts. It didn't even matter who sent the letter – hadn't she thought at one stage it might be Rory's mother? That was laughable.

Andie came back with the painkillers and a glass of water. Natalie swallowed the pills down and Andie took up position on the sofa, looking like she was about to explode.

'Say it,' Natalie said, 'whatever it is you're busting your hole to say.'

'How…? Umm, I was thinking we could watch a film tonight. I've got some good ones downloaded and we could watch them on my laptop. We could get some vodka. Mammy and Daddy have an account in The Snug. It might cheer you up.'

'Thanks, Andie, it's a nice thought, but watching a film with you isn't going to help.'

'What if we went out to The Snug? That could be fun.'

Natalie gave Andie an irate glance. 'The Snug? Fun? Easy seeing you don't get out much.'

Andie turned her eyes to the floor.

'Look, Andie,' Natalie said, realising she should try not being so cutting to the person who was giving her a roof over her head, 'I know you mean well, but I'm not having a down-in-the-dumps moment that a night on the tiles is going to sort out. This is really serious and I honestly don't know how I'm going to get through it.'

'Do you want me to stay over?' Andie asked. 'I could be company for you at least.'

'That's nice of you, and I mean it, but I might be better off on my own tonight.' She had a bottle of vodka in one of the cupboards and that would make better company than Andie.

'I should get back home then,' Andie said.

'Good idea,' Natalie said. 'I'll see you tomorrow.'

Andie got up, unable to hide her disappointment. Natalie didn't have the energy to give a shit. In minutes, the front door closed and Andie was gone.

Natalie felt tired – dog tired, like she might fall into a coma if only this thumper of a headache would fuck off. She leaned on the armchair and waited for the painkillers to kick in, glad to be alone without Andie lurking around. Honestly, that girl had no life of her own, no other friends, no hobbies nor interests. She was a limpet, clinging to Natalie for something to do outside of working in that shop and running errands for her parents. And, mad as it sounded, Natalie almost believed Andie was enjoying this whole shitshow and being needed. What had she said the other day? "I have you all to myself now."

Natalie shivered. Andie could be creepy as fuck at times.

The pain began to ease, finally. She nearly cried with relief. At last, she could rest. She just needed some rest…

*

A drumming sound woke her. Natalie slowly opened her eyes. The drumming, she realised, was heavy rain bouncing off the windowpanes in an endless, repetitive, monotonous rhythm. She groaned. She'd fallen asleep in that rickety armchair and now she had pins and needles in her legs and a crick in her neck so bad it was as though she'd broken a bone.

She sat up and stretched carefully. The curtains were open and it was dark outside, except for a streetlight that kept the black night at bay. A car drove by, the tyres swishing on the wet tarmac. She leaned over and switched on a corner lamp. A soft, golden ball of light popped out, chasing the gloom.

Natalie's stomach growled. She was hungry, though she couldn't be bothered to fix something to eat. A dull throb filled her head like a mist, blunting her thoughts. If only it could do likewise to her feelings – those were sharper than scalpels.

She'd been dreaming. Dreaming about Rory.

They were at the wee beach on Inch Island and it was the most beautiful day. They were sitting on a blanket on the sand and the tide was going out. But then, without warning, it was dusk and the last of the sun was dropping behind the horizon. She suddenly heard a tiny, far-off voice, calling her name, from out in the sea. She looked and she spotted somebody in the distance waving. She turned to tell Rory, but Rory was gone. She was alone. She looked back at the sea and realised the person waving was Rory and he was calling her. She set off into the water, wading out deeper and deeper, getting closer and closer, close enough to hear he was calling for help. She waded forward until she couldn't touch the seabed anymore. Rory was screaming now, begging her to hurry. She could see him bobbing up and down, gulping in whole mouthfuls of water, calling out between gulps. He was drowning. She had to hurry. She was really close. A few more feet and she'd be there. She stretched out her arm. So close. Her fingertips brushed against his face. He bobbed up and down, and up and down, and up and under, and then… he was gone, lost to the deep.

The dream ended. Her heart was like a lump of lead in her chest. Why had she dreamed such a terrible dream? Some people said dreams had meaning – they were trying to tell us something. She thought that was hokum. And yet this one…

She brushed away tears from her cheeks and stood up. Time to hunt down that bottle of vodka. She needed more painkillers, too. Andie said she'd brought a load from the shop. And Natalie knew she had a prescription of co-codamol still intact from a sprained ankle the previous year. She remembered packing them into her toiletry bag.

She pulled on a cardigan and padded into the kitchen.

Maybe she knew fine well what the dream was telling her.

She began opening and closing cupboard doors, looking for the vodka. She found it and she washed a half-pint glass that was lying in the sink. She didn't have mixer, but she'd manage fine without.

Did she have the guts to face what she knew to be true, what she knew right down into her DNA? *Go on, say it.* That annoying voice was back, whispering from the caverns of her mind, goading her like a cheeky schoolgirl.

Natalie stuffed the boxes of painkillers into the pockets of her cardigan and brought the vodka and the glass into the sitting room. She drew the curtains and plopped herself on the armchair. She threw the boxes of painkillers onto the coffee table – she'd hunt for the co-codamol later – and filled the half-pint glass with vodka.

The debt. The fucking debt. Had she really not guessed there was something amiss about all that money Eoin was spending? Wasn't she even a tiny bit suspicious that they were living the lives of movie stars? Or was she enjoying it all too much to care?

You fucking knew, the voice said. *Grow a spine and admit it.*

She wanted to scream and drown out that voice. But the thing was, the voice was right and no amount of screaming was going to change that. So, yes, okay, she fucking knew. Even before Eoin had told her, she'd guessed the truth. All that righteous anger at Eoin – well, that was bullshit.

Natalie lifted the glass to her mouth and let the harsh, bitter liquid dance on her lips for a second. The quiet before the storm. She swallowed down half the contents in one go, ignoring its burn and how it made her stomach want to heave.

Even when she had started seeing Rory behind Eoin's back, even when she had ended up falling in love with him – fuck, even then – she had let the mad spending go on. All the while knowing, down into her DNA, that the money was coming from a dodgy place.

And she could play the violin about her dirt-poor upbringing and how she never again wanted to go to bed hungry or live in a freezing cold house or wear hand-me-downs. That still didn't justify a thing.

If Rory had taken his own life because of debt, then the people to blame were her and Eoin. Not just Eoin. Her and Eoin. That was the truth. That's what she hadn't been able to face all this time. That's what her poison pen letter finally made her face.

How could she have done that? No one normal, no one with a shred of decency in them, would do what she'd done. The very fact she cheated on Eoin in the first place – that, in itself, was as low as a rat on its belly.

But that's who she was. She was sick. She was an evil, selfish bitch who deserved whatever the consequences were. She deserved her wrongdoings to finally catch up with her.

Natalie took another drink – the burn of the vodka now a comforting feeling in her stomach. Soon, that comfort would go to her head and maybe help her forget.

Here was the thing, though. Now that she'd held her hands up and admitted she was guilty, it had left her terrified. See, the person who did those sickening things, the real person she was inside, she couldn't stand to be around that person.

Come on, coward, say it properly. The annoying voice popped up again.

All right then, she hated herself. She hated her-fucking-self. And, worse still, she knew she'd probably do the same all over again. It was her nature; it was who she was. What did that make her? Like a scorpion or something; a thing that would always choose to sting. She shivered.

The voice in her head surprised her by remembering a saying she thought she'd forgotten. *Life's a bitch and then you die.* Natalie sniggered. First time she heard it, she had no clue what it meant. Of course, now she understood it perfectly.

'Sláinte, bitch,' she slurred and held her glass in mid-air. 'You win.'

She finished off the glass, grimacing as the last drop went down, and poured another half-pint from the bottle. She thought about how she wanted to get lost in the bottom of that bottle. Oblivion. Anything to get away from herself.

She slid one of the boxes of painkillers towards her. A box of thirty-two. They could take her well down the road to nowhere. She opened the box, pulled out one of the blister packs and swallowed down a couple of the pristine white pills with a gulp of vodka. She felt them slide slowly down her throat. Her stomach gurgled.

She was a waste of fucking space. Always was. Probably always would be. That was an unbearable weight to carry. Unbearable.

She lifted the glass to her lips. She took a large swig, sending the liquid straight down her throat and avoiding the sides of her mouth as much as possible. It whisked past her tongue and cheeks, its harsh chemical fumes filling her nostrils and almost taking her breath away. She slammed the glass on the table and gasped for air. Paint thinners couldn't be any worse. Maybe a mixer would be necessary, after all, to take the hard edge off. If she kept going like this, she was liable to throw it all up and that would sort of defeat the purpose.

Natalie sank her hands into her hair and groaned. Tears came out of nowhere and pooled along her eyelids. She lifted her head and her hair fell in strands over her eyes.

The purpose. What was it anyway? She hadn't spoken it; she hadn't even thought it, not really. It was one of those ideas that skulked around in the dark, only coming into the light for a second or two every so often before running back into the shadows. It was peeking out now, though, getting braver, more confident.

Your life's so rotten, you shouldn't have to put up with it, her inner voice said.

'But what choice do I have?' Natalie said back.

Her words were loud in the empty room, echoing off the walls.

You know, it teased. *Come on, you know.*

'I do know,' Natalie said.

She reached for some more pills.

Take them all at once, the voice whispered. *Better that way, right?*

Right, better to take a lot and all at once. Dribs and drabs wouldn't get the job done. She'd heard the stories of people who hadn't taken enough quickly enough waking up in pools of piss and vomit. Worse still, taking enough to leave themselves on kidney dialysis for the rest of their lives. No fucking chance was she going to wind up like that. And no fucking chance was she going to wake up. It was all the way or nothing.

Hurry up and do it.

'I am,' Natalie said, 'I am hurrying.'

She emptied the blister pack onto the table, pushing each perfectly round pill out of its cosy plastic bubble. She kept pushing and pushing until the whole box was emptied and all the pills were free. She nudged them close to each other so they were gathered in a heap. She noticed they had a tiny letter imprinted on one side.

Never mind the tiny letter, what are you waiting for. Get on with it.

Natalie lifted half the pills into the palm of her hand. They felt heavy altogether like that. She stared at them, imagining lifting her hand to her mouth and pushing them in, their dry chalky taste on her tongue, and the harsh vodka helping them go down her throat.

You're a coward. A wee scaredy-cat.

She brought the pills closer. They touched her lips. She opened her mouth. And—

A sound, louder than a bomb, shattered the air. The whispering voice was frightened off and it scampered back into the shadows.

The pills fell from Natalie's hand. Her body jerked back.

'What?' she said, gasping. 'What am I doing?'

The sound went out again and this time she realised what it was. The doorbell. Somebody was ringing the doorbell. She dropped to the floor and scrambled around looking for the scattered pills. She gathered them up and threw them into the grate. She grabbed the box and empty blister packs and stuffed them under the cushion of the armchair.

The bell rang once more. Natalie stood up and walked unsteadily out to the hallway. Blood thumped in her ears and she was suddenly out of breath. She opened the door. Her eyes widened. On the step was one of her cousins, the rain bouncing off her head. Behind her, sitting in a car, Natalie could see her mother and her aunt.

The shock, or maybe the relief, of seeing their faces sent a rush of emotion through her body, like a hurricane, from the bottom of her stomach up into her heart. Sorrow, pain, fear, joy, love – they were all there, whirling around inside her.

'Oh, Maggie,' she wailed, 'I'm so glad to see you.'

She fell forward and Maggie caught her in her arms.

'You're all right,' Maggie said. 'You're all right now. We're here to take you home, Nat.'

33

A splash of icy rain from the grey sky landed on Ciara's nose. She was at the entrance to The Snug, about to go inside, when a few doors up she spotted George Grant on his morning rounds.

'Yes, George,' she called, 'what's the craic?'

He looked up, startled, almost nervous. When he saw her, his face relaxed.

'Aww, it's you,' he said, coming towards her, his large postbag hanging off his shoulder.

'Are you all right, George? I haven't seen you in the bar for a couple of days.'

He glanced up and down the street. 'I've been keeping the head down, like,' he said. 'Staying out of the way of people as much as my job lets me.'

His eyes were strangely alert, like he was a scared little animal on the lookout.

'Jesus, what's going on?'

Before he could answer, Mairin Kelly walked past. Ciara nodded and said hello.

'How's Ciara?' she asked, ignoring George.

George's gaze dropped to the ground.

Ciara waited until Mairin was out of earshot before speaking. 'What was that about?'

'That's why you haven't seen me in a while. I'm a suspect.'

'What?'

'It's this fucking poison pen thing,' he said. 'There's a rumour going round that I'm the one sending the letters.'

'Come on, that can't be—'

'Since I'm the one delivering them, like, I could be the one writing them.'

'Who the fuck started that?'

George shrugged.

'Well, nobody's mentioned a word to me,' Ciara said. 'If they do, I won't be a minute putting them straight.'

'That's good to know. I need people in my corner. It's melting my head. You want to see what they're putting up on Facebook. My Rosie's stopped telling me cos it was driving me to distraction.'

The pained expression on his face said it all. Ciara had never seen him so out of sorts.

'You can count on me and Joe to stand by you. If the rest of the village have lost the run of themselves over this bullshit, we definitely haven't.'

'Being a postman's the worst job you could have with something like this going on. I have to go round every house, even knock on the doors if it's for parcels. People I've known my whole life just blank me as if I'm not there. I've had a few choice words thrown at me, too. Only the odd person is treating me as usual.'

'I don't know what to say, George. It makes no sense why people would think you'd be writing these letters. Just cos you're the postman? For fuck's sake! Whatever happened to not shooting the messenger?'

'I suppose I'm as likely a candidate as the next man or woman, like.'

'But it's not you,' Ciara said, 'and we know that.'

'I wonder who it actually is,' George said.

'Have you any suspicions?'

'Well… not really…'

'That sounds like you do.'

'Maybe. I've no evidence, mind you, but I can't help thinking it might be one of our local gossips.'

'The same thought crossed my mind,' Ciara said. 'I don't think it's important, anymore, who sent the letters. Or even if they're a hoax.'

'Why do you say that?'

'I dunno,' she said. 'I was talking to Shay and it got me thinking. The letters have taken on a life of their own; they've set events in motion that can't be wound back, regardless of whether the person's caught or the letters stop.'

George shifted the postbag to his other shoulder. 'You could be right. At least the Gards are looking into it now,' he said.

'Is there any update on their investigation?'

'Only that they've started interviewing everybody on the list I gave them.'

Ciara sighed relief. She and Joe had their house in order. There wasn't a drop of *poitín* anywhere near The Snug. And they had a play-dumb story all rehearsed about why they got a letter, just in case. If the Gards arrived right there and then, they'd have nothing to hide.

'I heard there's going to be a community meeting,' George said. 'Edel McDaid at the village hall was on about organising one to see if there's something that can be done to support people.'

'Good, sounds like a sensible idea.'

'I intend to be at it. I intend to make it pretty fucking clear I've nothing to do with this shite.'

'I'll be there. I'll back you up,' Ciara said. 'Look, George, I have to go back inside. We've got a delivery coming. But why don't you call into the kitchen after work today? It'll be nice and private and I'll serve you a pint there.'

George managed a small, weak smile. 'Aww, Ciara, that would mean the world to me.'

She touched his shoulder and smiled back.

'You know, Ciara, for all the madness we're seeing from the folks who got letters, there are some that's keeping very quiet. Makes me wonder what they're hiding if they're saying nothing, like.'

'That never occurred to me.' She thought about herself and Joe.

George looked right into her eyes and shook his head slowly. 'This whole village is like a powder keg just waiting for a spark.'

34

The email from David Woods wasn't very long, but it was enough to give Shay a change of heart about Lorna.

David was one of Rory's closest friends, along with his cousins, Sean and Liam Lafferty. The four had been pals since they were little and had been pretty much inseparable growing up. They had stayed over at her house so much over the years that, at times, it was like she had four kids instead of one. They were good boys, good friends to Rory. Sean moved to Australia just before the lockdown kicked in. Talk about bad timing. He had to spend his first weeks in isolation. He sent her a card with the nicest heartfelt message not long after Rory's funeral. Liam was living in Belfast, and he'd been at the funeral along with the rest of his family. David went to San Francisco for a gap year in college and ended up staying there – his parents were none too pleased he dropped out of his course. He sent Shay a lovely card, just like Sean did. He even called her up a couple of weeks after the funeral and they chatted for a while on FaceTime, remembering the old times, remembering Rory.

Shay reread his email from her phone:

Dear Shay,

Rory was on my mind last night and I thought I'd email to say hello. I won't ask how you are.

I miss chatting to him, we used to FaceTime every couple of months after I moved out here, just to shoot the breeze, catch up. Though, I hadn't heard from him a good while before everything happened. I think the last time I talked to him might've been March, not long after he split up with Lorna. He was so cut up about that because he messed things up with her, drove her away. He mentioned something about his business not going so well too. I regret not picking up on that one. I took for granted he'd sort it out, the same way he sorted out whatever else life threw at him.

I'm planning to come back home next summer and I'll call round for a visit. We can talk about the old days and all the stuff us kids used to get up to.

Take care, Shay, love always,
David.

Shay smiled, touched that Rory was in his thoughts, that he'd bothered to email. And even though he hadn't said much at all, she drew comfort from his few words. She hadn't replied to him yet but, when she did, she'd not bother mentioning that by the time he came home next summer, she wouldn't be there. He'd find that out soon enough. She wondered what David, or any of Rory's friends, would make of her poison pen letters. They'd think she'd lost the plot, no doubt.

That nightmare was raging on. Apparently, the village had turned its suspicions on George Grant. It was so awful and it was her fault, but she didn't know how to make any of it right.

And then there was the shocking news about Eoin Devine. A hit-and-run? Who knew what ugly shit people were hiding? She wondered if her letter had been responsible at all for his arrest.

He might have thought that's what the letter was pointing to. She hoped so. Regardless, she didn't regret for a second sending him a letter and his arrest was a good thing. In some ways, the hit-and-run just reinforced her view of him – that he was a low-down, conniving piece of scum. The fact he'd handed himself in didn't redeem him in the slightest. He was facing prison time and he was going to be punished, even if not for Rory. That pleased her.

She turned back to David's email and her eye wandered to one particular line. It mentioned Lorna: *He was cut up about that because he messed things up with her, drove her away.* Shay pondered the words. Maybe she'd been wrong blaming Lorna for running out on Rory. Maybe Rory wasn't the injured party.

Shay remembered her call with Lorna; her saying she loved Rory, how she wanted a chance to explain. That made more sense now. And her request to meet Shay, and Shay agreeing to contact the girl to confirm. A barefaced lie. But after David's email… Yes, after David's email, perhaps Lorna deserved better than a lie.

35

The village hall was a practical, no-frills affair and big enough to seat a couple of hundred people. The walls were painted a dull yellow and dotted with noticeboards, and the floor was polished wood – Shay thought she could catch a faint whiff of floor wax – and decorated with stuck-on coloured lines and semi-circles that marked out areas for playing games. A table at the top of the hall, set with four glasses and a jug of water, stood empty and waiting.

A low mumble of voices droned in the background, broken now and again by the odd loud guffaw. The air was warm and stuffy, only made worse by her face mask. Shay was on the right-hand side, fourth row from the front, in a seat next to Ciara.

'The whole village must be here,' Ciara said, through her mask, 'and then some.'

Shay looked around. She knew almost everybody, if not personally, then at least who they were and who their family was. Most were wearing masks, some were not.

She noticed Francesca sitting a few rows back and thought it curious. Village gatherings weren't the kind of thing she usually came along to. She mixed in far more cultured social circles and Shay suspected she saw herself above the simple folk of the village. Yet here she was, sitting up straight and staring ahead; an expectant, even excited, look on her face.

'The place is packed,' Ciara said, 'and people are still coming in. Look at them, they're having to stand wherever they can get a space at the back and along the sides.'

'I can't believe there's so many,' Shay said.

'This poison pen's a massive deal,' Ciara said.

That was the last thing Shay wanted to hear, though the size of the turnout made it hard to deny. She felt her whole body sink into itself. This was her fault. Not quite all her fault, but she'd started it. The copycat only existed because of her, and whoever the fuck that was had gone on a letter-writing spree.

Edel McDaid, the centre manager, was racing up and down the aisle, her face the colour of a fire engine, making sure the older people had seats and trying to get the crowd to move near the front where there was more standing room.

Two Gards made their entrance, a male and a female. They strode confidently up the aisle towards the top table. George Grant was hot on their heels. The Gards and George sat down and Edel joined them.

'Looks like we're about to kick off,' Ciara said.

Edel called the room to order. It took a while, but eventually it fell into a hush.

'Thank you,' Edel said. 'Thank you for coming here tonight to talk about this very worrying issue. The big turnout shows just how much this poison pen has been affecting us.'

She turned to the Gards and George.

'I've got Garda Duggan, Garda O'Hagan and George Grant here at the top table. Thanks to you all for attending.'

The Gards nodded to the crowd and George gave a nervous wave.

'You probably already know,' Edel went on, 'that the Gards have launched an investigation into the poison pen affair and Garda

Duggan is heading it up. The poison pen was reported to them by *An Post* after George here had the good sense to alert his managers to what was going on. Well, I'm not going to talk all night—'

'That'd be a first,' came a shout from the back of the hall.

Even from behind her mask, Edel looked disgusted. 'There's a first for everything then. Without further ado, I'll hand over to Garda Duggan to say a few words.'

Whispers and mumbles rippled through the crowd and then the hall went quiet again as Garda Duggan got to her feet.

'Good evening, everybody,' Garda Duggan said. 'Clearly this poison pen is causing a lot of concern and understandably so. We see all sorts of situations in the Garda Síochána but, I have to say, this is a new one to even our more experienced people. You might not be aware of this, but there's a new law known as the Harassment, Harmful Communications and Related Offences Act and it criminalises the sending of threatening communications. These letters fall squarely under that law.'

Shay turned cold. 'Could the person sending the letters be arrested?' she whispered to Ciara.

'Maybe,' Ciara whispered back. 'I hope so.'

'So, we're taking this very seriously,' Garda Duggan went on. 'We've allocated resources to the investigation. We have a list of people who received poison pen letters and Garda O'Hagan and myself have already been in the area talking to some of you. We'll continue interviewing until we've spoken to everybody.'

Garda Duggan took off her yellow-and-navy waterproof jacket and hung it on the back of her chair, before tucking her blue shirt into her waistband.

'However,' she said, 'we can't be sure if our list is complete and contains all recipients so, if you got a letter, or know of somebody who did, please get in touch. I'd also appeal to anyone who might have information to come forward – no matter what that information is; no matter how trivial or irrelevant you think it is. Best to talk to us if you have a niggling doubt because you never know what might be useful.'

Garda Duggan shot a glance in Edel's direction and sat down. Edel took the floor again.

'Thank you for that, Garda Duggan.' Edel faced the crowd. 'I hope you've been reassured that the Gards are dealing with this and that you'll all do your best to cooperate with the investigation.' She turned to George and gave him a nod. 'And now George Grant's going to give us a rundown of how he discovered there was a poison pen active in the village. Go ahead, George.'

Edel sat down and a purple-faced George pushed his chair back and slowly got to his feet.

'Oh, God help him,' Ciara whispered. 'He looks terrified.'

The hall waited in a tense silence for George to start.

'Hello all,' George said, clearing his throat. 'You probably know me, ah-umm, or at least know me to see. I'm the postman for this area. Right, well, I'll get on with it, like.'

'Aye, get on with it,' a man in the crowd called out.

George cleared his throat again. 'I suppose I have Sarah Maguire to thank for putting me wise to the letters. Is Sarah here?' He stopped and checked.

'Mammy wasn't able to come out tonight,' someone said, 'but I'm here in her place.'

Shay turned around and saw Helen Maguire stand up and then sit down again.

'That's grand, Helen,' George said. 'Well, Sarah stopped me one morning to show me a letter she got and she was very upset about it. I told her not to be worrying, that it was just somebody acting the eejit.'

'We wanted to report it to the Gards,' Helen Maguire said, 'but Mammy wouldn't hear of it. She just wanted to tell you, George, and I trusted you'd take care of it. Did you report it at the time? To the Post Office, at least?'

George sighed. 'Not right away,' he said. 'In hindsight, I should've, but I thought I'd keep an eye on things for a while first – see if anybody else got one, like. I didn't want to jump the gun and go to head office too early with a half-baked story, only for them to tell me it was nothing.'

Garda Duggan piped up. 'You should've reported it right away, Mr Grant.'

'So you should've,' a woman from the floor called. 'What was in your head not to?'

George's face fell, like a chastised child. Guilt burned in Shay's cheeks.

'Leave him alone,' Ciara shouted out. 'He did his best.'

'Ciara's right,' Edel said, 'no point crying over it now. Gone ahead with your story, George.'

George gathered himself. 'Well, right or wrong, I said nothing. I watched out for similar-looking envelopes. Sure enough, I spotted more. I couldn't open them so I had to take an educated guess they were the same as Sarah's, and I kept a wee note of the people they were addressed to.'

The crowd listened as George went on telling his story his way. He took a deep breath and straightened himself.

'That went on for about a week 'til Mary-Margaret Walsh reported her letter to me.'

A few sniggers escaped from the left-hand side of the hall.

'Have a bit of respect,' Edel said.

The sniggers got louder, turning into a guffaw here and there, but soon quietened down. Shay squirmed. George started again.

'Mary-Margaret was in a wile state,' he said, 'and it took a right bit of cajoling to calm her down.'

There was an outbreak of stifled giggles.

'It was then,' George said, 'I knew it was high time I took action. I told my manager, she called head office and we had a meeting. After that, they went to the Gards.' George wiped the sweat off his forehead with the back of his hand. 'It worries me that this is going on in our community. We're all friends and neighbours here, like. We all know each other. We look out for each other. The idea that one of us could do a thing like this and cause that much harm, I can hardly take it in. And I heard rumours that some folks think it's me doing this. For the life of me, I can't believe anybody could think that. It's terrible altogether, terrible.'

'It's all right, George,' Edel said. 'Don't get yourself worked up.'

George sat down, a sense of relief on his face. A loud mumble and a few raised voices sounded out. By now, Shay wanted the floor to swallow her up. That person George was talking about – it was her, partly her at least. What on earth had been in her mind to send those letters to Peter and Eoin? This wasn't how it was supposed to play out.

Edel stood up and called for quiet. 'I'm going to open the floor to questions, but we need to do this in an orderly way. If you put your hand up, I'll note your name and I'll take you all in turn. Is that fair enough?'

No one answered, but a lot of hands shot up. Shay shifted in her seat, unable to get comfortable. She didn't know if she could just sit there and listen to what people had to say.

'Maybe we should go, Ciara. What do you think?' she whispered.

'We can't leave now,' Ciara said. 'It's only getting started. Let's stay a while to see how it goes.'

Staying to see how it went was as appealing as swimming in sewage. Shay leaned back in her seat, wondering how she was going to get away. She knew Ciara wouldn't let her leave alone and yet wild horses weren't going to drag Ciara from the place.

'Eamonn O'Sullivan,' Edel said, 'I'll take your question first.'

'I didn't get a letter, but my wife did. How do we know this isn't some kind of threat and that we're not in danger?'

'Garda Duggan?' Edel turned to the Gard.

'While we can't rule that out as a possibility,' Garda Duggan said, 'we've had no evidence to suggest we should expect danger. Apart from the initial letters, we haven't seen any follow-up, any next step. And the fact that there were so many letters makes it less and less likely that the sender actually "knows" anything. The recipients seem to be random and the threat in the letter is generic, like a scatter gun. We're being cautious, of course, but, at this stage, as I said, we don't believe anybody to be in danger.'

'Even though the letters mention paying the consequences,' Conor Mullan, who wasn't in the question queue, piped up. 'Isn't that a threat? Or what if one of the letters isn't a bullet from a scatter gun and it's pointing to a specific thing, you know, like some of the letters are just decoys but there's an actual target?'

Edel looked put out about the disruption to her orderly approach. Garda Duggan answered the question anyway.

'We think it's highly unlikely that the letters are referring to anything specific. And, yes, the letters mention consequences and that could be construed as a threat, but, as I say, there have been no follow-up letters.'

'So will we have to wait 'til somebody gets hurt before you take it seriously?' Aoibh Friel shouted.

'Will you all stick to the rules and put up your hand if you want to ask a question?' Edel asked.

'I want to answer this one, Edel, if you don't mind,' Garda Duggan said. 'We're treating this case with the utmost seriousness. We've assigned resources to it and are actively pursuing a course of action, but we want to avoid creating undue panic. We're proceeding with caution.'

'No more shouting out questions, folks,' Edel said. 'Put up your hand.' She pointed in Shay's direction. 'Daisy, you have a question?'

Shay turned behind her to where all of the McBirney-Smiths were seated – none of them wearing masks. Daisy was on her feet,

Rodney and Andie were sitting on either side, and Louisa Allan was next to Rodney. Shay was about to turn away when her eye caught Andie's. The girl smiled at her and Shay smiled back, uneasily. Andie's smile was so wide and jolly, it made her look… well, it made her look a bit maniacal.

'I think the letters are one massive practical joke, so I do,' Daisy said, folding her arms like she was just gabbing behind the counter in the shop. 'A bit on the sick side, but still a joke. I agree with Garda Duggan: the sender hasn't a clue; they're just bluffing. I don't understand why people are getting worked up.'

'Did you get a letter?' an angry voice shouted from somewhere in the middle of the crowd.

'No, but—'

'Well, then shut your mouth and stay out of it.'

Daisy sat down in a huff.

'And that wasn't even a question, anyway,' a wisecracker called from the group standing at the back.

'I don't think it is a joke,' Orla Ryan called out, 'not a bit of it.' She sat a couple of rows in front of Shay. 'Let's remember what happened to Mary-Margaret Walsh. I know there's people here tonight who seem to think it's amusing, but you should be ashamed of yourselves.'

Shay's stomach fluttered. The copycat was to blame for Mary-Margaret, but Shay was to blame for the copycat. So, however she looked at it, everything came back to her. Everything was her fault.

'Thank you for that, Orla,' Edel said. 'And we should note that you, yourself, were attacked, and that could've been very serious if your husband hadn't intervened. Next question… ah, you, Francesca.'

Shay looked back again, surprised that Francesca was getting involved. She had the same expectant look on her face as before, only now it seemed even more exaggerated. She was enjoying it, maybe not as much as Andie McBirney-Smith, but she was enjoying it.

'Are you any closer to discovering who's writing these letters?' Francesca asked.

'We're in the process of carrying out interviews,' Garda Duggan said. 'The case is proceeding.'

'That's the kind of answer you'd get from a politician,' Paul Brennan said, jumping in. 'Just tell us straight: are you any closer to catching the poison pen?'

'We can't make our findings public at this time.'

'Does that mean you haven't got a notion and you're telling us a load of shite?' Paul asked.

'It means we can't make our findings public at this time.'

Disgruntled mumbles permeated the hall.

Shay wondered about the progress Garda Duggan had mentioned; whether they had a suspect in their sights or whether her name been caught in their crosshairs. They hadn't interviewed her yet and she took that as a good sign. She was uneasy all the same.

'Do you think they know anything?' Shay whispered to Ciara.

'Naw, definitely not,' Ciara said. 'That's all waffle she's coming out with.'

'Do you really think so?'

Ciara was distracted with what was going on and didn't reply. Shay breathed slowly in and out, again and again, trying to create an inner sense of calm. She wished she hadn't come, yet she knew it was important she had. She needed to see what the letters were doing to her village. She had to witness that first-hand.

Edel called on Aidan O'Brien.

'I'm in Daisy's camp,' he said. 'Aren't we making a big fuss out of nothing here? At the start, when we were getting letters and we didn't know anybody else was getting them, I can understand we might've thought they were making a real threat. But now we know a load of us got these exact same letters and there's been no consequences other than what we did to ourselves. We should take no heed of them.'

Shane Hamilton stood up. 'You're missing the point, Aidan. It's the harm this fucker's done by sending the letters in the first place. Joke or no joke, real threat or not, people are afraid and upset. We have to find whoever's done this and dish out some justice.'

Mutters of agreement could be heard.

'I can't believe how we're all turning on each other like rats in a sack,' Helen Maguire said. 'Not that long ago, we were in a pandemic and we pulled together as a village and took care of each other. It was amazing. To have come through that crisis only to let these horrible letters beat us seems, I dunno, wrong or something. Why can't we pull together for this as well? Maybe these letters could be used for good, to bring us closer again.'

'Fair enough but even if we did,' a man in the front row said, 'one streak of silver lining wouldn't make this cloud of shit okay.' He stood up and turned to face the crowd. 'This needs to be sorted and sorted now! We won't stand for it anymore.'

The crowd clapped and cheered in agreement.

Edel put up her hands to settle them. 'Please, folks, calm down. Order, please.'

She was completely ignored. Shay felt lightheaded. The hall around her blurred in and out of focus.

'This is a nightmare,' she said to Ciara. 'It's a horrible nightmare, isn't it?'

Ciara wasn't listening. She was looking around like an unsettled hen, her head going every which way. The crowd was getting louder and more belligerent.

'I lost Rory,' Shay said, quietly enough not to be heard above the din, 'and I only wanted someone to suffer. I didn't want this. Why did all this have to happen?'

Ciara was engrossed in the unfolding scene. Shay leaned forwards, her face buried in her hands. The hall was now in uproar on all sides. She thought she was about to collapse.

'There's a vendetta against the village,' a man from somewhere in the madness bellowed.

'No, it's from inside the village,' a woman shouted. 'Somebody inside the village is doing this. Somebody who didn't get a letter.'

'It's whoever didn't get a letter,' a second woman screeched.

'It's George Grant,' a man near Shay called out at the top of his lungs. 'If anybody's a suspect, it's him.'

'You're right,' a woman at the back shouted. 'It's him.'

'Will everybody calm down, for the love of God?' Edel screamed.

Garda Duggan stood up. Garda O'Hagan stood up with her, his first move since the start of the meeting.

'Edel is right,' Garda Duggan called in a commanding voice. 'You need to calm down. Right now.'

Slowly, silence spread from person to person, uneasy and more fragile than a piece of bone china.

'That's better,' Garda Duggan said, 'thank—'

'I meant what I said about George Grant,' the man called out again, not so loud this time.

Ella McMonagle spoke out. 'Do the Gards know he's down in The Snug every day after work, spilling his guts to Ciara McCann? How do you think that might affect the investigation? He should be sacked.'

'We've already interviewed Mr Grant and have no reason to suspect him,' Garda Duggan said.

She was still standing, as was Garda O'Hagan. Voices began to rise again, murmurings were swelling.

'But he's sitting up at the top table tonight and not down here with the rest of us because he knows stuff we don't.'

'He's taking a hand out of the whole townland.'

'So he is!'

The uneasy quiet eventually broke and the crowd worked itself into a frenzy for a second time. Ciara shot to her feet.

'This is fucking mad,' Ciara shouted. 'George has nothing to do with sending the letters.'

To Shay, the noise was distant and muffled like she was hearing it from the inside of a barrel. She saw Edel McDaid, now standing on top of the top table, squealing for order and calm and almost in tears. The Gards were yelling right along with her. This time, no one was paying any heed.

'It's him. He's the poison pen.'

'It's him!' a chorus of voices echoed.

People began to move out of their seats and towards the top table. George got to his feet. The Gards stood in front of him.

'Get back!' Garda O'Hagan screamed. 'Get back. We'll arrest anybody that touches this man.'

'Holy fuck,' Ciara said in a wail, horror in her eyes. She crouched down beside Shay, clutching her shoulder. 'Are you seeing this? They're descending on George.'

Shay swayed to the side. 'I want to go home.'

'What? Shay, what's wrong?'

'I'm not feeling well. Get me out of here.'

An unnerving howl went up, louder than the cries of the crowd, drowning out Shay's words.

'That's… oh, Jesus, that's George,' Ciara shrieked, standing up again. 'Oh my God, they're like savages. They're going to attack him. I have to do something.'

Shay fell on her knees. She couldn't depend on her legs to hold her up. She began to crawl between the feet and legs of the chaotic crowd.

The last thing she heard was Ciara's voice screaming, 'Leave him alone, you stupid bastards!' After that, everything went silent and she could hear nothing. She could only see what lay ahead, the wooden floor and the way out, as she crawled on all fours. Shoes and boots stamped on her hands and legs, but she didn't care – maybe didn't rightly notice. She kept on crawling until she got out of the hall and as far as the exterior door.

Shay caught her breath and leaned against the cool brick of the wall, closing her eyes. The light-headedness began to subside a little and her senses slowly came back. The riot in the hall and the primitive attack on poor George had left her stunned. If she hadn't been there to see it with her own eyes, she'd scarcely have believed it. The devastation the poison pen was causing was like some black death creeping through the village.

And going from bad to worse, there she was on the floor, dealing with her own black death – one that ate at her brain a little bit more every day.

This insane, unpredictable madness couldn't be allowed to continue. She groaned and lobbed her head from side to side. She wished she could make it all go away.

36

'Mr Feeney?' Harry Parkes greeted him. 'How are ye?'
Peter Feeney thought Harry looked genuinely surprised by who was on his stoop, surprised in the way somebody would be if they'd been expecting to win a million Euros only to find out they'd won a toaster instead.

'I'm well,' Peter said curtly. Under his arm was tucked a thick, black walking cane with an ornate silver handle.

Peter hadn't been so up-close to Harry in years. The old goat hadn't changed a bit. Way back, he looked seventy and now he still looked seventy, with his face as wrinkled as a dried-out apple.

The two men eyeballed each other for longer than necessary; Peter on the stoop, Harry with his hand on the door. A bitter wind whistled round the house and driving sleet pounded Peter's face.

'Are you going to leave me on your step like some stray hound with this weather battering me or are you going to ask me in?'

'Oh, right you are,' Harry said, standing aside to let Peter through. 'Come on in, then.'

The front door opened into the kitchen and Peter stepped inside, glad of the calm and the warmth of the house.

'Fierce weather,' Harry said, closing the door.

'They said we were in for some storms. I suppose this is the start of it.'

'S'pose so,' Harry said. 'Grab a chair by the fire, Mr Feeney. I'll make us a cup of tea.'

The dimly lit kitchen was small with a low ceiling and smelled faintly of disinfectant and boiled cabbage. A table and chairs were tucked away in a corner. A few cupboards ran along the nearest wall and beside them a sink and a washing machine. At the far wall stood a dresser and next to it was an old range cooker that gave off more heat than a small sun. A dented aluminium kettle hissed on the top of it and at either side a couple of armchairs beckoned occupants. The kitchen was drab and miserable, Peter thought, and not a place he wanted to stay in longer than he had to.

He chose the left-hand side of the range and hooked his walking cane on the back of the chair. Shedding his heavy overcoat and draping it over the back of the chair, too, he removed his leather gloves, finger by finger. He pushed them into the pocket of his coat and sat down. The chair was comfortable, though it had seen better days, like most everything else in the hovel.

Harry filled a fat teapot with boiling water from the kettle and threw in a couple of tea bags.

'I'll let that draw a while.' Harry motioned at the pot.

Peter focused his gaze on a square of golden light flickering on the mat in front of the fire, a reflection of the glowing coals from the open door of the range. He gathered his thoughts in preparation for what he was about to say.

He hadn't rushed into making this visit, unlike the efficiency with which he usually acted. His driver Vincent happened to mention something or other about people in the village getting strange letters and, for a while, that had him wondering if his letter was connected. In the end, he decided against that notion. His gut told him Harry was behind his letter and his gut was never wrong. There was also Harry's confab with Ursula about Aggie's anniversary, which had only added to his certainty.

No, whatever claptrap was going in the village, well, that had nothing to do with him. Weren't they all meeting in the village hall that very night to jabber about the things that little people like them jabbered about? The village and its dramas never intersected with his life and had no impact on his decisions. For him, confronting Harry was essential – something he should've done a long time ago.

Harry grabbed the teapot and carried it to the table to fix their beverages.

'Do you want any milk or sugar?' he asked.

'Neither,' Peter said.

'I like both,' Harry said.

He handed Peter a mug and pulled a rickety wooden stool over from the table. He set it in the middle between them and then made himself comfortable in the other armchair.

'I wouldn't usually be this ill-mannered, Mr Feeney, but I'm going to ask you straight out what you've come here about. A man like you doesn't visit the likes of me to chat about the weather.'

'I appreciate your candour,' Peter said. 'Since we're getting down to straight talking, I'll get to the point. Why did you send me that heinous letter?'

Harry frowned.

'Listen to me.' Peter's voice went slow and deep. 'I'm not here to fuck around. Why did you send that letter?'

'I sent you nothing – a letter nor anything else. If you didn't notice, Mr Feeney, we haven't had anything to do with each other in many a year.'

'And I wonder why that is? You used to work for me and then… you didn't.'

Harry shifted in his chair and his eyes dropped to the floor.

'You left very suddenly, if I remember.'

'Ah, I… it was… my Annie wasn't keeping well, you know. I was needed at home. I told you that at the time.'

'That's what you told me, right enough.' Peter straightened himself so he was sitting tall and ever so slightly looking down on Harry. 'It never made a lot of sense, though. Didn't you start working on Ciaran Hanlon's farm not long after?'

Harry started wringing his hands.

'Well? Didn't you?'

Harry mumbled something.

'I didn't catch that.'

'Annie came back to herself,' Harry said, just a bit louder.

'You don't sound very sure.'

'That's what happened. It's the truth.'

Peter narrowed his eyes and trained them on Harry, laser-like. 'I believe you, though thousands wouldn't.'

Harry lifted his tea to his mouth and Peter saw his hand was shaking.

'Careful you don't spill that,' Peter said. 'Why didn't you ask for your old job back instead of going to Hanlon? You would've known I struggled for a long time to get a reliable replacement.'

Harry choked on his tea, coughing.

'I didn't think you'd want me back after I left like that,' Harry said.

Peter pursed his lips. 'You could've asked.'

'I could've but, shure, it's all in the past now.'

Peter tutted. 'Is it?'

Harry shot him a look.

'I've often wondered why you really left,' Peter said, slowly.

Harry stuttered in an effort to say something, but Peter talked over him.

'It wasn't about your wife, not *your* wife. Maybe it was to do with *my* wife. What do you think?'

Peter's gaze bored into Harry. It was hard to tell in the dim light and the flicker from the range, but had the colour drained from his face? Outside, the wind wailed and unrelenting sleet battered the windows.

'It was all about my wife, wasn't it?' Peter said. 'And what happened to her… that night.'

Harry's eyes narrowed. 'Are you talking about the night Mrs F fell? Is that what this is about?'

'Continuing to play dumb, Harry? You know you're trying my patience.'

'That was a terrible thing that happened, sir. Poor Mrs F – she was a good woman, the best.'

'That night isn't one I like to remember much, but these past weeks… seems I can't think of anything else. I'd been out at a business dinner, a very fruitful one, and I'd come home late. I was tired but happy with my evening's work. You'll probably never know what that feels like, to win a big customer, to succeed at that level. When I got home, all I wanted was to sit in the comfort of my home, feet up, with a large brandy. Not too much to ask.'

Harry straightened himself. He had an interested but slightly confused expression on his face, Peter noted.

'Not too much to ask,' Peter said, 'but still too much for me to ask. I was making my way upstairs to change out of my suit and got as far as the mezzanine when I heard her. That voice of hers, slurring and whiny. She was drunk. As always. My heart sank, my happiness disappeared.' Peter took in a long breath through his nose. 'Did your wife drink like a navvy, Harry? Did you have to put up with the shame of her making a fool of herself every time she left the house?'

Harry turned his eyes towards the range. Peter sneered. He knew Harry wouldn't want to say a bad word about Aggie but, at the same time, it was hard to argue with the truth.

'She was at the foot of the stairs,' Peter said, 'glass in hand. Straight vodka, I knew. She didn't waste good alcohol on mixers.

Funny, I can even remember what she was wearing: a full-length nightdress – satin and burgundy, I'm nearly sure – and a pair of stiletto slippers with a fluffy, feathery affair of some sort going across the foot. I remember those well because I couldn't help thinking they were such impractical footwear for someone who was drunk.'

Peter could see her in his mind's eye, as clear as yesterday, putting the glass down on an adjacent console table, just feet away from her portrait that hung near the bottom of the stairs. He'd had it commissioned the year Dan was born. He saw it, presiding over her in an almost jeering reminder of her former beauty and how far she'd fallen. People used to say she looked like Sophia Loren, though, personally, he could never see it.

'You showed up at my door that night,' Peter said.

'For my wages,' Harry said, in a low voice. 'It was Friday and you hadn't left them for me like you usually did.' He cleared his throat. 'Mrs F was embarrassed and she told me to call round later. She insisted.'

Peter smiled, dryly. It was the wages that had started the whole damned row. The events of the night flashed in front of Peter's eyes in an instant as he privately remembered…

*

'Damn it, Aggie, I don't need the hassle tonight.'

'It's not much hassle,' she said. 'You only have to open the safe and put his money in an envelope.'

Her continuous slurring voice was maddening. Peter stiffened.

'You talk as though money appears in that safe like it's a magic pot,' he said. 'Somebody has to earn it first and put it in there, you know.'

'Oh! The safe isn't magic?' She smirked.

The muscles in his neck tensed. Aggie took an upwards step towards where he stood on the mezzanine.

'You disgust me,' he said.

'I know, I'm so disgusting.'

'And you're stupid, incredibly stupid,' he said.

'Stupid, too,' she said, moving farther up the staircase. 'Shure, whatever y'say, Peter.'

Her voice didn't raise a decibel. If anything, she sounded bored. And that slurring.

'Take me seriously when I talk to you.'

She looked towards him. 'So that's what y'call what this. I thought you were insulting me.'

He gritted his teeth. 'Be careful of that loose mouth and remember who I am.'

She was halfway up the stairs by now. 'How could I forget?'

'You have no respect,' Peter said, 'for yourself or me.'

'I suppose next thing you're gonna say is I don't care.'

'Well, you don't. Look at yourself. You don't care about me or the children.'

'Don't you mention my children!'

Something awoke in her previously dull eyes and their hazel-brown flashed orange sparks of anger. Now it was his turn to smirk. Mentioning the children never failed to change her cavalier attitude, never failed to get her riled. For all her faults, no one could say she lacked as a mother. She'd given Dan and Ursula everything and even managed to control her drinking when they were growing up, never letting them see her liquored – but he wasn't the kind of man to let the truth get in his way.

'I wonder what they think of having a lush for a mother.'

She was one step from the top of the stairs. He towered over her, blocking her way and preventing her from going further.

'Fuck you,' she said, pushing her hair back, spit flying from her mouth. 'They're old enough now to know why I drink.'

'What do you mean by that? I hope you're not poisoning them against me.'

'I don't need to. You've done that all by yourself.'

Her voice was finally raised, shrill and frightened. He was close enough to smell the drink on her breath, stale and bitter.

'If I find out you've been saying things—'

'Ursula told me she never wants to get married,' Aggie said, 'cos husbands are just bullies. And Dan, you broke his heart making him spilt up with that Dunne girl.'

'Shut your mouth. I saved Dan from a lifetime of misery. That girl was a gold-digger and that baby isn't his.'

'But he is,' Aggie wailed. 'Of course he's Dan's and now I've a grandchild out there that I'll never be able to hold or love or…' Tears streamed down her face, blotching her mascara. 'You bastard.'

She swayed sideways, her eyes closed, and lobbed against the wall. Peter glared at her, his jaw clenched, his neck and face growing hot. Did she really think he was going to allow her to blame him for her problems and, in the process, turn his children against him?

'You owe everything to me,' he shouted, leaning his head towards her. 'Everything! The roof over your head, the food you eat, that fancy car out there, those flimsy, flouncy slippers you're wearing – everything. It's all because of me.'

Her eyes flew open, wide and mad. 'And I want none of it,' she screamed, standing away from the wall. 'I want nothing from you. I want to get as far away from you as I can.'

'Well, go. Now. And I won't give you a fucking penny to live on. Then you'll see how hard life is.'

'It couldn't be as hard as living with you.'

She reached up her hand and swung it, about to slap him across the face. He stopped her before she landed on her target and squeezed her thin, frail wrist so tight he thought it might snap. She squealed in pain.

'Lemme go,' she cried. 'You're hurting me.'

He twisted her arm, without relaxing his grip.

'Jesus, let go!' She struggled to break free, almost losing her balance as she went over on one of her slippers.

And in that moment, he knew what would happen if he did what she asked – if he let go. He knew.

He opened his hand. He did it so gently, so slowly. And he let gravity do the rest.

'As you wish, darling,' he said.

Her mouth opened to speak but couldn't form words, as she watched his hand retract. She teetered on the stair and reached out to grab his lapel. Her hands flapped like a circus seal's flippers but missed.

For the fleeting seconds before she plunged to the bottom of the stairs, their eyes locked. Drunk though she was, she knew what he'd done and what was going to happen. Her eyes begged him to save her. He stood stark still, staring straight back into those hazel-brown orbs.

And then she somersaulted backwards, in a downward dance to the bottom of the staircase, with thuds and thumps and grunts and yelps, until she landed with a crack on the marble floor below. Peter's heart stopped, half-expecting her to stand up and start accusing him. But she didn't. Her body lay horribly twisted, but still and at peace.

His heart restarted and, without giving himself time to think about what he'd just done – though what had he done? – he raced down the stairs, two at a time, towards where she lay.

Just before he got to the last step, the doorbell rang with a grand, echoing ding-dong. He halted, his heart now hammering against his chest, in near disbelief that someone could be calling right at that moment. He contemplated not answering, but doing that would look suspicious later on. He had no choice.

He swung the door open and, before bothering to check who it was, shouted out, 'It's Aggie. Oh Jesus, help me. She's fallen down the stairs.'

'Is she hurt?' the man asked.

Only then did Peter realise who was at the door. Harry Parkes. He pulled Harry into the grand hall, launching fully into the role of a panic-stricken man – which wasn't completely untrue. He ran to Aggie's body and fell to his knees beside her. He saw her up-close for the first time. She was like herself, but not herself – her face frozen in a surprised expression, her eyes blank. She was dead. She was really dead.

His gaze turned to Harry. 'She fell,' he said.

Some tears dropped onto his cheeks. Harry stood motionless near the door, his eyes fixed on Aggie.

'She'd been drinking,' Peter said. 'You know she drinks.'

His words came out, unintentionally, as a plea – a plea to Harry, who would surely understand.

Harry slowly looked towards him and that was when he saw it. In Harry's eyes, in the maelstrom of shock and grief and confusion and panic, there was also incredulity...

*

'Why was it you didn't believe me?' Peter asked.

'What do you mean?' Harry said.

The kettle wheezed on the range while the storm raged louder beyond the walls of the house.

'When you came in and saw Aggie, you didn't believe she just fell, did you?'

'I don't know what you're talking about, Mr Feeney.'

'Stop lying. I know you're lying; just tell me the truth.'

Harry fidgeted, shifting from side to side. He was still holding his mug and a little of the tea spilled onto his hand. He set the mug on the stool.

'This is ancient history,' Harry said. 'All in the past. That's where we should leave it.'

'You have some nerve saying that after what you've done.'

A nervous tingle rose up through Peter's torso and his jowls tightened – telltale signs his temper was beginning to break.

'Tell me right now,' Peter raised his voice, finding it difficult to stay seated. 'Why didn't you believe me?' He slammed his fist on the side of his chair. 'Tell me right fucking now.'

Harry's eyes widened. Was it the surprise of Peter swearing or of him slamming his fist? Peter didn't know which but Harry finally gave in.

'It was the way you were looking down at her.' He spoke in a whisper.

'What?'

'When you went over and kneeled beside her, you were like a man inspecting a hedgehog his car ran over. That's when I knew. That's when I knew you did it.'

Peter went to speak, but his jaw just flapped up and down a few times. He couldn't quite find the words. A chill rippled through his body, like an icy finger had run up his spine. For Peter, this was the proof that Harry had sent the letter.

'Why now?' he said, finally gathering himself. 'Why, after all these years later, do you dare to raise this abomination, to out me – and wrongly, too – to threaten me, to… to…?'

'I don't know what you're talking about,' Harry said.

'Answer me! Why did you send it?'

'You're not still on about that letter? If you got a letter, it wasn't from me. There's somebody sending letters, you know, to people in the village…'

Peter could hear a tremble in Harry's voice. The man was terrified and yet he remained defiant, unwilling to admit what he'd done.

'It *was* you and I'm going nowhere 'til you tell me it was you.'

'Mr Feeney, please, I want you to leave.'

Peter sneered. 'Is it money? Do you want money? Is that why you raked up this muck after all this time? You want money to keep your mouth shut?'

Harry was close to tears. 'I never said a word to anybody about that night – not then, not since, not a single word. And shure, what good would it do? Who'd believe me? How could I prove anything, and who'd care now anyway?'

Peter jumped to his feet quicker than his age should've allowed, quicker than his bad leg should've allowed. The armchair scraped back along the oil cloth. 'I've had enough of this. All I'm asking is that you come clean. Why won't you just do that?'

'I won't own up to something I didn't do,' Harry said.

Peter thought his head was going to blow. This pathetic man simply wouldn't confess to the letter.

'It's time you left my house, sir,' Harry managed to say.

'You'll not dismiss me like some servant girl! How dare you?'

'I want you out,' Harry said.

Peter could see that Harry's entire body was trembling, and yet he wouldn't relent, he still had enough left in him to demand that Peter leave.

'I don't want you with your black heart in my house again,' Harry said.

Peter reached for his walking cane and gripped it tight.

'I'll go when I get what I came here for,' he said.

Harry got to his feet, using the arms of his chair for support. 'I'll see you to the door.'

Peter heard a loud snap in his head. He could take no more from this insolent cur. He stepped forward and brandished his cane. Harry backed away towards the corner.

'Jesus Christ, man,' he shouted, 'put that fucking stick down.'

'Tell me you sent that letter, Parkes, and I'll leave,' Peter growled, like a savage wolf.

'I never sent the letter.'

'You're making me do this,' Peter growled again, raising the cane above Harry's head.

Harry cowered. 'You've gone mad.'

Peter felt his senses go dim; everything got quieter and duller and further away as he brought the cane down in a blow that struck Harry across the skull. Harry staggered, dazed. His legs wobbled like they were marshmallow. He reached out to keep his balance. His hand found the top of the range and he howled in pain as the hot surface connected with his skin.

Peter struck again – on the other side of his head this time. A thread of blood appeared, tracing the track of where the cane had hit Harry's cheek and temple. He dropped to his knees and tried to say something, but Peter couldn't make out what. His eyes stared in stunned betrayal, reminding Peter of Aggie's in those seconds before she fell.

Peter looked down and saw Harry, writhing and moaning. Peter hit him again, raining blows on his torso and legs. Harry crashed onto the floor. A pool of blood began to form beside his head, spreading out over the floral pattern of the oil cloth.

And then Peter's senses returned. Suddenly, his anger was gone. He was left with the horror of what he'd done. Blood throbbed in his ears. He dropped the cane and it fell to the floor with a clang.

Harry lay deathly still. Peter hunkered beside him. He felt for a pulse but could find nothing. He retreated, using the nearest armchair to hold himself steady.

This wasn't supposed to happen. If only Harry had admitted his guilt, things could've been so different. But no, the stubborn old bastard had stuck to his lies.

Peter looked round the kitchen, eerily silent now. For the first time, he noticed an ancient TV fitted snugly into one of the corners and beside it a small table with a phone on top. Odd, Peter thought, how the house had none of the modern trappings of technology; no mobile phone, no flat screen TV, no computer nor laptop.

Peter recalled that the letter had been typed on a word processor and then printed, along with the address on the envelope. His stomach churned one way and then another. All of that from a man who didn't seem to have as much as a remote control for his old TV.

'What have I done?' he said.

Doubt edged into his thoughts. It had to be Harry, he argued with himself. No one else could've sent that letter. No, it had to be him.

Peter let his breath out slowly. He couldn't permit himself think about any of that right now. He had to keep his head and jump into action.

A plan sprang to mind. He'd make the scene look like a robbery gone wrong. He thought for a moment, without moving. His gloves. He'd need his gloves. He retrieved them from his coat.

Grabbing his mug, he rinsed it at the sink and put it in the cupboard with the rest of the crockery. Once done, he set to ransacking the place, one room after another, starting with the kitchen. He pulled out drawers and opened cupboards, scattering their contents. He used his cane to sweep clear the top of the dresser near the range. Next, he made his way to the sitting room, causing the same upheaval there. He smashed the cane into the glass doors of a small display cabinet and from the debris he plucked out a silver salt and pepper set and popped them into his pocket.

Adrenalin pumped through the veins in his body, filling him with energy not normally his. He should've been feeling exhausted, but instead he felt like a gladiator – ready for anything. He scaled the stairs with the speed of an athlete and found himself on a small landing.

Outside, the sleet had stopped but the wind was higher than ever. At this part of the house, it made an unnatural scream, almost human – the way he imagined a banshee might sound. A sound all the more disquieting now he was in the house alone with a dead body. He had to make haste and finish the job.

Upstairs were three bedrooms and a small bathroom. Peter set to work, disturbing anything that looked like it might be hiding money or other valuables. He came across Harry's wallet on a bedside locker in the biggest bedroom and relieved it of the few Euros inside. A cardboard box on the top shelf of a wardrobe was most promising and it didn't disappoint. Peter found a roll of bank notes, personal papers and a few bits of jewellery – probably belonging to Harry's wife. He secreted the notes and jewellery in his pocket along with the rest of the swag.

His work was done – the house looked convincingly robbed. Not before time. He'd spent much too long there already. He took himself downstairs as fast as he could and made his way to the front door. Before he stepped out into the stormy night, he gave the kitchen a final look.

It resembled the aftermath of a riot. Harry lay motionless on the floor. Nothing moved. Peter shivered. He closed the door quickly behind him.

The adrenalin propelling around his body began to slow and he was relieved. He wasn't sure if he could withstand much more. The trick now was to get away without being seen. Peter didn't think he'd have any problem doing so since Harry's cottage was in a remote area and at least a mile from the nearest house.

He jumped into the Bentley, revved it up and started down the short laneway that led to the road. The wind rocked the car and a fresh burst of sleet returned, hitting the windscreen so hard the wipers could barely keep the glass clear.

Peter turned left onto the road and had just begun to pick up speed when he saw lights a couple hundred yards back in the rear-view mirror. The car behind him slowed and indicated left. They were turning into Harry's lane.

'Fuck,' Peter howled.

He swerved, almost going into the ditch. He couldn't be certain if they'd rounded the corner in time to realise that he'd just come out of Harry's and, if they had, whether they'd made the model or make of his car.

'Fuck,' he said again, slapping the dashboard with his fist.

He'd been so close to getting clean away without sight or sound of anything.

'No, they didn't see me pull out of the lane,' he said, confidently, looking at his reflection in the rear-view mirror. 'Anyway, it was too dark to make my car.'

But Peter's confidence was hollow. His luck might have run out. If it had, only time would tell.

37

The sun shone high in a clear sky, belying the coldness of the day. Shay was perched on a bench along the Foyle embankment, waiting for Lorna. She'd driven to Derry – risky for her these days – and was relieved the journey had been symptom-free.

The freezing metal of the bench seeped into her bones as she stared out at the water, dark and pockmarked with eddies from the current. That river rolled on for miles, ever expanding to become a lough before finally getting swallowed up by the Atlantic. She thought about Rory. The same lough had swallowed him up. Tears brimmed along her eyelids, turning icy.

The tears didn't go away as she remembered the village hall meeting the night before. It still rang in her ears, the uproar and the din – and, as she had crawled away from the attack on George, the look on his face when he had realised the crowd was closing in on him. Ciara hadn't been one bit happy to find out that Shay had taken off without a word. She arrived at the house not long after Shay had gotten home. She read the riot act. She was also able to tell Shay that the men and women of the village had finally come to their senses and George hadn't been injured. That, at least, was something.

Shay shifted on the bench, wiping her eyes and trying with no success to get comfortable. Her legs were stiff. She scanned the quay, left and right. A man walking a little Yorkie strolled past, the dog curious and sniffing everything in its path, including Shay's boots.

'How's it going?' the dog owner said to Shay on his way past.

'How's it going?' Shay said, with a faint smile.

As the pair walked away, Shay's mind drifted to thoughts of Lorna. She wasn't quite having second thoughts about meeting her, but maybe it hadn't been the wisest of decisions after all. Too late to turn back now, although it was possible Lorna herself had done exactly that. It would explain why she was late.

Shay looked up the quay again. This time, at last, she could see Lorna. She was about to wave when she stopped. She did a double take. Lorna wasn't alone. The girl was pushing a baby's buggy.

When Lorna arrived at the bench, Shay stood up, slowly and carefully – mindful of her leg.

'Nice to see you, Lorna,' Shay said.

'And you,' Lorna said, her cheeks blushed with the cold. 'I hope you don't mind, but I brought this wee man to meet you.'

'I, um, I… is he your little boy?'

'Yes,' Lorna said.

She lifted a purple and green woolly hat from his head to reveal a smiling, bright-eyed baby with tufts of chestnut-brown hair and ruddy cheeks, nestled like a chick in the puffy folds of the buggy's chair.

'I didn't know you had a baby,' Shay said, looking at him and thinking how cute he was.

Lorna brimmed. 'Say hello, wee angel,' she said.

The baby giggled, revealing gums devoid of teeth.

'Say hello to your nana.'

The world swooned. Shay thought she was going to fall. Suddenly, Lorna's arm was around her.

'Are you all right?' Lorna said. 'I'm sorry. I probably gave you a shock. Do you want to sit down?'

Shay steadied herself. 'No, I'm grand,' she croaked.

She stared down at the baby, who was cooing and kicking.

'Are you saying he's Rory's son?'

Lorna nodded. 'He's called Rory, too.'

Shay bit her bottom lip to stop it from shaking. Stinging tears filled her eyes. A bitter-sweet mix of sorrow and joy.

'He's… he's beautiful,' she said, her voice thick. 'Oh, not just because he's Rory's, but because he is anyway, if you know what I mean, or maybe I'm not making sense—'

'It's okay,' Lorna said. 'I know what you mean.'

Shay could only keep staring. The pain of seeing little Rory, but knowing her Rory was gone brought her heart to bursting point. She breathed deeply to catch her breath.

'Are you sure you're all right, Missus Dunne,' Lorna said.

'It's a lot to take in,' Shay said. And it was. 'By the way, just call me Shay… what age is he?'

'Just over two months old. He was due at the end of September but he was premature. He was born on the sixteenth of August. It was like he couldn't wait to get out into the world.'

Lorna gave a wistful smile. She lowered her hand to let him wrap his tiny fingers around her index finger.

'That was very early,' Shay said. 'Was he okay?'

Lorna shook her head. 'It wasn't looking good for a while. He was kept in hospital for three weeks before they let him out. And I had him at home another three weeks before I decided he was strong enough to leave the house.'

'You must've been out of your mind with worry.'

'And then some. I was so focused on him getting well, I couldn't deal with anything else.' Lorna looked out onto the river. 'That's why I didn't come to the funeral. I wanted to. I really need you to believe that. I even got dressed to go but, at the last minute, I got too afraid to leave him.'

Shay felt shame burn her face as she remembered her anger

at Lorna not being at the funeral. Lorna's gaze returned. Her face carried an air of melancholy, like a ghost that haunted her.

'I understand,' Shay said, in a whisper. 'Now I get it.'

'The DMs you sent me,' Lorna said. 'You must've hated me for not replying. I wouldn't blame you.'

Now it was Shay's turn to look away. Of course she'd hated her.

'I got really sick around the middle of July,' Lorna said. 'I was rushed into hospital. They thought I might lose the baby. They told me I'd picked up an infection, don't tell me how, but it was the worst experience of my life. They got me stabilised after a week and I was able to go home, but they warned me to do nothing and to make sure I had no stress. So, I hid away my phone and my laptop and went to bed and just read books.'

'I'm so sorry that happened to you,' Shay said.

'No stress,' Lorna said, 'and then I hear Rory's missing?' She wiped tears from her eyes with the back of her hand. 'Although, honestly, I didn't think he was really missing. I was convinced he'd be back, that he'd only taken himself off somewhere to clear his head.'

Funny how that's what Shay herself had thought.

'When the police or, you know, the Gards phoned me,' Lorna said, 'and asked me about the last time I spoke to him, I knew then something was badly wrong. I tried not to freak out but it was nearly impossible. I wanted to get back on my phone and laptop to see if I could contact him and keep up with what was going on, but my parents stopped me, told me I had to put the baby first. I never saw your DMs 'til after he was born and, by then, well, as I said, he was so sick I could think of nothing but getting him well. I should've replied all the same.'

Lorna took a tissue from her coat pocket and dried her eyes. Shay stood watching, wanting to say or do something to comfort her, but not sure what.

'Would you… do you want to hold him a while?' Lorna said. 'I know it's cold, but he's well wrapped up and a few minutes out of his buggy won't do any harm.'

'Can I? Would that be all right?'

'It would be more than all right.'

Lorna unbuckled the brace that held little Rory in place and lifted him out. His body was lost inside a light-blue all-in-one snowsuit.

'You forget how small they are,' Shay said, reaching for his hand.

Tears spilled over onto her face, streaking a moist path all the way to her lips. She absently dabbed them away. Carefully, Lorna handed over her precious bundle.

'Here,' she said. 'Give your grandson a cuddle.'

Shay cradled her arms around him and held him close, somehow certain that in this sacred moment her disease wouldn't dare let her drop him. She gave his forehead a gentle kiss.

'He smells so lovely,' she said. 'All new and clean, all full of hope and possibility.'

She played with his fingers and he flailed about happily as she did.

'He's got Rory's eyes,' Shay said, 'and his hair colouring. But other than that, I think he's more like you, Lorna, with his swarthy skin and perfect little nose.'

'I'll make sure he doesn't pierce it,' Lorna said, laughing and pointing to a tiny gold stud sitting snug in the side of her nose.

'I hadn't even noticed that.'

Shay looked more closely and thought the stud looked pretty on Lorna's face. It was a kind face, too, Shay decided, along with being sad.

'I hope you're not annoyed with me,' Lorna said, 'that I didn't let you know about him before now.' Her voice wavered. 'I waited 'til he was strong and healthy, but maybe I waited too long.'

'Don't feel bad. You had to do what was best for you... and him.' Shay brushed her cheek against Rory's forehead. 'You've told me now and that's all that matters.'

'I was hoping...' Lorna said, 'hoping you might, you know, like to be part of his life.'

Shay swallowed hard against her pain. 'Hoping I might?' she croaked. 'I'd want nothing more.'

It would never happen, but it didn't make wanting it any less true.

Lorna beamed. 'Will I put him back in the buggy and we can walk?'

Shay returned him to Lorna and she tucked him snugly back in before the trio started off.

'Have you been managing okay with him?' Shay asked. 'A new baby can take a bit of getting used to.'

'It took a while, but I'm finding my feet. He's a good wee boy, sleeps sound at night, is happy so long as he's warm and fed – oh, look, he's nodding off.'

As if on cue, little Rory's eyelids began flapping together, his mouth hanging open. Lorna stroked his cheek.

'When I told my parents I was pregnant, they weren't too thrilled. They thought after all my hard work at college, becoming a single parent was like throwing my chances away.'

'I remember Rory saying how clever you were,' Shay said. 'Weren't you doing a science course?'

'Marine Science, at the university in Coleraine, which is ironic because until the age of eleven, I was afraid of going into the water. I finished my degree in May, just before all the trouble started. I'm due to start my PhD in January.'

'I'm so impressed. A PhD?'

'I'm going to do it on marine pollution. I even got in touch with that journalist who broke the big waste-dumping scandal in Co Derry. Do you remember her? Belle McGee?'

'I remember the story in the papers. They got a few convictions, didn't they?'

'They did, but nobody was made to pay for the clean-up.' Lorna leaned over to check on Rory. 'I wouldn't be able to do the PhD without my parents' support. They've been so good and they just dote on little Rory, so do my two younger brothers.'

'I like knowing he has so many people to love him,' Shay said, 'and that he has a mother like you. You should feel very proud of yourself… and him.'

'I'm definitely proud of him,' Lorna said.

Her face lit up like fireworks in a night sky. *The first time that haunted look has left her*, Shay thought. She felt a pang. She thought her heart was shattering and yet she was utterly happy.

'You've changed my whole life, Lorna, bringing him here today, letting me see him.'

'Oh, I—'

'No need to answer, I don't expect you to realise just how much it means. You've no idea. These past months, I've been so… so lost, like a rickety old rowboat drifting out to sea with nowhere to go.'

She stared into the distance as the words came out of her mouth. Stingy, salty tears blurred her vision.

'And all this time I thought my son was gone…' she said, half-thinking aloud, 'gone off the face of the earth like he never existed. Gone forever before he'd been able to make anything of his life.' She pulled herself back as though coming out of a trance. 'It's not like that anymore. Because of the baby. And you.'

'I wished I'd told you about him earlier,' Lorna said. 'I feel like I've denied you something, but I'll make it up to you – I will.'

Shay couldn't bring herself to tell Lorna she wasn't going to get the chance to keep that promise. She'd find out soon enough. Shay reached over and squeezed her hand.

'Will you promise me something else?' Shay asked.

'Anything.'

'Will you make sure little Rory knows who his father was? Will you tell him about my son, the good things about him? Don't let him grow up without knowing he had a father who would've loved him.'

'That goes without saying,' Lorna said.

They walked a little further. Shay was lost in the silence of her own thoughts; Lorna was silent, too – maybe equally lost in hers. As they inched along the river, Shay realised one piece of the story remained unknown to her.

'Something I need to know,' she said. 'I hope you don't mind me asking. Did Rory know? About the baby?'

Lorna looked at her. 'He knew. I told him at the start of June.'

Shay had to stop so she could properly process the news. 'He knew? And he still did what he did, took his own life?'

'That's the thing, though,' Lorna said. 'I'm not convinced he did. That's why I didn't think it was anything serious at the start when I heard he was missing. It didn't make sense at all.'

They started walking again.

'What made you think that?' Shay asked.

'I should explain from the start,' Lorna said. 'You knew Rory and me split up, but you said you didn't know why.'

'He never told me.'

'I'd say that's because he didn't want you finding out he cheated on me.'

Shay almost tripped. 'He, what?'

She'd gotten that one wrong, too. She'd blamed Lorna for bailing out on him in his hour of need when, all along, Rory was the guilty party. She could scarcely believe he had that in him.

'He had an affair with Natalie O'Donnell, do you know her?'

Shay rummaged in her mind and found the name. 'Right, Eoin Devine's girlfriend.'

She recalled a memory of Natalie at the funeral, upset and barely able to give her condolences.

'They started seeing each other around November, practically a year ago. I didn't get wind 'til February when my cousin told me. She spotted him one day with a girl outside a café at the top of Waterloo Street. When she described the girl, I knew right away it was Natalie. It broke my heart and what made it worse was being pregnant. I was over two months gone at that stage. I hadn't told Rory yet. We hadn't been getting on well, very badly actually, and I was still trying to process the news for myself. He was so preoccupied with his business and I was so preoccupied with college. We were both working all hours and hardly ever seeing each other. I suppose we were drifting apart. It's still no excuse for what he did.'

'Did you confront him about cheating?'

'Right away. I hoped and prayed right up to the end that it wasn't true, but he admitted it. Worse still, he tried to justify it, saying Natalie seduced him at a time when we weren't getting on so well. That just made me so angry and we had a flaming row. We calmed down after a while and he apologised, said he wouldn't see her again, it was all a mistake and he wanted to be with me.'

'I'm guessing you didn't say yes to that.'

'I said I had to think about it and I needed a break. I came so close to telling him about the baby, but I knew if I did, he'd only beg me to stay with him and I'd give in. I wouldn't get the time away from him that I really did need. I had to make up my mind if I wanted him – if I could ever trust him again.'

'Did you contact him after that?'

'Yup – around the middle of June, I called him. I'd come to a decision.'

'You didn't want anything to do with him,' Shay said, predicting what Lorna was going to say.

'We had a long chat on the phone.'

*

'Hi, Rory,' Lorna said, 'how's it going?'

'Wow, it's you,' Rory said. 'It's good to hear from you. It's great.'

She could hear a tremble of excitement in his voice. She was pleased.

'I finished my degree,' she said. 'I got a First. Gets me straight onto the PhD.'

'That's amazing. Didn't doubt it for a second. Congratulations. I'm proud of you.'

'Thanks. And how have things been for you?'

He groaned. 'I had a nasty shock to do with the business,' he said. 'Things are somewhat fucked. I found out in April that Eoin dug me into a hole of debt – long story that I won't bore you with, but the bottom line is I'm in deep.'

'Jesus, Rory, that sounds awful.'

'In a weird way, it was a relief. For months, I was busting my nuts and working all hours, and even though I was making money hand over fist, the finances never seemed to get any better. I couldn't understand what was going on and it was pulling me under.'

'So, what're you going to do about this debt?'

'I talked to Mum,' he said. 'That helped. She can give me a bit of money, so can Dad. Between them, it's enough to get the loan sharks off my back, I think. They're the scary bastards, so it'll be good to see them off. The rest, I'm still figuring that out. I was in a bad way for a while there, but I'm in a better place now. I'm determined to beat this. The business is still making good money, that's a major plus, and I'm getting the legal work done to have Eoin removed from anything to do with it.'

'You have it under control then,' Lorna said.

'Not quite, but it's moving in the right direction. And I've taken up sea swimming. You wouldn't believe what a dip in the cold Atlantic does to the brain. When I come out, I feel on top of the world, like I could take on anything. I love it.'

She fell quiet, smiling. Rory sounded like his old self – the one she fell in love with; the one she might be able to trust again.

'Are you still seeing Natalie O'Donnell?'

Rory didn't answer right away. A lot was riding on what he'd say next – what decision she'd make.

'I won't lie,' he said. 'I've met her maybe three times since we split up. Each time I wanted to tell her it was over but, each time, I chickened out. I couldn't dump her. She's not a horrible person and, whenever I went to end it, she'd say something that made me feel sorry for her and I'd just think, "Fuck it, I'll do it next time."'

'At least you told the truth. Do you still have feelings for her?'

'I don't love her. I don't want to be with her. I've just been putting off the inevitable because I'm a coward.'

Lorna believed him. Not just for what he said, but how he said it. The matter-of-factness and, at the same time, the compassion for another human being.

'Listen, Lorna,' he said, 'I know I fucked up. I was a total bastard and I'm sorry. There's no justification for what I did. I was in the wrong – full stop. I get that now and I have to live with the consequences. I—'

'Rory, I want to tell you something.'

'Hang on, I need you to know this. I deserve to be brokenhearted, to live with the regret. And you didn't deserve what happened. You're a beautiful, kind person and I was too stupid to know how lucky—'

'Rory, I'm pregnant.'

Rory stopped. Lorna heard him gasp.

'Yuh… you're… am I…?'

'You're the father. I was over two months gone when we split up.'

Another gasp. Then silence.

'What're you thinking?' she asked.

'That I want to be with you, that I want to be a dad.'

Something in her body leapt and she started to cry. 'I hoped you'd say that,' she said.

'And I hoped you'd say that,' Rory said.

She could hear his sobs over the digital space between them.

'My ma's going to be over the moon,' he said.

'Rory, please don't go telling her or anybody yet,' Lorna said. 'I've only told my parents. Not even my brothers know. Can we keep it quiet for a while? I'm still coming to terms with it.'

'Okay, it's your prerogative.' He paused. 'But it's all good, right?' he asked. 'We're good.'

'I think so.'

'I've some business to take care of,' he said. 'Natalie, for a start. Then this debt shit. I need to think a bit more about how I'm going to get rid of it. But I promise I'll be ready for when the baby comes. I'll have my house in order.'

She smiled happily, relived. 'I know you will. I know you will.'

*

Shay hardly knew what to say when Lorna finished.

'Sorry to bombard you,' Lorna said, and that melancholy was back again. 'I know there's a lot to take in.'

Wasn't that the truth? Shay didn't know where to start. Rory was cheating and with Natalie O'Donnell, then he was in touch with Lorna again. He knew he was going to be a father and that he and Lorna were probably going to get back together.

Little Rory stretched and gave a whimper. Lorna leaned forward.

'It's all right, wee man.'

She rubbed his tiny forehead and he settled down for a second sleep.

'There's something that bothers me,' said Shay. The pieces of Lorna's story were floating around in her head and something didn't quite fit. 'You told Rory about the baby and it seemed like you were both going to get back together, am I right?'

'Right, he was excited about the future.'

'See, it doesn't make sense,' Shay said. 'He had everything to life for. You, the baby, even the debt thing… but from what you've said, it wasn't a problem he'd take his own life over.'

'Well, that's exactly what I've been thinking all along. Why would he do that when life was looking up? So, the question then is: why does everybody believe he took his own life?'

Lorna looked right at Shay, her eyebrows raised with expectation. The question wasn't rhetorical, Shay realised. Lorna was waiting for her to answer.

'Because,' Shay said, 'umm… because he drowned in the sea.'

'And?'

Shay scrambled to follow the trail Lorna clearly wanted her to follow. 'And you'd only drown in the sea because you wanted to.'

'But what if you didn't want to? What if you'd taken up sea swimming?'

A big, beaming light went on in Shay's head, blinding like a floodlight.

'Jesus,' she said, 'he was on his own and he swam out too far and…'

Lorna's eyes pooled. 'It was an accident,' she whispered.

Shay didn't know if it was joy or grief that caused the swell in her chest. His death was an accident. An accident. He hadn't taken his own life, after all. It haunted her to think of how he'd been driven to end it all. Weren't the damned poison pen letters just her way of coping with that? To know it was an accident didn't make it any less painful, but it gave her solace that his last days had been happy.

She put her arms around Lorna and she felt Lorna's arms embrace her, too. They were practical strangers and yet this truth about Rory united them like they'd known each other their whole lives. They stood on the quay, the baby's buggy beside them, holding each other. They didn't speak a word. They didn't need to.

*

Darkness had fallen by the time Shay got to the house. For the whole of the drive back from Derry, she'd focused on nothing other than getting to her destination safely, without crashing, forbidding her thoughts to run riot. But now, in the refuge of home, she could give vent to whatever was inside.

As soon as the front door closed, a dam of tears burst through, their release like shackles coming away from her feet. She slid to the floor, feeling the soft carpet beneath her. Everything had changed. Meeting Lorna, finding out about the baby, the near certainty that Rory's death had been an accident – especially that, oh God, especially that. Everything had changed beyond recognition. She had changed.

The soreness in her broken heart didn't seem so raw anymore. Little Rory's face was ever present in her mind. His happy, beautiful little face. His smile, his eyes, his chubby cheeks took the hard edges off the pain somehow. Her anger, too – maybe not quite gone, but subdued and fading. She felt a sort of peace – a quiet, gentle joy. It surrounded her like an aura, distancing her from the sour pool of emotions she'd been swilling in for too long. Losing Rory, being diagnosed, facing her own mortality – it all seemed too cruel. It was only natural for her to want to lash out. Not anymore.

Shay heaved herself up off the ground, flinching. Her whole body was as stiff as a plank of wood and her left leg was cramped so badly that the touch of a feather would have made it hurt. She limped to the sitting room. Her disease had stayed away all day, as though permitting her that time with Lorna and the baby. Now it was back, taunting her and ready to make up for lost time. She just about got to the sofa and she stretched out her gammy leg in the hope of easing its pain.

Lying there, she thought about the revelation of Rory's death being an accident. She planned on telling everybody what had really happened. Whether they chose to believe her or not was up to them.

She'd quit her job, too, and claim sickness benefit. She didn't feel the need to hold onto it as a sign of independence any longer.

There was Dan to consider, too. She'd have to tell him he had a grandson. He had a right to know, after all. She'd seek Lorna's permission first; she didn't think Lorna would have a problem, but it seemed right to ask anyway.

After today, she'd make out a new will. The house would go to the baby – a nest egg for when he turned eighteen. She had a few trinkets of Rory's she wanted to leave him, too: the Postman Pat bell from his bike and the *Barnaby Buckle* book, for starters. And her photo albums would be his – on second thoughts, she wanted Lorna to get those right away. She'd post them off tomorrow. Between the covers of those albums were hundreds of photos of Rory, practically his whole life captured in a mountain of still images, from the biggest moments to the smallest, year after year – his first tooth, his first step, his first bruised knee, his first haircut, his first day at school, his First Communion, Christmases, birthdays, summer holidays, family gatherings, camping in the backyard with his friends, playing on the school football team, passing his driving test.

The baby would never meet his father. Rory would never get the chance to tell his son about his life or his family – that history we like to pass on to our children – but the photos would be the next best thing. They'd do what Rory couldn't and the baby would know something about his father.

Shay thought back to what Lorna had told her about Rory's infidelity. That news had both surprised and disappointed her.

He'd redeemed himself in the end, though, she thought. He was going to make it right, be a good partner to Lorna, a good father to little Rory. Of that, she had no doubt.

Shay sat up on the sofa. The cramp in her leg had eased. She felt better – a little bit, at any rate. She might make a toasted sandwich and a cup of tea. That would be nice.

She got to her feet, stretched again and found she was able to walk without limping, which was an improvement. Her vision blurred for a minute and now she had a pain pushing against the back of her eyes. She got as far as the kitchen and flicked on the kettle. Maybe she'd forgo the toastie and just take a couple of painkillers – a couple of the high-powered ones the hospital prescribed.

The day's revelations brought something else to mind: her cringe-inducing plan to punish Peter Feeney and Eoin Devine. At that moment, nothing seemed so utterly preposterous. Had she lost her facilities when she'd dreamt it up? How could she have believed a scheme like that was ever going to make her feel better or do any good? And the whole thing had backfired so badly.

Her head thumped relentlessly.

She filled a glass of water from the cold tap and popped out two tablets from a blister pack. She was tired enough to sleep for a year. She laughed dryly. She wouldn't live long enough to sleep for a year.

38

Ciara was lost in thought as she walked up the slushy-wet street to McBirney's, a shower of rain turning to sleet as she went. She'd taken Shay to the solicitor the day before to make a new will. Now, there was a shocker. Turned out Rory had a son. Astounding news. And poor Shay, she was buzzed about it. It wasn't the only news Shay had had to share. She had a new theory that Rory didn't take his own life. He was sea swimming, Shay claimed, and drowned accidentally. Could that be true? Shay believed it – said Lorna did, too. If it made Shay feel better, Ciara was willing to play along.

The slush on the pavement squished under her boots, the sleet pattered against her umbrella.

But Ciara was worried about Shay. Her condition was getting worse and, according to the consultants, she was deteriorating faster than they'd expected. Each day, it seemed, brought some new development that bit by bit chipped away at who her sister was.

The sleet fell harder, big drops bouncing off the waterproof material of the umbrella in a rhythmic beat. Ciara fixed her gaze on the ground. What needed to happen now was for Shay to move in with her and Joe. The downstairs bedroom was ready and waiting and it wasn't a case of "if" anymore, it was a case of "when". Shay would resist and Ciara couldn't blame her. It would be another piece of her independence eroded away. But that was happening, whether she liked it or not, and it was either move in with them or move into a care home. There was no way she was going to let Shay end up in some home being looked after by strangers. Anyway, Ciara was tired of worrying about her being alone and something happening. It'd be easier to have her living at The Snug.

Tears threatened. Ciara refused to let them through. She reached the shop and, quickly donning her face mask, stepped inside. She said hello to Louisa Allan, who was on her way out and in a hurry.

'Morning, Ciara,' Daisy said.

Daisy was smiling with a cat-that-got-the-cream sort of smile and Ciara guessed that smile was because of whatever juicy tittle-tattle she and Louisa had just been sharing.

'How's Daisy?' Ciara said.

She grabbed a shopping basket and did a quick tour of the shop, picking up a few essentials as she went: a litre of milk, a brown loaf, a small block of Cheddar cheese, a roll of bin bags. She bumped into Andie, literally, as she rounded the corner at the bottom of the main aisle and nearly tripped over the girl hunkered on the floor stacking a ground-level shelf.

'God's sake, Andie,' Ciara said, irritated, 'I didn't even see you there.'

'Sorry, Mrs McCann,' Andie said.

She stood up but kept her eyes on the floor. Immediately, Ciara felt guilty at snapping. Sometimes Andie was so dumb you just wanted to shake her 'til her teeth rattled, but she meant no harm.

'It's all right, Andie,' Ciara said. 'I didn't hurt you, did I? When I banged into you?'

'Umm, no, I'm all right.'

Ciara brought her goods to the checkout where Daisy looked ready to bust.

'I hear the Gards are nearly finished their interviews about the letters,' Daisy said, as she began ringing in Ciara's basket.

Ciara's ears pricked up – sometimes Daisy's news could be useful.

'Are they going to be calling on you at all?' Daisy asked, narrowing her eyes as though penetrating Ciara's brain.

What she was really asking was whether Ciara had gotten a letter. Ciara had zero intention of telling Daisy-McBirney-Smith that, yes, they had gotten a letter and, no, they hadn't been interviewed yet.

'I wouldn't think so,' Ciara said. 'What about you?'

'Oh, I wouldn't think so either.'

'Good for you.'

Andie appeared behind the counter and set to tidying a shelf. *Here to catch the news*, Ciara thought, *moreso than to put the shelf in order.* She was her mother's daughter, that was for sure.

'Did you hear the craic about Mary-Margaret?' Daisy asked.

'Last I heard she was in St Bart's.' Ciara pulled a reusable bag from her coat pocket and went about packing her goods.

Daisy's face brightened. 'Oh, she got out, so she did. A couple of days ago.'

'Well, that's good to hear,' Ciara said. 'Could you give me some Ibuprofen?'

Daisy turned to a shelf behind her. 'Twelve or twenty-four?'

'Twelve, thanks.'

'But she's been put on extended sick leave,' Daisy said, adding a pack of painkillers to the rest of Ciara's shopping. 'Chances are she might have to take early retirement.'

'All because of one incident? Seems a bit harsh.'

'Maybe it's a good thing. She wasn't exactly Florence Nightingale, according to some of the stories I've heard.'

'I heard stories, too. Even so, it's sad.'

Daisy rang up the last item. 'That's eighteen-forty-three, Ciara.'

Ciara checked her wallet for notes and spotted a twenty.

'And wasn't it wile what happened to Harry Parkes?' Daisy said, adjusting her face mask.

'It was shocking,' Ciara said. 'He has a severe head injury, so I was told, and he's still in a coma.'

She handed over the twenty Euro note and Daisy took it.

'He's lucky to be alive, so he is, and there's no guarantee he'll pull through.'

'Jesus, it's unreal.'

Daisy gave Ciara her change.

'So, the craic is,' Daisy said, 'his daughter, you know, the older one, Alison, I think, or is it Amy, I never can tell the difference in them. Anyway, whichever one it was arrived at the house very soon after the attack and was able to get an ambulance straight away. They say if he hadn't been found so soon, he would've died.'

'Do the Gards think it was a robbery?'

'The place was ransacked so it could've been. My bet is that it's to do with the poison pen.'

'Ach, Daisy, you can't know that.'

'Well, we'll see. Once he wakes up, we'll know for sure. That is, if he wakes up at all.'

'Who would do a thing like that?'

'Did you know the daughter saw a car pulling out of the lane?' Daisy said.

'That, I didn't know.'

'Oh aye. She couldn't get the number plate, but she said it looked like a Bentley.'

Ciara did a double take. 'A Bentley?'

There was only one person who owned a Bentley. She couldn't wait to tell Shay this one.

Daisy folded her arms and raised her eyebrows in a knowing look. 'A Bentley.'

39

'So, Eoin, how've you been?'

'Okay, I suppose,' Eoin said.

He was across the table from his solicitor, who was leafing through a stack of papers from a tan leather document folder. They were in the kitchen of his mother's house. He'd been staying with her since making bail. It was the same house he grew up in – his grandparents' house, now his mother's, maybe his someday.

'It's good you're here,' the solicitor said, twirling the pointed tip of his beard. 'Quiet, with family. That's what you need right now.'

'It's hard on me ma,' Eoin said. 'She's not doing well with it.'

He stared out of the window at an overcast sky that matched his mood.

'Only to be expected,' the solicitor said. 'She's just worried about you.'

'And I'm worried about her. She doesn't need this shite. My grand-da would kill me if he was still alive for bringing this trouble to her door.'

His solicitor joined his hands and frowned.

'She depends on me,' Eoin went on, 'to give her a few extra

Euros, sort things out round the house. Who's going to look out for her?'

The solicitor shook his head. 'You need to prepare her for what's to come.'

'I don't know what's to come.'

'Well, that's why I'm here today.'

Eoin slid a cigarette out of a box on the table and put it to his mouth. He nodded to his solicitor.

'I don't smoke,' the solicitor said, 'not anymore.'

'I should probably knock them on the head, too,' Eoin said. 'Sometime.'

'They've set the date for your hearing.'

'When?'

Eoin could hardly bear to be told. He lit his cigarette and took a long drag, releasing a billow of smoke that wafted in the direction of the solicitor. The solicitor cleared his throat.

'Sorry,' Eoin said, stubbing out the cigarette.

The solicitor nodded. 'It's exactly two weeks from tomorrow. Letterkenny courthouse.'

Eoin's stomach twisted. Two weeks. They'd fly in and, at the same time, he knew they'd drag. The days might be going by like weeks as he waited and waited in his childhood home for what was about to happen, yet two weeks wasn't long for the decision that was going to change his life forever.

'Your barrister has your file,' the solicitor said, 'and we've prepared the case for her, so she'll be ready when the time comes.'

'How do you think it's going to go?'

The solicitor twirled his beard again, a habit that was beginning to play on Eoin's nerves.

'It's a serious case,' the solicitor said. 'A man lost his life. What we're going to argue is manslaughter – involuntary manslaughter, not murder. I think that'll be the verdict of the court, too.'

'Manslaughter, murder, who cares? What difference does it make if I'm guilty? Which I am. I'm not disputing it.'

'There's a big difference when it comes to sentencing. We want to get you the lowest sentence possible.'

'I want that, too, but maybe it's not what I deserve.'

'It's not the job of your legal team to judge the ethics of what you did. Our job is to give you the best legal defence we can. If we win a plea of involuntary manslaughter, you could be looking at a sentence as low as two years, max fifteen. The hit-and-run will be the fly in the ointment, but we can major on the fact that you did eventually hand yourself in. That'll count for something.'

'I'll never understand why I did that,' Eoin said, watching the sky outside darken, 'just left that man lying there. I'll live with that my whole life.'

'You'll have plenty of time to deal with your conscience, Eoin. The focus right now is on getting the lowest sentence we can.'

'How low do you reckon it'll be?'

'It's hard to tell. I don't want to raise expectations.'

'But you must have some idea, if you were a betting man.'

'I'm not.'

'I suppose you don't drink either.'

The solicitor was not amused.

'Give me your best guess,' Eoin said.

'I think you'll do well to get eight to ten, though you're likely to serve half your term in prison and the other half outside on licence.'

Eoin swallowed and reached for his cigarette pack. 'Jesus.' He pulled out another cigarette with a trembling hand. 'Hearing it spoke out like that for the first time… well, shit, it doesn't sound great.'

'You might as well get used to it because that's the reality – the best-case scenario.'

'You've got such a reassuring bedside manner.'

'Eoin, I'm not here to hold your hand and say it'll be all right. I'm here to give you the facts and do the best legal job I can.'

Eoin put the cigarette down and began gnawing the inside of his cheek. He looked across at the solicitor. Pointy beard or no pointy beard, he was deadly serious – cold.

Eoin realised, maybe properly for the first time, what lay ahead for him. He was going to prison and not for a little while. He was going to prison and he'd be on his own in there. No one would be looking out for him. His solicitor, his mother, his uncles, his cousins – they'd all be on the outside and he'd be locked away in a place where none of them could protect him. His life, the one he knew, would be over. The nice things, the fun things, the creature comforts, the safety of his mother's house would all be lost to him. In their place would be a barren cell and hostile inmates.

For some reason, he didn't know why, he thought about Rory. Maybe this was the kind of fear that had run through his mind before he made his fatal decision to kill himself. Paying off debt was a less scary prospect than going to prison, yet Eoin had no notion of taking his own life. Everybody was different, he supposed, and one man's cake walk was another man's last straw. Poor Rory. It crossed Eoin's mind that if he'd known how bad Rory was taking it, he could've done something to lift the debt burden off him before it was too late. And then the thought left his mind as quickly as it had entered. Like the solicitor said, he'd have plenty of time to ponder the whys and wherefores where he was going, and for now they could wait.

'I'm scared,' he said, in a whisper.

The solicitor's eyes softened. 'I know,' he said, his voice suddenly kind. 'I won't sugar-coat it. It's not going to be easy. But you'll push through. And some day you'll have done your time and you'll be out again. You'll have a life after this.'

'The stories you hear about prison,' Eoin said. 'Are they true?'

'Stories? Like getting beaten up or raped?'

Eoin felt a shiver, like the touch of an icy breeze on the back of his neck.

'That's not common.'

'But it does happen?'

'It can but, as I say, it's not common. It's never happened to any of my clients and I've never heard of it happen to anybody else's. Once, I think, I heard a fella got stabbed, but he was mixed up with a gang inside and there was a feud. The majority of people go in and do their time. They keep their head down, make a few friends, get through.'

Eoin took in the solicitor's words as though they were a warm blanket on a winter's night. He'd keep them with him as a reminder when the terrors crept in.

'There'll be others like you, you know,' the solicitor said. 'Not the career criminals, but others. You'll find each other. You'll find a way to get by.'

Eoin stared at a burn mark on the table. He half-smiled remembering how it had come to be there: a stray cigarette dropping out of the ashtray one night that his family were gathered at the house for a few drinks and a singsong. His mother hadn't been one bit happy about the damage to her kitchen table.

'First things first,' the solicitor was saying, 'we focus on the trial.'

40

The pain in his head was the worst he'd felt in his life. With every breath, every move, it was as though a knife was going through his brain. It sat in front of his eyes, pushing on his forehead. Worse than the pain was the constant buzzing. The only thing he could compare it to was the test card they used to have on the BBC years ago. Between the pain and the buzzing, Harry was just vaguely aware that the rest of his body wasn't in any better shape.

He was in a private ward, not much bigger than a prison cell. He touched his head very gently with the tips of his fingers and felt a bandage. His left leg was in a sling and, somewhere in his midriff, he felt an ache, though not as bad as his head and only if he tried to move. His right hand, bandaged under many layers of dressing, felt as though it was on fire.

'Do you feel up to talking to the Gards, Daddy?'

Harry's youngest daughter, Alison, was at his bedside, holding his hand, the worry in her face saying everything he needed to know about his condition. His other daughter, Amy, stood at the foot of the bed beside a uniformed Gard, a hulking figure with hair combed into a side part. They were all wearing masks.

'I, ah, I—' Harry coughed. His throat was too dry to speak.

'Do you need some water, Daddy?'

Alison brought a glass of water towards his mouth and placed a straw on his lips. He sipped, his head clamouring like a brass band.

'That's grand,' he said, pulling back from the straw.

'Are you still very sore, Daddy?' Amy asked, the redness around her eyes and cheeks giving away the fact that she'd been crying.

'Aye,' he said, 'I'm in a wile state altogether.' He leaned slowly back into the pillow.

'At least you're out of the coma now, so that's a good sign,' Alison said.

'I was in a coma?'

'For the last four days,' Alison said, 'but today you came out of it, thank God. We're all relieved like you can't believe.'

'The doctors said you're lucky to be alive,' Amy said.

'I don't feel that alive or that lucky.'

'Give it time, Daddy,' Alison said, rubbing his hand.

'Why's there a Gard here?'

'The Gards have been waiting for you to come round so they can talk to you,' Alison said. 'You were showing signs of waking up today and we let them know.'

'But why?'

'Somebody attacked you,' Amy said, 'do you not remember?' She looked like she was going to cry again. 'They gave you a couple of blows to the head and you have two fractured ribs and a fractured leg. And there's a burn on your hand.'

'Dear God,' Harry said. 'Where did that happen?'

'In your own house,' Amy said. 'I found you lying unconscious on the floor and I saw a car coming out of the lane as I was driving up and—'

'We'll get to that later,' the Gard said. 'I want to find out what Mr Parkes remembers first.'

'Ah, okay, understood,' Amy said.

The door to the ward opened and in walked Harry's son, Arthur. He took up position beside the Gard.

'How's everybody?' he asked. 'You're back in the land of the living then, Dad. Glad to see it.'

Harry nodded.

'The Gard's going to find out what Daddy remembers from that night,' Alison said.

'I don't think I remember anything,' Harry said.

'With head injuries, Mr Parkes,' the Gard said, 'it's common for people to have a very cloudy recollection of the event that caused the damage. That's why I'm here, to help jog the memory.'

A bolt of pain shot across Harry's skull and he winced. 'I can't believe this.'

'When you get out of here,' Arthur said, 'you can come and stay with me and Jane 'til you feel up to going back to the house.'

'You can stay with any of us,' Alison said, 'for as long as you need.'

Amy nodded.

'I'm blessed to have you three wains,' Harry said.

The Gard spoke up. 'You were alone in the house, Mr Parkes. Can you recall if somebody came to the door?'

Harry tried to cast his mind back. Whatever he had in there, in his brain – what was it they called it… the mind's eye? – it was nothing but thick fog behind a brick wall of agony. Random pictures of things popped up for a second, before disappearing again. He focused on them as best he could.

'I remember earlier on in the day,' he said, 'I went and got shopping in town. I bought them pastries Amy likes cos she was coming over.'

'Oh God,' Alison said, 'not them terrible custard things.'

There were a couple of sniggers, including from the Gard.

'After you got the shopping,' the Gard said, 'what happened then?'

Harry closed his eyes. It helped him dredge up more images from wherever they were hiding.

'I fed the dog and locked him in the shed for the night,' Harry said. 'I remember that.'

A memory of rain… no, it was sleet… coming down heavy and the wind picking up.

'It was blowing a gale,' Harry said. 'Weren't they talking about a bad storm on the weather forecast?'

And then another memory… somebody in the house talking about the storm.

'Somebody did come to the house,' Harry said. 'They knocked on the door. They knocked because I remember not being sure if it was a knock or just the wind.'

Harry opened his eyes, only slightly because the light hurt.

'Go on, Mr Parkes, you're doing very well.'

'The person who knocked, Daddy,' Amy said, 'did you let them in? I mean, did you know them and let them in? Or did they push their way in?'

'Umm, I—'

'Let him tell it his own way,' the Gard said.

Harry concentrated, in spite of his throbbing head, and closed his eyes again. This time, he saw the range in his kitchen and a man sitting beside it with a cup of tea.

'I made him tea, I remember that. I made him tea.'

'Very good,' said the Gard. 'This is very good. You remember a man and you remember this man was somebody you let in the house and made tea for.'

'But who was he?' Arthur asked, impatience in his voice.

'Let's take this at a slower pace,' the Gard said.

'Oh, right, sorry,' Arthur said.

'Did I fall down the stairs?' Harry asked. 'Could that be how I hurt myself?'

'Daddy,' Alison said, 'I told you, this wasn't a fall. You were attacked.'

'It's just I keep seeing stairs.'

And so he did: a misty picture of a whole lot of stairs and a banister and they weren't straight, they were curved. But that wasn't the stairs in his house. His stairs weren't much more than a dozen steps and they were straight and they didn't have a banister. They just had a handrail going along the wall and…

The stairs he was seeing were in somebody else's house. They were… oh God. Harry's eyes shot open, causing a flash of pain to explode across the front of his skull.

'She fell down the stairs.'

'What?' Arthur asked.

'Daddy, who're you talking about?' Arthur looked at Amy. 'Is he starting to ramble?'

'I'm not rambling, Arthur,' Harry said, 'not one bit of me. I know she was pushed down those stairs, though I didn't see it with my own eyes.'

'Oh God,' Amy said, 'he's going into some delusional state. I'll get a nurse.'

The fog in Harry's head cleared for the briefest of moments and he saw a man, one he knew very well. He saw him standing in his kitchen. His face, frowning. No, his face distorted in a rage. And the man was shouting.

Harry gasped. 'He had a stick.'

Amy had her hand on the door, ready to go, but stopped.

'A walking stick… with a fancy silver handle.'

The picture in Harry's head fogged up again, all except the stick. The thick, heavy black stick and the hand holding it. It hovered above him. And then it came crashing down.

'Peter Feeney,' Harry said. 'It was Peter Feeney that set upon me.'

What sounded like a sigh of relief rippled across the room.

'That's whose car I saw,' Amy said.

The Gard nodded. 'Very good, Mr Parkes. You did well. We now have you and your daughter, independently of each other, placing Peter Feeney at the scene.'

'So, you already knew Peter Feeney was the one who did this?' Harry asked.

'Not quite. Your daughter saw his car, but that alone didn't prove anything other than he'd been at your house, or somebody driving his car had been at your house. Your statement proves he was the attacker.'

'Are you going to arrest him?' Arthur asked. 'His walking stick'll have DNA evidence, won't it? His clothes, too, maybe.'

'I'll radio into the station right now for his arrest to take place. As for evidence, DNA or otherwise, that'll all be taken care of. We're trained in our jobs, you know.'

Arthur blushed. 'Ah, sorry, I've been watching too much CSI.'

The Gard smirked. 'Thank you, Mr Parkes,' he said, 'you did a great job there. I'll have somebody visit you tomorrow to take a formal statement.'

He waved and left.

Arthur came up to the bed and took his father's hand. 'Good on ye, Dad.'

The girls were in tears and fussing round him.

'Why did Peter Feeney hurt you, Daddy?' Alison asked. 'It makes no sense.'

Harry could see the confusion in her eyes. The same went for Arthur and Alison. Harry frowned, in spite of the pain it caused him.

'He did something very bad a long time ago and he got away with it. He took a notion I knew about it and was trying to blackmail him.'

The three of his children were confounded. They all started speaking at once.

'He thought you were blackmailing him?' Arthur said.

'What was it he did?' Alison said.

'We need to tell the Gards,' Amy said.

'I can't stay awake, wains,' Harry said. 'Let me sleep a while first and then I'll tell you the whole story.'

41

The ringing tone pulsed in her ear. Natalie had finally plucked up the courage to ring Eoin. Part of her hoped he mightn't answer but, at the same time, she needed to make this call. The phone rang a few more times. She was about to give up when she heard his voice.

'Natalie? Nat, it's you.'

She bit her lip. Too late to change her mind now. 'It's me.'

'It's good to hear your voice, babes,' he said, and she could tell he was smiling. 'I mean, it's fucking-A to hear your voice.'

'Yours, too.'

'Are you doing okay?' he asked.

She thought for a moment. Best not to tell him how low she'd sunk. He had his own shit to deal with. 'I'm doing good.'

'That's great.'

'I'm back home, with my mother. It's not as bad it sounds. I got a part-time job in a local clothes shop – that nice one beside Asda.'

'I know it. Hope you're getting discount on the merch.'

'You better believe it.' She gave a little laugh. Eoin always had an eye out for the perks. 'I've applied for a foundation course, too.

My cousin, Maggie, suggested it. She's at uni doing medicine. A foundation course is a way to get onto a degree if you don't have A-levels.'

'Aww, seriously? That's great, Nat.'

'Just hope I can get the grades.'

'You will. You can do anything you set your mind to.'

She smiled. Their conversation was nice… kind… normal. They sounded like a couple of old friends catching up. Only that wasn't quite what they were, and they hadn't always been so nice and kind to each other.

'How've you been doing?' she asked.

'So-so,' he said. 'I'm back at home, too. Mum's looking after me well.'

He stopped and Natalie thought she heard the tiniest crack in his voice, though maybe not.

'I've a really good solicitor,' he went on, 'and he's building a decent defence for my barrister.'

'When's your trial going to start?'

'Not sure; the hearing's in a couple of weeks, so I'll know better then.'

'Are you scared?'

Another pause. He breathed out, shakily. 'Aye. Terrified.'

'Maybe you'll get off, you know, for coming forward.'

'I'm going down, Nat. It's not a case of if but how long. I've accepted that.'

Natalie shivered. Her mother would say somebody stepped on her grave. The finality of his words sat heavy on her heart.

'I'm sorry,' she said.

'Don't be. It has to happen. My Grand-da would want me to do the right thing. I'll accept the sentence they give me. I'll serve it with dignity. Atonement and all that jazz.'

Silent tears blurred her vision.

'My solicitor keeps telling me there's life after jail, you know. I can rebuild when I get out. That's what I look ahead to. That time when I get out.'

'I'm happy you're taking that attitude,' she said, hoping he wouldn't hear she was crying.

'Well, you know me, babes, I'm a glass-half-full sort of guy.'

He forced a laugh and she thought her heart would burst. She swallowed hard, dreading what she had to say next.

'I need to tell you something, before… before your trial. I know you have a load of shit to deal with, but it's, well, I don't want you thinking our break-up was all your fault.'

'Natalie,' he said, 'there was fault on both our parts. Let's leave it at that.'

'This is hard enough for me to go through with, so please just let me say what I have to say.'

She heard him inhale.

'I was cheating on you.' There, she'd said it. The words sounded awful out loud.

A pause from the other end of the call. Then, an answer.

'I knew, Natalie,' he said. 'I knew.'

'You knew? But how… no, don't tell me.' Tears trickled out despite her resolve to keep them contained. 'Do you know who it was with, too?'

'Umm-humm.'

'How come you never said anything?'

'I hoped it'd fizzle out,' he said. She heard the smile in his voice again, not joyful, more rueful. 'I thought you'd come back to me if I let you get him out of your system.'

'Oh.' His answer took her by surprise. 'How come you didn't hate me?'

'Hate you? I could never hate you. I loved you. I didn't always act like I did, but I did. The best way I could. And maybe I deserved it after what I did to Rory.'

Natalie couldn't hide it from him any longer that she was

crying. He tried to soothe her and she wished he could hold her and rock her like a baby.

'You know this is probably the last time we'll ever talk,' she said.

A gasp came from his side of the call. 'I guessed as much.'

'Saying goodbye seems like a total fucking anti-climax.'

'I never could understand what was good about goodbye,' he said.

She laughed through her tears.

'We don't have to say it,' he said. 'We could do it another way. What if we just wish each other a good life and press end call?'

'Okay.' She sniffed. 'You first.'

'Me first. Have a good life, Nat. Have the most amazing, fantastic, beautiful life.'

'Have a good… you have the same.'

She pressed end call. The phone went silent. He was gone.

'Have the most amazing, fantastic, beautiful life,' she whispered.

The phone dropped from her hand. She was crying too much to notice.

42

'Did you hear what I said?' Dan asked. 'Pop?'

'Something about the meeting with the, ah, that crowd in Dublin,' Peter said.

'That was five minutes ago,' Dan said. 'Is there something wrong? You don't seem... yourself.'

'I'm grand. A bit tired, that's all.'

Peter felt Dan's stare. Of course he knew something was wrong. It was hard to miss. But how could he tell Dan the truth? *I got a letter a while back, son, and it was from Harry Parkes making a veiled threat about the time I pushed your mother down the stairs – oh, by the way, I didn't tell you that your mother's death was my handiwork. Sorry about that. And when I went to Harry to confront him and he denied all knowledge, I lost my patience and struck out at him. I thought I'd killed him, thank god I didn't, but unfortunately that means he'll be able to identify me as his attacker once he comes to. So, forgive me if I seem a little preoccupied, if every minute of every day has me waiting to be taken away in handcuffs and thinking of nothing else.*

'Maybe you should, you know, take your foot off the pedal for a while,' Dan said.

Peter noted the caution in his voice, not wanting to cause a row on a subject that usually created tension.

'Everything's in hand,' Dan went on. 'Things are running smoothly. Don't you think? A few weeks R and R?'

Peter heard his son take in a deep breath – waiting for the backlash, no doubt. There would be none this time. Peter ran his hand through his hair. A robin landed on the decking outside the patio door. Its head jerked from side to side before it took off again.

'Maybe I spoke out of turn, Pop.'

Dan again, this time backtracking, maybe taking Peter's silence for anger that was about to blow up.

'No,' Peter said, finally, 'no, you didn't. In fact, I need to talk to you about the business, the future.'

He turned to face his son, observing his surprised expression.

'I made you CEO last year,' Peter began, 'but I didn't really let you off the leash, did I?'

Dan shrugged.

'But you've proved yourself.'

Peter saw more surprise in Dan's face.

'You know the ropes well enough, Dan, and you haven't needed me for a long time now.'

'I, umm, I wouldn't say that… I—'

'It's true.' Peter sighed. 'I've never said this before – I probably should've, though – but I trust you with the company. I trust you to run it entirely on your own.'

Dan's mouth opened, his eyes widened. He looked like he was about to speak. If he was, Peter didn't wait to find out. He knew if he didn't go ahead and say what he had to say, right there and then, he never would.

'I'm, ah, very proud…' he said, clearing his throat, 'of you. Of the manager you've become… of the man… you've become. I'm very proud.'

Dan went scarlet from his neck to his forehead. His jaw moved up and down and he emitted a croak that perhaps was meant to be a word.

'Don't answer,' Peter said, putting his hand up like a halt signal. 'No need. I should've said these things long ago.'

Peter lowered his head and looked at his shoes. They were sunk into the deep-pile carpet. Silence descended like snowfall.

'Are... are you all right, Pop?' Dan asked, after some time. 'I mean, health-wise. You didn't hear bad news, did you?'

Peter smiled. 'You think I need to be diagnosed with a terminal illness to say what I said?'

Peter pondered for a moment. Dan was right. Or nearly right. Bad news was on the way, just not the kind Dan thought.

'Let's get back to work,' Peter said. 'Tell me again what you were talking about earlier.'

Peter took his seat at the dining table and Dan continued with the business at hand. Peter listened as attentively as he was able. Not that it was easy. With each new breath, he expected to hear it. The knock at the door, quite literally and metaphorically. That life-changing moment. Although hadn't that moment already happened the night he paid his visit to Harry Parkes?

And then there it was. The ring of the doorbell. It surprised him despite his expectation.

'Shush a minute, Dan,' he said.

He strained to hear the voices at the front door. Louisa's was the only one he recognised. The other one was unfamiliar, but he could tell it was a southern accent. Wasn't that likely to be a Gard?

'Dan,' he said, 'no matter what happens, I want you and your sister to know that you were all I ever cared about.'

Dan scrunched up his face. 'What?'

'I achieved all I did to make a life for the both of you.'

'Pop, you're scaring me. Are you having a breakdown?'

Dan got to his feet and came closer. Peter saw the fear in his eyes.

'Listen to me,' Peter said, 'I want to—'

The door to the dining room opened and Louisa came in. Three men appeared behind her – two in Gardaí uniforms, the third in civilian clothes, but clearly a Gard too, all wearing face masks. Dan straightened himself.

'What's going on?' he asked, looking first at the Gards, then back to Peter.

Peter almost pitied him. The confusion on his face begged for answers and Peter could see the little boy he used to be – the little boy who could rely on his father to give him the answer to anything he asked.

'It's okay, Dan, you've nothing to worry about, son. The business is all yours.'

The plain clothes Gard said something to Louisa and she pointed.

'He's the gentleman sitting down,' she said.

'Mr Peter Feeney,' the plain-clothes Gard said, 'I'm Inspector O'Sullivan.'

'Hear me?' Peter said to Dan. 'The business is all yours to run now.'

'Pop...?'

'Mr Peter Feeney,' Inspector O'Sullivan continued, 'you are under arrest for the assault and attempted murder of Harold Parkes on the night of the thirtieth of October 2021.'

*

The ringing tone reverberated as Shay waited for Dan to answer. When he finally did, he sounded strained – unhappy that she was calling, no doubt.

'This is a really bad time,' he said.

'Isn't it always?'

'No, I mean it. Your timing couldn't be worse.'

'I'll call you back then.'

He hesitated. 'Ahmm, no, it's okay, what were you ringing for? Is anything wrong?'

His voice was unsteady, trembling, and Shay realised maybe it actually was a bad time. She'd be better to hold back on her news until a better time.

'Has something happened?' she asked. 'Is it one of the kids? Francesca?'

'No, it's...' He cleared his throat. 'It's my father.'

Shay pursed her lips but kept silent. She didn't care if Peter Feeney had dropped dead. But that wasn't quite true. She'd like some suffering to come to him first. After that, he could go to hell.

'Is he sick?' she asked.

'Worse,' Dan said.

She thought he might start sobbing.

'What do you mean?'

'He's been arrested.'

Shay staggered, almost falling backwards. By some miracle, she managed to keep her balance and her grip on the phone.

'Are you still there?' Dan said.

'I'm here,' she said.

'You're not... taking a turn or something like that.'

'No, I'm trying to process that news. Jesus, Dan, that's fucked up.'

'The Gards took him away about an hour ago. I've been sitting here since, staring out the fucking window like a shop dummy.'

'What did they arrest him for?'

'They've accused him of attacking Harry Parkes.'

Shay sucked in a mouthful of air. The idea that Peter Feeney had been arrested and arrested for assault – it was the stuff of fantasy. Ciara had mentioned something about Harry's daughter seeing a car that people thought was Peter's, but she didn't believe for a second he was responsible for hurting Harry.

'There's no way he did that,' Dan was saying. 'It's impossible.

I'm going to call Burley's – they've been our solicitors for decades. Jonathan Burley will know what to do. And as soon as I clear my father, I'm going to sue those bastard Gards. They're going to be so sorry. They can't accuse a man like my father of attempted murder. He could get a life sentence for that.'

Shay imagined Peter Feeney sitting in a jail cell, alone and looking very small and insignificant. A smile danced across her lips. She hoped he was worried and scared… and guilty. *Fucking karma coming at ya*, she thought.

Though what would've possessed him to do such a thing? She knew he was a nasty piece of shit, but this? The dimmest of notions flickered in her mind. Was the letter she sent him responsible in some way? If that was the case, wouldn't it make her as bad as Peter and Eoin? She honestly didn't have the space in her head to be haunted by that guilt. She pushed the notion away, choosing to believe her letter had played no part and Peter Feeney was driven to his act of violence all on his own steam.

'I'm sorry you're going through this, Dan,' she said. And she was. Sorry for Dan.

'Ah well, I'll get it sorted.' Dan sniffed. 'What was it you were ringing me about anyway?'

With the shock of Dan's news, she'd almost forgotten her own news. 'I have two things I want to tell you. They might come as a bit of a bombshell.'

'Can't imagine being any more rattled than I am already.'

'Well, let's see. First thing. Rory didn't take his own life. He drowned accidentally.'

'He… who told you this, Shay? Was it the Gards?'

'The Gards aren't worth a fuck and I'm sure you won't argue with me on that score. His ex-girlfriend, Lorna, told me. Do you remember her?'

'He mentioned going out with a girl called Lorna, yes, but where did she get her information?'

'I'll give you her number and you can talk to her yourself. She'll explain it all. But when you hear what she has to say, it'll make sense.'

He sighed heavily. 'Somehow, I don't think I'll be contacting my son's ex-girlfriend, Shay.'

'I think you will when you hear the second thing I have to tell you.'

'Oh God, what's this going to be?'

'Rory has a baby son.'

Silence came from the other end of the call. Shay waited, giving Dan a chance to let the news sink in.

'Oh my God,' he said, eventually, 'a baby. I was absolutely not expecting that. It's… it's… can I see him? What's his name? Is he being cared for?'

'He's called Rory, isn't that great? And he couldn't be in better hands. He's with Lorna and she's a great mother. She's lovely and she has her whole family round her. She said she'd love to meet you and have you meet the baby, if you wanted.'

'I, um, I'd like that. And he's named after Rory? It's so… it's amazing.'

His response filled Shay with joy. A lump squeezed on her throat.

'Dan,' she said, swallowing, 'I want you to promise me something.'

'What?'

'That you'll be part of his life, that you'll make sure he knows who Rory was. Will you do that, please, for me? I won't be able to. I won't even be here for his first birthday.' She breathed in hard. 'Promise me, Dan, you'll do what I can't.'

'I promise,' Dan said, his voice breaking. 'I swear on my life.'

Shay heard his sobs.

'I'm sorry,' he said.

'About what?'

'About us,' he said. 'Our lives, the way things ended all those years ago, and me not standing up to Pop when he drove you away – things might've been so different. And then what happened to our Rory and now… this… this horrible fucking disease.'

'Ah, Dan.' She tried not to cry. 'Thank you. Thank you for saying that. But all that stuff, you know, all that stuff is life. It's just life.'

43

'The day after tomorrow is the day,' Ciara said, 'right?'

'The day after tomorrow, it is,' Shay said.

The time had come for Shay to move in with Ciara and Joe. No more putting it off. Ciara was taking no more excuses. They were in Shay's living room, lit only by the subdued glow of a table lamp in the corner and the flickering flames of the wood burner. Shay was curled up on a corner of the sofa and Ciara was standing in front of the stove, unable to settle.

'I'm relieved,' Ciara said, 'that I'll have you under my roof and know you're safe.'

Shay smiled and nodded.

'I know it's hard for you,' Ciara said. 'I know you want to keep as much of your independence as long as you can.'

Shay went on smiling and nodding.

'You're very quiet,' Ciara said. 'You seem calm. I thought you'd be putting up more of a fight.'

Ciara's face was full of concern. Here she was, taking on an invalid and all she was worried about was whether the invalid was okay. That was Ciara all over. How Shay would've managed half the shit in her life without her sister, she didn't know.

'Don't worry, Ciara,' Shay said. 'I'm fine with it.'

'It has to be done, you know. I wish it didn't, but we have no choice at this stage.'

'It's okay.'

Ciara fidgeted with her hands and looked away.

'This isn't your fault, Ciara, so stop beating yourself up.'

'Am I beating myself up?'

'It looks that way.'

Ciara tutted. 'Maybe a bit. It's just I still can't believe… aww fuck, I can't talk about it.'

'So don't,' Shay said. 'We've talked it to death and it doesn't change the facts.' Shay stood up. 'You're twitching there like a bag of cats, you're so nervous. Tell you what, why don't you get back to The Snug and leave me to get my few bits and pieces packed up?'

'I can help you with that.'

'Don't be silly, I can manage.'

'Are you sure?'

'Go,' Shay said, feigning a smile.

'Okay, then, if you're sure.'

Shay went over to her sister and hugged her. Ciara hugged her back. They kept the embrace longer than usual.

'You're the most amazing sister anybody could wish for,' Shay said, her voice muffled against Ciara's shoulder.

'You are, too,' Ciara said.

'I mean it, Ciara. You've always been there for me down the years. In the worst and hardest times, when I hit rock bottom, when I had few others, you were my constant. I knew I'd never fall because you were there for me.'

She felt Ciara hold her closer.

'Whatever happens from here on,' Shay continued, 'I want you to know that apart from Rory, nobody in the world means more to me.'

'Shay, there's no need to say all that. I know it and you've been the same for me.'

Shay pulled back, her eyes filling up. Ciara's were, too.

'What are we like, the pair of us?' Shay said, forcing a laugh. 'Now, go on, before Joe sends out a search party.'

Ciara wiped her face with her sleeve. 'I'll drop in with you tomorrow to check things are okay.'

'No, not tomorrow, I'll send you a text as I normally do,' Shay said. 'I'd like to spend the last day in my house on my own – to say goodbye to it, if that makes sense. And I'm going to take a walk to the graveyard, too. It's not too far, so even in my sorry state, I'll manage it.'

'I could drive you.'

'No, I'm looking forward to the walk.'

'If you change your mind…'

'I know where to get you.'

Ciara hugged her again. 'Well, I'll go then,' she said.

She grabbed her coat from the armchair.

'Before you go,' Shay said, 'I meant to ask, is there any update on Harry Parkes?'

'Harry? They say he's going to be fine.'

Shay gave a satisfied nod. The sickening thought she'd had when Dan told her about Peter's arrest, that her letter had something to do with the attack, popped into her head again. She dismissed it for the nonsense it was. What mattered now was knowing Harry was going to be okay. She'd get him a card, wishing him well, and she'd post it today so it would be waiting for him when he got home from the hospital.

'I'll head on,' Ciara said. 'See you bright and early, day after tomorrow.'

Ciara left. Shay eased back onto the sofa, mulling over her plans for the next day. She had plenty to do, but she'd pace herself to make sure she'd get it all done. She felt heavy, like the air was pressing in around her.

A ping from her phone jolted her, a reminder that the world

was still going about its business. She leaned over to the coffee table and slid the phone towards her. She had a text from Lorna. She opened it:

Hi Shay, letting u know Dan Feeney reached out. He wants to be part of little Rory's life! Thx for telling him. Means a lot. Been showing little Rory the photos u sent of his dad. Hope we'll c u again soon. L.

Shay read the text a few times before she left the phone back on the table. A smile found its way to her lips through the wretchedness of everything. She was relieved… no, jubilant. She was jubilant the baby would know his grandfather. And Lorna was showing him the photos. Oh, that made her heart want to sing. He was too young yet to understand what he was seeing, but understanding would come when he got older. And for as long as that baby was on earth, a little piece of Rory would be on earth, too.

A bolt of pain shot through her and she grimaced. Her left hand began to tremble uncontrollably. She breathed deeply a few times and tried to relax her body. After a while, the trembling eased to a slower shake and eventually stopped altogether. Shay slumped onto the sofa.

This disease was fighting her and it was winning hands down. She was tired of fighting back and losing. And she knew it was only getting warmed up. The next stages would bring hellfire. This disease wouldn't stop until everything she had was stolen away. Not the material things – they were as important as a grain of sand on the shore – but the things that made up your marrow, your soul. The things you should be no more separated from than colour should be separated from a flower.

She cowered as she imagined herself completely incapacitated, laid up in bed, unable to do anything, not even speak, getting fed through a tube, pissing and shitting into a nappy like a newborn, and all the while, her legs and arms going into those nasty, painful spasms – all this would happen very soon as, according to the consultant, she had less time than they thought. The burden of looking after her in this horrific state would fall to her sister and Joe.

But even greater horrors lay in wait. As her body decayed, so, too, would her mind. The details of her life, the happiest times, the saddest times and everything in between, the memories that were hers and hers alone, the people she loved and the people she didn't, her family, her neighbours, her lovely little village – every last trace of these would be gone like they were never there in the first place. Her mind would be one vast abyss of blackness and nothingness with no meaning, no roots, no purpose.

And when she reached those unfathomable depths, if she were to see a photo of Rory before her eyes, would she know who he was? Would she look at the picture and see a nice boy but a stranger looking back at her, or would she know he was her life and her light and her whole world, or would she be capable of thinking anything at all?

Life had already robbed her of Rory, but the disease would rob her of his very memory. What then would life be?

Shay couldn't, wouldn't, bear it.

She clenched her fists so tightly that her nails dug into the soft flesh in the palms of her hands. She began to weep. Her wails echoed off the walls as though the house was crying with her.

In time, her sobs ebbed away, partly because she was too shattered to cry another tear, partly because she remembered the baby. The baby was something beautiful and pure in her broken, doomed life. She leaned into the sofa and hugged a cushion close to her chest.

The peace she felt that first day after meeting him returned, only stronger. It settled inside her, like calm, contented acceptance, like somebody who was ready to go.

And she was. Ready to go.

44

'That's good news about the arraignment being this Monday,' Dan said. 'Jonathan Burley said he could've organised it sooner, only tomorrow's the weekend.'

Peter was sitting on an uncomfortable plastic chair that wobbled every time he breathed. Dan was on another plastic chair that looked equally uncomfortable and wobbly. They were in an interview room that was only slightly bigger than Peter's holding cell.

'Jonathan's certain you'll get bail,' Dan said, 'and when you do, I want you to come and stay with me and Francesca until the trial. I don't like the idea of you rattling about in that big house on your own.'

'If I get out on bail,' Peter said, 'I'll be more than capable of staying in my own house.'

'I know you will, but that's not what I mean. As the trial gets closer, you mightn't want to be alone. It might be nice to have family around, even as a distraction from ruminating.'

'I'm not afraid of ruminating. And where I'm going, I'll be doing little else.'

'Don't say that, Pop. You don't know how it's going to pan out.'

'Dan, you need to accept the fact that I'm going to prison – and probably for a long time.'

'You didn't do what Parkes is accusing you of. And Jonathan Burley found us the best criminal defence in Ireland. They—'

'Dan, you have to accept this: I did exactly what Parkes is accusing me of. I'm guilty. I'm also prepared for the worst. I expect to die in prison.'

'Don't. I can't hear you talk like that.'

Peter saw the pain in Dan's eyes. He found it touching that his son genuinely cared so much. Pity his daughter couldn't muster even an ounce of that. She hadn't bothered to get in touch since his arrest. Maybe she knew better than Dan, sensed something off in him, like milk that was about to turn, and didn't like being around him. Once Dan knew the truth, he, too, might be the same.

'Have you ever wondered why I did it?' Peter asked.

'No. I don't believe you did do it, never mind why. It makes no sense. You couldn't have.'

'It wasn't my intention to hurt him. He sent me a letter, you see, and all I wanted was for him to own up, explain why he sent it. But the man kept denying it. Why did he do that? He kept denying it. The very notion he wouldn't admit what he'd done, I couldn't stand it. I lost control.'

'Pop, I don't get what you're saying. And what letter are you on about?'

'I got a poison pen letter and—'

'You got a poison… but you couldn't have, I, uh—'

'You're probably surprised I took something like that seriously.'

'Wuh-well, that's not what—'

'I took it seriously because—'

'Pop! Listen!' Dan shouted. 'You got a letter, but I intercepted it. I took it home and destroyed it. So that must mean you… you got a second letter.'

'You intercepted my post?'

Dan's face turned red. 'For your own good. I... I knew the letter was bullshit and I didn't want you worrying. I... I never did such a thing before. I won't again.'

Peter opened his mouth to give Dan the tongue lashing of his life. He thought better of it. Instead, he tried making sense of why he could've received two letters. Was one letter from the ridiculous poison pen who was taunting the village and the other from Harry Parkes taking advantage of the poison pen so he could torment him? Possibly. Though what did it matter, for what was between them – him and Parkes – was there regardless of letters or anything else.

He breathed out with a sigh deeper than an ocean. Perhaps, in the final analysis, it was no bad thing he'd been forced to face his transgressions. The truth had a knack of coming out, no matter how long it took, like a thorn embedded deep in the flesh. It wasn't gone, only slowly working its way through to the surface until it broke the skin and was born into the world.

'What's done is done,' he said.

He could see the relief on Dan's face.

'You're not mad at me?'

Peter shrugged.

'So, why Harry Parkes, Pop? Why did you connect him to your letter?'

Peter eyed him.

And then Dan's jaw dropped, like the proverbial penny that was probably dropping in his head at the same time. Peter couldn't help thinking how utterly dumb he looked as realisation reached his son's eyes. They widened. Astonished. Horrified.

'You did something, oh God, you really did something old Parkes knew about and... and... you thought he was going to...'

'Don't you want to know what it was?'

'No, I don't,' Dan snapped. 'I don't care what it was.'

'I want to tell you before I go to trial and it comes out there.'

'Stop, I don't need to hear this.'

'Yes, you do. I'm going to tell you and you're going to listen.'

'Fuck you, I won't listen.'

It was as though his son knew what he was going to say and, in that moment, to his surprise, Peter felt compassion for him.

'I didn't push her, not intentionally, not really—'

'Shut up,' Dan roared.

45

A proper storm raged, the kind that usually stayed out at sea but had decided to come ashore. The wind screamed and rain and hail battered the windows.

Inside Shay's bedroom was a sanctuary of tranquillity. The pool of light from her small bedside lamp mingled with the darkness in a soup of shapes and shadows. She was sitting up in bed, about to turn in for the night. She reached across to take her medication, an array of blister packs on her bedside locker. There were so many; a waste of money for somebody who was as good as dead. She swallowed the pills, grimacing at their taste in her mouth – drier than an Egyptian parchment and more bitter than sloe berries.

Her head was light and she slid down on the bed. Her entire body ached, even her toes, even her brain. Shay's gaze turned to an envelope addressed to Ciara that was on top of the bedside locker. Ciara was to call over first thing the next morning to bring Shay to The Snug. She hoped the letter inside that envelope would go some way to leaving things right. She hoped.

She nestled into the pillow, lavender-scented and moist with tears that spilled down her cheeks like droplets from a trickling waterfall. Her eyelids were heavy. Sleep beckoned. She wouldn't fight it. She was done fighting. She was ready for surrender.

A hail-filled gust slammed against the bedroom window, the room trembled and the rafters rattled. She smiled. Rory would've loved this. He'd have been sitting by his bedroom window, his nose pushed against the glass, savouring every second. Wild weather, thunderstorms, high winds, torrential rain, hail showers, snowfalls – he delighted in it all.

Snowfalls… Rory's first snowfall had been like her first snowfall. Their everyday, predictable world was transformed into an enchanted land of brilliant white. The two of them wrapped up in woolly layers and raced outside to immerse themselves in this frozen new place. They stood with their faces up to heaven to watch the mesmerising descent of each fluffy flake; they had a snowball fight and built a misshapen snowman. And only when they could take the cold no longer did they drag themselves back inside to the heat…

Shay's stomach gurgled and she flopped over on her side. The room spun as she did. Sleep was moving in fast. Too late to escape it now. Not that she would try to.

In the summers, they spent every day they could at their favourite beach, the one down in Moville, near Shrove… Shrove, where the end had come for him. So many times, she couldn't count, they'd traced the weaving, meandering path carved out of the rock face that rolled into the sea between Moville and Greencastle. She fancied she could hear the gentle lapping of the waves below and feel the heat of the sun on her face… and there was Rory leaping around the shore with a fishing net and bucket, hopeful of scooping crustaceans from the rock pools…

She turned on her other side as the room went in and out of focus. Another gust shook the house. A giggle that came from nowhere escaped through her mouth, although her tears didn't stop.

'Why are you crying?' a voice said, loud and real in the quiet of the room.

Impossible… the voice was Rory's.

'Are you here?' Shay asked.

'Don't cry,' the voice said. 'There's no need to cry anymore.'

'Rory?'

No answer. She wondered if Rory was with her mother, if he was with her father and her grandparents and all the others who'd passed. Were they waiting for her tonight to finally come to them?

'Wouldn't that be grand?' she slurred and another giggle slipped out.

Her eyelids dropped like a lobster's claw shutting closed. She sank further into her drowsy trance, as though sinking into a bottomless pillow, embracing, enveloping. A thought sneaked up on her. What if Rory wasn't waiting for her? The doubt floated, feather-like, towards her. Immediately, she blew it away, clear out of her mind. She wouldn't entertain such thoughts. She'd always believed there was more than just this life and she was damned if she was going to let herself believe anything other than that now, not now.

Suddenly, her body went into a spasm and she bolted upright up in the bed, as straight as a steel rod, more awake than she'd been in her life before. She understood everything with startling clarity, it seemed. She could see the world around her – not just what was in front of her eyes here in this bedroom, but for miles beyond – in amazing technicolour. A hundred thousand images of families and homes, and streets and towns, and fields and hills, and trees and woods, and then back to the lough below her village. She sped along its surface like a bird in flight until it met the Atlantic – a cold, black expanse swallowing the horizon, and above it the eternal night sky and its lightshow of stars and planets and moons. Up into the heavens she went, up into the heavens.

And then the vision was gone, as fleeting as a shooting star, gone, and all she saw was her room.

Shay flopped onto the pillow, shattered and spent. As sleep wrapped its dark cloak around her, her sobbing slowly waned until she was quiet. Finally, the torment fell away from her tear-soaked face.

Shay, like the room, was still.

46

Ciara gripped the door of the bar and swung it open. Joe was behind the counter. He looked up as she came in.

'Ciara, love,' he said, 'is Shay not with you?'

'I need you to come with me, Joe.' Ciara's voice was little more than a croak.

'But there's no one to mind the bar,' he said. His face showed bewilderment. 'What's happened?'

'Just lock up and come with me,' Ciara said, feeling her head go light.

Joe rushed over. 'Jesus, Ciara, what's going on?'

'I can't explain. We have to go. Now.'

He looked at her. Did he see her desperation?

He asked no more questions. In minutes, the bar was closed and they were ready. Ciara took his hand and they raced to the car.

'Where are we going?' he said.

'Shay's. Where else?'

*

Ciara stopped at the threshold to Shay's bedroom. The curtains were shut, dulling the glare of daylight but not preventing it from seeping through the satin folds to give the place an eerie gloom. The air was stony silent and stifling, making it hard to breathe.

Joe was directly behind her.

'Aww, fuck!' he wailed.

He turned and walked to the other side of the landing.

'I can't fucking handle this.'

'Don't fall apart on me, Joe.'

'Are you sure she's really…?'

'Yes. I checked. She's…'

Ciara couldn't bring herself to say it out loud. To say that Shay was actually gone.

She started to sob. Joe came back to the doorway and wrapped her in his arms.

'I don't know what to say,' he said, his voice thick. 'I'm heartbroken.'

They stood locked together, holding each other up, for what seemed like an eternity. Ciara eventually pulled away.

'We have to call an ambulance,' she said, rubbing her hands across her cheeks, tugging free some strands of hair that had stuck to the tears. 'And the Gards, too.'

'Why the Gards?'

'She didn't just die in her sleep, Joe,' Ciara said. 'Have a look.'

Ciara pointed to the bedside table where a little lamp still burned.

'Nearly all them blister packs are empty. My poor sister… she poured that shit into her stomach before she'd face the rest of her life.'

Ciara started to weep again and Joe held her again. She could hear him weeping along with her.

'We have to try to keep it together, love,' he said, eventually, ''til we get the formalities over.'

'I know,' Ciara said. 'You're right, but I can't bring myself to believe it. Every time I think of it, it's like the first time and I'm stunned all over again.'

Joe stroked her back. 'Let's do right by Shay. Let's get this situation sorted out.'

Ciara nodded. She left Joe's side and stumbled over to the bed. She could hear him dab 999 on his phone. The formalities were in progress.

Shay was tucked into the bed, her head poking out from under the quilt. She looked like she might only be sleeping. But, of course, she wasn't and the telltale signs were there to be seen: the grey-pale skin; the mouth skewed at an unnatural angle – a blob of dried vomit stuck to the side, Ciara was ashamed for noticing – the absolute stillness of her body; no lift and drop, not in the slightest, of an intake of breath. It was like a grotesque photograph.

Ciara felt her heart had been hollowed out. Her eyes were swollen with crying. She wanted to sit by the bed and put her arms round her sister and hug her. But she couldn't. The body in front of her wasn't Shay. She knew it would be cold and stiff and wouldn't feel like a human being at all. She didn't want to remember Shay that way. She wanted to remember her warm and soft, as she'd always been.

Joe was talking on the phone, giving Shay's address to the emergency services. Ciara willed them to hurry. She glanced across to the bedside locker, the blister packs, a glass tumbler, a bottle of vodka almost empty. And one final thing she hadn't spotted before: an envelope with her name on it, sitting unassumingly on top of the locker, inviting her to look closer.

Ciara grabbed it and hunkered on the floor, pushing against the back of the bed for support. Her stomach churned and she hoped she wouldn't throw up.

'Joe,' she said, as he finished his call.

He came walking over. She handed him the envelope.

'Would you open this, love?' she said.

Joe did as she asked. 'Shit. Her will's in here and there's one of those wee USB sticks. And a handwritten note.'

'Oh, Jesus. What does it say?' Ciara pushed harder against the bed.

Joe slid to the floor beside her. She rested on his shoulder, taking solace from their closeness.

'There's not a lot to it,' he said. 'It goes: *"Ciara, the USB is for you. Start with the document called 'Read me first' and then you'll understand."*'

'What does that mean?'

'Maybe she's going to explain why she, you know, why she…'

Joe handed the note and the USB to Ciara and then pulled her close. She sank into his embrace.

'Umm,' Ciara said, 'that must be it.' She closed her eyes. 'I've got a headache coming on – a real whopper.'

'Do you want me to look for some headache tablets?'

'No, don't. Knowing what Shay did, I'd rather put up with the pain than be anywhere near pills. Just stay here with me.'

'I'm here,' he said.

They sat on, without moving, without speaking, until they heard a commotion outside.

'Sounds like the ambulance,' Joe said, 'or the Gards, or maybe them both.'

Joe got up, helping Ciara up with him.

'I'll run down and let them in,' he said.

He was about to make a dash for the door when Ciara grabbed his arm.

'Wait!' she said. 'Say nothing about the note and the USB.'

He threw her a quizzical look. 'But they're going to ask us about that kind of thing.'

A thunderous knock shook the front door.

'We can tell them about the will but say nothing about the rest.' She slipped the will back into the envelope and returned it to where she'd found it. She stuffed the note and the USB into her jeans pocket. 'I swear, I'll tell them as soon as – but first I want a chance to see what's on there. I need to know. If I tell the Gards now, they'll take everything away.'

'I don't like the idea but, fuck it, Shay's more important than the Gards.'

Another knock came, this time so loud it might've taken the front door off the hinges. Joe bolted downstairs.

In no time, the room was bustling with medics seeing to Shay and Gards handling the scene, all masked and suited up. One of the Gards interviewed Ciara and Joe, though Ciara didn't remember much of what they asked nor what she and Joe said in reply. The main thing was they kept quiet about the note and the mysterious USB.

Not an hour after arriving, the medics and Gards had done their job and were packing to go. Ciara and Joe stood on the landing, leaning on each other like a pair of broken reeds, looking out at the driveway below. Villagers had come out to the street to watch the goings-on. Shay's body, encased in a body bag, was being placed in the ambulance. Ciara sank into Joe's chest.

'Do you want to go down and see her off?' Joe asked.

'I couldn't bear it,' Ciara said, lifting her head.

The Gard in charge approached. His face was sombre.

'That's us finished, Mr and Mrs McCann. We can leave you in peace. I'm sorry you had to go through this, but it's the process we must follow for suicides.'

'No problem,' Joe said. 'We understand.'

'We didn't find a note,' the Gard said. 'Only an envelope with the will in it. There isn't always a note, of course. You didn't happen to notice one?'

'Definitely not,' Ciara said; not too forcefully, she hoped. 'Didn't we not, Joe?'

'No, definitely not,' Joe echoed.

The Gard studied them with a probing stare that seemed to go on forever. Ciara's nerves tingled like somebody was going at her with a cattle prod. If he was trying to psych them out, he was doing a half-decent job. They had to hold out. Ciara squeezed Joe's arm tighter, hoping he'd know what he had to do.

'Oh well,' the Gard said, mercifully breaking the uncomfortable deadlock. 'Shure, if you do happen to find something that would be useful, you can always let us know later.'

'Will do,' Ciara said.

He began to walk away, stopping before he reached the door. 'Coming to us later,' he said, 'we'd be fine with that. It wouldn't be a problem.' And with that, he finally left.

With everybody gone, an uneasy stillness descended – like before, only now with Shay gone.

'Shay's house without Shay in it,' Ciara said. 'It's unnatural.' She shivered. 'It feels like a big, huge empty… cave.'

'Is this really happening?' Joe asked.

'I don't know if I can get through this.'

'You will.'

'I couldn't do it without you, Joe.'

'That's what I'm here for.' He held her. 'Do you think that Gard knew we were hiding something?'

'I think he knew surely, but we'll worry about him another time.'

'We'll have to get word out… get in touch with your brothers, first of all, then the wains… and Dan. We have to tell him before he finds out from somebody in the village.'

'I was talking to Eddie just the other night on zoom,' Ciara said. 'It was the first time I mentioned Shay being sick and he didn't take it well.'

'It's going to be some shock for him, and Mickey and Paul.'

'Seems like no time ago when we were all gathering for Rory's funeral.'

Fresh tears stung Ciara's eyes, but she held them at bay. 'It's not fair, what Shay had to go through these last two months. How could life be so cruel?'

'It was too much for her at the end up.'

'We'll have to get an undertaker, get things ready for the wake – oh God, there's so much to do.'

'It'll be all right,' Joe said. 'We'll do what's needed.'

'Look.' Ciara held up her hands. 'I'm shaking.'

Joe hugged her. 'We'll get through this, Ciara. We'll do Shay proud.'

Ciara's heart weighed like lead in her chest. She pulled back from Joe.

'She had all her affairs in order before she did this,' Ciara said. 'She had everything organised.'

'She was always organised,' Joe said. 'She went about her death the same way as she went about her life.'

Ciara nearly smiled. 'That's our Shay for you… I mean, that's what she used to be like.'

She dug into her jeans pocket and pulled out the USB.

'We shouldn't forget this contraption. It has to be important if Shay left it here. I've got to know what's on it.'

*

Fifteen minutes later, Joe and Ciara were crowded into the box room where they kept the accounts for the bar. The Gards had taken Shay's laptop so they had to come home to check the USB. Ciara was perched on a leather swivel chair, while Joe hovered over her shoulder.

She rubbed her eyes as she waited for the USB to load. She thought about Shay being taken away in the ambulance.

'Do you think she's in the morgue by now, Joe?'

Joe squeezed her shoulder.

'Will they take care of her?' she said.

'Good care,' he said. 'The best.'

A window popped up on the screen and the contents of the

USB were finally revealed. Sure enough, "Read me first" was there. But it wasn't the only file. There was one more, titled "Letters".

'What's that about?' Joe said.

'I... I don't rightly know,' Ciara said, as confused as Joe.

She double-clicked on the "Letters" file, ignoring Shay's instruction about the "Read me first" file. Ciara's body ran cold.

'Fuck!' Joe said.

'Oh God, this can't be… it can't be what I think it is.'

'Shay,' Joe said. 'Fuck. Shay was the poison pen?'

Ciara's mouth hung open. 'Shu… she wouldn't do that. She just wouldn't do that.'

'Open "Read me first",' Joe said.

Ciara wasn't able to make her index finger move, so Joe opened the file for her and began to read out loud:

'My dear sister, Ciara,

First things first. I'm sorry. I know you'll be upset now, maybe so upset you'll have Joe with you reading this. I'm sorry. I'm sorry for what I did, what I'm about to do. I'm sorry you'll be the one to find me when you come to the house in the morning. I can't say it enough, how sorry I am. You'll never know how deeply I mean it. But I hope you can forgive me, if not when you're reading this for the first time, then some time.

You might be asking yourself why I'm about to do this or you might already have guessed. But I'll tell you either way.

It's this simple. I can't face what's left of my life, ending my days in a twilight dream where nothing's real as I creep towards death. You said you and Joe would look after me when the time came but the more I think about it, the less I want that burden to fall on the two of you. And I wouldn't want anybody else doing it. This'll be hard for you to take in. I realise that. But I want you to know, and this is from my heart, it meant the world to me that the two of you were prepared to look after me. How blessed I am.

And then there's waiting for that disease to take away my memory of Rory. I can't bear it. Being alive without him is already agony. But the idea of being alive and not even being aware I'm without him, that's beyond any pain I could tolerate. Getting out now, it seems like the smartest thing to do. I can go on my own terms, with dignity.

And now it's time I gave you some answers about why I have that file called Letters. *I could nearly predict that you peeked into it first.*

Why did I send those poison pen letters, you're probably wondering? Is Joe wondering, too?

It was after Rory's funeral, you see, I was so ruined. Empty. Angry. So angry. I'd lost my beautiful, bright, happy boy. I was forced to accept he'd taken his own life. I wanted someone to hate, to blame. I didn't have to look far. Peter Feeney and Eoin Devine. I don't have to explain why they were obvious choices.

My Rory was six foot under and they were happy as sand boys living their lives. How was that fair? Well, it wasn't. Not to me. I wanted to give them some pain.

That's when I came up with the idea of the letters. I didn't reckon they'd connect the letters to Rory but I hoped they'd have a secret or two lurking in their past that might bubble to the surface... my God, as I write it down now, in black and white, I can't believe I actually did it. Part of me thinks the whole scheme was mad nonsense. Part of me thinks it worked, a bit anyway. Did my letter nudge Eoin Devine into fessing up to the hit-and-run? That wouldn't be a bad thing. I entertained notions for a while that the letter I wrote Peter was behind what he did to poor Harry but that doesn't hold any water.

The very worst thing about my letters was that they gave somebody else the idea to write their own letters. I mean, can you actually believe it? I have to take some of the responsibility for the crazy shit they caused, especially the trouble it caused you and Joe. I only wish I could take it all back. All except wanting to vent my anger on Eoin and Peter. I don't regret that, not even now when I know Rory didn't take his own life.

But will you do something for me? Will you tell the village the truth? That I sent the letters to Peter and Eoin though not to anybody else, and that I'm sorrier than I have words for, I'm sorry for the hurt. Put it down to my illness if it makes it easier, just as long as you tell them. What I hope for most is that when you get the truth out, the copycat will stop. This whole awful thing will stop.

And will you explain to Lorna why I made the decision to take my own life? Will you do that? Tell her that finding out about the baby was the one thing that gave me joy at the end. The beauty of that moment when I saw him for the first time, I knew I couldn't bear to keep seeing him, growing more and more attached as my death drew closer.

I want to finish now, though not before I tell you I love you, Ciara. You made my life better in a million different ways. Tell Joe and the kids I love them too, and our brothers and their families. I love you all so, so much. And when you think about me, think about the person I was before all this business.

I'm about to die. I'm afraid but I'm ready. I believe I'm going to see Rory again. I believe I'm going to see Mammy and Daddy and everybody else that passed on before us. I really believe that. And I believe I'll see you again too. Death isn't the end, no, it's not the end.

Your loving sister, Shay.'

A surge of emotion, more powerful and sudden as a lightning bolt, came over Ciara. She leaned back into Joe's arms. Ciara should've felt betrayed, but she didn't. Instead, she understood. Ridiculous and misguided as it was, she understood.

Ciara laughed wryly. 'You know, Joe, for a while I thought the poison pen might've been Daisy McBirney-Smith. She's such a gossip and there's a nasty streak in her. But our Shay. I can't take it in.'

Joe scrolled down through Shay's letter, reading it again.

'It's not her fault,' Ciara said, 'what Peter did to Harry. That's all on Peter. The rest of us got letters, but it didn't make us try to kill somebody.'

Joe nodded. 'And Shay's not to blame for it all. What she says here is there's another person writing letters.'

'A copycat.'

'We'll probably never find out who it is but they're vindictive, the way they just went after us all and kept going and going.'

'We'll have to show this to the Gards,' Ciara said. 'They're bound to give us a bollocking when they find out we kept the USB from them.'

'Well, we'll just take whatever they throw at us, love.'

'The village won't be happy either.'

'We'll take whatever they throw at us, too. It's up to us to tell Shay's story and do right by her.'

Ciara pulled herself up from the chair. 'I'm dreading it.'

'It's okay, love. We can get through this. Together.'

Ciara knew they would, she and Joe and the kids together. For Shay.

47

Business was slow, unusual for a Saturday morning. Mrs Dillon was at the counter getting her head talked off. Andie was putting out bread, fresh from the oven.

Andie had lost count of the number of times she'd heard the story about Shay Dunne and the poison pen in the last week. Her mother hadn't missed an opportunity to bring it up with every single customer she served. Didn't she get tired of it? The same story over and over. And once that story fizzled out, Andie knew, she'd only replace it with some other shit that she'd repeat over and over, and on and on, 'til she dropped dead, probably behind that bloody counter.

Andie seethed. When it came her time to run the show, things would be different around here. She was—

'Andie!' Her mother was shouting in that shrill, bossy voice of hers. 'Andie! Wake up, girl! Go and get a box of cornflakes, will you, for Mrs Dillon from the storeroom, and you can restock the cereal shelf when you've done that.'

Andie put her head down. 'Okay, Mum.'

She headed off to the storeroom, catching part of the conversation as she went. 'That girl does nothing but daydream, so she does,' from her mother, and 'Ach, shure, they're all the same at that age,' from Mrs Dillon.

All the same, indeed. A knot of resentment tightened in her gut. Her mother didn't seem to realise that she, Andie, had feelings. She didn't seem to realise that ordering her about and belittling her in front of customers was humiliating. She didn't seem to realise that her daughter might want to be more in life than a gopher. Or maybe she did realise and she didn't care. Her father didn't care, that was for sure. Nobody cared.

Most of the customers hardly gave her a second glance, except maybe when they were looking for some item they couldn't find. Some, like that Shay Dunne, looked at her as though to say: "Poor, pathetic Andie". She had seen it in Shay's eyes when she went to pick up the Friday night takeaways. Her son, Rory, had been no better. He'd always been nice to her, but Andie knew he didn't mean it and was only pretending. Then there were the people, like her mother, who always seemed to be annoyed with her. She hated them all. They had no respect for her. It wasn't fair.

Even Natalie had turned on her. Oh, how she wished she'd grassed her up for cheating with Rory. Would've served her right. She'd been Andie's first proper friend – her only friend, well, since school. And now she was gone, too. What had—

'Andie! Where the hell are the cornflakes?' Her father was at the door of the storeroom. 'Mrs Dillon's waiting on them.'

'Oh, sorry,' Andie said, 'I've got them here.'

He grabbed them from her. 'Aren't you supposed to be sorting out the fridges this morning?'

'Okay, Dad.'

He disappeared and she was left alone again, with her thoughts. She slipped her phone out of the pocket of her shopkeeper's coat. Her parents insisted they wear these hideous khaki coats in the shop – that was another thing she was going to change once the shop was hers. She took a sneaky peek at the last text she got from Natalie. It had come through the day before and she'd read it a hundred times, as though if she read it enough, it might eventually look different.

Stop ringing, stop texting. U have to leave me alone.

The words cut her like the blade of a sharpened butcher's knife. She couldn't understand why Natalie had to be so harsh. Though it certainly explained why she hadn't answered any of her calls or messages since disappearing from the village. Ungrateful bitch.

How could she do that? Andie had been so good to her. She'd listened to her endless whining on and on about her relationships and her job and her life. Moan, moan, moan. And not once was she interested in hearing what was going on in Andie's life. But Andie had tolerated it because she wanted a proper friend her own age, and a self-centred Natalie was better than no Natalie at all.

Andie had been there for her when Eoin was scooped by the Gards and she was left homeless. She visited her every day and brought her supplies. No one else did that, not even her own family. Natalie had needed her then, for that short while, and she'd been sort of nicer when she was down on her luck. Andie liked being needed. She liked it so much she hadn't wanted Natalie to stop needing her. Of course, it came to an end. And abruptly at that. She'd gone to the cottage one lunchtime with two lovely chicken salad baguettes for them to have with a cup of tea, and when she got there, the place was empty. All Natalie's stuff was gone and the keys were lying on the kitchen table. No note, though. She didn't even leave a fucking note. And now she'd ghosted her. How dare—

'Pity's sake, are you still out here?'

Her father again. Andie swore under her breath. Why couldn't they leave her the fuck in peace?

'Will you get the bloody fridges done?' he said. 'And once you're done with that, your mother wants the cereal shelf restocked.'

'Okay, Dad.'

'Come on,' he said. 'Out you go.'

He waited at the door for her to lead the way.

She set to work tidying the shelves in the fridge, able to see and hear her mother from her standpoint. She was talking about the poison pen story to yet another customer. This time, it was Sally Brennan getting the full treatment. Jesus wept!

'Terrible sad about Shay Dunne taking her own life, so it was,' Andie's mother was saying.

'Terrible,' Sally said, 'and after her son doing the same.'

'Though before she died, Shay was telling everybody what happened to him was an accident.'

'God help her. Maybe that was her way of coping,' Sally said.

'That's what I think, too, but did you hear that she was the poison pen?'

'Shay? The poison pen? I can't believe that. She was such a lovely woman.'

Andie had been as shocked as Sally to hear that news. She wouldn't have guessed in a million years that it was Shay Dunne. Although, after hearing her mother repeat the story so many times, the shock had long worn off.

'Oh, it was her all right.'

Andie's mother folded her arms and narrowed her eyes. Andie raised her face to the heavens. That stance was a sure sign there was a long story on the way.

'Ciara McCann's insisting that Shay only sent the first two letters,' her mother said. 'To Peter Feeney and Eoin Devine. Ciara didn't say why.'

Andie checked the dates on the cheddar cheeses, rearranging them so the oldest were to the front.

'According to Ciara,' her mother said, 'all the rest of the letters, other than them two, came from a copycat. That's the story the McCanns are putting out, so it is.'

'A copycat?' Sally said. 'I've never heard the likes of it.'

'It's hard to believe that though, don't ye think? A copycat? Seems a bit far-fetched.'

Sally slowly shook her head as though trying her best to make sense of all she was hearing. Andie smirked. Sally had the same reaction as everybody else her mother told.

'Not likely, is it?' Andie's mother said. 'Not one bit likely that the village hasn't just one, but two poison pens. If you ask me, the McCanns are covering up for Shay. Though, God save us, she probably wasn't in her right mind after losing Rory. And I heard she was very ill, too, but I don't know how true that is.'

'Poor Shay,' Sally said.

'But we'll soon know for definite if it was all Shay's handiwork, won't we?'

'How's that?'

Andie sighed quietly. It was either that or scream aloud. This was the bit Mrs Daisy McBirney-Smith lived for. The analysis. Her wisdom being applied to whatever the situation was.

'If there's no more letters, then there never was a copycat.'

Andie stopped what she was doing and looked across to the till. That was new, she thought. In all the times her mother had told and retold the story, she hadn't come out with that one. It rang true, though. For once, her mother had said something that made a bit of sense. Andie closed the fridge and headed for the door to the storeroom that also led to their house.

'Whatever the truth is,' Andie heard Sally say, as she tiptoed away, 'I hope Shay's at peace now and I hope the village can get back to normal and we can put this terrible mess behind us.'

*

Andie trotted up the stairs to her room. Her sanctuary. It was where she went when she needed to get away from her auld pair. She went inside and closed the door, locking it just in case one of them decided to barge in.

Her mother's words spun around in her head – *If there's no more letters, then there never was a copycat* – as she flopped down on a desk chair that was adorned with a fluffy pink throw.

She clicked the on button of her laptop and it whirred to life.

The village having one poison pen was unbelievable enough. But two? Like her mother said, the idea of a copycat was highly unlikely. It was so unlikely it was probably impossible.

Andie moved the index finger of her right hand over the laptop's touchpad, guiding the cursor to a folder on her desktop.

The McCanns might want to convince everybody that Shay wasn't to blame for all the trouble the letters brought to the village, but they hadn't a hope.

She clicked twice on the folder and browsed the alphabetical list of documents. She was after one, in particular.

The problem with the copycat story was it was too far-fetched. See, people liked simple explanations and they chose the simple over the complicated every time. They didn't want to have to think too hard; they wanted the easy, all-worked-out answer handed to them on a plate. That was human nature and Andie knew it.

She found what she was looking for – a document called "Fun and Games". She clicked it twice to open.

There probably wasn't one person in the whole village who'd give her the credit for having the shrewdness to understand human nature. Not one. Those horrible people all thought she was stupid.

The document popped up on her screen. She felt its bright whiteness reflecting on her face.

The fact was it was them that were stupid. They were nothing but fools who underestimated her. They couldn't see what she was capable of. Not even Natalie. Especially not Natalie.

Andie scrolled down the document. A smile danced on her lips.

When people were as stupid as all that, they were so easy to play with, so gullible. They'd never let it cross their tiny brains that sometimes the complicated explanation might be right one.

Her smile morphed into a wide grin and then she started giggling as her eyes meandered across a list that took up the whole first page.

She heard footsteps thumping up the stairs and then a loud rap.

'Are you in there, Andie?' It was her father. He tried the door. 'For fuck's sake, get yourself down to the shop right now.'

Her giggles erupted into an uncontrollable howl of laughter.

'What are you doing in there?' he called, knocking hard.

The list was made up of names. Andie picked out a few. Mary-Margaret Walsh, Ciara and Joe McCann, Sarah Maguire, Angie O'Sullivan, Aidan O'Brien, Shane Hamilton, Ella McMonagle, Brendan Kelly, Peter Feeney, Tracy Johnson, Natalie O'Donnell. Sweet, sweet Natalie. Even Shay Dunne. Oh, that was fucking priceless. Even Shay Dunne.

The list went on.

'Andie, I'm giving you to the count of ten.'

By now, Andie was laughing so hard she could barely stay upright on the chair. If people were too stupid to understand anything else, she'd let them have their simple explanation. The complicated one? Well, that would be her delicious secret and hers alone.

Tears rolled down her cheeks as she scrolled to the next page. On it was just one sentence:

I know what you did. Prepare for the consequences.